Sapphire Scars

Book Three
The Jewelry Box Series

by

New York Times Bestseller
Pepper Winters

Sapphire Scars
Copyright © 2024 Pepper Winters
Published by Pepper Winters

All rights reserved. No part of this book may be reproduced or transmitted in any form, including electronic or mechanical, without written permission from the publisher, except in the case of brief quotations embodied in critical articles or reviews.

This is a work of fiction. Names, characters, businesses, places, events, and incidents are either the products of the author's imagination or used in a fictitious manner. Any resemblance to actual persons, living or dead, or actual events is purely coincidental.

This book is licensed for your personal enjoyment only. This book may not be re-sold or given away to other people. If you would like to share this book with another person, please purchase an additional copy for each person you share it with. If you are reading this book and did not purchase it, or it was not purchased for your use only, then you should return it to the seller and purchase your own copy. Libraries are exempt and permitted to share their in-house copies with their members and have full thanks for stocking this book. Thank you for respecting the author's work.

NO A.I OR OTHER SOFTWARE WAS USED IN WRITING THIS BOOK.
ALL PEPPER WINTERS TITLES ARE HUMAN WRITTEN ONLY.
The only tools used were imagination and a keyboard.
That's it.

Published: Pepper Winters 2024: **pepperwinters@gmail.com**
Ebook Design: Cleo Studios
Paperback Design: Cleo Studios
Alternative Cover Image: Julia Cherrett Valareign (etsy)
Internal Images: Julia Cherrett Valareign (etsy)
Editing by: Editing-4-Indies (Jenny Sims)
Proofreading by: Christina Routhier
Indian Sensitivity Reader & Hindi Translation: Shabnam Arora & Sonal Phansekar
French Translation: Aurélie Gordio
Audio Narration: Luke William Bromley & Lucy Jessica

OTHER WORK BY PEPPER WINTERS

Pepper currently has close to forty books released in nine languages. She's hit best-seller lists (USA Today, New York Times, and Wall Street Journal) almost forty times. She dabbles in multiple genres, ranging from Dark Romance, Coming of Age, Fantasy, and Romantic Suspense.

For books, FAQs, and buylinks please visit:

https://pepperwinters.com

Subscribe to New Release Newsletter by following QR code

STEAMY STANDALONES

Spectacle of Secrets Standalones
One Dirty Night
(Roommate to lovers)
One Stalker Night
(Stalker to lover)

(Steamy, spicy standalones with plenty of heat and swoon)
Plenty more to come…

Destroyed
(Grey Romance)

Can't Touch This
(Romantic Comedy)

Unseen Messages
(Survival Romance)

DARK ROMANCE

The Jewelry Box Series
Ruby Tears, Emerald Bruises, Sapphire Scars, Diamond Kisses

Monsters in the Dark Trilogy
Tears of Tess, Quintessentially Q, Twisted Together, Je Suis a Toi

Goddess Isles Series
Once a Myth, Twice a Wish, Third a Kiss, Fourth a Lie, Fifth a Fury,
Jinx's Fantasy, Sully's Fantasy

Indebted Series
Debt Inheritance, First Debt, Second Debt, Third Debt,
Fourth Debt, Final Debt, Indebted Epilogue

Dollar Series
Pennies, Dollars, Hundreds, Thousands, Millions

Fable of Happiness Trilogy
Fable of Happiness Book One, Book Two, Book Three

FORBIDDEN, EROTIC, COMING OF AGE ROMANCE
The Luna Duet
Lunamare and Cor Amare

The Ribbon Duet
The Boy & His Ribbon, The Girl & Her Ren

Spinoff Standalone to The Ribbon Duet
The Son & His Hope

Truth & Lies Duet
Crown of Lies, Throne of Truth

Master of Trickery Duet
The Body Painter, The Living Canvas

Pure Corruption Duet
Ruin & Rule, Sin & Suffer

INSPIRIATIONAL / CHILDREN
Pippin & Mo
(Picture book based on Pepper's own rabbit)

UPCOMING RELEASES

For 2024/2025 titles please visit www.pepperwinters.com

RELEASE DAY ALERTS, SNEAK PEEKS, & NEWSLETTER
*To be the first to know about upcoming releases, please join Pepper's Newsletter
(she promises never to spam or annoy you.)*

Pepper's Newsletter

SOCIAL MEDIA & WEBSITE
Facebook: Peppers Books
Instagram: @pepperwinters
Facebook Group: Peppers Playgound
Website: www.pepperwinters.com
Tiktok: @pepperwintersbooks

Dedication

To those swallowed by darkness…light always finds a way.

Letter from the Author

The Jewelry Box Series is a work of fiction, but it is a dark read. Almost every trigger that can exist, exists within this tale. Blood play, breath play, non-con, dub-con, degradation, pain, despair, betrayal, hope, and faith.
Please take the warning seriously. This book is explicit, erotic, despicable, and downright monstrous in some places. There is love, yes, but first, you have to go through a hell of a lot of depravity to find it.
Please read responsibly.
Pepper x

Prologue

THE CURSE OF BLOOD & DARKNESS
by
Henri Mercer

I THINK THERE COMES A POINT in everyone's life when you wake up.

You wake to the truth of who you are, what you're doing, and who you're meant to be.

Some people wake and realise they're on the right path already.

Others wake and come face to face with all their mistakes.

Near-death experiences can cause such an awakening.

Reaching rock bottom can slap you into seeing.

Sickness and burnout, terror and tragedy—they're all feared but can grant such freedom if you submit.

Pity I didn't submit.

Pity I wasn't ready.

Because when my awakening happened…

I broke.

Chapter One

Ily

"THIS WAY!" PETER HOBBLE-RAN beside me, dripping with pain and grunting with every stride. "I know a shortcut to Neverland!" He chuckled, but it came out more like a sob.

Every jewel spurred onward, so used to obeying Peter when he was sober and smart, not questioning his judgement now he was high and hurting.

The way we ran as a group reminded me of track at high school. How we'd always start as a group and slowly thin out the more distance we covered.

Would that happen here?

Would jewels fall back? Would we slow to stay together? Or would some bolt ahead, chasing after hope that they might find escape, if only they ran quick enough?

Gasping for breath, I glanced at Peter. The target mark on his chest rivered into streaks of black, white, and red. The paint smudged and soaked into the band of his nude-coloured boxers. His glazy eyes and feverish skin far worse than even ten minutes ago.

Rachel scowled, holding her full breasts as we ran, preventing them from bouncing too much. "You are not Peter Pan, Pete. There is no such thing as Neverland."

"Pretty sure I am." Peter spread his arms. "Share his name, don't I? Bet you I could fly if I threw myself off the cliff."

"No one is throwing anything off the cliff." Rachel grimaced. Shooting me a look, she couldn't hide the depth of her terror. "He's lost it," she whispered to me.

"Fly faster, friends!" Peter shouted, almost falling to his knees from running on burned feet. "Shortcut ahead!"

Rachel reached for him, but he shrugged her off.

Sighing heavily, Rachel let fear braid with her temper. "How the hell do you know a shortcut? What shortcut? You're as high as the clouds, and if you say you can fly in those clouds, I'll—"

"Rachel." I shook my head. "It's okay."

Tears instantly welled in her eyes. Gritting her teeth, she looked away.

Peter stumbled as we bolted down the lush grass of Victor's runway and past his private plane. A split-second idea of stealing the plane and flying everyone out of here tantalised. If only I'd studied to become a pilot instead of a gemmologist.

As we dashed past, the roar of the ocean crashed against the cliffs to our right, almost deafening us.

Everything was louder out here, alive out here...wilder out here.

The forest we sprinted toward beckoned with bark and leaf, promising to protect and hide us.

A few running jewels looked at the cliffs.

A guy I hadn't spoken to and Suri—the girl who'd been on show with Kirk the night of the treasure hunt—gravitated toward the edge.

"Don't you dare!" Peter bellowed, tripping again as if his burned and blackened feet were moments away from snapping off. Shaking his head to clear the clouds Rachel mentioned, he added, "Ignore me. I can't fly. No one can fly. No one jumps, do you hear me?"

"What's the point in running?" Suri gasped with tears as she did her best to keep pace. "They're going to catch us. They *always* catch us." She broke ranks, drifting toward the cliffs. "I-I can't take anymore."

Peter cursed and charged after her. Wrapping his bleeding, brutalised hand around her cuffed wrist, he dragged her back into our midst. The drugs in his system faded just enough for seriousness to bleed through his fantasies. "It's almost over, Suri. I promise." He looked at me with pure agony in his gaze. "Ily and I are going to get you out. I swear."

"Hell, not this again, Pete. Stop saying shit like that." Dane put his head down and ran harder, grabbing the elbow of a small dark-skinned girl flagging beside him.

Suri wrenched out of Peter's grip and couldn't stop her tears.

Hauling the girl he'd grabbed into speed with him, Dane shot me and Peter a look. "You're collared, Pete, just like us. You live under the eye of a million cameras, just like us. You're a *slave*, just like us. How the fuck are you going to get us out?"

"I don't know yet, but we are." Peter did his best to keep

going even though it cost him. "Just trust me, okay? One day…one day soon…you'll be back with your families and—"

"That's so fucking cruel." Citra darted toward us. "You can't give us false hope like that. There's no getting out of here—"

"I vow on my life," Peter spat, his naturally dusky skin going white with agony. "I know you think I'm high, but I've never been more serious. I'm done. We are *all* done. Just…trust me."

"I trust you." Rachel gasped for breath, her face blanching with pain from Victor's beating. "But I have no idea how you're gonna keep that promise."

"Oopsies." Peter stumbled, almost face-planting in the grass. He laughed as if it was the funniest thing in the world.

"Shit." My hand snapped out and grabbed his left arm just as Rachel grabbed his right. Together, we managed to keep him upright.

He stopped laughing and swallowed hard as if he might throw up.

Just because he had drugs in his system nullifying his pain didn't mean his body wasn't completely saturated with trauma.

God, how much longer can he run and not pass out?

Getting his rhythm back, Peter swiped at sweat running into his eyes. Looking at every fleeing jewel around us, he vowed, "I'll kill you myself if I fail to give you freedom. How about that?"

I didn't know if he was joking or serious.

He glanced at Suri who ran close by. Her black hair flew behind her; her slim figure covered in thin silver scars. "If we fail to get you out in a few months, I'll kill you. I'll make it as quick and as painless as possible." He snickered. "You can even request the method. Pillow over the face? Drowning by bath? I'll be the full-service assassin, how about that?"

Suri cried harder.

"Goddammit, Peter." Kirk changed his trajectory to wrap an arm around Suri's waist, awkwardly hugging her while running. "Don't listen to him. He's flying with the fairies. I've got you, Su. You can't leave me, alright? Just…let's get through today, and then we'll figure shit out, okay?"

Suri gave Kirk an adoring, wet-eyed look.

The porn they'd been ordered to perform as the housewife and handyman might've been forced, but…the way they looked at each other screamed truth.

Oh no…

So *that* was why Kirk got so angry with Peter the night I'd sobbed in the vault. Why he'd warned Peter not to catch feelings for me.

He caught them himself.

I could imagine the helplessness of that. The sheer inability to protect the one person who held your heart.

Henri sprang into mind as we left the manicured grass and spilled into the forest. Immediately, the soft thunder of our footfalls turned into crunchy cracking over twigs and leaves. Our speed dropped as our tight group fanned out, dodging trees and falling into lines, following animal trails and slightly overgrown paths through the thick undergrowth.

I'd trusted Henri, and he'd broken that trust.

I'd felt something for Henri, and he'd scrambled my feelings until I had no idea what I felt anymore.

I'd come here as someone and transformed into something *else.*

Something I didn't really like.

A nice girl turned nasty. A girl who would happily murder every Master she could get her hands on…but if a miracle happened and Peter's vow came true…then what?

If we somehow got everyone free and made the Masters pay…could I kill Henri too?

Could I look him in the eye and hurt him the way he hurt me?

Because if I can't, then…what does that say about me?

I glanced at the orange splodge on my upper thigh.

He'd shot me with his paintball gun.

He'd chosen me and fired, punching my leg with a horrible bullet that stung and bruised and exploded.

But…he hadn't shot Peter.

He'd aimed at him, prepared to pick on him like he always had, yet…his eyes had glowed with horror as he'd noticed what Victor had done to my friend.

And then, he'd shot me instead.

And that made me…grateful.

Hopeful…

"Enough about murder, please. You didn't answer me before." Rachel panted as she avoided a thick bush and hissed between her teeth as she ran over something sharp. "Where are we going, and how do you know a shortcut?"

Peter bent forward, his stamina rapidly failing the deeper we charged into the forest. "I know the same way I know what happens at a Diamond Kiss ceremony." He almost bumped into a tree. It took a swift yank on his elbow to keep him on the path. "Victor has made me serve at a few." He almost dry-retched as if the memories were too much. "You only know that a Diamond Kiss is death. You know that when one of us is selected, they don't come back." He giggled blackly. "But lucky ole me? I get to watch them die. I get to clean up. I get to see things even my nightmares can't conjure. And let me tell you…all of that shit? It haunts a person."

Rachel shot him a terrified glance. "W-What happens?"

Up ahead, Suri looked over her shoulder, listening to Peter.

I wanted to tell him to hush. To not give the jewels any other reason to end their lives.

But he grunted, "There's a cave. He calls it the Temple of Facets. There's a table. He calls it the Altar of Awakening." He laughed once. "There's a knife. He calls it the Blade of Beauty—"

"H-He stabs them to death?" Suri choked.

"Worse." Peter sighed, tripping. "He's the Master Jeweler, right? He thinks of us as his uncut gems. The ceremony ensures we sparkle." He didn't laugh this time, his horror drowning out his high.

Waving with a heavy, sweat-glittering arm, he pointed deeper into the trees. "Keep going straight. The forest spills onto the beach, and the entrance to the cave system is there. Temple of Facets is the third largest cave, but it leads to others."

"H-How do you know?" Suri asked.

"'Cause I've gone exploring…before he comes back to get me." Gulping down air, he forced himself to continue, "After the ceremony, I'm tasked with clean-up. Vile Vic doesn't want his cleaning crew seeing what he gets up to in there, so it falls on me. Not that there's much left by the time he's done." He smirked. "The blood is all gone—drunk by the Masters and—"

"What the actual *fuck*?" Kirk slammed to a stop and spun to face Peter. "They drink our motherfucking blood now?"

"Says it's rejuvenating." Peter almost swooned into a sapling as we skidded to a standstill. He laughed out loud, hobbling on shredded feet. "Did you know we make a chemical in our blood when we're about to be killed? It gets stronger the more shit-terrified we are. The ritual isn't about some religious practice but ensuring we're completely drowning in this chemical. And then…they harvest it. Like a crop." He laugh-cried. "We're just expensive vegetables—"

"*Harvest* it?" Kirk looked like he'd vomit. "What the fuck do you mean, *harvest* it?"

Peter rubbed his face, smearing blood on his cheek from his hands. "He says it's a time-reversal tonic. The most expensive commodity on earth—more sought after than gold or diamonds or…"

"I can't listen to this." Rachel shook her head and backed up. "I might take the cliff. I can't…"

"Shit." Peter put his bloody, oozy hands on his knees and sucked in lungfuls of air. "I didn't mean to say that." He groaned under his breath as a couple of tears escaped. "I'm sorry. Just…ignore what I said. Doesn't matter anyway 'cause we're getting out." Sucking back his grief, he stood upright. "We'll hide in the cave system. We'll stay hidden until dark, and then…we'll go to the pier and see if Master K's boat is docked."

Kirk grabbed Peter by the shoulders and shook him. "If you weren't burned to a crisp right now, I'd punch some goddamn sense into you! What the hell are you talking about? A boat? There's a boat? Why are we standing around talking about blood-drinking psychopaths when we could sail—"

"Boat won't be there." Peter's knees collapsed, leaving Kirk holding him up instead of shaking him.

"Damn, someone help me," Kirk barked.

Stepping forward, I slung Peter's arm over my shoulder and took as much of his weight as possible. The moment his cold-sweat slick body stuck to mine, Peter choked on a silent sob, then buried his face into my hair. "*Mujhe maaf kar do. Mujhe bohat afsos hai. Mera matlab yeh nahi tha, shaayad mujhe unhen koodne dena chahiye tha. Shaayad hum sabko koodna chahiye.*" (I'm sorry. So sorry. I didn't mean…maybe I should just let them jump. Maybe we should all jump.)

Rachel wrapped an arm around his waist from the other side and gave me a despairing look. "What did he say?"

I swallowed hard, squeezing Peter close. "He says he's not feeling well and hallucinating. None of what he said is true, but the cave system is close, and we should keep going."

Both Rachel and Kirk gave me a searching look, not believing me.

Kirk stepped into Peter with a menacing growl. "Tell me why

we aren't running to the pier, Pete. Tell me why you kept all of this to yourself. Tell me why you haven't told us what the fuck goes on out here."

Unable to stop tears tracking down his cheeks, Peter looked at Suri hugging herself behind Kirk and sighed. "Ily's right. I'm bullshitting, man. Making shit up." He forced a laugh. "Funny, huh?"

"The boat, Pete. *Now*."

Pushing me and Rachel off him, Peter staggered forward, kissed Suri on the cheek, then broke into a hobbling run. We all took off after him, our ears straining over the sounds of rustling bracken as he said, "Master K—Kyle—helped Victor burn me. He's leaving tonight…or was. He's one of the few who travel here by sea, but Victor doesn't let them moor for long. The yachts are only docked at the pier for an hour or so before Vic has them towed out and moored a kilometre or so away."

"So…we swim."

"Yeah, okay." Peter scoffed. "Give me a moment, and I'll summon the dolphins with my perfect whale song. They can tow us."

"We can swim a kilometre," Kirk argued, flicking Suri a look. His heart lived in his eyes every time he looked at her. "We have to try."

"We *are* trying." Peter nodded with a sickening sway. "Hide until dark. Wait until Master K goes to leave and his yacht docks. We'll swarm him in sheer numbers and sail into the sunrise." He nodded as if it were the perfect plan, either forgetting or ignoring the fact that Victor would be hunting all night, and guards would most likely patrol the pier for this very reason.

But…even as I saw nothing but holes in his plan, the others sucked up hope as if it were their last meal.

Their strides lengthened, our speed increased, and no one said another word as we ran.

Chapter Two

Henri

I RAN WITH THE REST OF them.

Across the drawbridge, down the grassy runway, and into the forest beyond.

Masters spread out, stalking through the dense trees like true hunters.

I felt like a fraud.

I'd never hunted a damn thing in my life, and the gun felt obscenely heavy in my hands.

Didn't matter that the bullets were rubber and detonated with paint, not lead. It still went against every bone in my body to hunt *people*.

Wrapping my fingers tighter around the weapon, I tried to figure out how I could win a game that had so many moving parts. I couldn't exactly kill every man on this island like I'd tried to do with Daxton, Roger, and Larry.

Out of three men, I'd only killed one.

My jog faltered a little as the true weight of that sentence punched me square in the face.

I killed someone.

Someone not exactly fit to stay alive, but…I'd still taken a life.

Did that redeem me because I'd removed a piece of evil, or did it shove me further into hell?

Does it matter?

You earned a one-way ticket the day you were born.

Gritting my teeth, I ran faster.

Trees reached out to grab me, branches swatted me in the face, and bushes clawed at my jeans. My ears rang for any sign that a Master had found a jewel and shot them.

Then again, the gunfire wasn't loud.

I'd been surprised at how quiet my shot had been when I'd fired at Ily. I couldn't rely on explosive bangs to point me in the right direction.

You need to figure this out and quickly.

How the fuck was I supposed to protect Ily when Victor had unleashed every monster in this place? They were free to do whatever their rotten hearts wanted. Victor had to be an idiot not to see what he'd offered and completely moronic if he thought they'd play by his rules.

Why would they?

Why would they permit only one winner when the prize was that tantalising?

The minute a slave was caught, I had absolutely no doubt that slave was most likely fucking dead.

A gush of sourness coated my tongue.

Tonight at rollcall, when this game was done, I had a horrible feeling jewel numbers would be far less, and the only one to blame would be Victor himself.

Find Ily.

That was my only objective.

What I'd do when I found her was a future problem.

Sprinting through the trees, I caught sight of three Masters picking and choosing the best trail through the undergrowth. A couple of them wafted their guns through bushes and ducked around trees as if expecting to spot a jewel huddled for cover in the bracken.

They wouldn't be in the forest.

Too risky. Too close.

Peter would've rounded them up...*if he's still standing.*

If I'd learned anything in my time here, Peter wasn't just a serving slave. Somewhere along the line, he'd become one of Victor's trusted servants, and if anyone would know this island...it was him.

You're making shit up, Ri.

As if he'd be allowed out of the gates.

He'd be as clueless as the rest.

In that case, he'd probably lead them to water.

That would be my plan.

I'd take the chance to swim, even if I couldn't steal something that floated.

My mind ached with memories from this morning.

Victor said Daxton boated here.

He'd been one of only a few Masters permitted such freedom. Maybe another Master was staying right now with the same privileges. Another boat moored somewhere. The smallest chance that a crowd of jewels could clamber onboard and sail out of our reach.

I ran harder.

The crash of heavy surf beckoned me forward.

The forest sloped downward, guiding me toward watery boundaries.

It didn't take long before the trees thinned and spat me out on a rugged beach. Dull sand glittered with blue and green sea glass, almost as if Victor tossed all his broken bottles into the ocean and let the sea turn them into wave-tumbled gemstones.

My loafers crunched over them, scattering a few as I jogged down the small embankment and leapt over a few larger rocks. Seaweed clung to an outcrop of boulders, the scent of salt and dead fish in the air.

Stopping in the middle of the sea-whipped beach, I looked left and right.

A few Masters spilled out onto the sand, glancing around like me.

The beach curved around a headland to my left.

In the distance, a long table, a few plastic tubs, and two youngish men worked under the scrutiny of four guards. Sunlight glinted on sharp filleting blades, followed by the glitter of fish scales.

Well, that explained the stench.

I supposed living surrounded by the ocean, Victor had his staff go fishing rather than import seafood. Did he have his own lobster pots and crab stores too?

Turning away from the staff preparing tonight's dinner, I held up my hand to ward off the sunlight spearing off the waves.

Before me stretched an incredibly long pier.

Buoyant and locked together with black flotation pieces, they interlocked like a giant puzzle snake, stretching far out to sea. With every wave, it rolled and crested, riding the water with its interconnecting pieces.

Whatever vessel sailed in could dock without any worry of shallows and hidden reefs.

Farther down the pier, a few posts stabbed the sky with tethering ropes...

But no boat.

No way free.

Two Masters jogged past me, heading to the right and the sweeping cliffs. Victor had built his stronghold at the very top, leaving the downward run through the forest to spit us out at the bottom. Huge granite rockfaces towered above, acting like speakers for the roaring surf. The weathered stone dotted with white-feathered seagulls.

The Masters disappeared into a black crack, swallowed up by the island.

I swayed to follow.

"Ah, Henri, there you are." Charles panted as he slowed to a stop before me. "Isn't this fun?"

Swallowing down my sarcastic retort, I forced a smile. "You betcha. Great fun."

He grinned and pointed to where the other Masters had vanished. "Come on. We better follow. I bet my ass our little gems are hiding in the cave system."

"Just invite everyone, why don't you." Another Master pulled up beside Charles.

I didn't recognise the guy, but he smirked and swiped back oily brown hair. "Peter knows how to get to the Temple of Facets. I reckon he'll try to hide in there. But stop announcing it to the entire island, Charles. Less fun for those who find them first."

"And what do *you* classify as fun?" I asked carefully, fisting my weapon.

The stranger chuckled. "Buy me a drink first, and then I'll spill my secrets."

Charles rolled his eyes. "That's Kyle." He glanced at his wristwatch. "And he's right. Come with us, Henri. We'll hunt together, but then it's every man for himself when we find them, fair?"

My guts churned at the thought of teaming up with the same men I wanted to slaughter.

But…we'd cover more ground as a group, so…I nodded.

Once I found Ily, then I could deal with them.

"Fine." I fell in behind them. "Let's go."

"That's the spirit." Charles slugged me in the arm, then broke into a lumbering jog. I could walk at his turtle speed. None of us spoke as we headed toward the cliffs and the shadowy crack just above the surf line. Waves lapped at the rocks below the entrance, frothing white and noisy.

Charles stumbled to a walk, breathing hard. "Damn, I need to work on my cardio. Can we stroll a bit?"

Kyle scratched his jaw, raking his fingernails through a thin chin strap. Skinny but strong, he reminded me of a feral chihuahua my old neighbour had. Tiny but absolutely lethal, with a stare that could frighten a fucking Doberman. "You're a liability, Charleston."

"*I'm* the liability?" Charles chuckled, coughing up a hair ball and spitting it on the sand. "You're the reason Victor started with all his rules and cameras in the first place." He rolled his eyes in my direction. "I was quite happy with my little needs. I could cut Dane in private, and no one needed to know. But then *he* came along." He scowled. "Want to know who has a fascination with dismemberment? Him. That guy. Right there."

Kyle threw me a smirk. "What can I say? I wanted to be a doctor when I was a boy."

"Heaven forbid you ever become a surgeon." Charles shuddered dramatically. "Your patients would walk out missing pieces."

Kyle laughed. "Isn't that the fun part?"

"Pretty sure that's the opposite of what the Hippocratic oath says," Charles shot back.

Kyle snickered and hefted his gun onto his shoulder. "My version says I shall do harm and enjoy it."

Everything about him put my teeth on edge.

Looking at me, Kyle sighed happily. "Can't help what we like, hey, H? Just like I can't help liking the way they scream."

"You can make them scream without removing body parts, you know." Charles rolled his eyes. "I could teach you if you'd like. You lack finesse."

"And you're getting soft in your old age." Kyle poked Charles in his spreading belly. "You have a wife at home who has no idea you like cock. Don't think I haven't noticed the way you look at Dane when he's giving you a blowy." Kyle winked in my direction. "He's got feelings that he shouldn't have. Then again…so have you."

A cold draft shot down my spine that this feral creature had noticed what I liked or didn't. The thought of him finding Ily before me…of removing her pieces and making her scream.

My finger twitched around the trigger.

I wished my gun was full of death, not paint.

"It's not really up to you to say what feelings I'm supposed to have," I muttered.

"You're weak." Kyle sniffed. "Just pointing it out."

"I could be weak." I nodded. "Or I could finally be learning the power of emotions and all the other shit that comes with them."

"Ah, that's right. You're a poor little broken boy who didn't get a hug from his mother." He laughed and rolled his soulless eyes. "Tell you what...when you stop searching for love and accept that you're top of the food chain and those little jewels are ours to slice, dice, fuck, and shoot, then we'll talk. Until then...you're wasting my time." He scoffed at Charles and his winded breathing. "Actually, you're *both* wasting my time." Breaking into a run, he dashed toward the black maw in the cliffs. "See you later, losers. I'll be sure to leave a few pieces for you."

"Asshole." Charles watched him go. "Always has been."

And that asshole was hunting Ily.

"See ya round, Charles." I took off after Kyle.

No fucking way would I let him out of my sight.

Charles tried to call me back, but his wheeze faded beneath the surf.

My feet pounded over sand and sea glass, chasing Kyle as he leapt over a few rockpools and scurried up the boulders toward the black crack in the cliffside. Taking the path of least resistance, he scaled the rocks and pulled away as I slogged through soft sand.

Changing my direction, I followed his, leaping onto the rocks and praying I didn't break an ankle.

The sly fucker kept up a pace my damn loafers couldn't. The slippery shoes offered no traction as I did my best to leap from rock to rock. Slinging my gun over my shoulder with its black strap, I tried to go faster—to stop him, kill him, only...

A strange rumbling beneath my feet.

A roar of power; a shake of earth.

A flock of seagulls took wing.

"Watch out!" Charles yelled behind me.

Too late.

Kyle vanished into the cave just as a gush of heavy seawater exploded beneath me.

It felt as if the ocean formed a fist and sucker-punched me right in the balls, throwing me backward, slapping me with a tower of salt.

My back bellowed as I landed on craggy rocks.

My temple thwacked against a sharp outcrop.

My gun broke from my weight, the muzzle snapping in half as I tucked and rolled, wincing as a curtain of punishing rain pummelled from above just like it'd pummelled from below.

A few seconds and it was over.

The roar faded, the violent water nothing more than wetness glittering on rocks.

Fuck!

Cupping myself, I rode through the flush of icy-hot agony as my balls throbbed from the ocean's beating. Everything hurt. Everything dripped.

Goddammit!

Clucking his tongue, Charles appeared by my pounding head.

Planting his hands on his hips, he looked at where I lay contorted and in motherfucking agony. "Blowhole got you good, huh? Avoid the rockpools. You have no idea which one will turn into a waterspout."

The torture in my dick slowly faded, seeping into my lower belly and down my legs. I wished the pain in my head would do the same thing. "Yeah, thanks." I groaned, gritting my teeth and forcing myself upright.

"Oh shit. Guess you're out of the game." Charles cocked an eyebrow at my broken gun. He chuckled as his eyes dropped down my jeans. "And I hate to tell you, but that's not just seawater you're dripping in."

Ignoring the contusions throbbing in my spine and the black dots dancing over my eyes, I stood and brushed at my soaking clothes. A rush of nausea—that had nothing to do with morals and was more about a head injury—had me locking my knees so I didn't fall back down.

At least the spots in my gaze faded as I looked at the bright orange paint coating my left side.

Great.

Fucking wonderful.

"Definitely out of the game. You've smashed all your paintballs and broken your gun." Charles shrugged with fake grief. "Ah well, better luck next time, old chap. I'll be sure to tell Ily you said hi." Licking his lips, he bent a little closer. "I have to say, after watching you two at dinner, I've been dying to know how she tastes."

I bared my teeth as the world swam a little.

Backing out of my reach, he chuckled. "You know...Kyle might like to cut them up, but what he doesn't know is, if you don't cause too much damage, you have a never-ending smorgasbord."

Rubbing at my blood-streaked temple, willing the beach to stay still, I frowned. "Smorgasbord?"

Lowering his voice so even the seagulls didn't hear him, he whispered, "I'm saying I've eaten a few strips off Dane over the years, and as long as you don't cut too deep or take too much, the body heals itself in the most miraculous—"

"Wait." All my pain vanished. "You're saying you fucking *eat* him?"

He laughed with a whimsical sort of obscenity. "Ah, don't be jealous. I used to be like you. Blood was my dessert of choice, but after a while...I needed more. You'll reach that level too, eventually. And I'll be here to teach you."

My ears roared.

My mind went blank.

I'd seen some sick shit in this place, but that?

Knowing that this seemingly normal man—this man who had a wife and a career and was old enough to have existed in society with no one the wiser—*dined* on people?

Yeah...he has to die.

"Go rest up," he said. "That head wound looks nasty." Breaking into a waddling run, he waved. "Bye!"

I lurched after him.

The world tilted.

I landed on my knees.

The cartilage in my joints crunched against barnacle-sharp rock.

"No, no, don't follow!" Charles glanced back. "You're really not looking so good. Don't worry, plenty more games to enjoy if you sit this one out." Laughing again, he clambered toward the cave entrance where Kyle had disappeared.

Scrambling to my feet, I went to chase.

Vertigo kicked my ass.

I tripped to the left, the surf dragging me toward it with its salty song.

FUCK!

Unslinging my useless gun, I tossed it into the sand with a snarl.

Closing my eyes and balling my hands, I focused on getting

my shit together.

I couldn't think about Charles or Kyle or the other two Masters already in the caves.

Focus.

Breathe.

I tried to do what Ily did every morning and ground myself. I pictured the pain in my head trickling down my body and into the beach.

I felt ridiculous standing there with my eyes closed and pain tearing through me, but…slowly…breath by breath, my mind quietened just enough for the pain to cascade through my bones and seep out the soles of my feet.

What the hell?

Meditation, she called it.

Wrong…it was a fucking miracle.

My eyes snapped open, clear and focused again.

How had something so simple as shutting out the noise and concentrating worked so well?

Sure, I still hurt.

Sure, I was still cold and drenched and bruised in places I really wished I wasn't, but…it was no longer debilitating.

The wooziness was gone.

The pain manageable.

I ran.

I chased after Charles and his sick confessions.

I had nothing but my bare hands, all while two guys—who just admitted they got off on chopping up human flesh and turning cannibal—hunted Ily.

If they find her…

The animal inside me prowled and snapped at its tether.

The darkness sucked me deeper.

I'd tried to play this smart.

Tried to stay human.

But…the ocean had either decided to condemn me or free me.

I wasn't meant to play this as a man.

I was meant to play this as a creature unbeholden to rules and regulations.

Stiff with pain and breaking beneath monstrosity, I stalked Charles right into the darkness of the cave. He stumbled and grunted as he navigated uneven ground, sounding like an elephant seal as I hunted.

Every step, I turned my back on sanity.

Every breath, I embraced anarchy.

I'd eaten with this man.

Spoken with this man.

I hated this man because he was filth and rot, but…so was I. And there wasn't enough room for both of us.

I cleared my throat as the cold, dank stone snuffed out sunlight. "Charles."

He sucked in a breath and turned to face me. His nose wrinkled at my sorry state. "You don't give up, do you? Look, go back and have a hot shower. There'll be plenty of other games." He reached out and patted my shoulder. "Go on. Have a beer and just, *guhh*—"

His voice cut off as my hand lashed out and wrapped around his throat.

Every hideous part of me sprang out with fangs.

I couldn't stop it.

I had no control over the diabolical savagery within me.

He *ate* people…

Sick.

Vile.

Dead.

Slamming his well-padded spine against the wet rock, I wrapped both hands around his throat.

He tried to speak.

He scratched at my wrists.

He drew blood as he thrashed.

But I just kept *squeezing*.

The more he struggled, the worse I became.

He turned suicidal in my hold.

Kicking, groaning, flailing.

His weight almost threw me off balance as I kicked away my slippery shoes and planted bare feet on slimy stone.

But I didn't let go.

I didn't speak or look away as his eyes bugged wide, his mouth gasped like a dying trout, and his soft body went slack in my hold.

I killed him slowly, personally. I watched his lifeforce sputtering, ending…

I'd killed Daxton in a fugue of fury. I hadn't been aware when I'd stolen his life.

This was different.

This was cold, ruthless, merciless.

With a soft grunt, he slithered down the cave wall, collapsing between my spread legs.

I went with him, crouching over him, never loosening my grip.

Another roaring.

Another pebble dancing shake.

But it wasn't a blowhole exploding this time.

It was me.

My soul.

My immortal spirit shot out of me as I dug my thumbs deeper into his fleshy neck and *squeezed*.

I squeezed until he switched from sleeping to dead.

I squeezed until there was no chance he'd ever wake again.

I squeezed until the beast inside me stopped snarling and accepted that it'd won.

Only then did I wipe my hands on his shirt, steal his gun, and stride barefoot into cave-wrapped darkness.

Chapter Three

COULD A PERSON KEEP LIVING IF their heart stopped beating?

Because mine did.

The moment we entered the Temple of Facets...

It stopped.

Just like that.

Salty tang and chilly rock entombed us as we traded the sea glass-pebbled beach and stumbled into the cave system. No one spoke as Peter collided from stone wall to stone wall, guiding us deeper into the island's belly.

The first circular space looked like any other cave. Scraggy and sharp, wild and wet where no humans were welcome. Enough light spilled from outside to etch every step with shadow. The second was larger, with massive stalactites descending from the roof—some so long we had to weave around them as we followed our feverish tour guide. We travelled through a narrow rock corridor, light fading with every metre, forcing us to rely more on touch than sight.

But the moment we exited that narrow alleyway—decorated by nature and its mercurial tides full of seaweed and broken bits of coral—and spilled into a cavernous catacomb…my heart ceased beating.

Flickering sconces in the shape of burning torches granted us soft, dreamy light, trying to hide the nightmare before us.

My knees buckled.

My stomach threatened to revolt.

All around me, jewels reacted in their own way.

All skin colours turned shock-white.

All eye colours went horror-wide.

No one could wrench their gaze off the table in the centre.

No, not a table.

An altar.

Carved from the very cave itself with a thick pedestal and chunky stone platform.

A *human*-sized platform.

Shaped like a flat coffin, grooves cut into its edges, ready to capture liquid and funnel it to the end where a glass cauldron swung, greedy and grasping for every drop.

An ancient ache worked through me.

Time seemed to overlap.

My mind filled with similar scenes. Historical sacrifices, pages from books I'd read, and scenes depicted in the old castles and manors I'd explored.

In every era of humanity, evil had presided.

Today was no different.

And standing in that oppressive cave with stone pews circling the sacrificial altar and torches adding a patina of misery, I struggled to believe in innocence. Struggled to hold faith in hope.

Even Mother Nature seemed in on this hellscape with stalactites dripping like fangs and mineral-deposited stalagmites spearing like demon fingers.

I'd never felt so small or so stupid.

Historic brutality couldn't compare to the energy pouring off my fellow jewels.

The indescribable shattering of thirty broken hearts as we all came to terms with our fate if we didn't find a way free.

One day, each of us would be buckled and bled on that altar.

One day, every single one of us would cease to exist.

For an age, no one breathed.

But then…a gasp.

A cry.

A stumble.

The spell broke, and the jewels all reeled back as one. Bumping into one another, choking on wails, scrambling for strength, and finding they had nothing left.

"Don't…" I whispered, gagging on my own dead heart. "Don't…."

I wanted to tell them not to give up hope.

Not to envision what'd happened in here or to picture themselves on that table.

"Stay," Peter ordered as he clung to a stalagmite, doing his best to remain standing. "Forget what you see. Ignore it. We'll travel deeper into the cave system where they will never find us, and then we'll—"

"We'll be caught!" Nancy screamed, her bright red hair looking like flames in the gloom. "We'll be caught like always and hurt and raped and…and—" Slashing at her wet cheeks, she trembled. "We'll end up on that." She pointed at the altar. "No matter what we do. No matter how well we behave. No matter how long we serve. We'll all end up on *that*. Oh God—" Hugging herself, she backed up. "Zach and Seline…Paula and Thandi—"

"Don't do that," Peter commanded weakly. "They're dead. They're free—"

"And they died *right here*." Nancy sobbed with no sound, shook with no rattling. "No. I can't. No more. I-I can't do this." Pushing past the other jewels blocking her exit and darting around the dripping stalagmites, she snarled at Peter as he snatched her wrist.

"Let go of me, Pete! I'm leaving. Right now. I can't stay in here. I can't stay here period. I'm swimming. I don't fucking care—"

"You swim, you die." Peter groaned, swaying on the spot as Nancy ripped her arm back.

"I've heard drowning is an okay way to go." Rebecca, the blonde with small breasts and weary eyes, drifted to Nancy's side. She looked at all of us before linking fingers with Nancy's. "Nancy and I are going to try. If anyone else wants to come—"

"I will." Dane stepped forward. "I reached my limit the first time that Charles bastard made me cook a strip of my skin for his appetiser."

"Me too," Suri whispered. "I can't stomach Branson and Azhar sharing me again."

"Fuck, if you're going, I'm going too." Kirk wrapped his arm around Suri's slim shoulders.

"You don't even know if there's land close by." Peter winced, doing his best to stay standing. Any sign of his drug-addled state was gone. "Please, guys. Don't do this. I know you've all been hurt. I know you're at your wits end. I know death seems like a vacation at this point but…just trust me. We need to stick together. If we do, we can—"

"I'm sorry." Kirk shrugged. "This might be the only time we're allowed out without our collars electrifying us into soup. If we don't try now…we might never get another chance." Stepping forward, bringing Suri with him, Kirk clutched Peter around the nape and squeezed. "Be safe, brother."

Letting Peter go, Kirk glanced at the jewels who'd stepped forward to join him and nodded. "Let's go."

They left before any of us could stop them.

The emptiness of their sudden departure made the Temple of Facets all the more oppressive, as if the cave sucked their souls into its ghostly collection.

With a guttural groan, Peter buckled to the ground.

Rachel and I dashed toward him just as another group of jewels banded together and headed toward a black crack to the right. Shooting Peter a look, a brown-haired girl who I thought was called Harper said softly, "We don't want to swim, but I agree with Kirk. This is our one shot to find a way off this island."

"*There is no way!*" Peter shouted. "Not unless we stick together and take them down."

Harper gave him a sad smile. "You're talking about war. But all I'm hearing is suicide."

"Harper's right," a curvy Asian girl muttered. "It's too risky to stick together, and it's far too risky to think we can fight back. We'll spread out in the caves. We'll stand a better chance at hiding in small groups. When it's dark, we'll make a raft or something and get the hell away from this place."

Peter shook his head with a cold laugh. "A raft? Now who's deluded?"

Harper and her friend didn't reply.

They just waved and stepped into the crack.

Peter blanched. "No, wait!"

Too late.

More jewels vanished after them, slipping through the stone and swallowed by cave-black darkness.

"*Shit!*" Peter pushed me away, trying to stand just as a third group of jewels headed toward the left and another crevice partially hidden by a stalagmite and dancing with fake firelight from the torches.

"Don't even think about it," he snarled. "There's no way out that way." He held up a bleeding, charred hand. "There's a blowhole that erupts at high tide. You'll drown—"

"You might've been in here before, Peter." A dark-skinned girl sniffed. "But you can't know every crag."

"We'll go find our Masters," the strawberry-blonde girl who'd asked if Victor would forgive them before we'd been told to run, said softly. "If we willingly go to them, then they'll be lenient, and we can forget about this." Glancing at the small group, she braced her shoulders. "Ready?"

"Ready." The dark-skinned girl nodded.

I stepped toward them. "Please, don't. Listen to Peter—"

They vanished too.

And just like that…our thirty somehow became nine.

My knees locked as I smiled at a few familiar faces.

Peter, Rachel, Citra, Mollie, Sonya, myself, a Chinese guy missing two fingers, and two other girls who avoided eye contact.

"Help me up, Rach." Peter did his best to clamber to his oozing, charcoal feet.

With a heavy sigh, she did as he requested, wincing with her own pain.

I went to them and took my share of Peter's weight.

Rachel gave me a soft smile and nodded.

I nodded back.

Somehow, a fierce friendship had sprung between us. We'd barely spoken, yet our bond felt stronger than any of my old high-school girlfriends. I supposed a common goal and utmost determination not to let this island and its monsters beat us forged feelings that went above mere like and straight to sisterhood.

Breaking our stare, Rachel pushed Peter's damp hair off his forehead. "Okay, Pete. We're all yours. Where are we going?"

He blinked at her touch, then swooned as if she'd robbed the last dregs of his energy. His chin flopped onto his chest; his knees buckled again.

"Ah, crap." Rachel and I clung to him, stopping him from collapsing. "Let's put him down for a bit," Rachel said. "I'll see if I can find some water and cloth. If we wrap his hands and feet, he might be able to—"

"I'm fine. I'm fine," Peter slurred and stood on shaky legs. "We need to hurry. We've spent too much time in here already." Arching his chin at the closest pew, he muttered, "Set me there and then raid that chest." He pointed at a weathered-wooden chest with brass fixings. It was large enough to hide a folded-up body, and I honestly didn't have the stomach to see what was inside.

Peter gave me an understanding grimace. "It's full of tools. Vials. Siphons. Goblets…that kinda thing. Victor doesn't keep the Blade of Beauty down here, but he does keep other knives."

"You planning on stabbing a Master now?" Rachel rolled her

eyes as we both stumbled with Peter between us. We deposited him on the pew he'd requested.

My spine protested as we set him down and backed up.

"If it comes down to it. Yes." Peter nodded and placed his ruined hands upright on his lap. "Now, hurry. Take whatever weapon you find. I want to be out of here in sixty seconds."

"Gotcha." The Chinese guy strode forward and reached for the chest.

I expected it to be locked.

It wasn't.

Flipping it up, he stumbled back and raked a hand through glossy black hair. "Man, this just keeps getting worse."

Peter stood and hobbled toward him. He didn't get far before he fell face first against the altar and clung to it. The image of him touching that rust-stained stone threatened to make me sick.

"Ignore the canopic jars, Caishen," Peter muttered.

"The *what* jars?" Rachel spun around from where she rummaged through open shelving where black-wax candles and huge gemstones glittered.

If those gems were real, the size of the sapphire alone would be enough to buy a house in expensive London suburbs.

Needing to do something, I headed toward the large intricately carved cupboard to the left. The design looked like entwined souls imploring the heavens to save them, all while shadowy things tried to pull them down.

"The Egyptians used to use them," Peter groaned. "To hold organs in the mummification process."

Caishen ripped his hands away. "*Cào nǐ mā.*"

Peter actually chuckled, as if anything was amusing at this point. "I had a friend from Canton. Doesn't that mean 'fuck my mother'?"

Caishen shot him a smirk. "Not your mother, obviously. *His* mother. Fucking Vile Vic's."

"Ah. Well yes, she's partly to blame for birthing him." Peter pressed his forehead against the altar. He breathed heavily; all signs of mirth gone. "I promise there's nothing inside the jars anymore. Just grab the knives and—"

"Was there something in them before?" Rachel asked. "Are you telling me they cut out our organs as well as drink our blood, Pete?"

Peter didn't reply.

Instead, his gaze shot to me as I yanked open the cupboard. "Ily, *don't*—!"

Too late.

Oh God, what—

I tripped backward, rolled my ankle against a small stalagmite, and fell painfully on my ass.

Oh God.

Oh God.

Oh God!

Just like my heart stopped beating, my soul threatened to fly free and abandon me.

"Close it!" Peter snarled with energy I hadn't heard in a while. "Close the fucking doors, Ilyana!"

Scrambling to my feet, I couldn't tear my gaze off empty sockets where eyes used to be.

Skulls.

So many, many skulls.

All stacked neatly side by side, bleached white and dust-free, rows upon rows upon—

The doors slammed closed. Caishen stood with his back to it. "Time to run, don't you agree?"

I tried to swallow.

To nod.

The cave spun.

My lungs burned.

Peter broke my rising panic attack—or added to it—by whispering, "Now you know why I was so adamant about finding that Diamond Kiss chit." Hobbling toward me, he tucked me under his sick-sweaty wing. "At least none of the Masters have come forward with it. If any of them had found it, they would've said something by now." Kissing my temple, he breathed, "It's okay, *jaanu*. We'll get them out. You convinced me to try. Don't give up on us now."

Spinning in his hold, I flung my arms around his slim waist, not caring I smeared his streaky bullseye all over my own. "How the hell have you survived this long, Paavak? It's bad enough being a jewel and putting up with the nightmares in that castle. But this?" Pulling away, I studied his tortured black stare. "Watching this? Seeing what they do? Cleaning up what they've done?" I couldn't hold back the tears. "Please, *please* tell me you don't have to…they don't make you—"

"Cut the heads off?" He winced. "No. I just have to gather the parts, toss away the bits he doesn't want, and preserve the pieces he does. Acid does most of the work."

And that was my limit.

Breaking out of his embrace, I vomited.

A pitiful little pile of dismay and disgrace as the reality of Peter's life slapped me stupid.

Five years.

Five years, he'd not only endured but done things that would forever haunt him.

How wasn't he catatonic?

How was he still sane?

Peter went to hold back my hair but cursed under his breath as his bleeding hands stuck to my strands. "We've got to go, Ily. I don't mean to belittle your reaction, but…save the throwing up till tomorrow, okay?"

Caishen planted a hand on Peter's shoulder. "I've always respected you, even if you pissed me off for being such a stickler for the rules. I'm sorry for every mean thought I ever had that you got preferential treatment for being our little leader."

"Respect me by getting her moving." Sucking down his agony, Peter looked at the other jewels scattered in varying degrees of dread. "None of us will end up in that cupboard. I promise you. I meant what I said. I'll kill you myself before I let anyone else be brought into this temple. But right now, forget everything you saw and follow me. As fast as you can. It's dark the deeper we go, but use your hands, and you'll get by."

Shuffling behind the small podium—another rock that'd been chipped and chiselled to make a platform—he beckoned us to hurry. "Fuck the weapons. We've run out of time. Let's go."

Vanishing behind a thick outcropping of stalagmites, he limped into the darkness.

Rachel bounced on the spot, urgency flooding her. "We've got to go." Waving at the other girls, she ordered, "Come on. Move. Quickly."

Citra led the pack, following Peter through the secret passage.

Caishen gave me a worried look. "I don't know about him, but I'd feel better if I had a knife."

"Me too." I flew toward the chest.

Together, we flung out canopic jars and tossed away heavy black velvet robes. Almost in sync, I found a few battery-fed torches, and he found a single knife with a nicked blade as if it'd been used against stone.

"Let's go." Holding out his hand, Caishen gave me a kind smile as I threaded my fingers with his.

We didn't say a word as he pulled me through stone into hell.

Chapter Four

Henri

I LOST TRACK OF TIME AND sanity.

The deeper the cave system swallowed me, the worse I lost myself.

The cave—with an altar, cupboard full of skulls, and carved seating for devils to watch fucked-up ceremonies—chilled my bones until I turned numb.

The energy in that place coated my skin with goosebumps.

I wanted to leave as soon as I stepped foot inside it and only stayed long enough to ransack the boxes and cupboards, looking for something to help me do whatever it was that I would do.

Nothing.

Nothing but a torch with half-dead batteries.

I had no idea what my plan was.

I was barefoot, freezing, and frankly, I feared myself.

Feared how fucking *good* it'd felt to squeeze the life out of Charles.

How empty my mind was as I added yet another soul to my tally.

I felt no guilt.

No remorse.

Nothing but single-minded determination to find Ily.

Fisting the torch, I eyed up the crevices leading from the large cave where death dripped down the walls. The one to the right was the largest. The one slightly to my left utterly uninviting with its ill-fitting crack and jagged rocks.

I chose that one.

If I wanted to hide, I'd probably go that way. Choosing the least inviting direction to dissuade those chasing me.

Twisting a little, I stepped into the dank, damp chill.

My stolen paintball gun whacked and cracked against the narrow walls, hindering me a little as I clicked on the torch and left behind fake sconces and a blood-stained altar.

I stopped counting minutes as I followed the long seam, heading deeper and deeper into the earth.

Every step, the blackness inside me billowed, matching the blackness swallowing me whole.

I feared the beast within me.

The thirst for blood.

The hunger for carnage.

All around me, heavy rock suffocated the sounds of existence, making it feel as if I'd been buried alive. I walked in a grave with no ending, laid to eternal damnation beneath soil full of saltwater.

On and on, I walked.

Heard no one.

Saw nothing.

Flashes of what I'd done to Charles popped like holograms in the gloom.

His eyes as I snuffed them out.

His lips as they turned blue.

His death had been satisfying but also…hollow.

It hadn't granted me peace.

If anything, it'd opened a clawing, rabid hunger inside to do it again. And *again*. To eradicate every son of a bitch on this island until I was the only one.

I sniffed back the whiff of paint on my soggy clothes as I travelled through perpetual cave-dark night.

The journey acted like a sedative on the snarling mayhem in my veins.

It gave me space to think instead of act impulsively, and by the time the narrow pathway spat me out into another cave, I bordered human once again.

The click of my torch as I turned it off echoed in the rock-wrapped chamber. I didn't need any light as the cave had electricity—burning brightly from exposed light bulbs suspended from the ceiling by thick plastic-wrapped wire.

Glancing around, I spied a few things of interest.

The uneven ground was soaked with the black-crimson of dried blood. A heavy wooden box tucked to the side looked like a treasure chest of murder. A heavy-duty hose hung, coiled and sleeping against the wall. The whiff of ocean filled the space, doing its best to tease my nose with wild water instead of the lingering stench of viscera.

Whatever went on in here would make even the sickest serial

killer blanch.

It looked like a butcher's workshop—an abattoir to chop up meat.

Swallowing hard, I stepped toward the box. With gritted teeth, I lifted the lid and found things that made my spine shiver.

A bone saw.

A small axe.

Heavy-duty scissors, filleting blades, even a small battery-powered chainsaw.

If I wasn't so numb, I might've done something foolish like throw up.

But the blackness kept me anesthetised.

The darkness kept me shielded.

Running my fingers over the tools of dismemberment, I chose the small axe and continued on my way.

Another crack to the right.

A short, muffled scream echoing down its path.

My hands curled around the torch and axe as I squeezed into the chasm. My toes turned to ice, and the stupid gun slung across my back kept catching on jagged rocks.

I hoped Kyle was up ahead.

I'd teach him a lesson of what it felt like to be sliced and diced.

Ducking beneath a low outcropping of stone, I scowled as my torch flickered and dimmed.

Victor will murder you if you go on a killing spree.

My steps slowed.

The faintest nudges of commonsense acted like shards of light through the dark fog of my mind.

I was a guest and governed by certain laws.

I couldn't let myself go.

I still had to live here. Still had nowhere else to go—

Another scream.

Followed by a masculine laugh.

My jaw clenched.

The urge to join in the pain almost consumed me again.

The fog grew thicker. My heart turned blacker.

But…reality made me pause.

I could explain away Charles.

I didn't have to explain anything at all.

No one had seen me kill him.

Anyone could've done it.

No cameras out here—

At least, I don't think so.

My eyes shot to the craggy roof as I followed the snaking stone path and stepped into yet another cave. No blinking red lights recorded my every move. No signs of cameras anywhere.

My torch beam skimmed this new cave, dancing over salt-encrusted stalagmites and sweeping over shadowy pockets. Seemed Victor hadn't brought electricity any farther—

A bloodcurdling scream pierced my eardrums.

I froze.

"That's a good girl," a man crooned. "I love it when you succumb. Such a good, wonderful girl." A man. A psychopath.

"Don't!" a woman begged. "Stop. Please don't—"

I moved before I could stop myself.

Dodging a few boulders, I followed the natural shape of the cave into another chamber.

My feet slammed to a stop as I stumbled onto a scene straight out of a dirty BDSM porno.

Two jewels. Two Masters. Coarse rope binding their prey to conveniently tall stalagmites. Neither of the jewels were shot with paintballs. In fact, they looked remarkably unbruised.

The strawberry-blonde jerked as she noticed me. Her golden collar twinkled against her throat thanks to unusable cellphone torches that the men had arranged as uplights against the cave walls.

"What the fuck are you staring at?" a bald Master spat. He stood before the pretty strawberry-blonde with his hand in his undone slacks and his hard cock in his fist. Shirtless, he showed off a gym-toned body all while his annoyance faded beneath smug arrogance. "Like what you see?"

Keeping the axe hidden behind my right thigh, I shrugged. "Where did you get the rope?"

"Always come prepared." The other Master with receding black hair and piercing ebony eyes tapped his nose. "Once a Boy Scout. Always a Boy Scout."

Strolling forward, ensuring I kept my posture intrigued instead of threatening, I cocked my chin at the surprisingly calm jewels. "How will you determine who's the winner? None of them are covered in paint."

"Meh." The bald one shrugged. "We're not really into

competition. Penny and Abigail know they've got it good with us. They came to find us, didn't you, girls?"

The strawberry-blonde, who'd practically begged at Victor's feet for redemption before Emerald Bruises started, nodded. "We know we're lucky." She glanced at the auburn-haired girl. "Don't we, Pen?"

"Master S and Master B are very good to us." Penny nodded with a soft smile. "We're grateful we found them so easily. We're safe with them."

My ears pricked for lies.

I found none.

Strange...

"Which one was screaming?" I asked quietly.

The blonde blushed. "I was, Master H. But...it's a game, you see—"

"A game?" My eyes widened.

"A game where we're the big bad assholes, and they're our meek little toys." The bald guy released his dick and pointed at his friend. "We indulge in all sorts. Have you never heard of mutual fun *without* pain?" He scoffed. "Stewart and I like to stick to ourselves, alright? It was pure luck we stumbled onto our girls, and we have no intention of giving them up, so run along and—"

"Did I say I wanted a piece?"

"You're certainly watching them like you do."

"I'm looking for my own." My voice turned thick as I asked the blonde, "Where's Ily?"

She flinched. "W-We separated. I'm not sure which way they would've gone after we left."

"They?"

"She was with Peter and Rachel and a bunch of others," Penny answered.

"Fuck's sake, you're ruining the mood, man," Stewart muttered. "Go away."

The urge for bloodshed rushed up my gullet.

These men were just as bad as all the rest.

I should exterminate them. Slaughter them. Save the jewels and—

Condemn myself to Victor's wrath.

I'd already pushed my limits where he was concerned.

What if he snapped and killed me, and Ily was left all alone? Alone and at the mercy of Kyle?

Swallowing hard, I stepped back.

It wasn't my job to save these jewels.

It didn't even look like they *wanted* to be saved.

I wouldn't interfere, but I would threaten them…just a little.

Casually holding up the axe, I made eye contact with the two Masters. "I'm not sure if you've heard the castle gossip, but I killed Daxton Hall and permanently disabled a guy called Roger. Instead of punishing me, Victor gave me a job."

"Yeah, we heard." Stewart nodded with a wince. "You're his in-house exterminator." He glanced at his partner. "Ben and I are fully aware how strict Victor runs his home, and we've never given him any reason to discipline us." He crossed his arms. "We pay our membership fees, come for some R and R, and leave."

Stewart took over. "Like we said, we, eh…we're not like the others."

I laughed under my breath. "Bullshit."

"It's true," Ben, the bald guy, jumped in. "We have tamer tastes than the rest." His eyes narrowed. "Compared to you and the rumours circulating about your love of blood, we're probably pathetic, but…we run a stressful company together. We're the bitch of every board member we stupidly appointed, and this is the only time we get to de-stress."

"By fucking slaves." I sniffed. "If you're rich enough to visit Victor, then you could afford a good fuck out in the real world." Stepping forward, I lowered my voice. "You're fooling yourself that you aren't one of us."

"We're not fooling anyone," Stewart said. "We know our limits. Ben and I don't have time to date, and we can't hire prostitutes if that's what you're getting at. Our company is public and of a sensitive nature. We're watched every fucking moment. The board would steal our company if there was even a *whisper* of controversy. In fact, they've been trying to do exactly that for years. The one time I risked going on Tinder, the girl I matched with was one of their spies. So…fuck you and your judgement. We want companionship as much as the next guy. It sucks we've had to resort to this, but…Victor provides us a safe space to play and—"

"What Stewart is trying to say," Ben said with a sharp edge, "is…fuck off and leave us alone."

Lowering the axe, I glanced at the jewels.

I studied their trusting eyes.

I vibrated with both man and beast and felt the nudges of that idiotic hero who'd come here hoping to save them.

But...that wasn't my path anymore.

Without a word, I turned on my heel and left.

My torch stopped working in the fourth hour.

Four fucking hours and I still hadn't found her.

I trembled with a deep-seated chill, and my ancient Casio hinted the morning had well and truly bled into afternoon.

I'd heard nothing.

Seen no one.

Just me in this ancient tomb, slowly dying in the dark.

Every crevice led to a blacker cave.

Every alley spat me out into emptiness.

I was lost and turned around and—

Pinpricks of light.

I stopped moving and peered at the cold ceiling above.

My eyes slowly adjusted to the claustrophobic blackness, aching with the need to see.

And...bit by bit, glow by glow...I did.

Raising my arm, I touched the forever-wet rock and stroked the faint luminescence.

A rustle of legs. A wriggle of insects. The light glowed brighter, then vanished as the critter scrambled behind a crag.

More light blinked on around me—like bluish stars falling from the heavens.

For the first time in my miserable existence, I stood in awe as more and more dots began to glow, following the contours of the cave, lighting up the space with cool teal radiance.

It felt as if I'd stepped into another dimension.

Found a portal and fallen through.

Glow worms.

The name popped into my head, followed by a stabbing memory of sitting on the rug in my childhood lounge and watching David Attenborough. He'd bewitched me with his iconic voice, filling my young mind with facts about all sorts of animals. His documentaries were the highlight of my weekends, all while my mother stayed locked in her room.

I'd been lonely and lost and living without any kind of guidance.

I was raised by the TV and consoled by the radio.

Enough!

Shaking my head, I pressed my fingers to the lump on my temple from the blowhole sucker-punching me.

I had to have a concussion.

No way would such a pointless, ridiculous memory dare trespass otherwise.

No way would the pathetic little boy inside me dare, fucking *dare*, make himself known.

Hefting the axe, I tossed away the useless torch and followed the path of glow worms.

I heard them before I found them.

Laughter and grunts.

Glee and despair.

Stepping from the seam that'd grown so narrow I'd had to travel sideways, I blinked at the brightness of lanterns. The four Masters didn't notice me as two of them fucked two jewels on the ground while the other two watched.

Their paintball guns were tossed in the corner, forgotten. My stolen one clung to my back, occasionally pressing against a bruise. My jeans and t-shirt hadn't dried. My feet were blocks of ice. And I had no doubt I was now filthy as well as orange.

Five hours I'd been stuck in this hellhole.

Five hours was a long fucking time to stay sane when every bend and shadow whispered with nightmares.

A jewel screamed as a Master rutted into her like an animal.

The cries from these jewels weren't like the ones with Stewart and Ben. They weren't given with an edge of acceptance or trust that their Masters wouldn't go too far.

These men weren't here just because they had nowhere else to go.

These men were here for pain.

Seconds ticked past as I watched.

The longer I witnessed their monstrosity, the less control I had over my sanity.

Their thrusts scrambled my mind.

Their lust seeped through me like a disease.

The loneliness of my childhood twisted into a toxic thing.

I didn't know if it was the silence down here. The burial down here. The vacuum of everything I thought I knew and all the hauntings of memories I daren't recall, but I'd never felt so...adrift. So lost. So fucking confused.

I'd been alone for so long.

But now I'd found men who shared my sins.

My bare feet shifted to join in.

I grew hard.

My heart pumped for the first time in hours.

I wanted Ily.

I wanted her on her back.

I wanted her heat, her fight, her kiss.

Fuck, that goddamn kiss.

I wanted to lick her again, taste her again.

I needed her to yank me back from this abyss.

This timeless, endless abyss where I became nothing more than death.

My hands balled.

The axe grew heavy.

I backed deeper into the shadows as my instincts roared into power.

As one Master came with a snarl and another moved to take his place, I fell.

Deeper into darkness.

Harder into sickness.

I no longer knew who I was.

Boy or man. Saint or sinner. Good or bad.

Watching these men...seeing myself in them...it enraged me, corrupted me, gutted me, *redeemed* me.

Why was I fighting it?

Why exist in such suffering?

I could be free if I—

Stop it.

Wedging a fist in my belly, I rode out the sadistic urges.

You need to get out.

I needed sunlight to banish this nightmare.

I needed open skies to resurrect me from this crypt.

I need...

I *need*—

Blood.

And pain.

And *her.*

I crashed against the wall as my floodgates smashed wide.

My teeth ached. My senses heightened. I lost myself to a creature with no name, no rules, no master.

Ily.

I have to find Ily.

I'd made the mistake of walking in darkness.

Of *killing* in darkness.

We were one and the same now.

Bonded by all the bad things I had done.

While Masters raped and celebrated, I stared into the black, and the black stared back, and it was over.

It opened its jaws and swallowed me down.

I sank into its belly and…*ran.*

Threading myself back through the chasm, I scuttled like a crab, sideways and breathing hard.

I had to get away.

I have to get the fuck out of here!

I wriggled and burrowed, desperation rising, claustrophobia clawing.

Desperate to taste fresh air.

Gasping for freedom.

Panic.

Fuck, *panic.*

It vised around my chest, gluing my ribcage to my heart so every breath wrenched and suffocated.

I tripped and stumbled.

Fumbled at the black wall.

Blinked with blind eyes.

With a groan that sounded as if it came from a tortured, pitiful thing, I tumbled out of the alley and back into the cave of wonders.

The glow worms flickered with indignation at my arrival.

They judged me as I collapsed to my knees like a pauper and gasped for redemption like a thief.

Pressing my sweaty forehead to the damp cave floor, I fell to my side and flopped onto my back.

Darkness.

Everywhere.

Fucking *everywhere.*

In me. On me. Around me.

But pinpricks.

Staring back.

Glittering like glowing sapphires, forming an entire galaxy above me.

I focused on them.

I clung to their light.

The angelical luminescence wasn't strong enough to forgive or absolve me.

I was unforgivable.

Unredeemable.

I was nothing but blackness and death.

Chapter Five

"WHICH WAY, PETER?" RACHEL TAPPED OUR broken friend on his pasty cheek.

Peter mumbled something and tried to lift his head, but unlike all the other moments when he'd been able to power through his pain…he no longer had the strength.

With the softest groan, he tumbled sideways where we'd placed him against the wall.

"Oh no." I caught him before his head cracked against stone, gently lowering his cheek to the cave floor. "Peter?" I shook his lax shoulder. "*Jaagate raho, Paavak. Chalo bhee. Aap theek hain.*" (Stay awake, Paavak. Come on. You're okay.)

Nothing.

None of us spoke for the longest time, all of us hoping for a miracle where Peter opened his eyes, sprang to his feet, and led us to victory.

When none of that happened, our small group of nine—our diligent, brave little group that'd bonded with trust and hope—fractured like crystals shattering under too much pressure.

"I don't know how much more of this I can stand." Caishen scratched his arms as if he'd grown allergic to the weighted dark. "I never thought I was claustrophobic but knowing tonnes of rock are above me? That any moment it could bury me alive…fuck."

"Me too." Kaya—a girl I hadn't spoken to before today—nodded. "It's taking everything I have not to run off screaming."

Caishen gave her a sympathetic smile, his face almost sinister thanks to the fading torch and its inability to banish the night.

"How long do you think we've been in here?" Catherine—the other girl I hadn't known—shivered. "Because I'm literally seconds away from losing it."

"No one is losing anything," Rachel muttered.

"Keep it together, guys," Mollie said, tucking dark blonde hair behind her ear. "If one of us snaps, we all snap."

Pressing the back of my hand against Peter's forehead, I hissed at his blazing fever. "If we don't find a way out soon, I'm afraid he'll die down here."

"No one is dying either," Rachel snapped. Rubbing her sore middle where Victor had repeatedly kicked her, she sighed heavily. "You asked how long we've been down here, Cath?" Shooting Catherine a look, she shrugged. "I'm guessing about five hours—"

"Five *hours*?" Caishen shot to his feet, almost bashing his head on a stalactite. The small cave we'd tumbled into barely gave enough room for all of us. "Right, that's it. I can't do this anymore. I need to leave." He clawed at this throat. "I-I can't breathe anymore." He jumped as if something stalked him in the shadows. "I-I'm seeing things, and I'm sick of fucking shivering. The game has to be over now, surely?"

"It has to be." Kaya sprang up from her crouch. "Victor said we all had to return before dusk. By the time we make our way out, it will probably be dark."

"Alright." Caishen nodded. "New plan. We retrace our steps and—"

"Peter's unconscious," I said quietly. "Are you proposing we leave him?"

"Course not. We'll carry him."

"Through all those narrow cracks?" I shook my head. "There's no way—"

"Leave him in here much longer and like you just said…he'll die."

"Yes, but perhaps there's a way out up ahead. We just need to—"

"Peter said it himself." Caishen crossed his arms, trying his best not to tremble from the ice that'd settled into all our bones. "Ever since we left that cave with the glow worms, he didn't have a clue which way to go."

My shoulders slouched.

For approximately five hours, we'd travelled as one, heading deeper and deeper into the island. At one point, Peter said we were directly beneath the fortress. A staircase and tunnel led from the dungeons to the cave system, but Victor had stopped using it two years ago because a rockfall had shut off the main path to the Temple of Facets.

We'd kept going, even when Peter admitted he'd reached the end of his knowledge and every choice was now guesswork.

He'd glanced at all of us, ready to pass up the leadership mantel. The wistful longing in his eyes said he wanted someone else to forge ahead and take responsibility, but...as awful as it was to keep the pressure on someone so wounded—none of us stepped up.

With unanimous, unspoken decision, we all rested a little and gave Peter a breather before hauling him to his feet and helping him hobble through puddled seawater and continue crawling into smaller and darker caves.

One of our torches had failed on the first hour.

The second only minutes ago.

If the third went, we'd be trapped in here. Completely lost with the very real fear of starving to death or drowning. That fear now overshadowed even the terror that the Masters would find us.

Catching Rachel's haunted blue eyes, I—

"Don't." She shook her head and bared her teeth. "Don't even say it."

"Caishen might be right," I whispered. "By the time we get out of here, the gong will go, and we'll be safe."

"Safe?" Her nose wrinkled. "Do you honestly think the Masters will obey Vic? After a day of chaos? Fuck that." She paced the small space, bumping into Sonya. "We go out there, and we're at their mercy."

"I say we take a vote." Caishen held up his hand. "Our fearless leader is out cold. We have no idea where we're going, and it's idiotic to think we're skilled enough to find a way out. I'm not even certain we can retrace our steps before that torch dies, but if we're gonna try, we have to go now."

Making eye contact with all of us, he demanded, "All those who want out, hands up."

Everyone but Rachel and Mollie swung up their arms.

Lowering my own, I glanced at the two girls. "I know you don't want Victor or Roland to find you, but...we can't stay here." I arched my chin at Peter. He barely breathed. His burned hands and feet covered in grit and dirt; his dusky skin far too pale in the dark. "We need to get him to Dr Belford...before it's too late."

Mollie sighed, her green eyes flashing. "How about a compromise? We'll wait here for an hour or two. Peter will hopefully wake by then, and we can help him walk rather than drag him. It should be nightfall in a couple of hours and Victor will have rounded everyone up, thanks to his guards. We stand a better chance of avoiding this game altogether if we let Victor wrangle his guests into order rather than go out there while they're being absolute maniacs."

"Peter might not have two hours." I stood too, balling my hands.

"Ily," Rachel muttered under her breath. "You have to understand. Roland is a fucking creep. If he knows he can get away with shit and finds Mollie…he'll kill her."

"He's a necrophiliac." Caishen shuddered. "I've seen him kill before. I was with a Master in the same room. Yumeko only survived because the guards dragged Dr Mel in with her resuscitation kit before it was too late."

The torch dimmed as if taking part in our debate and adding a fresh layer of panic.

Caishen's tolerance snapped. "Right, that's it. The batteries are dying. I'm leaving. All those who want to follow. Let's go."

"Go then if you're that afraid. I'm going to wait for Pete to wake." Rachel slid down the wall and sat beside Peter.

"Me too." Mollie sat beside her.

I stood in a dank, chilly cave and was absolutely torn in two.

I understood why they wanted to wait for him to revive. I was on board with that plan—none of us would have the strength to drag him for long—but…every minute was a minute he couldn't afford to spend.

"Just wait thirty minutes, Caishen." I stepped toward him. "Surely, you can—"

"If he's not going, we are." Sonya snatched the torch from Caishen's hands, sending the beam bouncing around the cave. "I'm done. How about you, Citra?" She arched her eyebrow at the Indonesian girl.

Citra rolled her shoulders. "I don't want to leave anyone behind, but…" She sniffed and rubbed her nose as tears dripped from her eyes. "I'm struggling. I feel as if I'm moments away from a full-blown panic attack and…I don't think I can stay."

Caishen grabbed his hair and tugged. "Fuck, I need air."

Almost as if the allure of sky and wind became too much, the jewels moved as one.

"Sorry, Ily. Follow us when you're ready." Caishen hung his head. "We'll go slow. We'll yell when we get out so you can follow our voices, okay? We won't stop shouting until you're with us on the beach."

"See you soon, guys," Citra whispered. "Please forgive us."

With apologetic winces, the five jewels all turned their backs and squeezed into the crack we'd just come from.

"You can't take the only light source!" I wriggled behind them, grabbing hold of Sonya's wrist. "We won't have any light to find our way out."

"Then I suggest you start walking," Caishen said sadly. "I'm sorry, Ily. I really am…but we voted, and this is what everyone needs."

"Peter didn't get a vote."

"Peter would want us to do whatever we can to survive, and right now…I'm gonna lose my ever-loving mind if I stay down here another second." Grabbing something from the back of his nude underwear, he passed me the knife he'd taken from the Temple of Facets. "Here. Just in case."

My hand shook as I accepted the knife.

And then…they were gone.

Rachel and Mollie didn't say a word as I fell back into the small cave.

The sounds of bare feet on stone faded with every heartbeat.

The pressure of the earth crushed my bones until I collapsed to my knees beside two awake jewels and one unconscious.

Thick, dank silence.

Heavy, hungry darkness.

And just our shallow breathing for company.

Water.

Icy, salty water lapping at my toes.

"Rachel," I hissed. "*Rachel.*"

Patting along Peter's feverishly hot body, I found Rachel's hand on his hip.

After the shock of being left behind, the three of us had agreed to rest for an hour and then leave. We'd do whatever it took to wake Peter and help him hobble back home.

Our plan was cruel, and terror whispered that he wouldn't make it, but…if he slept for an hour, hopefully he'd have the strength to get back to the castle so Dr Belford could heal him.

We'd all agreed to give him the best chance of recovery by sitting in a row and hauling Peter's dead weight onto our laps to protect him from the wet stone. With his head and shoulders on my legs, his torso on Mollie's, and his thighs on Rachel's, we'd done the best we could to stop him from dying any faster than he already was.

"Do you feel that?" I kicked my feet. The faintest splash answered. "Where's the water coming from?"

Mollie shifted beside me, removing some of her body heat. "Victor did say some of the caves fill up with water at high tide."

"I'm guessing the tide is coming in." Rachel sighed and upturned her hand to squeeze mine. She sounded exhausted and deflated and at the edge of her limits.

I blinked, willing the absolute darkness to fade. No glow worms like some of the other caves. No luminescent algae or light sources of any kind. We were blind. Completely and utterly blind and we needed to run.

Rocking Peter on my lap, I stole my hand back from Rachel's and raked my fingers through his sweat-wet hair. "Peter. Time to wake up, okay? We need to leave."

We'd been smart.

The game wouldn't be entirely over, but at least we were one hour closer to dusk. By the time we found our way out, Emerald Bruises would be finished and Victor's rules firmly back in place.

Giving Peter a few seconds to rally, I looked in Mollie's direction. "Did you mean what you said, Mollie?" I chewed on rising panic. "You sure you remember the way we came?"

A rustle as she nodded. "I've gone through the turns twice with you. I kept track of every direction we took. I can get us out, even without a torch."

"Mols has a bachelor in quantum physics," Rachel said with a stronger tone. "She's beyond smart."

"Didn't stop me from being snatched at a party, though, did it?" Mollie huffed. "I know how one particle can be in two locations at the same time, yet I couldn't see the pill dropped into my drink."

Rachel continued as if Mollie hadn't spoken. "Mols and I became friends through our shared love of science. I'm a research chemist turned war chemist, but Mols? She's on a whole other level. She can get us out. I have no doubt."

Mollie scoffed. "If I could get my hands on some household cleaning products, I could make a bomb big enough to blow up Victor's beloved Joyero. Then we'd *really* be out. We'd be free..."

Even with the tide creeping over my feet.

Even with Peter unconscious and barely alive on my lap...sheer blinding hope found me all over again.

"Wait. You could do that?" I asked on a sharp inhale. "Y-You have those skills?"

"Rachel does too." Mollie laughed sadly. "Between the two of us, we could destroy this entire island, but...knowledge is worthless without ingredients and action."

"Speaking of action, I agree with Ily," Rachel said. "The water is rising quickly. It's time to go."

It took some organisation and a lot of achy, chilly bones, but we managed to clamber to our feet and bring Peter with us. Among the three of us, we held him dangling in our shaking embrace.

Slipping the knife Caishen had given me into the back of my underwear, I hoped to God I wouldn't have to use it.

"Should we be worried that he's not waking up?" Rachel whispered.

"His system has shut down. A person can only survive in shock for so long." Mollie shifted her hold on him. "He might rally, he might not. I hope you girls are feeling strong."

"We need to talk about blowing up this island," I said, refusing to think about a scenario where Peter never woke up.

Rachel snickered. "Yeah, okay. Can we get out of the caves first?"

"The caves might be the best place to plan an uprising."

"Not if we drown, it isn't," she snapped.

"Everyone ready?" Mollie asked. "Focus."

Her voice seemed too loud in the pitch black, but her strength bolstered me.

We were moving. Finally.

We would be safe. Hopefully.

Today is almost over.

And tomorrow...we'll build a bomb.

"Lead the way." Rachel sniffed. "I'm so ready for a hot shower. I don't even care if I get raped for the privilege."

"Let's go." Mollie tugged on her part of Peter, guiding us toward the crack where the others had vanished.

We walked slowly, gingerly, blindly.

It took an age.

It took all our waning strength to half-carry, half-drag Peter, but we would make it.

None of us would give up.

I'd been lucky enough to find two of the strongest girls I'd ever met and—

"Oh shit." Mollie slammed to a stop, sending a ripple down our chain.

"Oh shit, what?" Rachel asked. "You know I don't like it when you say things like that, Mols. Makes my imagination go into overdrive."

I shivered as water lapped up my ankles, freezing my toes with insidious frostbite.

"The water is coming from the direction we need to go in," Mollie muttered. "And it's coming in fast."

"So…what does that mean?" Rachel asked.

"It means…we can't go that way."

"But that's the only way out." I did my best to stay calm. "If we hurry, surely we can make it. The tide doesn't come in that quickly."

"You obviously don't have a lot of experience with the sea. It can rise fast, and I'm not willing to take that chance." Mollie turned, taking us all with her. "Damn."

"Well, we can't stay here," Rachel gasped. "If the water is coming in that quickly, then…"

"We'll drown," Mollie snapped. "Yes, I'm aware."

"Well, what the hell are we going to do?!" Rachel shouted. "I can't…we can't just stand here and die!"

"Shut up and let me think!"

"We don't have time to think! We have to run."

"Run to where?"

"I don't fucking know, but—"

"Quiet, Rach. Your screeching is not helping—"

"Screeching? We're running out of time, and you're telling me to calm down?!"

"Perhaps the caves won't fill completely," Mollie mused aloud. "We could swim—"

"*Swim*?" Rachel's voice turned brittle with horror. "That's your plan? You study the damn universe, and the best you can come up with is—"

I shut them out.

I couldn't listen.

Their energy fed into mine, braiding our panic into a living, gnawing thing. My lungs threatened to stop working. Every fear, every terror, every horror, pain, despair, and loss strangled me like a monster.

My ears rang as they fought.

My arms ached as I held Peter.

I was so, *so* close to snapping.

So...I did the only thing I could.

I pressed my toes against cold stone.

I ignored the rapidly rising water level as it kissed my calves and travelled higher, higher, *higher*.

I begged that quiet, wiser part of my soul to take charge.

Images of us swimming and clawing at the ceiling as the ocean suffocated us played behind my closed eyes. Nightmares of us taking our last breath without ever seeing the sun again.

Focus.

I ordered every muscle to relax.

I went against every instinct and compelled my nervous system to choose calmness instead of adrenaline.

For a few moments, nothing happened.

The cave bounced Rachel and Mollie's argument like a megaphone.

But slowly...thankfully...

My attention turned inward.

Light and sanctity, I found a pocket of peace.

I wasn't this form.

This form could be cut, bled, raped, and drowned, but I was just the watcher within. Panic came from not accepting the situation. Suffering came from railing against certain fate.

But thanks to a lifetime of schooling my chaotic mind, I opened my eyes to a tranquil reality and smiled as the grounding cord of light that'd granted such salvation continued to glow up ahead.

Subtle.

Barely there.

But...

Wait.

I froze.

T-That's not imaginary.

From this angle, I could see around the shadow of a stalagmite.

A shadow caused by the barest hint of deliverance.

"There's another way out," I whispered in shock, awe,

disbelief.

Tugging Peter, I sloshed forward, sending water waking around our shins. The girls tripped with me.

"There's light." My arms shook with Peter's weight. "The ground slopes up. It's higher ground."

Mollie and Rachel stopped fighting.

Rachel sniffed back tears. "W-What are you saying? I don't see anything."

A surge of energy filled me. I finally donned the mantel of leadership that Peter had always worn. "It's faint. But trust me. It's there. Come on."

I expected Mollie to disagree. I tensed for Rachel to argue.

But…as I stepped into my role of guardian, they slipped into following.

Without a word, the two girls mirrored my steps.

We made a wet, slow procession through the small cave.

I bumped my toes multiple times, my heart pounded from carrying my share of a person.

Finally, we stopped outside the small chasm.

Peering inside, I willed the light to get brighter.

It didn't.

It was just enough to see how hard this journey would be.

It veered up steeply, mimicking the longest tunnel I'd ever seen.

But…it was dry.

"It's narrow to start with, but I think it widens."

Rachel squished closer. "We can make it. We don't have a choice."

Mollie pressed her cheek to mine, looking at our unfortunate climb.

She sighed, but then…

…the faintest breeze.

A lick of cool.

A kiss of freshness.

I gasped on a sob.

Not dank and cave stagnant.

But alive.

Bracken and soil and trees.

We glanced at each other.

Without a word, we wriggled into the crack.

I went first and dragged Peter with me.

They went second and pushed.

Together, we inched our way into the light.

I'd endured some horrible things since Henri targeted me and brought me here.

I'd had to dig deep to stay sane and draw from strength I didn't know I had.

But that journey…good God, it was hard.

Time lost all meaning as we climbed and crawled, tugged and dragged each other up and up and up. At one point, it felt as if we traversed a ladder made of rock and pebbles. The next we were in a chute made of stone.

Everything hurt.

Every muscle engaged to pull Peter behind me all while the two girls shoved him just a little each time.

The knife dug into my lower back, and cuts decorated every part of us.

Little slices as we travelled as if the cave demanded a cost in the currency of our blood.

Peter flickered in and out of consciousness.

At one point, he woke with a start and fought our hold.

The next, he woke up screaming.

Luckily or unluckily, he didn't remain conscious for long.

And we had no choice but to keep going.

Climbing higher and higher.

Light growing brighter and brighter.

The air cleaner and cleaner.

Until eventually…freedom.

"I want to kiss you, Ily." Rachel laughed with pure giddiness as we limped, shuffled, and practically fell out of the widening crack and into the largest cave so far.

Not that it was a cave.

With a heavy exhale, I raised my face to the darkening twilight above.

Seagulls flew in the greying sky, squawking their daily news and getting ready to roost.

Greenery framed the scene above like a gorgeous painting.

The earth trapped us but the ceiling had fallen, creating the most wonderful skylight.

I would never take fresh air for granted ever, *ever* again.

I longed for rain.

I begged for the sun.

I craved the moon and stars and—

I gasped as soft lips slammed over mine.

Laughter spilled into my mouth as Mollie kissed me with great smacking affection before pulling away and kissing Rachel.

Rachel threw her free arm around her friend and kissed her back.

It wasn't romantic or lustful but pure emotion bubbling free in the only way it could…love and gratitude.

"Thank you, thank you, *thank you*!" Rachel flung her head back, basking in the dusk as if it was the hottest summer day. "God*damn*, it's good to be out of there!"

Mollie chuckled and gave me a soft smile. "Good spotting, Ily. You saved our lives."

I blushed. "Just luck."

"Whatever it was, I'm grateful." Hoisting Peter higher in her arms, she added, "Let's put him down, and then we'll figure out what's next."

We eyed up the driest part—a tussock padded undergrowth in the centre of this strange natural amphitheatre. Together, we half-carried, half-dragged Peter and gently lowered him as carefully as we could.

Rachel ensured his head was pillowed on the thickest part of the tussock while I rested his arms by his sides, careful to keep his oozy, charcoal hands from falling face down. Mollie arranged his legs and squeezed his knee as if telling him it was okay.

With streaks of paint from his bullseye and cave-smeared skin, he looked as if he'd been burned by a dragon and now lay cursed like some reversed Sleeping Beauty fairy-tale.

I studied his face, waiting for him to wake.

When he didn't, we all stood and stretched.

Our moans were identical as we worked out our many kinks.

My shoulders throbbed.

My spine blazed.

Every bone and muscle ached with a thousand bruises, but I would've carried Peter for days if it meant we ended up here…together and alive.

"I don't know about you, but I don't want to go back down there if we can help it." Mollie spun in place, glancing at every side of the bowl we'd found ourselves in.

The sides soared as high as a two-story building, the walls covered in twisted plants and stunted, ugly trees. No vines to climb. No convenient rope to scale. Unless we were rock climbers, getting out of here would be almost impossible.

And with Peter...

Almost as if the thought struck all of us at the same time, we made eye contact and slouched.

We could get out...possibly.

We could clamber to the top...maybe.

But Peter?

Even if he woke again, he wouldn't be able to use his hands and feet to scale anything, let alone a freaking mountain.

"Well, crap." Rachel scrubbed her face. "Perhaps one of us gets out and finds Victor? The gong will have gone by now." She pointed at the rapidly darkening sky. "It's past twilight, and he's a stickler for rules. The Masters will have to be on their best behaviour again."

"You could go." Mollie cocked her chin at me, her shoulder length blonde hair swinging. "Find Master H. He's Victor's latest pet project. He could bring a few guards to haul Peter out."

Henri.

The instant his name soaked into my ears, my dead heart fisted and came alive again. Its unwillingness to thump since we'd entered the Temple of Facets was now replaced with a very real, very annoying pounding.

I hated that it thrummed in longing.

That it turned traitor by whispering he could fix this.

I scowled.

He wouldn't fix this.

He would make this worse.

He hated Peter.

He tolerated nothing and no one.

I crossed my achy arms.

He tolerates you.

He kissed you...

I froze as our kiss exploded in my head.

My lips tingled.

My insides melted.

How had a simple kiss become the hottest thing we'd shared?

That damn kiss burned my blood and turned me into an addict for more.

"I hate to say it, Ily, but Mols is right. If you found Henri, he'd have to obey the rules. Victor's agreed to let him live here permanently, but that graciousness only goes as far as Master H's obedience."

"Did I hear someone mention Master H?"

All three of us spun around.

My heart leapt into my mouth.

Rachel cursed.

Mollie froze.

And I brandished the knife on instinct as four Masters appeared.

Sprigs of leaves and foliage debris caped their shoulders as if they'd brushed through an autumn garden. My eyes narrowed as I looked past them, studying the cave walls for a hidden exit.

They hadn't come in the way we had.

That means…there's another way.

Mollie and Rachel squished closer to me, forming a wall before Peter on the ground.

The Masters chuckled, their eyes skating over our bloody, dirty bodies.

An older one said, "Well, well, you have been in the wars."

A younger one with a thin chin strap and oily brown hair snickered. "Where on earth did you get a knife? It looks kinda cute on you."

My arm trembled, but I didn't lower the weapon. "Leave us alone."

The men all laughed, their amusement like sick music.

"I lost my blade somewhere in the caves." The Master with brown hair grinned like a jackal. "Thank you for giving me one. I would've hated to miss out on claiming my prize."

"Fuck you and fuck your friends." I bared my teeth. "It's over. The game is over. You lost."

"Oh, I never lose, little jewel." He cocked his head. "Besides, you look as if you've been warmed up nicely. Rather…tenderised." He laughed quietly. "I do love the sight of blood in the evening."

Chills scattered over my skin.

Mollie shivered just once.

Licking his lips, the Master kept his eyes locked on us, refusing to look at his companions. He stood alone as if he'd led the party but wanted nothing to do with those who'd followed him.

Hefting his paintball gun, he clucked his tongue. "Because you've done me a favour by bringing a knife to our party, I'll give you a favour right back." He pouted. "I do so hate being the bearer of bad news, but…if you're looking for Master H, he's not coming. Your worthless Master took a beating from a blowhole at the start of the game. He left, I'm afraid. I hear he's back at the castle, enjoying a beer at this very moment, all while sticking his dick in some other slut."

I wasn't prepared for how violently that picture hurt.

How the thought of Henri touching another made my insides knot into thorns.

He chuckled as I braced myself against such a ridiculous response. "A little possessive, are we? Fancy that you're his only plaything?" He shook his head and clucked his tongue again. "You poor deluded little thing." Raising his gun, he aimed directly between my breasts. "Tell you what, I'll put you out of your misery. I'll be the Master he never could and release you from all this pain."

The nude-coloured underwear barely covered me.
The bullseye on my skin distorted and smeared.
But the lines were still visible.
Marking the spot for his bullet.
Mollie and Rachel looked at one another.
The comradery between us faltered with fear.
We could've fought off one Master together.
Maybe even two.
But four?
God…

My knife seemed utterly useless against four Masters with guns—even just paintball ones.

If I charge them, I might be able to stab one…

I shifted, ready to run.

The other three Masters behind the scary dead-eyed one raised their guns too. "You can have that one, Kyle, but we're taking the others."

Kyle snarled and whirled on them. "No one else fires. You can do whatever the fuck you want to the others, but I'm the only winner, do you hear me?"

I waited for a battle to break out.

The whiffs of testosterone choked me.

But whatever they saw in Kyle's face made them lower their weapons and nod. "Fine."

"Good boys." Kyle blew them a kiss.

And that was my cue.

I bolted.

On silent aching feet, I threw all efforts of survival into attacking first.

"Kyle." Two of the Masters feinted back, arching their chins in my flying direction.

Kyle spun to face me.

Metres separated us.

Too many metres.

With a surprised, far too gleeful laugh, Kyle swung up his gun and grinned. "Time for some fun, little jewel."

I feinted to the side.

I tried to get close enough to kill him.

Bang.

The punch of the paintball shot all the air from my lungs.

A burning pain feathered from my sternum.

Choking, I reeled back.

Bang.

This time in my belly.

I doubled over.

Bang.

Pain in my shoulder.

I stumbled sideways.

Bang.

A wallop on my wrist.

I dropped the knife.

Bang.

Agony in my thigh.

I tripped.

And then…there were too many to count.

Bang.

Bang.

Bang.

I fell backward.

My feet tangled with Peter's.

I collapsed.

In a blur of speed, Kyle ran toward me, kicked away my knife,

and towered over me on the ground.
    With an evil smile, he emptied his entire clip into me.
    Pain.
    Everywhere.
    Pain.
    All over.
    Pain.
    Pain.
    Pain!
    I screamed—

Chapter Six

Henri

THAT SCREAM.

It poured into my ears and struck a match in my dark-soaked heart.

I ran.

I no longer knew who I was or what I'd become down there.

But I knew that scream.

Every part of my soul recognised it just as I'd recognised her that first night.

Different.

Familiar.

Mine.

I tripped and almost fell over a fallen tree.

My bare feet found every sharp stick and agonising debris.

I ran on dregs.

I powered on fumes.

But I didn't stop.

The scream came again, followed by two others.

Fuck!

I raced faster, climbing the hill and cutting to the left toward the cliffs.

Birds chattered in the trees.

Clouds clotted as night quickly fell.

Exhaustion didn't touch how I truly felt.

My endurance had peaked an hour or so ago as I'd swam out of the caves, fighting the tide and fearing I'd drown. I'd made it just before a heavy wave slipped through the crack and prevented any others from exiting.

No more blowholes or rockpools.

The beach and its sea glass sand were gone.

I'd swum to the treeline and hauled myself out of the sea.

And then, I'd started to climb.

I'd left Charles' paintball gun behind.

I'd lost the axe when I'd gotten trapped in a dead end—
Another scream.
This one cut short with a heart-ripping gurgle.
The trees thinned; the ground opened wide.
I almost fell into an open-top cave.
Skidding to a stop, I grabbed a gnarly branch for balance and peered down.
Someone had rested a cellphone against a boulder, shining its torch at a corner of the cave and casting huge shadows on the walls. He loomed over his prey, looking like a twelve-foot-high demon.
Beneath him, I barely made out the bare legs of a jewel.
A jewel covered head to toe in scarlet red.
Blood.
Her blood—
Everything switched off.
Every longing.
Every loneliness.
Every need for love.
That was the moment.
The last moment.
The final moment of my humanity.
I dropped over the lip of the cave and descended into hell.

Chapter Seven

Ivy

GOD, *EVERYTHING* HURT.
So, so much.
Too much.
I couldn't breathe. Think. Or move.
Hands on my body, smearing the crimson paint.
Red gloop in my eyes from him shoving a handful of pigment over my face.
The clatter of the knife as he picked it up.
The first sting as he—
"What the fuc—"
A cursing Master never finished his sentence.
The sickest thwack followed by a thud.
Rachel stopped screaming.
I didn't know what was worse.
Knowing she was being hurt or not knowing if she was dead.
Mollie yelled something I didn't catch.
And Kyle, who sat on my belly with his knees on either side of my hips, paused his first cut and looked over his shoulder.
His legs tightened around me, holding me down.
I tried to raise an arm—to claw away some of the paint to see, but Kyle shifted and snatched me from the ground. Crawling behind me and wrapping his arm around my throbbing chest, he pressed the tip of the knife against my throat. "Fuck off and I won't kill her."
Rubbing my face on his arm, I blinked through the red and froze.
Henri.
Or at least…it looked like Henri.
Sodden jeans, torn t-shirt, dirty bare feet. Orange streaks on his face and remnants of orange staining denim. His dark hair

dangled over his forehead, dripping with the occasional droplet of ocean.

He looked like Henri, but…this man wasn't Henri.

The fire in his grey eyes…extinguished.

The longing in his handsome face…dead.

With his jaw tipped down, lashes lowered, and fists balled, he looked as cold and as merciless as the caves below.

He didn't look at me.

Didn't even seem to recognise me.

His focus locked on Kyle and only Kyle.

I gasped in fresh pain as Kyle dug the tip of the knife into my throat. "Fuck off, Mercer." His heart pounded against my spine, hinting he sensed the same unhinged ferocity in Henri that I did. "I won. Fair and square. She's covered in my paint. I can do whatever the fuck I want with Victor's blessing." He dared to laugh. "She was open game. He said it so himself. You can't do shit."

A darkness rippled beneath Henri's skin.

Nightmares flickered over his face.

Looking past him, I made eye contact with Mollie and Rachel. Beside Rachel, the older Master lay unmoving with a heavy log dropped by his head. The other two Masters stood side by side.

I'd seen how ruthless Henri could be.

I'd watched him turn into pure violence the night of the treasure hunt.

He'd taken on three men and won.

But…he didn't seem to even notice the others behind him.

The two men crept closer with the faintest nod from Kyle.

"Watch out!" I croaked.

"You little bitch." Kyle wrapped his hand around my neck.

Henri merely turned on his heel and glanced at the two Masters.

Quietly, coldly, he murmured, "I'll give you one chance to leave. Just one."

He flexed his fingers. His voice all wrong.

None of the passion I was used to.

No echoes of the man who'd confessed what he was and forced me to admit my own downfall.

Kyle spat on the ground, his fingers vised around my throat. "Gut him, Gary. I'll finish him off."

Henri shrugged and crossed his arms.

He didn't say a damn word, never looking away from the two

men.

His silence was absolutely petrifying.

An icy breeze whipped.

The heavy pound of surf against the cliffs sounded like the earth's heartbeat.

I flinched for carnage.

I tensed for war.

But then…the two Masters bowed slightly and held up their hands. "This isn't our fight. We'll go." With a quick glance at Kyle holding me as his shield, they marched toward the south end of the cave, brushed aside a curtain of dead shrubs, and vanished.

"Fucking cowards," Kyle spat.

The moment they were gone, Rachel and Mollie charged back to Peter. Resting their hands on his unconscious form, they never took their eyes off Henri as he took a single step toward Kyle and me.

I scrambled for air. I flinched from the knife.

Henri didn't drop his eyes to mine.

He seemed utterly saturated with darkness.

Kyle bristled behind me. "Take another step and I'll slit her throat."

Henri didn't stop.

Footfall after footfall. He. Did. Not. Stop.

Tears stung my eyes as the connection between us snapped free.

Emptiness flowed from him.

Vacant emotions and bone-icing nothingness.

Kyle cut me deeper. "I'll do it. I'll fucking—"

Henri flew.

One second, he stalked us. The next, he knocked me backward, using my weight to crunch Kyle to the ground. With cold, vicious hands, he tore Kyle's fingers off my neck, ripped him off me, then dragged him away, kicking and screaming.

Coughing and choking, I scrambled to my feet, swaying a little at the onslaught of so many pounding bruises. My skin glowed with crimson paint, but beneath the red sludge, my flesh already welted with purple and black. A morbid rainbow of bruises that marked me as the chosen one.

Rachel and Mollie charged to my side and clutched me close. "Are you okay? Did he—"

"Don't." Pushing past them, I limped forward, needing to

keep my eyes on Henri.

He felt all wrong.

Lost.

Broken.

Kyle kept yelling obscenities and curses, all while Henri tossed him onto his back and planted a foot against his chest.

"Get off me, you cunt." Grabbing a handful of pebbles, Kyle threw them into Henri's face.

With a grunt, Henri fell back. Clawing at his eyes, he gave Kyle a split-second window to shoot to his feet.

He launched himself at Henri.

The two men went wheeling back, fists flying, bodies twisting.

Kyle might be smaller, but his temper kept him evenly matched.

"We have to go." Rachel tugged my arm. "We'll follow where the other Masters went. I know them. They're sick, but they're afraid of Victor, so they won't touch us now the game is over."

"I agree." Mollie took my hand. "Let's grab Peter and—"

Henri bellowed as Kyle kicked him in the balls, then charged to the fallen knife.

"No!" I raced toward him, desperate to get the blade before Kyle did.

We arrived together.

I ducked for it.

Pain as he backhanded me and sent me flying.

In a blur of tears, I watched as he fisted the knife and bolted toward Henri.

"*Watch out!*" I screamed.

Lowering his hands from between his legs, blinking past grit, Henri braced himself just as Kyle launched through the sky and stabbed him.

The blade sank into Henri's bicep, the tip vanishing into his arm.

For a moment, nothing happened.

Nobody moved.

And then...whatever strings existed in Henri frayed completely.

He didn't seem real.

Not human.

With the smoothest arc as if he were a dancer in a past life, Henri snatched the knife out of his arm, grabbed Kyle by the throat, and shoved it into his jugular.

Kyle screeched.

A fountain of red exploded, covering Henri's t-shirt.

"Oh my God," Mollie gasped.

Rachel moved to my side.

None of us looked away as Henri deposited Kyle almost gently on the ground, dropped to one knee as he watched Kyle's lifeforce pump out of his throat, and then…withdrew the knife, wiped the blade on Kyle's slacks, and pierced it directly into his heart.

The crunch of ribs as he stabbed hard.

The whimper from Kyle as he died.

The blur of Henri's arm as he withdrew the knife and stabbed again and again and *again*.

He didn't stop.

He kept going.

A blood-covered savage as he turned a person into nothing more than a hunk of meat.

Chapter Eight

Henri

CARNAGE AND BLOOD.
Blood and death.
Nothing else existed.
Just darkness and dying and the despicable need to slaughter.
To eradicate this world of filth.
To end all life that didn't deserve to live.
To end *myself*.
I lost count how many times I killed him.
How many times I drove that blade into his flesh.
It became meditative.
Calming.
Freeing.
This was what I was.
Death.
And alone.
Always, always alone.
I would've kept stabbing if a voice didn't call me back.
A voice I recognised but wasn't the one that leashed me.
A voice that caused jealousy and annoyance and worry.
Such worry that I would never be worthy.
Such fear that I would always lose.
"Master H…"
A man's baritone.
I ignored him.
I drove the knife into another gristly part.
"Henri."
I shook my head from the unwanted noise.
"*Henri!*"
I paused.
The smog slowly lifted.

I blinked.

"Henri…"

I gulped at that one.

Feminine, soft, afraid.

Ily.

The world slipped back into focus.

I gagged on the mess I'd caused.

Shoving away from Kyle's corpse, I shot to my feet and glowered at the knife in my hands. My fingers thick with another's blood.

Such thick, cooling, congealing blood.

"Put the knife down, Henri."

That voice again.

Giving me orders when he had no right to do so.

"Put the knife down so you don't hurt her."

Ily's hand landed gently on my shaking forearm.

My head snapped up.

I looked past her to Peter.

He sat upright in a thicket of tussock. Bloody hands on his thighs, pain carved deep into his face. "Please, please don't hurt her."

"Henri…you're okay. It's over." Ily reached for the knife. "Can I have this?"

My fingers tensed but then relaxed.

Opening my hand, I presented it to her on my red-dripping palm.

But I didn't speak.

I didn't think I would ever speak again.

Animals weren't allowed the gift of words.

And only an animal could've done what I did.

"We need to get rid of the body," Rachel said, cutting through the buzzing in my brain.

"Tie a few rocks to it and toss it into the ocean," Peter muttered, faint and swaying. "The tide will drag it out to sea. That's how Victor gets rid of all his other…" He faded off, swallowing hard.

With a soft gasp, he fell backward.

Ily and the two girls dashed toward him.

I followed silently, almost as if a tether lashed Ily and me together, binding me to her even now.

I was her animal.

Her nightmare.

Towering over Peter, I let the girls stroke his pallid cheeks and mutter worriedly to one another. Things like how they'd get him back to the castle. And how much he needed Dr Belford.

In the middle of their whispered debate, his eyes popped open again.

They locked on me.

And he smiled as if he saw an angel instead of a devil looming over him. "I see what she does now." Almost dreamy and completely high on agony, he smiled. "You did come for us. You're going to free us. I know it—"

And then, he passed out.

Chapter Nine

Ily

IF THE OLD ILY COULD SEE ME NOW…if she watched me *willingly* leave behind her only weapon and walk over the drawbridge into Victor's fortress, she would've disowned me for my stupidity.

She would've screeched and shouted and ordered me to run and swim and do whatever it damn well took to get as far away from here as possible.

But…

But.

I sighed heavily as I glanced at the sorry company I kept.

I'd come here alone, yet somehow, I'd grown attached.

Three jewels and one Master.

All of us dripping in pain.

Leading the way, Henri prowled on bare feet. His left arm coated in blood from where Kyle stabbed him, his t-shirt soaked with murder.

We matched, him and me.

We all did.

He might be painted in blood, but the rich scarlet matched the red paint covering me.

Stars pinpricked the black velvet sky above. The hazy whirlpool of a galaxy gleamed brightly as if studying our sad procession.

Rachel walked beside me. Her own body covered in red paint like mine. When Henri had snatched Kyle's gun, checked the canister still had paintballs, and aimed at Rachel and Mollie, I'd leapt in front of him.

"Don't you dare shoot them." I'd balled my hands, fighting through debilitating pain from all my bruises. I'd studied his blood-streaked face for some reaction. But there'd been none. He was a total stranger with every emotion shuttered and every feeling hidden.

He hadn't spoken to me.

But he *had* spoken to them.

Arching his chin at the two jewels, he shrugged with indifference. "I don't know what we'll be walking into when we return, but I do know Victor will expect a winner. I'm claiming all of you. It's the only way I can think of to keep you safe."

Rachel and Mollie shared a look.

Keep you safe.

Such a protective sentence yet said with blood-tipped frost.

What did he mean by that?

Had he had a change of heart and seen the errors of his ways?

Is he going to help us?

Peter remained passed out, unable to offer his counsel.

What he'd said before…the comment about seeing something in Henri.

What had Peter seen?

Fragments of light?

Filaments of hope that Henri hadn't truly forsaken his task?

I sucked in an optimistic breath; pain daggered right in my ribs.

The urge to bend over and hug my bruised chest faded as Rachel cupped her belly, shielding her new pregnancy.

I sucked in shallow breaths as she bit her lower lip. Bracing her shoulders, she nodded. "You're right. Victor might be psychotic, but he's strangely fixated on rules. If you shoot us too, I doubt anyone else will have managed to shoot three jewels at close range. He'll add up the bruises and announce you as the winner."

None of us mentioned that the winner was entitled to do anything he wanted. And with how empty Henri looked, I honestly didn't know how far he'd go.

He turned Kyle into ribbons.

"This is nuts." I threw up my arms, immediately paying for the move with a flush of agony and that nasty stabbing in my side. "Let's crack open a few balls and just smear the paint over you."

"It has to be authentic." Mollie stepped forward, jutting out her chest and presenting her faded bullseye. "The game is called Bruises, remember?"

I shook my head. "The colour doesn't match. Henri was given orange paint." I pointed at the area of his jeans that used to be tinged with brightness but only found blood. No sign of orange anywhere, thanks to him wearing every droplet of Kyle's lifeforce.

"I don't think it will matter." Rachel dropped her arms and balled her hands. "Victor has a soft spot for him. I've never seen him be so tolerant to another Master before. That has to count for something."

"What about Peter?" I glanced at our comatose friend. "We can't shoot him while he's borderline dead."

Mollie nodded and pinned her brown eyes on Henri. "I agree with Ily. Just shoot us. Make every bullet count. But leave Peter alone."

Henri merely nodded.

And then, he let fire.

The canister held far more rounds than I could've counted. His aim stayed accurate as he worked his way down each girl's legs and then shot at their shoulders and arms. At the end, he shot once…directly at their bullseye. They staggered back in matching pain, but at least he hadn't shot anywhere in their soft middles.

Who was this ice-cold man who moved like rigor mortis had set in, yet had the foresight not to hurt unnecessarily?

I wished Kyle had been that considerate.

Every organ throbbed. My liver and kidneys, stomach and womb. Perfectly round bruises swelled and grew hotter the deeper night fell.

Tossing the empty gun at Mollie, Henri muttered, "Bring that with us." Then he strode toward the eviscerated corpse that used to be Kyle and hauled him over his shoulder like a dead deer.

My eyes widened as he headed toward the hidden exit where the other Masters had gone.

He disappeared, leaving the three of us to blink in exhaustion and try to figure out our next step.

I couldn't get a read on him.

I daren't ask him if he'd suddenly switched back to our side.

When he came back, minus a body, and headed toward the other Master he'd dispatched with a log to his head, he ordered, "Stay here."

Those two words ignited a fire within us.

We didn't listen.

All three of us fell into helping.

Henri staggered with his own injuries and exhaustion but didn't order us to stop as Rachel and Mollie took a dead Master's arm, and I helped Henri with the legs.

Silently, we'd carried the Master, slung like a hammock, out of the cave via a civilised tunnel and heaved our way up rough-hewn stairs that hinted the open-top cave was known and used, even if its wild appearance said otherwise.

Every step cost me.

Every shallow, painful breath not nearly enough for my winded, wounded frame.

I existed purely in the numbing shock of adrenaline.

At the top, we cut through the sparse trees and ended up at the cliffs.

Down below, the angry tide frothed and crashed.

Dusk had well and truly become night, and the half-moon granted just enough light to catch Henri's nod. Without a word, we all joined in the rhythmic swing as we gathered up enough momentum to toss the body over the side.

We let go.

The body went sailing through the air.

No splash.

No sign he'd fallen.

Henri raked both hands through his blood-soaked hair, looked at the moon with a heavy exhale, then slowly led us back to the cave.

Peter lay in a small puddle of moonlight, looking as if this wasn't just a resting spot but his new grave.

None of us said a word as Henri stumbled, righted himself, then headed toward Peter. His shoulders sagged with tiredness; his arm oozed with blood.

He towered over Peter with hands fisted and an unreadable black look. He studied my friend for so long, I feared he meant to dispatch him and leave him there.

Worry crawled up my spine.

If he means to kill him…

Both Rachel and I darted forward and barricaded ourselves in front of him. "What are you doing?"

He blinked as if the answer was obvious even though he didn't speak.

Pushing us aside, Henri ducked to his haunches, gathered Peter's unconscious limbs, and hoisted him into his arms.

My heart squeezed.

Hope, *delicious* hope.

All the pressure, the pain, and the fear of the day threatened to become too much as I witnessed a man who'd willingly bullied this jewel. A Master who'd judged him, ridiculed him, and been jealous of him—cradle him close as if he was a brother.

Tears stung my eyes as Henri swayed a little before clutching Peter closer to his chest.

Peter's head flopped back, his shoulders supported by Henri's arm and his legs draped over another.

Was Henri helping him because of tactic and schemes? Did he do this to stay in Victor's good graces? Or was he helping because none of this was right? All of this was wrong. So very, very wrong.

And…he'd participated.

Silently, we followed him as he carried Peter out through the tunnel and up the stairs. I'd left the knife tucked discreetly behind a rock, aware the guards would steal it the moment I stepped foot into the stronghold.

Every instinct ordered me not to go back there, but…what choice did we have?

Enter with Henri as our reigning winner and trust him to keep us safe or…risk our lives by swimming.

Krish would never forgive me if I drowned.

No one spoke as we padded silently through the forest, climbing higher and higher, following the same paths we'd sprinted down this morning.

Every day since I'd arrived here, the hours had defied the usual length of a normal trip around the sun. It felt as if I'd been a prisoner for years, yet that journey through the woods felt like it lasted an eternity.

My muscles burned with bruises, my ribs felt far too sharp, and my feet had long stopped screaming for walking over painful things. I didn't want to see how badly cut they were.

We were all spent by the time we broke out of the forest, sighing in relief as bare toes sank into the luscious grass of Victor's runway.

Rachel bared her teeth as the stronghold with its battlement walls, sniper guards, spotlights, and star-puncturing turrets appeared.

Uplights danced over every chiselled stone. Arrow slits and modern windows flickered like fireflies with illumination from within. With its caged balconies and gargoyles, angels and pointy parapets, Victor's home might be a nest full of monsters, but…it looked rather beautiful in the starry night.

"You're late," a guard muttered as our feet thudded heavily over the drawbridge and traded open air for stagnant imprisonment.

Henri sniffed. "Long day."

"The Master Jeweler is waiting for everyone to present in the ballroom. Rollcall should've finished three hours ago."

"Tell him he can keep waiting." Henri looked at Peter in his arms. "This jewel needs a doctor. Now."

Scowling, the guard spoke into a radio hooked onto his black jacket. Muttering something, his eyes skimmed the rest of us, growing wider as he noticed how paint-covered we all were.

By the time he got a crackly response, his face had traded annoyance for respect, and he bowed a little at Henri. "The Master Jeweler said he'll meet you in the foyer."

Stifling a sigh, Henri nodded. "Fine."

My skin crawled as we all started walking again.

I expected the drawbridge to clang up and lock us inside, but it seemed we weren't the only tardy ones. The three guards manning the entrance turned to face the dark runway again, their eyes peering through the night for more stragglers.

Rachel glanced at me. "I don't know if I'm hoping no jewels will show up for rollcall or all of them."

Mollie nodded. "What if a few jumped?"

"Then I guess they're better off than we are." Rachel staggered.

I grabbed her hand, stopping her from falling. Despite my pain. Despite our mutual exhaustion…we were in this together.

I glared at the castle as it loomed closer and closer. The manicured gardens with its animal hedges and fountains swallowed us deeper and deeper. Time quickly ran out of our hourglass, stealing our ability to speak.

I whispered under my breath, "What you mentioned in the caves…we need to talk about it."

Mollie stiffened. "We can't—"

"The kitchens. May—that kind cook—said no one hears what they say down there—"

"You want to use the kitchens as our war room?" Mollie hissed back.

I nodded, flicking Henri a look.

His shoulders bunched from carrying Peter. His back rippled beneath his bloody t-shirt. But he showed no sign of hearing us.

"The minute we can get away and meet there...we're planning something," I muttered.

"You're even more crazy than Peter, and he was high." Mollie rolled her eyes.

"Crazy or just determined?" I smiled sadly.

"I think it's the same word in this case."

"Hush, both of you," Rachel whispered. "No one speaks of this again until we can meet in the kitchens. Agreed?"

"Agreed." Both Mollie and I dropped our chins in silent acceptance. And just like that, we started gathering troops for battle.

A chill darted down my spine as we traded the empty beautiful gardens for the erotic tapestry-decorated foyer. The familiar sensation of evil wafted over me as my eyes landed on Victor.

He stood beside the curving staircase branching to the left.

Arms crossed, pristine navy suit soaking up the scant light from the crystal-dripping chandelier, his smile seemed crocodilian.

The sense of déjà vu from the night I'd been flown here threatened to overlap this one.

That night, I'd still believed I could escape.

Now...I wasn't so sure.

But I'll try...

"Ah, there you are!" Victor grinned with welcome, his greying-blond hair dancing with rainbows from the crystals above. "I was beginning to think you'd all drowned."

Henri shifted Peter in his arms and stopped before the man who ruled all our lives. "Vic." He bowed a little. "Like I told your guards, it's been a long fucking day. Can I have a shower and some sleep before participating in whatever annoying debrief you have planned?"

"Found even more ego out there, I see." Victor looked past him with a raised eyebrow, smirking at the three of us, red and bruised behind him. "My, my, it *has* been a long day. I told you to shoot one gem, Henri. Not all of them."

Henri forced a tired chuckle. "I got lucky."

Victor frowned at the red coating Henri. "And you also shot yourself?" Reaching out to smear Henri's bloody bicep, he scowled. "Wait, that's not—"

"You're right." Henri backed up, Peter dangling over his arms. "It's not paint. Not all of it, at least."

Victor's friendly welcome turned arctic. "Explain."

"I was attacked by a Master in the caves. He stabbed me." Angling his arm, Henri arched his chin at the wound in his bicep. "I retaliated. It got…messy."

Victor huffed. "Please tell me you haven't killed any more of my guests, *mon ami*."

"No." Henri kept a cool expression. "I've learned my lesson not to disobey you. I…I merely defended myself. I got injured for the effort, but I left him alive. He was still in the cave when the tide came in. I didn't see what happened after that."

"You're saying a guest drowned? Who?"

Playing a dangerous game, Henri gave a name. "Kyle."

"Kyle?" Victor gave him a careful look. "Kyle drowned?"

"Well, he said his name was Kyle. I didn't exactly ask for ID."

"I wasn't aware you'd had interactions with him."

"I haven't." Henri huffed, rearranging Peter again. "He was with Charles when we first met. Charles introduced us on the beach."

"I see." He inhaled a little harder as if sniffing for lies.

"They went ahead. I didn't see Charles again, but I did bump into Kyle. He was…having some fun with a jewel and a knife."

I shivered and fought the urge to touch my neck where Kyle had started to slice.

Victor didn't speak for a while before nodding slowly. "It's true he is a violent fellow. I've had to educate and discipline him more times than he's worth."

"Charles said he was the reason for all your cameras."

"He was." Victor nodded again. "Alright, tell me the rest. You interrupted his little filleting fun, and he ordered you to leave. I'm guessing you didn't?"

Henri shrugged, his biceps bunching under Peter's unconscious form. "He seemed high as a kite, if I'm honest. The moment I stepped into the cave, he came at me because he knew I'd tell you what he'd gotten up to."

Mollie, Rachel, and I didn't dare move as Victor mulled over Henri's half-truths. "Okay…say I believe you on that. What happened next?"

"I got lost in the caves and barely made it out as the tide came in. I managed to swim, but in my escape, I saw a few bodies floating that weren't so lucky."

"*A few?*"

"Three maybe?"

"All Masters?" Victor asked far too calmly.

"I can't be sure. But there were definitely a few bodies floating around." Henri widened his stance as if Peter's weight grew too much. "Look, Vic, as much as I want to—"

"Rachel." Victor narrowed his eyes on his favourite gem and the unwilling mother of his unborn child. "You're very good at telling me the truth, my pet. Did you see any of this?" He waved at Henri's bleeding arm. "Did you see him get stabbed? Is what he said true?"

I stopped breathing.

Henri didn't look over his shoulder, but the muscles in his back tensed.

Not looking at me or Mollie, Rachel bit her bottom lip.

She had the power to murder Henri.

She could collaborate or deny, and Victor would decide who he believed.

"Start at the very beginning if you'd be so kind." Victor never took his reptilian gaze off her. "Don't spare me a single teensy detail."

What she said before the bullseye was painted on us echoed in my ears. She'd said she was on our side. That she was in on whatever suicidal mission Peter and I cooked up. But that didn't mean her courage would hold up beneath direct questioning from the very man who'd made her doubt her feelings several times.

Goosebumps covered me from head to toe as Victor added, "Before you answer, my sweetling, allow me to tell you what will happen if you lie." His face turned dead and terrifying. "If you lie and I find out you hid something from me, I will carve out that child from your belly while you're still alive, then serve it to you as a special snack before killing you in the most drawn-out way possible." He crossed his arms. "Now, go ahead. In your own words. What happened out there?"

Mollie fought a tremble, but Rachel didn't so much as blink with fear.

Either she'd tipped over the edge of terror or gone into shock just like Peter. "From the beginning? Sure, Sir V. Your wish is my command, as always." She practically curtsied. "You saw us all run as one. We left the castle and ran through the forest. Some of the jewels thought about swimming away—"

Mollie gasped, cutting off Rachel's story and adding weight to what she'd said.

Victor smirked, enjoying Rachel spilling everyone's secrets. "Go on."

"If you're missing a few jewels tonight, Sir V," Rachel murmured. "You might find more took you up on the offer to jump than you would've liked."

He shrugged. "No matter. It was getting a little stale in here. I'll just tell my team to gather a few more while on their hunt."

Rachel nodded, still numb, still vacant. "We managed to stay together until we reached the Temple of Facets."

Victor sucked in a breath, arrowing a look at Peter. "Naughty boy. Seems as if someone has been tattling."

Rachel didn't stop. "Most of us couldn't handle what we saw in there, so…we split up. I don't know where most of the jewels ended up, but we chose the wrong direction and got stuck."

I gave her a subtle look.

If she mentioned the cave with the skylight, Victor could easily go and see how much she fabricated. He'd see all the blood. See the droplets as we carried corpses up the steps and tossed them over the cliffs.

But all my doubt in her loyalty vanished as she said, "We had to backtrack. Wading into water when the caves were filling up was petrifying." She shivered dramatically. "We stumbled into the cave where Kyle was having his own little party and witnessed him stabbing Master H. They were fighting."

"Please," Victor said softly. "Do go on."

"I'm aware of Master K's tastes and didn't stick around to see if he'd kill Master H. We scattered. We barely made it out before the sea poured in. But…" She swallowed hard as if resisting the urge to gag. "I-I saw what Master H saw. I'll never forget the sight as a few bodies floated past and—"

"Mollie," Victor snapped. "If you lie to me, I'll allow Roland to share his ultimate fantasy with you." He paused with a smile, knowing full well what that fantasy was and how painfully Mollie would die. "I'd like to hear your version."

"Yes, Sir V." With a shallow inhale, Mollie bowed. "I saw the bodies too, Sir V. Masters, not jewels. I spotted Master H wading out after us. His arm bled so much it left a ribbon of red on the water."

Victor pinned his eyes on me. "And where was Peter in all of this?"

I swallowed hard, hoping I wouldn't let the team down.

The fact that they covered for Henri?

That they banded around a Master and implicated him in our war effort without even knowing if he was on our side sent my entire nervous system fizzing with fear.

"Peter was unconscious." I fought the urge to copy my friends and use Victor's title with respect. I'd refused to do such things. If I started now…wouldn't that look suspicious?

Instead, I braced to be reprimanded and snapped, "You burned his hands and feet then sent him off running. You knew he might not survive the day. It's taken the three of us to keep him alive this long."

Victor shot Henri a look. "How did *you* end up carrying him?"

Henri's voice was low and bored as if this entire conversation fucked him off. "I watched the tide spit them out of the cave system. They looked half drowned, and it was well past dusk. I figured you'd be pissed if I didn't get them home where they belong. That's also when I shot them." He smiled like a killer. "They were too tired to run."

Victor grinned. "That was very considerate of you to carry Peter, *mon ami*. Especially seeing as you were wounded yourself."

"It's fine. Peter's useful to you." Henri sniffed. "I figured you'd miss him for whatever odd jobs he helps you with around here."

Victor stroked his smooth chin. "You're quite right. He's a handy boy to have. But I need to ask…why do you even care? You've made it abundantly clear you're not a fan of his."

Henri hoisted Peter once again and looked down at the unconscious jewel with a sneer. "He pisses me off, and you're right, I don't like him. But…this is my home, and you are my friend. So…here we are."

"Here we are indeed." Victor let heavy silence fall, studying each of us with terrifyingly intelligent eyes.

My skin crawled the longer he dragged out the pause.

My breath caught on the nasty sharpness centred in one of my ribs.

I almost sighed in relief as he chuckled under his breath. "So you saved my jewels then shot my jewels. Fitting, I suppose." He shifted a little, looking at our red paint. "My memory can be a bit fuzzy sometimes, but…didn't you have orange bullets this morning?" He glanced at my thigh where Henri had shot me in the line-up.

Not even a streak remained, completely branded over with scarlet.

"You're right, I did." Henri nodded. "I had an unfortunate incident with a blowhole and broke my gun at the very beginning. I would say you'd find the useless weapon on the beach, but the tide would've washed it away."

"And where did you get the replacement from?" Eyeing the weapon hanging off Mollie's shoulder.

"Kyle." Henri grinned. "He stabbed me, we fought, I grabbed his gun and left him to it. I figured he wasn't using it and had already caught the jewel he wanted, so…"

"Did you see who he cut?"

"No." Henri shook his head. "Sorry."

"Quite understandable. It's a high-stakes game. It's why I don't play along. I prefer my position as referee and live vicariously through you."

"Well, you missed out." Henri gave him another rancid smile. "It was fun."

"It definitely seems so, seeing as you've returned with three of my jewels as your spoils. I hope you don't think—just because you covered them in bruises and brought them home safely—that I'll allow you to keep all three?" His eyes glinted. "Besides, I thought you were only interested in one."

"I am," Henri snapped. "I just…got trigger happy. Look, Vic, Peter weighs a fucking tonne. He needs your doctor, and I'm—"

"Yes, yes, you're tired and want to rest." Wrinkling his nose, Victor nodded slowly. "I admit you stink of seaweed, and Peter looks as if you should've left him for the gulls." Leaning in, he flicked up one of Peter's eyelids before letting it snap back down. "The doctor is in her personal rooms, not the surgery. She's had a long day, and the patient rooms below are full. Go upstairs to her. However, you might've wasted your energy carrying him back. He smells as if death has already found him."

"That's his hands and feet, you bastard," I hissed.

Henri turned on me, roaring in French. "*Tiens ta putain de langue, Ilyana, ou je vais te la couper. J'en ai marre de ton attitude, tu m'entends?!*" (Hold your fucking tongue, Ilyana, or I'll cut it out. I'm sick to death of your attitude, do you hear me?!)

I recoiled and tripped backward on throbbing feet.

My heart spasmed with the sharpest pain.

I'd *never* been spoken to that way before.

Scolded that harshly.

Never had my entire soul tuck tail and hide, desperate to run far away from such violence.

Victor chuckled. "You better go rest up, Henri, before you butcher your favourite, hmm? I know what it's like when your temper is on the edge." Stepping aside from the marble stairs, Victor waved his arm for us to pass. "Tell Dr Belford to treat you first. You wouldn't want to die from sepsis. She can then tend to Peter with my blessing." Looking at us behind Henri, he purred, "Rachel, Mollie, return to the jewel quarters and shower off that paint. Report to me so I can count your bruises."

Stopping me with a hand on my shoulder as I followed Henri toward the bottom step, Victor grinned. "And as for you…"

I forced myself not to squirm as he dragged me close. Too close. "It looks like you got most of the bullets because your Master is finally seeing the errors of your ways." He chuckled as his horrible blue eyes skimmed down my hurting body. "You definitely didn't hold back, Henri." He clucked his tongue. "I'm impressed."

Henri growled under his breath. "She deserved it."

I fought the very real, very awful urge to sob.

Victor let me go with another laugh. "I suggest you rest before you discipline her any further. I would hate to tell you off for going too far."

"Understood."

"What are you two still doing here?" Victor barked, looking at Rachel and Mollie.

With a flinch, they shot me a look, then dashed to the left and the corridor leading to the jewel stables.

The corridor swallowed them whole.

I longed to go with them.

The thought of staying in Henri's company after he yelled…

God, I felt like a naughty child about to be spanked.

"See you later, Mercer." With a quick salute, Victor strolled toward the games room.

"Night." Giving me a guarded look, Henri snapped, "Come on."

He started a weary, slow climb up the stairs.

And I had no choice but to follow him.

Chapter Ten

Henri

EVERYTHING FUCKING HURT.
My arms.
My toes.
My *soul*.

I'd struggled to stay sane the entire walk back to the castle. Carrying Peter had drained the rest of my nonexistent reserves, and having Ily, Mollie, and Rachel stare at my back as I led them home drove me closer and closer to the bottomless black pit in my mind.

I'd snapped when I'd stabbed Kyle a million times.

I'd snapped when I'd strangled Charles.

I'd snapped on my own in that glow worm-dotted cave, drowning in the darkness—screaming into the abyss all while it swallowed me whole.

I needed to be alone.

I needed to rock in the motherfucking corner and figure out how to fix the mess inside me.

They vouched for me.

My rotten heart fisted all over again.

Why?

Why put themselves at risk?

I didn't have time for such questions.

Didn't have the capacity to care about the answers.

Shutting everything down, I ignored Ily's quiet breathing behind me as we finished climbing and headed down the corridor toward Victor's dead zoo and Dr Belford's chambers.

Peter moaned in my arms as I pounded a fist on the door.

A cold draft cut through my damp clothes, and my chilled bones added another level of torment.

My temper fractured.

I felt borderline insane. Itchy with the need to get Peter far away from me and to shove away all the mistakes I'd made today.

"Open up!" I bellowed. "*Now*."

The door swung wide.

I didn't give a shit about etiquette anymore. Victor's cornering had well and truly bled me dry; I had nothing left to give.

Bowling past the doctor as she finished drying her hands on a paper towel, I spied a white sheet-covered table by the wall and marched to it.

The relief in my arms and spine as I placed Peter onto it sent fresh waves of pins and needles through me. I put him down as gently as I could, but I suppose it wasn't gentle enough as the doctor gasped and darted forward, carefully rearranging his legs so they straightened out before tucking a starchy pillow beneath his head.

Raking both hands through my blood-saturated hair, I snarled, "Do whatever you want with him, but give me some painkillers and stuff for bruises first."

Ily.

I needed to fix Ily before I lost my mind.

Her keen eye landed on my bleeding arm, her body tensing beneath light green scrubs. "I have orders to treat Masters before jewels." She shot a longing look at Peter before gritting her teeth and stepping toward me. "That looks bad. You'll need stitches."

Clamping a hand over the wound, I backed up. "Drugs and bruise ointments. While you're at it give me some bandages and salve too." I flicked a look at Ily, noticing her shredded feet. They looked as bad as mine.

Fuck, I'm sorry.

The door opened and closed behind us.

I whipped around as the nurse who'd helped take my blood when I'd first arrived on this godforsaken island appeared.

I couldn't remember her name, but the doctor snapped her fingers and ordered, "Rose, prep everything we need to disinfect and bandage Peter. I'll need intravenous antibiotics and—"

"Give me what I need," I said coldly, calmly. "I won't ask again."

Dr Belford scowled and shook her head. "While Rose starts on Peter, I'll sew you up." Her nose wrinkled at my sorry state. "You need tending to."

"You're not fucking listening! I don't care about me. Give me what I want, and I'll leave."

She flinched at my aggression.

A fracture in her medical professionalism appeared. "Please

don't raise your voice at me." She couldn't hide her true feelings or the hatred she harboured. "You're the reason I have a full-time job patching up sex slaves, so allow me to *do* that job and stop throwing your weight around."

"The supplies, woman. Or I'll make you instead of asking you."

Every second prevented me from tending the only one who mattered to me.

Ily wisely didn't make a peep as the doctor swallowed back her loathing and went to a cupboard full of narrow drawers, each typed neatly with white labels. Drawing out the things I'd asked for, she placed them in a kidney-shaped dish and shoved them at me. "Here."

She made the mistake of looking behind me. Of noticing Ily swaying on the spot.

Red-soaked Ily with bruises pockmarking her from head to breakable toe.

"Goddamn you to hell," Dr Belford hissed under her breath, pinning me with livid eyes. "You're all fucking monsters." Darting past me, she grabbed Ily's hand. "Sweetheart, you need to sit down. How are you even still standing?"

Ily shot me a worried look—a look full of true fear and wariness. She shook her head. "I-I'll be fine after I've showered and rested. I just need—" She swallowed hard as the nurse placed Peter's hand into a metal bowl stinking of antiseptic solution. Whatever the liquid was immediately frothed as if dissolving his flesh like acid. "Oh…" Ily wobbled. "I'm suddenly feeling rather faint."

"I'm not surprised." The doctor couldn't hide her horror at the number of bruises covering Ily. "You're black and blue. Can you breathe okay? Any sharp pains in your side?"

Ily nodded weakly. "I didn't want to say anything, but…it feels like there's a dagger in my ribs. I've done my best not to inhale too deeply, but it's super painful."

What?

Why didn't she fucking say anything?

"Here?" The doctor touched her battered ribcage, right over a particular nasty bloom of colour.

"*Ow.* Yep." Ily sucked in a groan. "But…please don't worry about me. I'm fine. Fix Peter—"

"It might be a fracture," the doctor spoke over her. "You

need to lie down."

Fury kindled in me all over again.

The image of that psychopath shooting her at close range.

The *pock-pock-pock* of bullets.

The explosion of red as if he pried her open to feast.

It'd taken everything I had not to tear off his hands, scoop out his eyes, and rip out his stinking entrails.

Ily shook her head again. "No, no. I'm okay. Honestly, it's just a bruise. Peter needs you far more—"

"If any of your ribs are broken, you might puncture your lungs if I don't treat you." She gave Ily a quick once-over. "Is there anything else broken? Fingers, toes, arms, legs? No sense of building pressure in your chest or abdomen?"

My ears rang with her questions.

Ily closed her eyes, her voice scarily quiet. "No, no. I'm fine."

"Are you lightheaded because of lack of food, or have you been struck in the head?"

Ily flinched as she looked at Peter and the frothing bowl. "Please don't mention food."

"How many fingers am I holding up?" The doctor held up her hand.

"Four."

Glowering at me, Belford hissed, "What exactly did you do to her?"

My hackles rose. "That's none of your concern."

"It is as her physician. Did you toss her about? Hit her head? Did you use toys on her? Fuck her? How roughly did you take her?"

Yeah, after the shitty day I'd had, those questions tipped me the fuck over.

"Fuck you and *fuck* your questions." I vibrated with enough rage to explode her rooms into splinters. "I'm trying *really* fucking hard not to hurt you but if you don't give me what I need, let Ily go, and shut the fuck up, I will snap. And you *do not* want to make me snap."

I swallowed blackness. Choked on madness.

Doing my best to leash myself, I hissed, "Give her back to me. Right fucking now."

Her fingers locked on Ily's arm. "She needs to sit down and be examin—"

"*Ahhh*!!" Peter suddenly woke up screaming as Rose cleaned

his maimed hand with cotton.

Ily backed up, breaking the doctor's hold on her. "I can't stay here. I can't—"

"It's okay. I can put you in my room—"

"She's coming with me." I shifted the bowl of supplies, ready to grab Ily's wrist. "I'm not leaving her here."

"She's covered in contusions. She might have internal bleeding thanks to the soft tissue bruises." Dr Belford almost spat on my feet as her rancour grew. "You shot her like an animal. I've had enough of you creeps. All of you. I wish you'd just—"

"*Melanie.*" The nurse left a catatonic Peter and darted to her colleague. "Remember where you are, who he is, and calm down, alright?"

Melanie's nostrils flared as she sucked in a breath.

For a moment, she looked as if she'd stab me with a scalpel, but slowly, the rage in her pretty older face turned into weary hate. "I'm sorry, Master H. Forgive me."

"Focus on Peter." Clicking my fingers and striding to the door, I ordered, "Ilyana, come. I've had enough of this place."

I had to leave.

Before I lost it.

Ily's gorgeous golden eyes met mine just as Peter woke up again, mumbling with hallucinations and knocking over the bowl of disinfectant.

He screamed in pain.

Ily shifted toward him.

And something terrible happened.

A soft cry on her lips.

A weak press of her hand to her head.

Then she staggered.

And fell.

Crumpling, tumbling—

Tossing the metal bowl away, I hurled myself forward and caught her just before she cracked her skull on the flagstone pavers of the doctor's lounge.

No one said a word as I gathered Ily into my arms and somehow found the strength to lurch to my feet.

My back protested.

My arms had no strength.

But having her close, feeling her fading heat soaking into me—the *rightness* of her after the wrongness of Peter—*fuck,* I needed that.

I hadn't been aware how much I needed that.

How desperate I was to stay human when all I could see and hear and taste was death.

My eyes met the doctor's. "If you try to stop me from taking her, I *will* hurt you."

"Just like you hurt *her*?"

I glanced down at Ily's slack face and closed eyes. I held her life in my hands, and instead of her fiery temper colliding with mine, her silent submission undid me.

"Pick up the supplies and give them to me."

Melanie crossed her arms. "You can't take her. I won't let you. She could die if she doesn't receive proper care. Especially if there's internal bleeding."

"I'll bring her back later."

"Are you a doctor, or are you just stupid? She's *my* patient. Because of you, we've spent the entire day doing our best to repair what you and your fucking friends broke. I thought it was over. I hoped I wouldn't have to see another brutalised person tonight. But no! I now have two unconscious patients to add to my overflowing surgery, and I'm telling you, Master or no Master, she belongs to the owner of this castle, and it's up to me to fix her!"

"Wrong." I stalked into her. "She's *mine,* and I'll take care of her."

Her eyes flickered to my cut arm. Her expression said she didn't give a rat's ass about sewing me up anymore, but she would fight me on behalf of the jewels in her care. Her backbone grew stupidly brave as she shook her head. "If you think you can have more of your twisted fun tonight with a passed-out, bruise-riddled jewel, you deserve to die from that knife wound."

I reeled backward. "Do I look like the type of man who would fuck her in this condition?"

"You're the one who *put* her in this condition!"

"Give me the fucking supplies, and let me pass!" I bellowed, making Ily flinch but not rouse.

"Go jump off the roof!"

"Mel, *enough!*" The nurse leapt into action. Jogging to the cupboard of many shelves, she hastily ripped out a few other things along with a vial of colourless liquid. "I'm sorry, Master H. Please…forgive her. We've had a long day with jewels being brought in from the hunt. Many of them are injured." Her voice turned small. "A few are dead. It's…just…forgive us."

Inhaling hard, feeling my own agonies, I nodded. "Forgiven."

Melanie sneered but held her tongue this time.

Rose padded back to me, scooped up the bowl I'd dropped, then carefully tucked the supplies onto Ily's stomach where she lay sleeping in my arms. "There's a guest room two doors down from here. Please stay there tonight so we can come check on you both when we've stabilised Peter, okay?"

The way she watched me.

Maternally.

Kindly.

It very nearly brought me to my knees.

The weight of the world crushed my shoulders, and all I wanted to do was beg this woman to fix everything. To reverse all my actions. To heal Ily and heal me. To stop me from ever being this way.

Swallowing around the rocks in my throat, I nodded. "Fine."

Melanie sucked in a breath as if surprised by my sudden amenability.

Stepping closer, Rose dared put her hand on my filthy forearm. "Do you give me your word that you'll look after her? That you won't hurt her anymore?"

I wanted to tell her it wasn't me who hurt her, but I couldn't.

Every wound she carried was because of me.

"On the memory of my mother, I swear I only want to help."

"In that case…may I?" Moving her hand from my forearm to Ily's cheek, she raised an eyebrow. "If you intend on bathing her and treating her bruises, she'll need something to withstand the pain. Once she's clean and resting, we'll come in with the portable X-ray machine and take a few slides of her chest and abdomen to make sure nothing is broken. I'm hoping she'll stay unconscious while you tend to her, but…if she wakes while you're still treating her, she might hurt herself by trying to get away. So…I'm willing to trust you, Henri."

My eyes flew to hers.

Another?

Yet another person willing to trust me when I'd done nothing to deserve it?

What Peter had said crowded my mind.

"I see what she does now. You did come for us. You're going to free us. I know it—"

I had no intention of doing that.

I had nowhere else to go.

If I stepped foot outside this place, I'd die. And I was a selfish, selfish man because I had no intention of releasing Ily.

"Peter informed us that Ily doesn't tolerate chemicals well. However, the usual over-the-counter medicines won't dull her pain enough. So..." She flicked a look at the doctor. "Do you think she could tolerate GHB, Mel?"

Dr Belford's eyes widened. "The date rape drug? Are you mad? You want to give a highly potent drug to someone who can't metabolise them?"

"Her system already makes GHB. We all do. Albeit in very tiny amounts. I doubt she'd have an adverse reaction to it as long as we got the dose right."

"I'd hope to God we got it right because the wrong one would be fatal."

"Fatal?" I backed up, hugging Ily closer. "No fucking way are you giving her anything that could kill her. Jesus."

Both the nurse and the doctor looked at me with matching questionable expressions.

I didn't care we were on camera.

I didn't care Victor would see his in-house doctor yelling at me or my responses to Ily's condition. He could taunt me or threaten me all he wanted, but under no circumstances would I put Ily through another experience like the one she'd had in Ruby Tears.

And the fact I could look back on that night—one of the most freeing of my life—and only abhor it now broke yet another fucking part of me.

Were there any pieces left?

How much could a man keep breaking before he shattered into dust?

Rose held up the tiny glass vial. "This is GHB in liquid form. It's practically tasteless and—"

"No." I shook my head.

"She's in a lot of pain, Henri." Rose used liberties with my name again. "She might've fainted because of Peter's treatment, but I think it's more about the fact she reached the limits of her endurance. The kindest thing you could do for her is to let her sleep while you tend to her. And this"—she wriggled the bottle—"is probably the only sedative she can have."

I stepped back again.

Rose followed me. "This doesn't work the same way as psilocybin. It's gamma-hydroxybutyrate, and in the dose I'm suggesting, all she'll feel is tired. If she wakes, her pain receptors will be dulled. The worst side effects would be slight inhibition and giddiness. That's all."

"I'm not fucking drugging her, alright?"

Ily moaned in my arms; her eyes cracked open a little.

Rose caught her hazy gaze and smiled. "Welcome back. How're you feeling?"

"Sore." Ily winced, trying to get away from my arm pressed against her ribs.

I shifted immediately, swallowing a hiss as her hair stuck to my stab wound.

Melanie darted forward, snatching the vial out of Rose's hand. "Now you're awake…you can make the choice." Smiling thinly, she added, "As you know, Peter's in a bad way, and we need to tend to him first. But…you're also in a state. Your Master has agreed to do the initial clean-up and tend to your bruises. It will hurt. You really shouldn't move. Rose has suggested you take a micro-dose of GHB to keep you still, and…I tend to agree with her."

Ily stiffened. "No, I can't—"

"You shouldn't have any symptoms like you did last time. All you should feel is drowsy and free from pain for a while. Does that sound okay?"

Ily laughed, then bit her bottom lip with a moan. "Is that a trick question?"

"Okay then." Unscrewing the vial, the doctor sucked up the barest amount into a pipette.

"Wait." Ily blinked and tried to be more coherent. "Are you sure it won't make me hallucinate? I don't think I can go through that again."

"No." Melanie shook her head. "You should just be a little spacey. However, I wouldn't be doing my job if I also didn't advise that it might cause feelings of euphoria and increased sex drive. In too high a dose, it could cause tremors, nausea, breathing difficulties, and or death. So it's not one I regularly—"

"No way." I bared my teeth. "No drugs. Give her some damn Panadol."

"Panadol won't touch the sort of pain she's suffering." Her hate-filled eyes met mine. "And it's not your choice, is it?"

Ily trembled as if the thought of existing for another moment in pain was too much. She didn't look at me. Didn't ask me to put her down. She just nodded. "If it will give me some peace for a little while...then, yes please."

I sucked in a breath. "Ily, no—"

"I've made my choice." She refused to make eye contact.

Melanie sucked in a breath and squeezed out all the liquid in the pipette until only a few drops remained. Holding it over Ily's mouth, she murmured, "Open."

Hesitantly, Ily parted her lips and grimaced as the medicine was administered. Hardly anything at all. A thimble size. Minuet really.

Catching my eyes, the doctor ordered, "If she falls unconscious again, I expect you to monitor her. Roll her onto her side and keep her airway clear. Seeing as Ily has a history of being a lightweight when it comes to substances, it's your job to keep an eye on her and request us if her care requirements exceed your capabilities."

"We'll pop by as soon as we can." Rose smiled, her eyes far kinder. Either she was far better at hiding her true thoughts or she didn't hate me as much as Melanie did.

"Fine." I gritted my teeth. "You have my word. I'll never take my eyes off her."

"I can walk, Hen—" Ily cut herself off. "Please, put me down, Master H."

"No. And don't ask again."

Melanie huffed and tucked the vial into her scrub pocket. "Two doors down. Make yourself at home. And Ily...don't fight the effects, okay? In ten to twenty minutes, you should feel a lot more relaxed and able to ignore the pain."

"Sounds wonderful." Ily nodded with a wince.

Spinning on my heel, I strode out of the room before the doctor could say anything else.

Obeying the doctor's commands, I guided Ily into the spare guest chamber and flicked on the lights. Slightly smaller than our room below, this one glowed in autumn colours. A bed frame made of dull copper, white blankets edged with burnt orange, and curtains a dark shade of bronze. A dresser lined most of the wall with a workstation, minibar, and TV. The view from the small Juliette balcony displayed more of the gardens, allowing us to look down upon the battlements in the distance and the beetle-sized guards patrolling with their spotlights.

The bathroom glittered with modern mosaic tiles, pearlescent white with burnt orange, making everything seem as if we were inside a crystal tangerine.

It felt odd to be in a different room, but Ily didn't seem to care as she turned on the shower and adjusted it to her preferred temperature of Hades.

I managed to keep my temper the entire time she stripped off her disgusting nude-coloured underwear—now grime-covered and paint-soaked. I chewed on self-hatred as I followed her into the shower and reached for the soap to bathe her.

But then all my fury twisted into despair as she held up her hand and shook her head. "Don't...please don't touch me." She kept her eyes downcast. "The bruises just keep getting worse. The pain is almost too much. I think...I think I'll pass out again if you touch me."

I wanted to ask her so many things.

I wanted a comprehensive list of her pain and how to erase it.

I wanted to drop to my knees and press my forehead to her badly bruised belly and just *hold her.*

But that black abyss smothered me down.

A dam of misery blocked my throat.

I merely nodded.

Leaving her to wash, watching how gently she touched her swollen, black-and-blue skin, I stood under the hot spray and fought the urge to scream.

I'd been too late this time.

I hadn't stopped him.

That blackness kept billowing, pouring, suffocating...

Rivulets of crimson poured off my skin, but the water didn't stand a chance at cleansing my insides. My soul was putrid, fetid, *corrupted.* Red water swirled around our feet, vanishing down the drain. Every drop rivered over my mind, a waterfall pushing me into the deep, dark depths of whatever entity that'd taken hold of me.

My stab wound blazed beneath the hot spray, giving me something to latch onto.

I liked the agony.

I deserved it.

The urge to find another blade and open the scar on my leg flickered in my coal-black mind.

For ten minutes, Ily and I shared a silent shower, taking turns to rinse beneath the heavy pummel of water. Our bodies became clean, but my soul? That became darker than death.

Wringing out her hair, squeezing clear water not scarlet, Ily swayed into the wall.

"Oops." She giggled.

My heart wrenched to a stop.

I'd never heard her make such a light-hearted sound before.

It was the quickest flare of brightness in my otherwise wretched existence.

Every atom in my body urged me to reach out and support her wobbly steps as she tripped drunkenly out of the shower and clung to the towel rail.

She giggled again as she patted the fluffy towel. "Sorry."

She's apologising to the furniture now?

I thought whatever that damn doctor gave her was supposed to be mild?

Wrenching off the shower, I stepped dripping wet onto the bathmat and caught my reflection. The glass above the white vanity fogged with steam, my image hazy and clouded. But even in the mist, my eyes seemed to burn a dull grey full of bone-deep exhaustion. A tiredness that didn't just come from physical activity or the mental weariness of murder, but something so much deeper.

If I didn't know any better, I'd say the wasted man staring back at me was on a slippery slope to burn out, and I didn't really want to stop it.

If I burned out...this all ended.

I can finally rest.

Alone.

Wrapping herself in a towel, Ily hissed between her teeth, then walked with great concentration out of the bathroom.

Snatching a second towel from the rack, I dried off my hair and swiped my body dry. Agony bellowed in every inch. My arm never stopped bleeding, hinting that the lightheaded wooziness might not just be from thickening depression but also blood loss.

Wrapping the towel around my waist, I strode into the bedroom and spied Ily resting on the bed.

She lay star-fished beneath her towel. Arms and legs spread as if not wanting to touch any part of herself. Flat on her back where Kyle hadn't been able to shoot her, she breathed shallowly through her nose, obviously still in a lot of pain.

I lingered over her.

The urge to cup her cheek and promise I'd make everything better almost broke whatever wasn't broken inside me.

Everything I touch gets hurt...

Turning away, I fought the urge to run into the night and sacrifice myself to the churning, clawing chasm inside me.

I couldn't cope like this.

I couldn't be this way.

I wanted out.

I wanted to forget.

I want...

Christ.

Pinching the bridge of my nose, I backed away.

What I wanted I could never have, and if I tried, I'd only hurt her worse.

With shaky hands, I grabbed the medical supplies Rose had gathered for us, then carted them back into the bathroom.

Wiping off the mirror, I rummaged in the packets of bandages, arnica cream, and other salves.

I found salvation in distraction.

I did everything I could to avoid looking into the black maw growing ever bigger inside me. Tendrils of midnight wrapped around me, tugging me closer, closer...

My breath came faster as I found a small packet with a sterilised needle and surgical thread. I stared at my stab wound and imagined sewing myself together like a cobbler with leather.

The room tilted.

My breathing turned raspy.

My chest expanded until the contusion on my side glowed with dirty colours.

I fell into that swirl of pain.

My eyesight blurred at the edges.

I hyper-fucking-ventilated.

Blackness exploded through me, strangling me, throttling me—

My knees buckled as a fear I'd never felt before hammered into every bone.

Clutching the sink, I bent over the vanity, and panted.

I fucking panted and gasped, shaking and quaking as frenzied panic ripped through me.

It vised my chest, gagged my throat, and murdered me with every bad thing, wrong urge, and despicable desire.

I almost lost her.

I came face to face with it all.

Every decision.

Every choice.

I fucking *despised* myself.

The things I've done—

I retched.

Empty stomach acid burned my throat and splashed into the sink. Black despair spewed up and out, purging with every choke. Sweat dripped down my back as I pressed my forehead to the tap and rode out the spasms. The familiar regurgitation that'd punished me my entire life did its best to cripple me.

And for once, I was grateful.

So fucking thankful that the overload of insidious poison inside siphoned down the drain. I didn't vomit food. I vomited up my very essence.

By the time I stopped, I could barely stand.

She needs you…

Groaning, I commanded my muscles to brace and spine to straighten. Catching my stare in the mirror, I flinched at the creature staring back. My skin was bone white and eyes haunted as a graveyard.

But at least I hadn't been devoured by the darkness…

Yet.

Finding a paper-wrapped toothbrush in the drawer, I brushed, rinsed, then grabbed the largest gauze in the medical supplies and slapped it over my arm. My blood dripped over the vanity and floor. I didn't want to bleed over Ily while I tended to her.

I couldn't exactly do much for her apart from coating her entire body in arnica.

I was familiar with the homeopathic cream, thanks to my mother.

She'd always been jumpy. If I walked into a room without her hearing me, she'd often crash into a cupboard or doorframe as she turned around and noticed me.

I'd hated seeing her hurt because of me.

I'd accepted that every bruise she carried were constant

reminders that even though we were family, she acted as if I was her enemy.

And now, Ily is bruised.

Because of you.

The clawing in my chest returned.

The swirling blackness and wretched depression.

While she'd been covered in paint, it'd been hard to see the totality of her bruises.

But now?

Fucking Christ, every inch of her wonderful body was a blazing reminder of what I'd done.

She hates me...

Swallowing hard, I did my best to shut down the slicing pain in my heart.

The abyss pounced all over again.

I sank into the black.

Chapter Eleven

AIRY, BUBBLY, FLOATY…
Uh-oh.
I blinked as my fingers dug into the exquisitely soft bed, clinging tightly as if gravity would let go of me at any moment, and I'd drift around the room like an untethered balloon.

The mental picture of me bouncing off the ceiling and rolling down the curtains made me giggle.

Oh God—

Slamming a hand over my mouth, I tried to stop the rapid rising of inappropriate humour. My arms throbbed where they bent at my elbows, a reminder that bruises covered most of me.

I hadn't dared look in the foggy mirror to see how bad I looked. Then again, the soft spinning in my head didn't really care.

The sharp savagery of agony had gone.

Buh-bye…won't miss you…don't come again.

Dropping my hand, I sighed into the sugary softness of peace.
I liked this room.

No painting of that demonic goblin murdering a unicorn. No four-poster where Henri almost bound me with his tie. No wall where he'd kissed me and punched me right in the stupid, traitorous heart.

I rubbed my chest, needing to delete that first and worse contusion.

The whole organ was black with pain. The arteries and veins blue from his kiss. Every pump was a reminder of the ache in my soul every time he looked at me.

He scolded me.

The way he yelled at me downstairs…the emptiness in his eyes…the nastiness in his voice.

God—

Okay, so the pain wasn't completely gone.

The cluster of bullets Kyle had fired where my bullseye used to be, shared their pain directly with the very thing Henri had pulverised.

Even when he'd cut me and commanded me, he'd never spoken to me that way before.

I hope he's okay…

I frowned.

He was mean, and you're worried about him?

The room swirled as I nodded.

Krish sometimes used tetchiness in lieu of pain. His anger came from an inability to express whatever feelings consumed him. When words failed him, he sank deep within.

I hope Henri's not sinking…

My fuzzy eyes locked on the closed bathroom door.

He's been in there a while.

Maybe I should check.

I flinched.

He'll just yell at me again…

The urge to curl into a little ball came swiftly, followed by a morbid giggle.

Keep it together, Il.

The fuzz in my head cleared a little.

I sighed.

God, what a mess.

What an awful, agonising mess.

The giggles were back.

I snorted.

I snickered at how absurd everything was. How I was a *thing* not a someone. How I'd almost died in a cave today.

I helped toss a body over a cliff—

A loud laugh spilled free.

Oh no.

Henri appeared from the bathroom. His left side looked like a scribbly, abstract mess—as if an artist had squirted every pigment of purple and blue onto him, then decided it wasn't worth the trouble to paint. A few other smudges marked his bare chest, leading my eyes down to the white towel clinging valiantly to his narrow hips. The V of his cut muscles pointed directly to the bulge between his legs.

My stupid heart fluttered.

My greedy body hummed.

He's so pretty.
Pity about his soul, though…
I scowled.
He's not ugly inside.
At least…not all of him.
I swooned against the pillows.
He carried Peter all the way home.
He stabbed someone for me.
He protected Mollie and Rachel.
I wanted to hug him.
He'd done all that while bleeding and hurt.
And then, he yelled at me.
I huffed and blew hair out of my eyes.
My gaze landed on his face. On his hollow severe cheeks, clenched jaw, and thick black eyelashes.
It isn't fair.
He was like a Venus flytrap.
Dressed up with pretty petals but with poison waiting deep within.
I laughed as I pictured myself as a hapless fly, landing on his petals for an innocent sip of nectar, only to be devoured.
Good grief, I thought this stuff wasn't supposed to make me hallucinate?
Henri shot me a sharp look as he padded closer toward the bed. His eyes searched mine as if making sure I was okay. But he didn't say a word. Not a single one.
His unspoken question echoed in my ears; I answered him anyway.
"I'm feeling great!" I nodded sharply, confidently. A slight twinge all over but nothing like before. I never wanted to feel that way again. The excruciation of so many bruises. The needling pain in my side.
No, thank you.
Another wave of softness descended as Henri sat carefully on the bed.
The mattress rocked a little under his weight, making it feel as if I lay upon a giant fluffy marshmallow.
My heart squeezed as I studied his drawn face. No light in his eyes. No aliveness or awareness or need.
He's not sinking…he's drowned.
Raising my arm, it hovered on its own accord. So light. Featherweight and flimsy. I tried to reach for him. To give him

touch. To give him something to cling to.

But he reared back as if I'd tried to strike him.

I recoiled, wincing in preparation for another scolding.

When nothing came—when he merely opened a tub of cream and shifted closer—I let my stupid heart guide me. Just like I always did. Just like I probably shouldn't.

With a quick breath, I pressed my hand on his thigh.

My fingers burned with his strength.

The towel around his hips slightly damp and cool.

So many things surged through me.

Needs, fears, desires, trepidations.

I laughed because I didn't want such feelings.

I giggled because my feelings were absurd, and everything about this was crazy.

He cut you.

Stole you.

He's hurting...

I squeezed his quad. "It's okay..."

He stiffened and sucked in a tattered breath.

The tension in his leg turned to granite.

I snickered as I squeezed him again. "You're made of stone." I poked at his rock-hard stomach. Cold. Unyielding. "Actually, I think you're an iceberg."

His eyes remained locked on mine, cataloguing my every move. Yet he still didn't speak.

An image of the *Titanic* floated into my head. I was the *Titanic*. I crashed bow first into the iceberg that was Henri. I sank into crystal-blue water where penguins swam and polar bears dived and cute fur seals—

Stop it.

Swallowing hard, I blinked past glittering icicles and refocused.

The fantastical images in my head left, but the soft candyfloss feeling remained.

I like this feeling.

Henri needs some.

It'll help...

"Here." I threaded my fingers through his on the tub of cream. "I don't like that you're unhappy."

He shot to his feet. "*Merde*, you really don't handle your drugs well."

Finally...he speaks.

I smiled and nodded.

That was the key.

The only way he could come back from the shadows in his eyes.

"Come back." I opened my arms. "Talk to me. You're usually so chatty."

His eyebrows swooped up; a flush covered his neck.

Swallowing hard, he scooped some goo from the tub and gingerly sat beside me. "Remove your towel."

I shivered.

Couldn't help it.

A lash of heat.

A lightning fork of need.

It bolted down the energy line from the top of my head to the base of my spine. It simmered unwanted in my core.

Oh no, no, no…

I could cope with spacey. I could handle a few daydreams. But uninhibited desire? Elevated sex drive?

No way.

Squirming a little, I shook my head. "You know what? I think I'll stay wrapped up. I'm fine like a burrito. See? Burrito is my new identity."

He looked borderline unhinged as his gaze dropped to my chest and his teeth ground together. "You're not fine. You look like a morbid Christmas tree. Open your damn towel. That isn't a request."

God, *why?*

Why did his curt command rush through me like the worst kind of aphrodisiac?

It shouldn't.

It really shouldn't.

But it did.

And it *always* had, and if the spacey feeling just faded for a moment, I'd have enough strength to crawl onto his lap, remove both our towels, and kiss him.

I moaned and licked my lips.

A kiss.

Yes…I'd like that.

He owed me one after scolding me so meanly.

"Why did you yell at me?" I asked, tears suddenly brimming. "You've never been that cross with me before."

His nostrils flared.

I waited for him to answer.

He didn't.

I hated his silence.

I hated his pain.

I hated that he'd drifted to a dark, dark place I couldn't reach.

With a sharp inhale, he reached for the folded ends of my towel and spread them open.

"Hey." I batted his hands away.

Too late.

Cool air licked my highly sensitive skin.

Another flush of peculiar numbness and want.

I relaxed into it.

My body floated down and down, spiralling deeper and deeper until I hit a shadowy, silky bottom.

Sleep cloyed at my eyelashes, sudden and immense, making me smile with relief.

Sleep was better. So, *so* much better than lust.

"That's it, just…relax," Henri whispered.

I sighed as something comforting soaked into my skin. The barest-there strokes. The gentlest touch. The way he touched me reminded me how Krish would hold his drink at dinner if Mum forgot and gave him a glass cup instead of his preferred plastic one.

He'd hold it as if he'd break it just by breathing.

He'd cradle it as if it were the most precious, wonderous thing. Nothing else existed for him. Just him and that cup—half terrified of breaking it, half mystified by its fragility.

That's how Henri's touching me.

Like I'm a cup.

I giggled for no apparent reason.

"Jesus, that stuff is strong," he muttered under his breath. His fingers traced over my ribs, adding a thick layer of cream.

My entire body turned ticklish.

My giggle became a laugh. "Stop. God, stop!"

"*Fuck*." Ripping his hands off me, he shook the bed with his horror. "I didn't mean…" He sighed heavily. "I'm sorry. God, I'm—"

"For what?" I frowned.

"For hurting you."

"Hurting me?" I shrugged. "No, you tickled me."

That seemed to make him worse.

His face flushed.

His pulse pounded in his neck.

He spiralled; I reached for him. "Hey…it's okay. Talk to me…"

Swallowing a groan, he leapt to his bare feet.

He paced and refused to look at me.

I'd felt many things for this man. Most of them were not very nice, and some far, far too intense, but in that moment, all I felt was panic.

The stranger from the cave kept smothering the man who'd asked me to play along with him. The man from the bar who'd made my very soul shiver drowned beneath a blackened murderer. "Henri…"

"*Don't*," he hissed.

"What's happened—?"

"Be quiet." He raked a hand through his hair, unable to hide his shaking. With effort that etched his eyes with stress lines, he sat back down and painted another bruise on my hip.

He kept his eyes trained on my injuries. Lips pursed. Chest heaving. His insides screaming so loudly he deafened me.

You need to get him to talk…

Doing my best to ignore the creeping fear that he was slipping away, I scrambled for something to say. Something he'd find interest in. Something that would cease his descent into whatever nightmares he fought.

I came up blank.

My mind danced with sparks.

Yes, sparks!

Blurting, I said, "My wand."

His forehead furrowed. His grey eyes flickered to mine. But he didn't speak.

My mind filled with memories of that day. A happier time. A safer time. Those happy feelings bubbled over, and I found myself doing exactly what he'd said I would: I willingly shared a piece of who I was in order to bring him back to me. "I was nineteen when I got my tattoo. I got it the week after I passed my gemmology degree."

I waited for him to ask for more details.

He didn't.

Instead, he hyper-focused on another bruise, and another, and another. Making a personal vendetta against them as if by removing them he could erase everything that'd happened.

"I got a wand because Krish drew me a picture when I went to sit my exams. He said to imagine my pen was a wand, and it would write all the correct answers." I smiled so big my cheeks hurt. "It worked. It brought me luck. And I decided I wanted to keep that luck with me forever."

No response.

Yet I had the sense he was listening…clinging to every morsel I gave him.

"You might say that my luck didn't work. That it ran out, and that's how I ended up here."

Nothing.

His lack of conversation and the wrongness of his silence forced me to continue filling it.

"But luck works in mysterious ways…" I closed my eyes for a moment, tapping into that endless knowing within me, letting it guide what I said. "I think…I think my luck drew me here. Drew me to you. To the jewels. I think—"

"*Enough*," he snarled. "Stop it."

I didn't flinch this time at his scolding.

I saw it for what it was.

Agony.

I overflowed with druggy forgiveness.

He'd killed for me. Twice.

Because of him, I hadn't been raped or mutilated.

He's good.

Peter was right.

He saw that light.

It's still there.

I pointed at the dinged-up watch on his wrist, needing to make him snap.

His eyes followed my finger, his shoulders stiffening.

"Why do you get all sad when you look at your watch?"

He gritted his teeth and moved farther down the bed, smearing cream on my thighs.

No reply.

I longed for his secretive whispers.

I craved for him to speak.

"Tell me," I urged.

Nothing.

"I gave you a piece of my past—"

Still nothing.

"Do you miss her?"

His eyebrows flew into his hair. "*What?*"

Finally.

I kept digging, deliberately stabbing him with memories. "Your mother. Do you miss her?"

He choked and shook his head. "How...how could you possibly know she gave this to me?"

The drugs in my system made me float. "My magical powers of deduction?" I winked. The room spun. My heart thudded sleepily, making my tongue far too loose. "Someone you loved gave you that watch. I can tell because that love lives in your eyes when you look at it. It can't be your dad, and you said you haven't had much success in relationships, so...it must've been your mum."

He bared his teeth. "Shut up, Ilyana, before I lose my temper."

Do it.

Lose it.

You need to break.

He couldn't keep bottling everything in.

Gagging on his darkness.

The softness in my head arrowed straight at his discomfort. I didn't try to second-guess. I trusted the nudges inside me. "You've missed her your entire life, haven't you? There's no difference between missing someone alive or missing them when they're dead."

"Fucking hell." He glowered as if he wanted to smother me with a pillow. "Shut up—"

"Or what? You'll hurt me?" I giggled. Even to my ears, I sounded a little—a lot—crazy. "You'll have to wait, I'm afraid. Not sure I could handle anything else."

"I'm not going to hurt you," he snapped through clenched teeth.

I laughed again, finding everything freaking hilarious and horrible. "But you *will* hurt me again." The drugs chose that moment to swarm me. "You'll hurt me because that's your *loooove* language." I shrugged with an unbecoming snort. "Your love language is pain." I burst into peals of giggles. "Wonder if there's a love bible for a sadist? Lesson number one on how to show affection for your slave: whip them until they're moaning for you, then kiss them stupid."

I moaned with need, then laughed and laughed and laughed.

If I didn't laugh, I'd try to seduce him.

And I wasn't that far gone...yet.

Unfortunately, Henri did not find me the least bit funny.

I couldn't take my eyes off him.

So tortured.

So beautiful.

So wrong.

"Come closer and kiss me," I murmured.

Ily, stop it!

I didn't care.

I wanted his lips on mine.

I needed his body filling, stretching—

"Please, kiss me."

He shot to his feet and latched his hands behind his neck. "I can't be around you when you're like this."

Poor man.

Poor tortured monster.

"I'll kiss you and make it all better. How about that?" I drifted around on my cloud made of GHB. "You're so hopeless, Henri."

He staggered.

I struggled to focus on his stony face.

I frowned. "No, wait. Am I the hopeless one?" I tried to make sense of the syrupy swirls in my head. "After all, you're the one who stole all my hope." I sighed with a relieved, happy chuff. "Buh-bye hope."

I waited for him to speak.

I'd grown so used to him chattering away with his confessions.

I didn't know how much I'd miss it when faced with aching quietness.

I drifted again.

Mollie popped into my head. Behind her, Victor's stronghold went boom, thanks to one of her bombs. Then Rachel was there, grinning and dancing, her pregnant belly almost ready to pop.

I stiffened.

"She can't have her baby here."

"What?" Henri dropped his arms, raw panic carving his face as if I'd lost my mind.

"Children weren't allowed in here." I couldn't look at him, remembering Victor asking him to exterminate Rachel. "But now, thanks to you making Victor keep it, he'll probably decide to breed all of us."

Tears bloomed.

Fresh laughter bubbled.

I didn't know which would win—sobs of horror or peals of inappropriate delirium.

In the end, they cancelled each other out, and I tried to roll onto my side to curl into a ball.

I started to crash—

Henri clamped a hand on my shoulder. "Stay on your back."

My nervous system tried to warn me a bruise existed there, but the magic of drugs said…*who cares?*

My eyes tore open, locking on his. "You…you won't expect me to have a baby too, will you?"

"Fuck, Ilyana." His face shot ghost white. "No, of course not." He stumbled away from me, pacing the bedroom and raking cream-smeared fingers through his hair.

I tracked him for a little while, but he made me dizzy. "Oh, good. Because if you ever got me pregnant, I'd jump off the parapet."

His feet slammed to a stop.

Marching back to the bed, he loomed over me. He panted as if he'd run a four-day race. He looked utterly in pieces. "Y-You'd kill yourself rather than carry my child? You hate me that much?"

"I'd kill myself so our child never knew horror."

He winced.

Another wave of numbness.

I sank into it.

The sensation of lightness promised me the ability to float right out the window and soar all the way over the sea back to Krish.

A pinch in my heart.

The only pain I could still feel.

Krish…

God, I missed my older brother.

I missed the way he used to say my name. The way he'd say it in that special wonderful way, reminding me how loved I was.

Love.

The exact opposite of hate.

Love…that was the biggest monster here.

The hulking elephant in the room.

I could never hate you, Henri…and that's the problem.

"Ily—" His hand grabbed my chin, his fingers gripping hard.

"Open your eyes."

Ily...

Whenever he used my name, it made me feel all itchy inside. Squirrelly and snarly because he didn't know what it meant. He mocked everything he wanted with his tone.

I had an awful feeling that each time he said my name, it only magnified the curse between us.

Oh, that's sad.

Cursed to always say the words but never earn them in return.

My eyelashes fluttered open.

He needs to know.

It might help.

Or it might destroy him.

I couldn't tell how he'd react if he knew what he said each and every time he called me Ily.

Would he find it funny or get mad?

Would he scream at me?

Hurt me?

With eyes far too heavy, I caught his stare.

He still didn't look like him.

He'd transformed into a colder, crueller, dead-eyed version of the man I'd fallen hopelessly in lust with. The puddle of golden light from the bedside lamp avoided him, allowing all the shadows in the room to cling to his body.

Darkness beneath his eyes. Blackness along his jaw. Shadows swirled over his skin like moving tattoos.

Licking my lips, I tried to pull my chin out of his tight hold.

When he didn't let me go, I slurred, "Do you prefer calling me Ily or Little Nightmare?"

He didn't answer the question, but he did let me go.

Sitting heavily on the bed, he rubbed his hand on the sheets as if his fingers stung from holding me.

I felt his anguish.

I patted his knuckles with commiseration.

"You know...Ily isn't really a name." I sighed with all the love I had for my brother. "Krish misread the note my birth mother left pinned on my baby blanket." Hot tears prickled before fading beneath love again. "It was just a short note. A scribble really."

Henri didn't speak but he did go achingly still.

His palm suddenly tipped up and captured my fingers, fisting me in a painful handhold.

I didn't know if he squeezed me to make me stop or squeezed me because he needed to know. Either way, this story would probably shatter him.

I'm sorry...

I recited the words scribed on my heart. *"You're perfect. But I'm not. And you deserve perfection. I.L.Y."*

Henri choked.

For a second, it looked as if he believed that sentence was about him—not the final parting phrase of my birth mother—but then his forehead creased, and he licked his lips. He whispered ever so quietly, "I.L.Y?"

"Krish read the note and in his six-year-old brain, he smushed the acronym together."

Shadows gathered tighter around him. "Acronym?"

"It gives away my mother's age. Shows she was probably a teenager stuck in a very bad place."

He swallowed hard. His voice scratchy and raw. "What does it stand for?"

The fact that he didn't know.

That he'd probably never been given those three little words even as a child.

Tragic really.

Terrible definitely.

But in the end, I'd been right.

Love was his greatest weakness.

Not me.

He thought it was me because each time he used my name, he mentioned the very thing that petrified him.

A surge of sleepiness.

A cloak of foggy night.

I snuggled deeper into the bed as I yawned. "I.L.Y....it means I Love You."

Henri leapt to his feet. "*Quoi?*" (What?)

"I love you..." I struggled to stay awake, a heavy anchor on my mind.

"You mean every time I use your name, I'm saying *I fucking love you?*"

"Yep." I nodded, the room swimming.

Yep.

What a strange word.

What are words anyway?

How did someone come up with letters and then squish them into a language?

Do we even need language?

I knew what Henri was feeling most of the time without it. I sensed him. Some people said they even saw auras. Perhaps our ability to speak got in the way of our truth because the truth was there for all to see if we just opened our eyes instead of our ears.

I skipped out of time.

I fought the undertow of rest and forced my gaze open.

Aww, poor guy.

He looked rather freaked.

I giggled at the way he strangled the tub of cream, eyes wild, legs braced. "It's okay, Hen."

Now he looked *really* freaked.

It was kind of adorable.

"Hen?" he coughed.

"You know…like the chicken."

I pictured him with feathers, scratching around in the dirt.

Oh God.

New laughter built. Pressure bubbled in my belly, desperate to release.

"My *name* is Henri," he said slowly, scarily.

"Hen." I nodded.

"No. Not Hen—"

"Cluck. Cluck." I couldn't contain the mirth much longer. "Aww, don't be mad. You'd make such a cute chicken. Wait…" I split into laughter. "A male chicken is a cock." I lost control over my giggles. "You're a cock."

He made a whimpering sort of noise as if I'd well and truly ruined him.

"Cock-a-doodle-doooooo!" I lost it.

He groaned so deep and low, my entire body reacted.

Need roared.

Desire poured.

My laughter threaded with reckless, ruthless lust, and I shattered.

I either needed him to kiss me or go far, far away so I could break.

I didn't know why I laughed anymore.

Everything was ridiculous.

Everything was hilarious.

If I didn't laugh, I'd cry, and I really didn't want to cry.
But oops, there went the tears.
People had died today.
Blood had been shed.
Pain had been given.
Peter might not wake up.
Rachel is pregnant.
And I'm in love with a broken beast.
I laughed.
And laughed.
I laughed until I cried.
I sobbed until I couldn't breathe.
And then…I passed out.

Chapter Twelve

Henri

SHE'D KILLED ME.

Stopped my heart and torn it bleeding from my chest.

Slaughtered me with mere words, then passed out and left me alone.

Alone to pick up my pieces.

Alone to realise those pieces were nothing more than ash and blood.

I stood transfixed as she sank into a deep sleep.

My mouth watered as salty droplets glistened on her cheeks. My torn-out heart pounded with so much goddamn pain.

Her name?

A curse.

The nickname she'd given me?

The antidote.

How could both cripple me so?

Why the fuck did a stupid nickname do such agonising things to me?

Hen?

It made me weak-kneed. Rock-hard. Trembling with the savage need to fall on her and kiss her stupid.

All over a ridiculous pet name.

I'd never had one of those.

No one had ever gotten close enough to shorten my already short name.

Her nickname would've shaken my world…if she hadn't told me the origin of hers.

That knowledge tore into my chest with a thousand knives.

I honestly couldn't function.

I had no idea how to survive knowing I said 'I love you' each time I called her Ily.

How did she keep doing this to me?

Rearranging the ground I stood on.

Tipping me over edge after edge until I lost sight of the sky and gave up fighting the fall.

I stood over her, waiting for her to snap out of her coma and start laughing at my expense again.

But she didn't.

It seemed whatever adrenaline she'd burned through had gone.

I couldn't help myself.

I *hated* that I couldn't help myself.

Sitting back on the bed beside her, I tucked loose sapphire-black hair behind her ear and fought every urge.

Lines bracketed her mouth even in sleep.

Stress etched her forehead as if she couldn't forget where she was and who was responsible even in her dreams.

She hates me enough to kill herself if I ever got her pregnant...

Fuck, that shouldn't hurt so much.

I hadn't even thought of children, yet...just knowing she'd rather die—

My eyes stung.

The urge to retch returned.

Rubbing my thumb through the tracks of salt glimmering on her cheek, I willed myself not to do it.

I *begged* myself not to do it.

And I cursed myself to a thousand realms of hell as I sucked that droplet off my thumb and shivered at the taste.

I lost all control as I bent over and kissed her exquisitely softly on the cheek. I didn't care if the cameras watched me. I didn't care that Victor might have questions. The moment my lips pressed to her tear-damp cheek and her sweet flavour soaked onto my tongue, I shuddered with an agony I'd never felt before.

I couldn't pinpoint the origin of that despair.

Was it in my heart? My bones? My soul?

Wherever it was, it pushed me further to burn out.

The blackness inside me celebrated, sucking me deeper, deeper.

I reared back and shook my head.

Not yet.

I could succumb to my nightmares soon.

I could sleep...soon.

But first, I needed to erase her bruises.

I couldn't look at them anymore.

Couldn't have the reminder that I'd caused this.

Just like I'd caused them on my mother.

I only ever caused pain to those I loved and—

Loved?

I froze.

I don't love her—

A surge of possession.

A cascade of emotion that siphoned hotly through my veins.

Love…

No.

I couldn't.

I can't—

Licking my lips from her salty, sad taste, I gritted my teeth and shoved away every thought.

The bandage around my arm grew wet with fresh blood as I forced shaking hands to finish the job of coating her in the entire tub of arnica.

Her breasts and belly had little circles bleeding outward. Spreading flowers of black, blue, and purple.

She was stunning.

Ruined.

Ily—

I choked on those three little letters, gagging on the three words they represented.

Another trembling panic attack turned my insides into a maelstrom.

Yanking the towel out from under her so she wouldn't sleep on something damp, I tossed it into the corner before working the bedding down and tucking her in.

I shook as I gathered her wet hair and draped it over the pillow.

I trembled as I stood over her, trying to find other ways to fix what I'd broken.

With a heavy sigh, I moved away and swallowed a groan.

Everything hurt.

Everything throbbed.

Yet nothing could touch the pain she'd caused.

Biting my lip, I glanced at my left side.

The colours had only gotten deeper. The sharp pain she'd mentioned whenever she breathed affected me too. I'd managed to ignore it while killing Kyle. I didn't have time to focus on it while carrying Peter, but now…all alone, my legs chose that exact moment to buckle.

The dizziness.

The faintness.

I crashed to the floor, bracing myself on my hands and knees as my heart flurried and the sick sensation of not being able to get enough oxygen made the room turn black.

Darkness pounced, not done with me.

I pressed my forehead to the floor as every sin throttled me with violence.

Sickness gushed, but I swallowed it down.

Sweat ran over my skin, soaking into my blood-soaked bandage.

I couldn't stop the crash.

Couldn't catch a breath or stop hearing Ily calling me Hen or me telling her I loved her every time I said her damn name.

I love you.

I love you.

Fuck—

Curling my fingers into the dark copper carpet, I willed the episode to pass.

It only grew worse.

Greyness snuck over my vision.

Weakness stole through every bone, and my body tipped with warning.

I had seconds.

Mere seconds and I didn't want to pass out on the floor.

Staggering to my feet, I turned off the bedside light, then stumbled, shuffled, and fell through the dark to my side of the bed.

I tumbled beside Ily.

I grunted in pain.

Darkness grabbed me and sucked me deep.

"It's okay, Hen. Truly." Ily cupped my cheek and pressed her nose to mine. "You can say it. Here…I'll teach you." She smiled and gave me the sweetest, softest kiss. "Don't think about what the words mean, and just say it…I love—"

"I can't." I groaned against her lips.

"You won't, you mean."

"No…I literally can't." Rearing back, I caught her sunshine-shining eyes. *"I can't say I love you when I'm not worthy of love."*

Her face softened. *"Don't you think I should be the judge of that?"* Kissing my eyes, my cheeks, my forehead, she whispered, *"I see what you are now. You did come for us. You're going to free us. I know it—"*

I choked and shot upright.

The dream shattered, leaving me blinking in a pitch-dark room.

My entire body screeched with discomfort.

I hated that Peter's words kept haunting me but in Ily's voice.

"I see what you are now. You did come for us. You're going to free us. I know it—"

The rush of sickness coated my tongue; I launched out of bed. Wrapping my good arm around my bad ribs, I tried to hold my pain together as I half-ran, half-staggered to the bathroom, and flipped up the lid on the toilet.

My skin flushed with sweat.

I shivered with an icy chill.

I waited to vomit for the second time tonight.

Waited for that familiar curse to remind me all over again that the things I wanted were wrong and toxic and had to be purged.

How strange that my dreams had been full of love and togetherness instead of darkness and screams. How tragic that I'd finally begged for someone to *see* me, and I couldn't stomach it when they did.

Breathing hard, the gush of nausea slowly faded.

I backed away from the toilet and crashed against the towel rail.

Ow.

Goddamn ow!

I couldn't do this anymore.

I didn't want to exist in so much agony, and I didn't trust my sleep not to torment me.

I'm done.

Grabbing a white bathrobe off the hook, I lurched toward the exit. Shrugging into it, I ripped open our borrowed bedroom door and looked left and right.

Track lighting glowed above the flagstones. Faint and barely there, it granted just enough illumination to slip into the shadows and close the door behind me.

I wouldn't be able to lock it, but I took the risk that Victor lived up here, and other guests wouldn't be stupid enough to trespass.

I needed a book.

A thousand books.

If I could lose myself in their pages, then I could—

"How's she doing?"

Jesus fucking Christ.

Holding my rabbiting heart, I spun around and groaned as a fresh wave of misery made me sweat. I blinked at the ghostly figure in the dark then swallowed a curse as I snapped, "Your attempt at giving me a heart attack failed."

"What a pity." Dr Belford came toward me. She flicked on a switch. The drafty corridor suddenly glowed with soft sconces. "I was just on my way to check on Ily."

Ily.

I love you.

Shut up.

"She's asleep." I sniffed. "Whatever you gave her knocked her out."

Not before she knocked out my heart.

The doctor sagged with relief. "In that case, I'll let her rest a little before I disturb her."

I nodded and did my best to be civil. "Goodnight."

Before I could turn away, her weary eyes locked on my left arm. Her brows rose as she noticed the pinprick of blood that'd already soaked through the terrycloth dressing gown. "You're still bleeding."

"I'm fine." Pushing off from the wall, I went to head downstairs.

The library would be empty.

I could peruse the shelves, select a thick, brutal story, then bring it back to bed.

I'd sink into someone else's misfortune for a change.

Only, the corridor flipped upside down, then back to front, and I found myself on my knees again.

Motherfucker.

Soft hands landed between my shoulder blades. "Come with me. I'll stitch you up and give you something for the light-headedness."

"I said I'm *fine*," I snapped.

Perhaps if I kept saying it, it would come true.

Maybe if I believed it, I could remember how to survive without a bruised girl, a broken heart, and a soul riddled with fucking rot.

I didn't like people caring about me.

I didn't know how to act, how to accept it, how to *deserve* it.

Her temper appeared. "If it were up to me, I'd leave you to bleed out on this icy floor, but...you aren't the boss, and the man who *is* the boss would gut me if I refused one of his guests the best medical care I can provide so...." She dropped to her haunches and stared me right in the face. "Get the hell up and come into my room. Hold your tongue while I sew you up, and then you can go back to bed."

Swooping to her feet, she marched away without waiting for me. Shoving her door wide, she tapped her no-nonsense white sneaker that didn't look so white anymore. "I'm tired and need to go to bed before a crazy day in a few hours. *Now*, Master H."

Cursing under my breath, I obeyed her for reasons unknown.

It took all my strength to climb to my feet; I wobbled as I entered her rooms.

I immediately looked at where I'd placed Peter.

The white sheet-covered table was ominously empty.

I swallowed hard. "Did he...did he die?"

"Who?" Her eyebrows knitted together. "Who died?"

I hated that I'd asked. That I'd shown I cared. "Peter. He's gone."

"Ah, yes." She nodded. "He's resting in Rose's room down the hall. I don't have any other beds available downstairs, and he's not out of the woods yet. Rose agreed to keep a careful eye on him while I was supposed to catch up on some sleep." She sighed heavily and marched to her cupboard of tricks. "Seeing as Ily is in the best possible place right now, I suppose that means I only have one more patient to treat, and then I can call quits on this awful, awful day. Now, sit down and let me sew you up so I can go to bloody bed."

Her attitude made my hackles rise, but...I had no energy to refuse her.

I didn't take the table, though.

The memory of Peter's hand bubbling in that bowl of antiseptic made my already delicate stomach extra queasy.

Cutting past the couch and coffee table, I headed toward the small dining table pressed against a window. Pulling out a wooden chair, I sat heavily and looked at the view. This angle focused more on the ocean cliffs and the stars twinkling so far above.

Somewhere down there, Kyle and some other Master were sucked out to sea. Perhaps they'd been found by a shark. Hopefully, Charles had also been gobbled by the tide so all my crimes would go unseen.

Noises echoed behind me as the doctor gathered whatever torture devices she needed, then joined me at the table.

Neither of us spoke as she motioned for me to slip the dressing gown off my injured side. She sucked in a breath as she noticed my colourful ribs, but her hands were steady as she unwrapped my self-administered bandage, then opened a similar packet to the one I'd found in our supplies.

Threading surgical thread through a wickedly sharp needle, her face etched with concentration. Wiping my slashed arm with stingy fluid, she grabbed a head torch from her supplies and jammed it on her head. The light blinded me as she leaned in and studied my wound.

I closed my eyes.

I didn't want to watch.

Something sharp stabbed me a few times.

Fucking ow again—

"The local anaesthesia should kick in quickly." Her bedside manner improved a little as she placed the empty syringe I hadn't noticed back on the table.

After a few moments, she tapped my red-raw skin. "Can you feel anything?"

"Only a thick numbness."

"Good." She gave me a tight smile. "Look away if you're squeamish."

Could a man who got turned on by blood be squeamish?

I'd never actually tested myself and stubbornly kept my eyes locked on my arm as she shrugged and threaded the needle through the first section.

The way my skin resisted the puncture only to fail and surrender. The strangest slithering sensation as she pulled thread through flesh and then jabbed me all over again.

Yep.

My teeth clamped together as a fresh wave of nausea rushed.

I'm squeamish.

Closing my eyes, I breathed through my nose and did my best to use the same technique I'd done on the beach. I imagined my pain flowing down my legs and into Victor's castle. I focused on nothing but my breath, in and out, in and out, in and—

"All done."

"What?" My eyes snapped open. "Already?"

Giving me a strange look, she glanced at the clock. "It's been twenty minutes."

"Twenty minutes?"

How was that possible?

I studied the neat gauze stuck over my arm, bumpy with a faint line of black stitches beneath.

Panic filled me to return to Ily.

Ily.

Goddammit, her name corrupted my entire system.

I didn't know if my heart or my cock reacted the most anymore.

One thing I did know…I would go out of my way to never use her name again.

How could I?

Now that I knew what it meant?

Grabbing the open half of my dressing gown, I went to shrug back into it, but the doctor caught my wrist. "Wait." Her cool hands landed on my roasting, throbbing side, probing none too gently.

I hissed and flinched but didn't move away.

Slowly, she leaned back. "I don't think any of them are broken but they're heavily bruised. I'll give you some antibiotics for your arm, just in case, and you can take some arnica tablets with Ily to ease your bruises. I also need you to drink what I'm about to give you to replace everything you lost today. Give one to Ily when she wakes." Pushing to her feet with a tired groan, she padded toward a small fridge next to her medical cupboard and returned with two bottles of glow-in-the dark blue liquid.

"Electrolytes." She gave me a half smile, passing me the bottles. "You've lost a fair amount of blood, but I think your dizziness is mainly from lack of sustenance and whatever else happened out there today. As long as you drink this and take a few days to rest, your body will make up the blood, and you'll feel better. If you're struggling to regulate your body temperature and think you can avoid falling down the stairs, go grab some food from the kitchen. That'll help too." Ripping off her latex gloves, she arched her chin at the door. "Now, go away. I'll pop by in the morning to check on Ily."

She didn't speak again as I slipped my no-longer bleeding arm into my gown, lashed the belt tight, then slipped back into the night.

Chapter Thirteen

I WOKE WITH A START.
I felt as if I'd lost something but couldn't remember what.
Echoes of Krish.
Of Peter.
Henri.
God, Henri…
I groaned as sleepiness switched into pure fire. Fire in my blood, my heart, my core.
Every part of me hummed.
Fragments of my dream taunted me and the wetness between my thighs hinted it hadn't been a platonic kind of fantasy. I felt empty after being full. Cold after being hugged. Lost and confused and lonely and—
Just a dream.
Kicking my legs beneath the suffocating blankets, I rolled onto my other side.
I hated that even the cotton acted like an aphrodisiac. I'd grown well acquainted with achy desperation since meeting Henri, but this was far, *far* worse.
This felt insidious…growing hotter and hotter—
Ignore it.
Burrowing onto my side, I winced at the slightest flares of discomfort. The softest twinges of pain as I did my best to ignore the heat in my lower belly and tingles in my breasts.
I made the mistake of opening my eyes.
I froze.
Him.
The smallest halo of white light bled over the sweet-smelling cream pages of a book. The nightlight, jammed into the thick story, gave just enough glow to read by—a tiny puddle in the dark.
In the shadows cast by the booklight, my gaze drifted over

strong masculine hands holding the binding spread. Veins popped over bruised knuckles, tendons threaded under tanned skin. Both marvels of the human form worked their way up powerful forearms.

I stopped breathing as my eyes locked on his bare chest.

Chiselled with darkness and sculpted by the monster housed within, his pecs twitched as I studied him. The flinch dragged my eyes to his stubble-decorated jaw, over the hollows of his stern cheeks, and up, up, up to his burning, blazing grey eyes.

Even in the pitch darkness, even in this fortress of blackness, he was beautiful.

So wonderfully, *horribly* beautiful.

The fire in my blood broke into an inferno.

Not thinking. Not feeling. Merely existing in this present, fragile moment, I pushed upright and let the blankets fall away.

I'm burning...

His sharp inhale as his gaze fell to my bruise-colourful breasts made my entire body shiver. He froze where he sat upright, supported by folded pillows, his chin tipped down and face cold.

The room switched from calm rest to savage awareness as we stared at each other.

Goosebumps coated me as he sucked in his bottom lip and bit down.

I couldn't stop looking at him.

How gorgeous he was holding a book. *Reading.* How stunning he was strangling a book that wasn't just a prop but a lifeline.

He'd been reading a while, judging by how many pages existed beneath his thumb.

He held the tale as if it would save him from himself and cursed me for dragging him out of it. This was his meditation. Words were his salvation, and I felt absolutely humbled to know it.

To know *him.*

I swayed closer.

He stiffened.

A plate covered in crumbs on the bedside table hinted he'd eaten something while I'd been asleep. A sandwich waited on another plate...*for me?*

How long had I been asleep?

Did it matter?

All that mattered was this.

This man.

This tortured, terrible man who liked to read.

An avenger who'd defended me. A monster who'd mauled me. A ghost, a nightmare, a lonely boy…

I shivered again, flames licking all over my body.

I'd always been drawn to intelligence. Always loved to debate books on history, gemmology, and faith. My parents had given me an entire library on my sixteenth birthday. Titles full of the truths about living and dying and finding a balanced middle way.

The trick to existing was accepting that every facet of life and death was impermanent.

I'd forgotten that in my fight to survive here.

The only law in this world was the law of change. *Nothing* was permanent. Everything began, endured, and ended.

Eventually, this stolen silent moment of sharing a bed with this terribly gorgeous bookworm would end, and…I mourned it.

I grieved every other moment I'd lived and cursed, valued and unappreciated.

The memory of the caves still haunted me.

The nightmare of dragging Peter still ached in my limbs.

It'd been one of the worst days of my life.

Yet…it was over.

It no longer existed.

But *he* existed.

I existed.

And we would never have this moment again.

I trembled as I reached out and plucked the book from his frozen fingers.

I didn't bother looking at the title.

I merely closed it reverently, turned off the booklight, and placed both on my abandoned pillow.

"W-What are you doing?" He croaked in the darkness.

I could barely make out his face. The glow of his uncertain eyes.

The flashing red dots of cameras watched us.

Could they record in pitch blackness?

I hoped not.

Because what I was about to do probably hadn't been done by any other jewel in the two decades this place had existed.

"Seeing you reading?" My voice came out sultry, husky. Coals simmered in my heart. Embers kindled in my blood. Flames grew hotter, greedier.

Pulling the blanket off his thighs, the faint gleam of his skin appeared. His stomach flexed as I uncovered him. The dark patch of trimmed hair between his legs. And the rapidly swelling erection crawling up his belly. "It's one of the hottest things I've ever seen."

He coughed and reached for the blankets.

I ripped them to his knees, leaving him as bare as me.

A growl rumbled in his chest. "Nightmare, stop it."

I shuddered at his nickname for me.

I smirked as I remembered mine for him.

"I need you, Hen."

"Don't." He shook his head. "Don't call me that."

With a pounding heart and racing desire, I crawled over him and sat on his lap.

He jerked and looked at the ceiling. "For the love of God, get off me."

"Nope." Nuzzling his throat, I sucked in his scent.

He smelled off.

Antiseptic with the faintest whiff of stone.

The white slash of a bandage on his arm hinted he'd returned to the doctor. Had he also patrolled the stronghold on his own? I sniffed again, dragging in the softer smells of soap and the wilder notes of sea and stars.

"Nightmare—"

"It's Ily." I giggled, the soft, giddy feeling of before tangled with the debilitating arousal pumping through my blood. "You know that. You know what it means. I love you—"

"*Don't*," he hissed.

"Don't what? Say I love you?"

He groaned.

I grew drunk on his torment.

I revelled in my power.

"You've told me 'I love you', oh, I don't know…two hundred times since you met me. Each of those three little letters. I.L—"

"*Enough*." He tried to toss me off, but his touch was too careful, too kind.

My body warned that just because I couldn't feel my bruises, they were still there…hurting.

I don't care.

I gripped him with my thighs and pressed us tighter together.

Cock to core.

Heart to heart.

His answering growl made my hunger become starvation.

I *needed* him.

I needed to rock and thrust and come and detonate.

Whatever this drug was, I liked it.

I'd been afraid before.

Fearful of yearning and wanting and *need*.

But now...I gave myself over to it.

I quivered and craved and rocked my hips, pressing myself deeper onto Henri's hardness.

"Fuck." His hands clamped on the top of my thighs, stilling me. "Stop it."

"No."

"You're hurt."

"I don't feel it."

"I'm not doing this. Not while you're injured—"

"You're injured too." I nipped at his sharp cheekbone.

He drew his head back.

He fell into silent darkness—tumbling into a place I couldn't follow.

No...

Come back.

"Kiss me." Pressing my hands against his slightly clammy cheeks, I pulled him close.

I wanted a repeat of that kiss back in our room.

I wanted to see him shatter as badly as he had the moment our tongues touched.

"No—"

"Yes." I pressed my lips to his.

He froze.

His hands spasmed on my thighs as if I'd deleted all his keen intelligence and replaced it with staticky-white noise.

"Kiss me, Hen," I breathed against his mouth, licking his plump, slightly too-hot lower lip.

I wanted him to snap.

I *needed* him to take control.

But a guttural groan rose from the depths of him, and with an almost pitiful whimper, he pushed me away.

He didn't speak, but I felt him.

Felt his need.

Felt so drawn to him, bound to him, stitched to him.

After living in fear for so long, this stolen moment felt

infinitely precious and wonderful.

Falling on him again, I kissed my way along his jaw. I gave him truth and vulnerability because in that moment, both were needed. Both were lifelines to keep him present. "I need you inside me. I *need* you."

"Jesus Christ." He let loose a string of filthy French. "The doctor will castrate me if she finds out I touched you while you're like this."

"I told you, I'm not in any pain."

He groaned, but it came out more like a sob. "Fuck, I am."

"Where? This pain?" I smeared my wetness over his cock, making both of us shudder and shiver.

He lost his ability to speak.

My blood turned to light as every molecule hummed for more.

The tease of a release poured yet more fuel on my fire.

I stopped fighting it.

Stopped fighting feelings and needs and knowings.

My hand dropped below and found him in the darkness.

"Ah fuck." He grunted as I fisted him hard. "Stop—"

"No." I grasped his length and squeezed.

He exhaled in a rush. "Don't—*ughhh*."

That noise.

That groan and growl and grunt.

It made my very spirit quiver as I stroked him, up and down, sharing my fire, making him burn with me.

Another groan fell from him, slashing at his self-control.

The timbre of his growl; the echoing, earthquaking tone. It vibrated through me, rearranging my pieces and sending me higher than the sun.

I squeezed the base of him, teasing us both as I rode his length, coating him in my desire.

His head tipped back. His lips pulled away as he snarled at the ceiling.

"I'm on fire, Hen." I stroked his erection with tight little twists.

He snarled. Loudly. "Stop saying that—*merde*."

I pressed my thumb into his crown.

He jerked and hissed, his voice nothing but black. "And you're on fire because you probably have a fever." He grabbed my shoulders, his thumbs finding sore bruises. "Get *off* me. I'm not doing this tonight. You don't want me. You're high and—"

"No, I *do* want you. I've never wanted anyone more."

His fingers squeezed, hurting me.

I sucked in a breath, hating that pain threaded with pleasure.

That pain only *added* to my pleasure.

That pain and pleasure somehow became a delightful, dirty thrill.

Memories of him calling me that nasty little M word clotted my mind.

Masochist.

After today, I didn't think that was right.

I'd hated every moment. I'd panicked the moment Kyle started cutting me. I'd almost passed out from the agony as he shot me with those horrible paintballs.

I didn't like pain.

In fact, I could safely say I loathed it and had had enough to last me a lifetime.

But…I liked him.

Oh God…

Memories from earlier tonight flooded me.

The way the drug made me swell with fondness and burn with friendship.

I didn't just like him.

I love—

Whoa!

I couldn't. Not possible. I could accept I lusted for him. I could tolerate appreciating him when he defended me, but love?

Nuh-uh. No way.

How could I love the man responsible for this tragedy?

I couldn't.

Ever.

But…you can like him.

I paused, sinking back into need.

Yes, it was tolerable to like him.

I liked his particular brand of pain. Delivered with feelings and fears—*his* feelings and fears. I liked that each time he touched me, he left little souvenirs of his lust, bruises of his desire, and scars of his affection.

A tidal wave of want flowed far too swift and savage.

I trembled on his lap.

My skin burned with the need to be marked, gripped, squeezed, and autographed. Facets of myself unlocked in the dark, unfurling and embracing without scorn or worries.

Who cared about right and wrong, love or hate?

Right now, I wanted him.

I wanted him to deliver bliss as well as brutality.

I wanted him to kiss me, then bite me, caress me, then fuck me.

No, I wasn't a masochist.

I was a Mercerchist…or a Wardchist… whichever surname he now went by.

I laughed under my breath.

I'm a Mercerchist.

It could be a new catch-phrase.

I could put it on a t-shirt.

He could tear that t-shirt off with his teeth—

Oh God.

Rolling my shoulders, I sat heavier on his straining erection. "It's not a fever." My vision became hazy, my eyelashes heavy. "I'm on fire."

"You need antibiotics."

"My blood is burning, Hen."

"Stop that—"

"No, *you* stop it." I moaned and fell onto him, burrowing my face into his strong neck.

With another bed-shaking growl, his hands slipped off my shoulders and landed on my hips. He went to shove me off—

"I had a dream," I blurted.

He broke out in goosebumps as I kissed his hot skin.

"I had a dream you were inside me."

His cock lurched in my hands. Words strangled from his self-imposed silence. "I-I'm not going to fuck you."

"Why?" I nipped his jaw.

He choked. "I've already told you. You're hurt."

"That never stopped you before."

He stiffened into stone.

He shut down.

Every connection between us sucked into a black void, and…I took matters into my own hands…literally.

Rising on my knees, I grabbed his erection and angled him up. Without second-guessing, I positioned myself over his crown and sank down.

"*Putain!*" (Fuck!) Henri snarled as I sheathed him completely.

I cried out as his long, thick length penetrated me in one slick glide.

The thick invasion of him felt so threatening, so comforting, so *familiar*.

Glimpses of my dream reappeared.

Henri thrusting into me in a meadow full of bluebells. Kissing me in a thicket of purple pansies. Fucking me in a field of red, red roses.

Every glade was the colour of a bruise. Every flower stained with pain.

We might've been surrounded by crushed and wounded things, but each pump inside me was pure pleasure, pure happiness, pure bliss.

My thighs stuck to his as I sank down the final inch.

My core pinched a little, not quite ready—despite my erotic dream—to fully welcome such an invasion.

Faint echoes of what my body had endured hinted maybe Henri was right, and I shouldn't do this. The needling in my ribs was back. My bruises growing hot. But then his cock twitched inside me, and…I stopped thinking.

Folding onto his chest, I found his mouth blindly in the dark.

And I kissed him.

Rode him.

He snapped.

I moaned as he surged upward. Seated himself deep, deep, *deep*.

Pain transformed into fire.

I became that fire.

He was fire.

We transformed into twin flames as he pierced my body and claimed me.

Twin flames.

Twin flames…

Those two words pushed over a domino of memories—

"He's a mystic as well as a Vedic astrologer, Khushi. Be prepared for him to scare you as well as enlighten you."

My heart fluttered as my darling brother called me by my nickname.

Khushi…it meant happiness. He'd named me Ily thanks to a mistake when he was six years old. My mother and father had extended that name by googling what Ily could be short for and had chosen a pretty Arabic one for sunshine, which matched my eyes. I loved my name, but I loved it more when he called me Khushi.

"I'll be fine." I wanted to hug him, but that would be too much. He'd come into society despite all its noisy smells, sounds, and people. He'd come to support me. He'd come because today, I'd find out my destiny thanks to the stars.

"Ilyana Sharma?" An old Indian woman with white hair and a hundred beautiful bangles on her wrists beckoned us from her desk. "He's ready for you now."

Krish sucked in a breath, fortifying himself to step into a room with a stranger.

I knew better than to offer comfort or touch him. Instead, I let him sink into his way of coping.

Opening the door to a small office with heavy scents of sage and bright yellow calendula flowers hanging in a drying bunch by the window, my eyes fell onto an elderly Indian man sitting primly at a desk scattered with astrological charts, notebooks, and Post-its.

The moment our gazes met, he shot to his feet and frowned.

Krish stiffened. I went to ask if he was okay, but my fear for my brother's wellbeing was utterly overshadowed as the Vedic astrologer, who was said to converse with celestial energies and far off planets, planted his weathered hands on his desk and said, "You are blessed with soulmates, child. In fact, you have one standing beside you. He found you in this life and recognised you as kin."

My heart warmed.

I'd heard this tale before. My mother often told Krish and me that we all had multiple soulmates. A clan of them. An astral tribe that could manifest as our siblings, parents, and friends throughout our lifetime.

I smiled but then that smile fell away as the astrologer sat back down and studied my star charts that couldn't be completely accurate, seeing as I couldn't provide him with my exact date or time of birth.

Scowling, he said, "You are blessed, but it seems as if you requested to endure adversity. Your karma is worthy of an abundant life, but you will soon have a choice to make."

I glanced at Krish as we each took a seat on the opposite side of the mystic.

"A choice?"

The astrologer grabbed my hand over my planetary charts and uttered a warning that haunted my dreams for weeks afterward.

"One day, you will meet your twin flame. This is different to a soulmate as soulmates are individual spirits drawn together by past lives and love. A twin flame is two souls from one source. One spirit split into two bodies. When you meet them, you will know. You will recognise them just as surely as they

will recognise you. You are the same. You are one. But karmically, you are destined to destroy each other. The moment you meet, your choice is already made. This match will not last. The intensity will destroy both of you. If you accept this union, you will both burn—"

My eyes flew open as Henri bit my throat and thrust harder, yanking me back from the past.

Burn.

God, yes.

Everything was burning.

Every nerve ending, every heartbeat.

But I burned the hottest where we were joined.

Letting my hair go, Henri tipped forward and sought my mouth again.

The moment our lips touched, I forgot about wizened old mystics and detonated with brighter flames.

He cindered me to ash as his tongue dived into my mouth.

Our lips parted wide, colliding with force and violence.

Just like our other kiss, this one transcended the act of sex and made it something *more*.

It felt as if we merged, melded, fused, and blended.

Tingles spread from my heart and into every cell.

My clit throbbed. My insides clenched around him.

His large hands swooped up my body and cupped my cheeks, cradling me so tenderly, so ruthlessly, all while his mouth plundered mine and his body stabbed deliciously deep.

He thrust hard.

Viciously hard.

He fucked me from below all while I rode him from above.

We turned wild.

Grunting and panting, we struggled to get a proper breath, breathing each other in, sucking each other down, all while the pain in my side hinted medically this wasn't advised.

Screw commonsense.

If I had any brain cells, I would've run from this man back at the bar in Paris.

If I'd listened to the Vedic astrologer, I might never have stumbled into Henri's orbit.

He sucked my bottom lip into his mouth as I threw my arms around his neck and pressed my chest to his.

"You are the same. You are one. You are destined to destroy each other."

Pinpricks of bruised agony blazed down my front.

A whimper of discomfort even as bliss coiled and spindled in my lower belly.

I couldn't see him.

The lack of sight only made our kiss that much richer, that much deeper, that much more terrifying.

Our tongues spoke for us, silently feeding each other our truths.

Our lips made promises, weaving our faults into one.

"This match will not last. The intensity will destroy both of you. You will both burn."

His every thrust forced me to gyrate and arch over him, riding him harder, faster, rushing toward the finish line that blazed like a comet in the dark.

"You will both burn."

Too late.

Too *late*.

I was alight.

Burning.

"You are destined to destroy each other."

With a moan, I broke our kiss and sat upright.

Henri didn't let me get far.

Chasing me, catching me, he wrapped his vicious arms around me and did something I never expected.

He *hugged* me.

Violently, wickedly.

He crushed me with pain and possession and pleasure.

Binding me to him, he found my lips again, and when he kissed me...the world ended.

He licked me. Fucked me. Suffocated me.

He squeezed me to him as if intent on breaking all my ribs with his depraved embrace.

His arms screamed danger. His thrusts delivered bliss. His kiss utterly destroyed me.

I trembled as he invaded my body with dominance and delirium.

And...something happened.

My mind went achingly quiet. All premonitions and warnings blanked out.

Nothing else mattered but us.

Together.

As one.

That strange kind of meditative quality from our last kiss cloaked my mind all over again. Like falling stars. Like breaking dawn. Like the best kind of sleep and dream and fantasy.

I descended into it.

I relaxed as everything became gossamer and gauzy while somehow becoming intensely carnal. Exquisite eroticism feathered out from where we were joined, seeping into my veins, and flowing through my bloodstream like pure light.

Each thrust echoed with miniature earthquakes in my bones.

Aftershocks rippled again and again in my heart.

The longer he plunged inside me, the deeper the sensations became.

I lost track of where I ended, and he started. Our breathing synced, panting and wild directly into each other's lungs.

In a rush of tingling, shimmering pleasure, my physical form dropped away, and I swore our souls weaved together.

I *felt* him.

All of him.

The dark spots of his childhood. The black shadows of his present. Our energies coiled and knotted, binding us together as our pace increased and his hug tightened, and I spiralled up and up and touched that blinding supernova where all rapture manifested.

I cried out as he took me so hard, so completely.

I sucked on his bottom lip as I begged him to come.

But...as wonderous and as euphoric as this moment was...I couldn't trip over that final edge. A barrier prevented me. The final hurdle before flying free.

"Come," he growled. "I can't last much longer."

God, yes please.

I wanted to.

So, *so* badly.

"I-I can't..."

Was it the pain my body suffered? The drugs in my system? The strange tantric magic I'd somehow stumbled into for the second time?

All three of those things ought to push me screaming into heaven.

Yet...

Not enough.

Not enough!

I impaled myself on him.

He grunted as he thickened inside me.

"More," I moaned. "I need more."

"Don't tell me that." He kissed me like a feral beast, teeth clacking, tongues knotting. "You should stop me. Fight me off…don't fucking encourage me."

He yanked me harder against his chest and sank his teeth into the side of my neck.

Sharp. Monstrous.

I almost came.

Almost.

He licked away the sting, stopping me from soaring into the stars.

I wanted his teeth. Needed those pinpricks of pain.

"Again. Bite me again."

"*What?*" His pace stuttered.

"Hurt me."

His eyes flashed in the darkness, full of silver fury. "No."

Temper made me sharp. "You made me this way, and now you're denying me?"

He couldn't reply.

"Do it." Leaning forward, I pressed my throat to his mouth. "Bite me. Mark me."

He moaned as if I'd torn out yet another vital piece of him.

The hot puff of his breath. The promise of his teeth.

"Please…" I arched again, offering myself up, begging him to take the bait.

His heart pounded against mine. A drumbeat full of tribal war.

"You've killed me twice tonight," he breathed just before he pounced.

"You are destined to destroy each other."

I gasped as his teeth sank into my throat.

The pressure of his bite.

The puncture of his incisors.

I screamed.

Not in pain.

But in ecstasy.

His hips pistoned up, bouncing me on his lap as he hugged me and fucked me, bit me and loved me.

I tumbled into that blinding light.

My body detonated with a million blazing shards. Rippling with ecstatic waves, I became one with life and loss and love.

Henri roared beneath me.

His orgasm spurted in thick, body-wracking jerks.

I lost track of time as we transcended that bed, that room, that fortress, and for a few microseconds of freedom, we weren't blood and bone but air and energy instead.

And then, it was over.

And the crash back to earth hurt worse than anything.

Every injury from today welcomed me back. Every awful bump and bruise.

"This match will not last."

Wincing, I sank into Henri's tight embrace.

I didn't care he almost suffocated me.

I didn't care I was trapped on his lap and his body still speared inside mine.

It was just us.

Clinging to each other in the dark.

"You will both burn."

I'd been injected with a contraception, collared, cuffed, and imprisoned. I'd been hunted, shot, abused, and tormented, and somewhere along the way, I'd become a different creature.

I still didn't know who that creature was.

I didn't know how I felt about needing a dash of pain to erupt my pleasure.

But what I did know was…I'd been warned about this.

Adversity had found me, and if I believed in fate and star-crossed destiny, then Henri wasn't just a man who'd targeted me and made my life a living hell…he'd been drawn to me.

Just like I'd been drawn to him.

Because we were the same.

We were one.

And this was fate in all its agonising glory.

Maybe I'd feel different in the morning.

Perhaps I'd laugh at myself for entertaining such crazy things like twin flames but…as his body twitched in mine, and he sucked in a haggard inhale, another bubble of hope expanded.

If our density was to destroy each other, what if I made a different choice? A choice to *save* him instead?

Maybe that was what the Vedic astrologer had meant.

That ending up with him wasn't a choice, but how I reacted to him was?

What if I stepped into his nightmares and maybe, *just*

maybe…figured out how to drag him back into the light?

Ever so slowly, I shifted off my knees, disengaged, then sat back on his lap and wrapped my legs around him. My feet burrowed beneath his stacked pillows, and I hugged him.

I clung to him like a koala all while fresh pain waked through me.

He fell on me, wrapping me in the biggest bear hug of my life.

The way he held too tight.

The way his biceps bunched, and his face burrowed into my hair.

It hinted this might be his first true embrace.

A full body enveloping.

And if that was true, I was sad as well as grateful.

I grew drowsy.

A drugged kind of sluggishness that made my tongue far too free.

Keeping my wits just enough to be wary of the cameras, I pressed my lips to his ear. "If the man who told me to play along with him is still in there, then…play with me, Hen."

His thighs stiffened to rock beneath me.

He sucked in a shallow breath.

I closed my eyes and poured my plea into his soul, all in order to save mine. "Play along with me, okay? You're still in there. I know you are. You're still good. We don't have to destroy each other." I kissed his ear as my eyes prickled with tears. "Get us out, Hen. *Please*..."

Sudden light-headedness tangled my tongue.

A rush of panic for asking such things.

And then nothing but deep, dreamless sleep.

Chapter Fourteen

Henri

VICTOR MARCHED AROUND WITH HIS hands in the pockets of his black slacks, looking like a furious headmaster. The ballroom echoed with his terse sentences while he scolded us. Every Master had been summoned to partake in breakfast and be witness to the winner of Emerald Bruises.

I swallowed another mouthful of bitter coffee.

The beans had been roasted to perfection. The frothed milk silky and creamy, yet it tasted like dirt thanks to *her*.

My nightmare.

I—

Nope.

Still couldn't say it.

Memories of last night refused to leave me alone.

I couldn't decide which had broken me the worst.

Her name.

My nickname.

Her tears.

Her initiating sex.

Her asking me to play along with her…

The way she kissed—

Fuck.

My throat closed up.

She'd destroyed me.

Utterly and spectacularly *destroyed* me.

You know what broke you the most.

I strangled my coffee cup.

Don't, Ri.

Don't—

The memory of her touch.

The heat of her closeness.

The exquisite sensation of *hugging* her—

Too late.

My cock reacted. My heart thundered. The urge to hug her again poured hotly down my weary, achy arms.

Adrenaline and anxiety, greed and gratitude all soaked my system, and my knees trembled beneath the table.

That hug.

That *damn fucking hug.*

My first.

My only.

And goddammit, I hadn't been aware how much I'd been starving.

Past starving.

Fucking *emaciated* for something I didn't even know I needed.

The strength it took not to wrap her in another hug this morning when she woke in bruise-shot agony. The sheer willpower I'd had to enlist not to scoop her into my arms as she limped out of the bathroom, her chest painted in a kaleidoscope of earthy, brutal pigments. The mark of my teeth on her throat almost pushed me over the edge.

Jesus Christ.

"I have to say, I'm severely disappointed in you, gentlemen." Victor's pompous speech cut through my thoughts, giving me a reprieve.

A few Masters grumbled over their fruit pastries.

"You were told the winner could do whatever he wanted. The key word in that sentence, my friends, was *winner.* Yet I hear from lovely Dr Belford that she currently has seven jewels all in various states of disrepair thanks to some of you anointing yourself as the winner *without* my consent."

Another grumble of dissent.

Victor stopped marching and glowered at all of us. "Seven jewels are out of service for the foreseeable future. Three of those seven are missing pieces. And another might not make it."

Ily stiffened by my feet, no doubt wondering if Peter was the one who might not make it.

He'd looked pretty messed up.

I didn't know how much a human body could endure before breaking down, but…he'd been close. Carrying him up the hill, I swore he'd stopped breathing a few times. I'd clutched him close, hiding his lack of living from the three jewels climbing exhausted behind me. I'd deliberated digging him a grave or running as fast as

I could for someone to resuscitate him.

But each time I thought he'd died, he sucked in another shallow breath and survived.

Ily moaned quietly as she shifted yet again on the hard oak floor.

I hated her kneeling on bruised legs.

I despised that the clothing Victor had deemed appropriate to order for her was a scantily short sundress that barely skimmed her ass. He'd provided G-strings, not knickers, and no bras, so her full chest stretched the bodice, turning a baby pink dress into something sinful, especially with the pricks of her hard nipples.

She was cold. Same as me.

My jeans and black t-shirt didn't fend off the draft pinching from the corners of the ballroom. The erotic statues and tapestries looked morbid and morose—the new day overcast and threatening rain as if grieving for the atrocities committed yesterday.

Flashes of stabbing Kyle.

Glimpses of strangling Charles.

A highlight reel of Ily waking at three a.m. and finding me reading. The way her golden eyes glowed like hunter moons in the dark, shimmering with lust. She'd never looked at me that way before. Never rode me, ruled me—

"I have a good mind to discipline all of you!" Victor suddenly lost control of his infamous temper. "I allowed you to play to let off some steam, and instead, you took advantage of my leniency. I'm aware each of you have your own needs, but I thought we'd cultivated a society here. A utopia where rules were welcomed. But…" He ran a hand over his mouth. "I see now I live with idiots and ingrates, and I'm done putting up with such *flagrant disregard for my fucking property*!"

A few Masters flinched.

Ferdinand had the bravery to ask, "Where's Kyle and Gary? I haven't seen them."

"Dead," Victor spat. "See, gentlemen? Balance. It always finds a way."

"They're *dead*?" A few Masters leapt to their feet. "Who the fuck killed them?"

A few eyes turned in my direction.

I stiffened as Victor met my gaze.

If he suspected me, I didn't think I'd be currently sitting unmolested and sipping my coffee. Not unless he had another trick up his sleeve. Another television demonstration or soap drama of five guards holding guns to my head.

Then again, in the mood he was in…he might not care I'd dispatched a few men who didn't follow his sacred rules.

The bump on my temple throbbed, amplifying my constant headache all while my stitches itched. It took a lot of discipline to sit still and act innocent.

Giving me an exasperated smile as if I were the only one Victor believed to be worthy, he sighed heavily. "Kyle has yet to be found, but Charles and Gary were recovered at dawn. Their cadavers were caught in my fishermen's nets and showed evidence of being bounced around in the cave system. I warned you!" Victor pointed at each of us. "I warned you about the dangers of my island. Yet you all ignored me, just like you ignored me on how far you were permitted to go." His navy eyes filled with rage again. "I told you to hunt and shoot. To allow democracy and good sportsmanship to crown a winner. But no! Most of you didn't even bother to fire! You just grabbed a jewel and did whatever the fuck you wanted!"

Waving at me, Victor added, "The only one who followed the rules was my newest member! And he shot not one but three! Without even counting how many bruises he caused, it's obvious he is the clear winner because the rest of you are fucking illiterate and arrogant, and I'm quickly running out of *motherfucking patience.*" He paced again, growing more and more irate. "Henri earned the right to keep his ownership over Ilyana and, thanks to no one else playing the goddamn game, he also claimed my Rachel and Roland's Mollie. And you know what? I'm going to honour that claim because someone has to be rewarded for good behaviour, and it certainly isn't you lot!"

Ah, shit.

My pulse picked up as Ily's shoulders tensed.

What did that mean?

I'd shot Rachel and Mollie to keep them safe.

Nothing more.

I didn't want them.

I didn't want to think what Victor would make me do to them and how the fuck I could refuse…

Ignoring most of Victor's speech, Ferdinand wrinkled his nose. "You're saying Charles and Gary drowned?" He crossed his arms. "I want an autopsy. If there's no water in their lungs, then—

"

"An autopsy?" Victor snickered. "Yeah, sure, I'll call the morgue director straight away." His humour vanished. "A fucking *autopsy*? Where do you think you are? Snivelling society where murder is investigated? This is *my* world. *My* island. I gave you rules. I warned you of the dangers. Some of you didn't listen and are now dead. Good fucking riddance." He sucked in a breath. "An autopsy!" Rolling his eyes, he added, "Oh, and while I have your attention, because no one asked me what I want, *I* want a fucking apology from those who are responsible for the five jewels I lost yesterday! But we don't always get what we want, do we?"

Wait…five?

I froze.

Ily swallowed a moan.

We both glanced around the ballroom.

No other jewels waited by their Master's feet.

No other slave but her.

If seven were receiving medical care and five were now dead…that left eighteen.

Even as the number blazed in my mind and Ily caught my stare, I sensed where this was going.

What Victor would do.

How he'd react to losing his precious toys, even if he had given them the option to jump and turned their collars off for the day. How many jumped, and how many were murdered?

He'll replace them.

At the soonest opportunity.

Victor stopped pacing and clasped his hands together. He stood on the podium where that Kirk fellow and some girl called Suri had put on a porno.

Were they still alive?

Who were dead?

And how many more would die before I managed to get out of here?

Huh.

Strange.

Was that a Freudian slip? I didn't want out. I'd accepted this was my permanent home now. I knew the moment I stepped off this island Q would slaughter me.

"Play along with me, Hen."

Ily's whispers strangled my heart.

How could she ask me that?

How could she expect me to go back to that heart-sick, nausea-riddled idiot from before?

I couldn't play along with her because I couldn't get her out of here.

If I freed her, she'd leave.

I'd be alone again.

And after that hug?

That miraculous, marvellous hug?

That profound embrace where I'd felt such a softening, a quickening, a *ruining*...

Merde...

No.

Just...no.

"Here is how today will go." Victor spoke calmly, collectedly. "I've decided I need a break from you lot before I do something ill-advised. I'm going to join my team who are currently hunting on my behalf. My initial order of gems will have to be doubled, tripled, to ensure my stocks are back to an acceptable number to entertain you degenerates."

"Jeez, tell us what you really think." A dark-skinned Master sniffed.

"I am." Victor smiled tightly. "Some of you committed treason against me when you murdered my precious gems. I tried to do something nice for you. I trusted you to respect me." He crossed his arms. "You didn't. You proved you're selfish and childish, and if this is the only way I can get through to you, then so be it." His lips pulled back. "You are all to vacate my home immediately and think upon the mess you have caused. My Joyero is *mine*, not yours. You are here by my grace and invitation, and your invitation has been revoked."

"*What?*" Every Master shot to his feet. "But—"

"Ah, ah, I'm not finished." Victor held up his hand. "You will be allowed to return in one month's time. This will enable my current jewels to heal and grow strong for your pleasure and for me to find some new gems to sparkle brightly upon your arrival. You will be flown home and will receive your new invitation on the encrypted message board like usual." He smiled and ran a hand over his perfect hair. "However, a few of you will *not* be allowed to return. I'll make those announcements privately. As for those who do get another invite, I suggest you use this time to reflect upon your actions because this is your one and only chance. We are predators, gentlemen, not unintelligent beasts. We have urges, yes. We are at the top of the food chain, of course. But there still must be order. There still must be rules. And unless you are willing to abide by those rules, you are no longer welcome."

"What about him?" Ian, the Master who'd almost raped Ily on Victor's command, pointed in my direction.

Yes, what about me?

All my scheming to stay so I didn't die might be moot if Victor flew me back to Paris.

I guessed I'd survive an hour. Maybe two before Q came for me…

"Henri Mercer is my permanent guest. He's tested me and frustrated me, but…he has stayed true to my laws and is exempt from leaving."

Was it my imagination, or did Ily suck in a relieved breath?

I wanted to run my fingertips over her honeyed skin. To tip up her chin. To kiss—

"That's fucking bullshit," Roland snarled. "He's a snitch, Vic. We all know it!"

"Yes, he is." Victor nodded. "But he's *my* snitch. He snitched on his brother, and I expect him to keep providing me with information about his family as and when I require it. But for now, he stays, you go, and that's all I have to say on the matter."

Clapping his hands, he smirked. "Now, enjoy your last breakfast in paradise, gentlemen. For those who live in Europe, you may join me on the first flight out of here. For those who live farther abroad, you will have to wait until my captain returns." He bowed with a twist of his lips. "Farewell, my friends. I hope next time we play together, you will remember this moment and *behave*. Otherwise, I might suddenly find myself with a few more jewels by collaring you instead."

He swept out of the room like a royal.

The Masters broke out into heated words.

And I tapped my little nightmare on the shoulder and got her out of there.

THE CURSE OF BLOOD & DARKNESS
by
Henri Mercer

I can't decide if this will be fiction or non-fiction.

If I pen this as fiction, then I can get away with embellishing all my best parts and downplaying all my worst. I can pretend that the monster who loves blood and tears isn't some sick freak who craves things he should never crave, but a messed-up man who feels closest to his woman when her essence is on his tongue.

If I keep it as fiction, I can weave a story about how that first splash of bitter, bloody wine bursts like a red, red orange in my mouth. How the zesty spritz fills my every synapse with more than just her lifeforce but her very fucking spirit.

I can bravely write down how hard her blood makes this particular character. How bestial he becomes from a single forbidden sip. He doesn't have to mention the dark depression that's taken residence in his soul. Doesn't have to look into that abyss that's replaced his heart.

As long as this tale is fictional...this man can go on living instead of listening to those ever-increasing whispers to end it before he goes too far.

But...

I can't write this as fiction because it's real.

I'm real.

I'm the beast.

I'm the man who can't say Ily's name anymore yet has fantasies of making her bleed.

I'm the monster who lives in constant fucking purgatory because I can't wake up from these urges, and I can't seem to run away from them either—

Looking up from re-writing the first page of my memoir/fantasy for the hundredth time, I stretched my fingers and sighed.

A week since Victor flew away without a goodbye.

Five days since the last Master hitched a lift back to their wives, families, and work commitments.

Three days since I'd had a check-up with Dr Belford and

learned the insistent itching of my stitches was a good sign—a healing sign—instead of an infection I feared (wanted to) kill me.

My head no longer ached so badly. The mild concussion had come and gone, and without Victor breathing down my neck, I didn't need to be quite as sharp as usual. The relief at being able to relax hit me like a fucking bulldozer, and I retreated inside.

I shut down.

I turned off.

I did what I'd always done when things got too much and found solace in words.

Sure, Victor could keep track of me on his cameras. Sure, he'd see me ignoring Ily and utterly unable to touch her. But…I didn't think he'd question my unwillingness to play. My ribs and arm still hurt like a bitch, and Ily's bruises had lost the round edging and turned into splashes of gruesome stains. Thanks to the arnica tablets we both took, an electrolyte drink every day, along with some antibiotics for the cuts on our feet, we were healing…albeit slowly.

Everyone in this godforsaken fortress was healing.

The entire vibe had gone from alive to dead. The furniture didn't have white sheets thrown over them like some abandoned manors when their Masters left town, but it might as well have.

It was so quiet.

Eerily quiet.

Far, far too quiet for the mess in my mind, and that was why writing had become my crutch. Without the laptop, I doubted I would've made it past the first day of loneliness.

Ily remained at my side, but every time I looked at her, the darkness inside me throttled my voice, refusing to let me speak.

The rest of the jewels either hobbled or limped, keeping to the shadows and not coming out of their quarters.

Massaging my nape, I struggled to shed the tiredness that'd dogged me since Emerald Bruises. Just like Ily and I crashed for three days after our initial welcome into this cesspit, we both turned inward and lethargic.

For a week, we'd barely talked and never *ever* touched.

Something had changed between us, and I had no idea what.

Whenever she looked at me, sad secrets danced in her bright tawny stare. She smiled instead of glowered. She acted eager for my command despite the pain of her heavily bruised body. Her energy had turned softer, acting like a sedative against mine.

And it hurt.

Goddammit, it hurt.

Her kindness, when I deserved no such thing, chopped me into bleeding pieces.

Swallowing hard, I glared at my laptop screen. The glare from the sun throbbed in my skull. I sat beneath an umbrella by yet another pool in the western gardens, where a running track looped close by, revealing a few jewels who hadn't been butchered a week ago.

Two girls jogged side by side, no doubt doing their best to expel the very real urge to run far, far away.

Dropping my arm, I flinched as darkness descended once again. Cloying and thick, veining over my heart until all I breathed was black.

He's replacing them right now.

Where was Victor hunting?

How many had he already caught?

Guilt crushed my bruised chest as Peter's and Ily's voices braided together in my head, repeating that damn sentence.

"I see what you are now. You did come for us. You're going to free us. I know it—"

Slamming my laptop closed, I swung my legs off the lounger and tossed the computer beside me.

Raking both hands through my hair, my eyes trailed to Ily where she exercised a few metres away. Carefully, slowly, hurt and healing, she flowed through a sequence of poses that had stupid names like bird of paradise, eagle, cat-cow, and tree.

She said it helped her pain and kept her muscles from seizing.

I said it was pure fucking torture.

Watching her contort into all manner of delicious positions?

Christ, it was unbearable.

Time slipped through my fingers as I became utterly entranced by her.

The way the sun glinted off her impossibly dark hair.

The way her body was strong enough—even after everything she'd endured—to plank and push-up, lunge and balance on one leg. I'd often wondered where she'd gotten her strength from.

Now I knew.

On her last sun salutation, she placed her hands into a prayer and bowed her chin.

I expected her to drop to the grass and slip into a meditation like she usually did, but she took a deep breath and lowered her arms.

Her eyes flashed to mine.

She froze.

I froze.

All that electrifying awareness that never stopped crackling between us increased to a thousand volts.

I grew hard as I pictured kissing her.

I trembled at the thought of going too far.

My heart squeezed in literal pain.

I.L.Y.

I love you—

Don't.

The sooner I forgot what her name meant, the better.

"You're still in there. I know you are. You're still good—"

I swallowed a moan.

She asked me to play along with her.

She believed everything I'd done up till now was an act.

But she didn't get it.

I didn't want her begging at my feet as she played along with me; I wanted her scratching my eyes out and telling me to stop.

I wanted to hunt her down. But I didn't want her to play dead and let me; I wanted her to scream and try to kill me.

Fuck.

Sourness filled my mouth.

It seemed my morality after murdering four men had returned, suffocating me under the very real knowledge that if I touched her now, I would pay for the privilege.

She only asked me to play along to earn her freedom.

I dropped my head and pinched the bridge of my nose.

She'd kissed me, *hugged* me, not because she felt anything for me but because she was so fucking brave and figured out how to manipulate me.

All it would take was making me fall in love with her—

I sighed heavily and stood.

She sucked in a breath, wrenching my eyes to hers.

Books and manuscripts might give me a way to survive each day, but seeing her standing there, brilliant beneath the afternoon sun…my attempt at a novel paled compared to her.

No fictional character would ever live up to her.

Christ, how did people do this?

How did they find the strength to care for someone and accept equal care in return?

I couldn't be in my chaotic thoughts anymore.

Snatching my laptop, I stepped away from the lounger.

Ily balled her hands as if ready to fight instead of obey.

That one act of defiance made me rock fucking hard and starving.

If she cursed me. If she showed me a *fraction* of defiance, I wouldn't be able to stop myself. I'd grab her by the throat and pin her against the willow tree. I'd be inside her before she gave me any sort of permission.

But slowly, she remembered her promises from a week ago and dropped elegantly to her knees.

She winced from her bruises.

She bowed her head with perfect subservience. "You're hard, Master H. Feel free to use me however you want." Her voice teased with falsity, but her offer was genuine.

I could have her.

I could have her any way I damn well wanted.

An awful surge of horror filled me.

This wasn't my Ily.

This obedient, docile jewel reminded me far too much of the broken ones. Their willpower shattered and strength torn to pieces. She became the very jewel I could never touch because I couldn't feel her fire anymore. Couldn't burn alive with her anymore.

I-I can't do this.

"You're free for the rest of the afternoon," I snapped. "Do whatever you'd like. Visit whoever you want. Don't come looking for me until dusk."

She was safe without other Masters around.

I might be safe if I could outrun this blackness.

I stalked away before she could reply.

Chapter Fifteen

MY HEART ACHED AS HENRI stormed away.

What had I done wrong?

I thought we'd reached an understanding.

The way he'd hugged me after I'd whispered for him to play along with me. The way his entire body enveloped me in such protection, such hope.

I thought that'd been his answer.

In my GHB high state, I thought it'd been a yes.

Yes, to playing along.

Yes, to the act of using me, abusing me, making me kneel and scream—proving to everyone in this damn place that he was the worst. I would play along and be the best-trained jewel in here. I'd do whatever it took to convince everyone that Henri was one of them and I was his, and then…maybe, just *maybe*, Victor would let him leave. He'd trust him with the location of this island, and Henri could tell his brother, and reinforcements could arrive and—

I slouched.

It wasn't a yes.

Dread-filled butterflies churned in my stomach as Henri vanished into the stronghold in the distance. He'd never left me alone before. Never run away as if he couldn't stand being in my presence.

My bruises and ribs still hurt.

My bones ached with matching pockmarks from nasty bullets, but those wounds were nothing compared to the pain of confusion. The scrambling of the bond I thought we'd formed.

Whatever I'd felt that night—all those stupid, *stupid* feelings…they were nothing more than a ridiculous fantasy.

Enough.

Climbing to my feet, I groaned as my body protested.

I had far more important things to worry about.

Peter.

Rachel.

The jewels.

I was finally free to visit them.

Brushing a few blades of grass off my black workout shorts and aqua sports bra, I followed Henri's footsteps through the manicured grass.

A shiver ran down my back as I climbed the deck and cut around all the empty tables.

This fortress was hell on earth when monsters were in residence, but empty—apart from inconspicuous staff and black-suited guards—it was eerie.

No sounds of pain around shadowy corners. No sick laughter as a Master whipped a jewel. No awful beatings in the gardens.

I hadn't noticed how much every scream and whimper curdled my stomach. The calcification around my heart at the sounds of abuse chipped away a little, thanks to birdsong and silence.

A sharp-eyed guard watched me as I padded barefoot through the dining room. He didn't stop me, and another guard took up his glower as I cut across the foyer and down the stone corridor leading toward Dr Belford's surgery on the ground floor.

I added each guard to the ongoing tally in my head.

So far, I'd counted twelve on the ground floor and five scattered in the gardens.

I had no idea how many patrolled the upper levels or the battlements.

For the past few days, I'd started keeping a record of guards and staff, adding their positions to the schematics in my head.

As much as I hoped Henri would snap out of his strange silence and reveal he was still good, deep, deep inside, it wasn't in my nature to sit around and wait.

We had three weeks before the Masters returned. Who knew when Victor would fly home and if we stood a chance at getting out...this was our best opportunity.

My feet—healed from their shallow cuts from running in caves and forests—slowed outside the carved door of the surgery.

I shuddered with memories of that first day. Of Peter flirting with the doctor and nurse. Of his false happiness doing its best to hide just how afraid and hurt he was.

God.

My heart ached as I knocked.

Guilt pressed heavily.

A week since I last saw him. It wasn't good enough.

The door swung open. Melanie Belford stared coldly. "Oh, it's you."

I flinched at her warm welcome. "C-Can I come in?"

Looking past me, she scanned the empty corridor. "Your Master isn't with you, I hope. I'm not exactly a fan."

"No."

She frowned. "That's a first. Letting you wander around on your own."

I shrugged. "I suppose he feels I'm safe enough without other Masters staying."

"Safe?" She clucked her tongue and moved aside to let me in. "I don't think it's anything to do with your safety, Ily, but more about his demented need to possess you."

Ily.

My name caught me off guard.

Henri had barely talked to me since the night I'd taken pleasure from him. The talkative man who'd broken me with his secrets had turned into a stoic statue who barely grunted responses. And when he did deign to speak to me…he never used my name.

A prickle of worry shot down my spine.

Was it because of what it meant?

Was he that allergic to love that he couldn't even say the damn word…even in an acronym?

"Is Peter awake?" I asked, brushing aside her comment.

Sighing heavily, she removed a pair of latex gloves and beckoned me to follow. "He is."

My soul leapt with relief. "So…he's okay?"

She gave me a hard look as she guided me to a second door and led me down another hallway. "Define okay."

"Healing? As happy as can be expected?"

"He's a long way from happy, I'm afraid."

"But he's not going to die?"

"Not from this incident."

Her pessimism soaked into me.

It suffocated all my other questions.

My teeth locked together the farther we travelled. The scents of disinfectant grew stronger as we spilled out into a long narrow gallery. The ancient castle that Victor stole his blueprints from would've used this sort of space as an art display or promenade track. But now, in this modern hellhole, it housed a long row of single beds all facing a bank of interconnecting windows. Each window was wide open, allowing sunshine and fresh air to circulate.

A few jewels I recognised looked up from where they crowded around a bed.

With no Masters to serve and no Victor to command them, they huddled around the only leader they actually respected.

Rachel smiled and waved.

Mollie gave me a nod.

Citra and Caishen, Nancy and Corinne. Some of them had made the choice to go their own way in the caves, and others had left us out of panic. I held no grudges. Only relief to see so many faces.

"I'll leave you to it then," Dr Belford said. "I need to help Rose change Yumeko's bandages."

She retraced her steps and left me alone.

Drifting forward, my pulse pounded.

As much as I was one of them with our matching collars and cuffs, I was still removed—thanks to Henri refusing to let me sleep in the slave quarters.

What if they thought I wasn't to be trusted? What if they no longer welcomed me?

Fear clutched my throat as I reached the end of the bed, and my eyes landed on a soulmate in friend form. I'd been wrong that he wasn't a soulmate. I'd forgotten what my family had taught me. Soulmates came in all forms. My brother and parents were soulmates.

And this man too.

Undoubtedly.

And Henri? What's he?

"You're destined to destroy each other…"

I sighed heavily.

If Peter was my soulmate as surely as Krish was…what did that make Henri?

Was he my twin flame like the astrologer said?

While Henri typed away on his laptop the past few days, I'd done my best to remember what I'd researched after we'd gotten home that day. Krish had helped me, and together, we'd found texts full of dire warnings. Things like: *You're drawn to each other against your wishes. When you meet, you just know. Your twin flame will feel different from everyone else. Unbearable sexual chemistry. Reflection of darkness and light. Difficult and painful. Can amplify feelings of loneliness and loss. Cause discord and hurt. Can only be a lover and most often as not, ruin each other if that is the karmic pattern.*

Finding your twin flame never seemed to work out well.

Shaking my head from useless thoughts, I blinked and focused on Peter.

His dark brown eyes met mine, his dusky skin drawn with pain.

Bare-chested and propped up by white pillows, he shifted his legs beneath the sheets and gave me a wobbly smile. "Hi..."

Every worry.

Every concern.

Gone.

Tears instantly erupted, and my knees threatened to collapse. "*Aap theek hain.*" (You're okay.)

He shrugged a single shoulder. "I'm alive."

"Alright, guys." Rachel suddenly stood and clapped her hands. "Let's give them a few minutes."

With soft smiles and sweet kisses on my cheeks, each jewel gave me a quick hug as they moved from Peter's bedside and went to visit the other jewels healing down the row.

I never took my eyes off Peter as Rachel hugged me last.

Pressing her lips to my ear, she whispered, "Meet me in the kitchens once you're done. We need to talk."

I squeezed her hand and nodded. "I'll be there."

"Mollie and I will be waiting." Turning to blow a kiss at Peter, she added, "See you later, Pete."

"Yeah, you too." He grimaced as if speaking took too much energy. "Do what I said and ask Mel to order you some prenatal vitamins." He swallowed hard, pushing himself to care about others instead of himself, even now. "Just because it's his doesn't mean it's not yours too."

Rachel rolled her eyes as if she'd heard it before. "Let's just focus on you first, okay?"

With another quick smile at me, she clasped Mollie's hand.

They headed back the way I'd arrived.

I didn't move until the other jewels had scattered.

I tried to see who survived that awful game, but my heart pounded, and I couldn't take my eyes off how frail Peter had become. How his body held no vitality. How his hands rested like white tombstones on the bed, wrapped in thick padding and bandages. How that damn, *damn* collar seemed extra heavy and extra cruel, cutting into his neck.

Moving closer, I sat carefully by his hip and drank him in. Tears plopped off my chin as I forced a smile. "I'm glad you're not dead."

He laughed, then winced. "Meh, I'm feeling decidedly mixed about that."

The urge to fling myself on him and hug him stupid came far too strongly.

I managed not to fling, but I still hurt him as I folded close and wrapped my arms around his slender shoulders. He felt even less substantial than before. No longer wiry with strength but thin with sickness.

"Hey." His arms came up, his thickly wrapped hands bouncing against my back. "I'm okay, *jaanu*."

I burst into tears at the name. A name reserved for lovers or husbands and wives. A name that didn't belong in this place or in our relationship, but I couldn't find the strength to stop him. "I'm so, so sorry I haven't been to see you. I tried. I wanted to. I've thought about you every second of every day and—"

"Ily…hush." He chuckled tightly as I pulled away, leaving a few of my tears glittering on his pillow. "I'm fine. It's fine. I understand why you couldn't come."

"Can I get you anything?" I looked around the suddenly rather empty gallery. "Some painkillers? Some water? I can get you something to eat—"

"Ily…" He smirked. "Seriously. Stop it."

I slouched with a heavy sigh. The mania of finally seeing him faded a little, and I laughed under my breath. "Sorry. I'm just…really, *really* happy to see you."

"Same." With a trembling arm, he reached up and pressed his bandaged hand to my cheek. Using it as a tissue, he sopped up my tears before the exertion got the better of him, and he dropped it down again. "You okay?"

I flinched. "Shouldn't I be the one asking you that?"

He scowled. "The past week has been the best in half a decade." He cocked his chin at the other jewels in the beds. "No Masters to summon us. No gongs going off. No games to be endured. It's a fucking holiday."

Plucking the starched sheets, I asked quietly. "Who…who

didn't return?"

He stiffened. "You sure you want to know?"

It was my turn to scowl. "Just because I'm not allowed to sleep with you guys doesn't mean I'm not one of you. Of course I want to know."

"Sorry…I didn't mean it like that." He swallowed hard. "I only meant the minute you know their names and how they died, it'll haunt you." He looked away. "I have so many ghosts inside me, Ily…so many I've seen die in that fucking temple. It's made even worse by knowing their names, knowing *them*. The minute I tell you, you won't be able to forget."

Lowering his voice, he added, "Right now, all you know is some of us passed on. If it were me, I'd want to stay in that place where it doesn't become too real."

My shoulders braced. "Tell me so it *is* real. They deserve to be mourned. They deserve to be remembered. Their families have no idea what's happened to them. It's up to us to carry their memory."

"You're right." Shuffling higher up his pillows, his voice turned almost cold. "The six jewels who are healing with me are Yumeko, Morgan, Harper, Gail, Jo, and Kirk. I won't go into our injuries, but let's just say a few are hurt worse than others. As for the five who didn't come back…" He swallowed hard and glared out the window. "Suri, Dane, Kirk, Rebecca, and Nancy did try to swim. I don't know how far they got before the guards went after them in a speedboat. Where they moored that thing, I have no idea, but we should find out for…future attempts. They dragged Rebecca and Nancy out of the water. They got Kirk next with a fishing net, but Suri and Dane snapped. They duck dived. The guards opened fire."

I sucked in a breath, my aching ribs stabbing my lungs.

"Their bodies floated back up, and Kirk…" Peter shuddered. "Kirk lost it. He was beaten, and…he hasn't said a word since." His haunted eyes met mine. "I didn't realise how deep his feelings for Suri went. He did a good job of hiding it, but now…now, I'm afraid he's going to do something stupid."

Looking down the row of beds, I spotted one with a larger blond guy, huddled in a ball and facing away. God…the pain of seeing the girl you'd fallen in love with shot to death. The horror of not being able to stop it—

Rubbing at my tears, I whispered, "So Suri and Dane are dead. Who…who else?"

"Sonya, Phillipa, and Bet. According to the gossip mill, Sonya had her throat cut, and Pip had been—" He shuddered and cut himself off. "Bet was always quiet. Her mind broke on her second week here. She had no injuries, so...I'm guessing she probably jumped."

I swallowed hard.

If only she'd waited.

If only the jewels trusted we'd get them out.

If only we actually could...

Taking Peter's chunky bandaged hand, I placed it on my lap and did my best to take away his thoughts of pain and worry. "Those are the last names you'll ever recite, okay?" I shivered at the sheer determination in my voice. "No one else will die here."

He sniffed. Exhaustion from his wounds, his fever, and the past five years of hell pressed him deeper into his pillows. "You still believe we can do it?"

I didn't bother looking at the cameras above us.

I just kept my gaze on my friend as his eyelashes dropped and his breathing slowed. "It's almost over, Paavak." I kissed his bandaged knuckles. "I feel it."

"That's nice." Giving me a dreamy smile, he sighed and fell into a sick-heavy sleep.

I sent him healing light and strength.

And then I went to find the girls to begin a war.

"This is absolutely crazy," Rachel said the moment I stepped into the kitchens.

May, the kind cook who'd given us muesli bars before Emerald Bruises, cocked her chin at a shadowy corner by the huge larder full of herbs, spices, and a mountain of pasta boxes.

"Go talk there, girls." She shooed us away with a tea towel. "There's a dead spot in the camera's sight. But...for the love of our maker, please keep your voices down."

Obeying May, the three of us huddled close in the larder's shadow, keeping our heads as near as possible, speaking with the quietest whisper. Even with all the boiling, steaming, chopping, dicing, and extraction fans, who knew how sensitive the cameras were.

Without guests staying, the kitchen still worked at a furious pace to feed the guards and Henri. I didn't know if the staff got the same meals, but they still needed food, and after my headcount over the past week, I'd tallied at least twenty of them, possibly more counting the gardeners and maintenance crew who didn't come into the castle.

"Are you guys okay?" I whispered.

"I can't believe we're doing this," Rachel quipped again, shaking her head.

"You were the one who started growing a countdown clock in your womb." Mollie smirked, brushing aside her blonde fringe. "Nine months and counting you said. Get me out before this spawn is born…isn't that what you whispered a few nights ago?"

"I know, but—"

"We have to try, Rach." I gave her a soft smile. "But I understand if you'd rather—"

"No. I'm in. I am." She braced her shoulders. "Doesn't mean it's not crazy, though."

"Oh, it's crazy." I nodded. "And dangerous."

"And that's why if we're doing this…we have to be slow, smart, and steady," Mollie said. "Nothing is in our favour. We're outnumbered, out-gunned, and out-powered. But…if we plan it well and luck smiles down on us, then it's possible."

"I agree." I smiled. "Adversity only makes us stronger."

"The supreme art of war is to subdue the enemy without fighting. Sun Tzu." Mollie grinned.

Memories of my father quoting his favourite poet spilled quickly. "Wonders happen if we can succeed in passing through the harshest danger. Rainer Maria Rilke."

"God, can you two stop trading bumper sticker slogans?" Rachel rolled her eyes.

Mollie and I snickered, grateful to be able to laugh after everything Peter told me and all the lives that'd been lost.

A short silence fell before we all sucked in a breath and unanimously got to work.

"So…anything I missed this past week?" I asked.

Mollie shook her head. "Nothing. Been one of the most boring weeks I've ever spent here. It's been sublime. I feared without Victor around, the guards would get a little trigger-happy, but…they don't seem to care." She flicked a look at one of them lounging by the exit to the kitchens. "No one has stopped us when we've done errands for Dr Mel and Rose. We haven't been reprimanded for getting soup for the patients. It's like we don't exist."

Rachel sighed with relief. "Mols is right. The past week has been a bit of a dream. For those of us not healing, of course...or dead."

We all flinched.

I sent a thought to those who were gone.

Clearing my throat, I said quietly, "Peter said the same thing about the castle being slow and guards being lax. That's a good thing. If they don't care about us moving around, and there's no Masters to serve...then this is the perfect time to—"

"Yeah, about that." Mollie cut in. "Rachel and I have been talking and...even if we could get our hands on cleaning supplies to make our little presents, we have no idea how we'd get them set up around the castle. We've sat up night after night wondering how we can build a big enough 'present' to achieve the best possible ending, and the fact is...we can't."

My heart fluttered. My bruises ached. I had no idea how to plan an insurrection, but...my family had always taught me strength came in bigger numbers. Our community always came together to help each other. The elders shared their knowledge, and the young ones helped the elders.

That's what we need.

Mollie, Rachel, Peter, and I couldn't do this on our own.

We need help.

It's risky—

Shutting up that fearful voice, I whispered, "We need to expand our little war effort."

"You what?" Rachel's eyebrows shot into her dark hair. "You want to tell *more* people? Are you insane? The more ears that know, the more mouths that speak."

"The other jewels already know," I said. "Most of them heard Peter's ranting when we ran."

"Yes, but no one actually believes he'll try."

"They will if we show them our plan."

"We have no plan," Mollie muttered. "We have the know-how, but without supplies and distribution—"

"Exactly." I nodded. "Having the other jewels in on this is all well and good, but they're just as restricted as us in what they can and cannot do."

"So...we're doomed from the start?" Rachel asked.

"No. We just need to think outside the box."

Mollie caught my eyes and cottoned onto what I meant. "Y-You can't be serious."

"What? What can't she be serious about?" Rachel cocked an eyebrow.

Squeezing her arm, I whispered, "You said it yourself, we need cleaning supplies for our ingredients. Therefore…we need a cleaner."

Both girls went still.

"We need someone who can move about with far more freedom than us. Someone who has access to the chemicals you need."

"You're saying we enlist one of Victor's maids?" Rachel hissed. She flicked a look at Mollie. "They never talk to us. They're warned to stay far, far away. I heard Victor threaten them once that if they spoke to his jewels, he'd ensure they instantly became one of us."

Nervousness fluttered in my belly. "So he's formed a class system in here?"

"No one wants to wear a golden collar, Ily." Rachel sighed.

"Good point. Well, we have three weeks to ensure no one else ever does."

May drifted closer from where she'd been eavesdropping. Hugging a mixing bowl, she stirred some sort of wet dough with a wooden spoon. "Did you just say you need a cleaner?"

I stiffened, but the other girls nodded, their trust in May obvious. "Know anyone who would be keen to help us with our extracurricular activities?"

May smirked and wiped the back of her hand on her cheek, smearing flour. "Faiza."

"Faiza?" Mollie asked.

"She arrived about six months ago. Said she was head housekeeper in a five-star hotel in Abu Dhabi. She went into Victor's room to clean. She thought he'd checked out, you see. Unfortunately for her, he was still there." May shivered. "He had one of his guards drug her and smuggled her here. She's been working with his maids—bringing their quality of attention to a higher level—but a few weeks ago, a Master noticed how pretty she is and requested for her to change roles."

Rachel shuddered. "They put her in a silver collar?"

May nodded.

"What's a silver collar?" I asked.

"It's a form of probation," Mollie said. "It shows that Victor has taken the Master's request under advisement and has collared the cleaner in question while he makes his decision. She still can't be touched in that way, but he usually agrees to change a staff's role if someone takes a fancy to them."

"So she has incentive," I said.

May nodded. "She keeps asking me how to make poison from hemlock and other garden weeds. Thinks she can poison the Master who noticed her and go back to being unnoticed. Unfortunately, her silver collar has announced her potential of being available to everyone. She's well aware it's only a matter of time before she's raped. But if she knows you're planning something, she'd help."

"Fine." Looking at the women, I tried to be a good leader while Peter healed. "May, next time Faiza comes into the kitchens, tell her to meet us. Mollie, decide how much and what chemicals you need. Rachel, figure out how we can get the gardeners and other staff on our side. The bigger reach we have, the more places we can hide our presents."

"You want to tell the whole damn castle now?" Rachel whisper-hissed just as Mollie tapped her nose. "Smart. I see where you're going."

I grinned. "You said we can't make just one big present…so…we'll make lots of little ones. Would that work?"

Mollie smiled at Rachel, and Rachel gaped at May.

Mollie said, "If we had someone to help position them, a way of delaying detonation, and something noxious to cause panic, we could create some serious problems."

"Excellent." I clapped my hands and made the mistake of looking outside.

The sun slid down the sky, glowing pink and gold and red. Dusk.

Damn, time went fast.

"I have to go." I backed up. "Let's meet here this time tomorrow?"

"We can't tell everyone," Rachel snapped. "Someone will rat."

I sighed, my shoulders slouching. "Look, if we're going to do this, we can't half-ass it. It's either die because Victor figures out our plan or die on that altar down in the caves when he's grown bored of us." I shuddered. "I know which I would prefer."

"Me too." Mollie nodded. "I'm willing to take the gamble in order to get more manpower. Who knows…maybe even a guard or two would be approachable."

"Crap on a cracker." Rachel buried her face into her hands. "You're both as crazy as each other."

"And crazy is what's needed," Mollie muttered.

Wrapping my arms around Rachel, I whispered in her ear. "I'm not going to let you have your baby in here, okay? We'll be smart. We'll only tell the ones we have a good feeling about, and…we just have to hope karma is on our side."

Sagging against me, Rachel nodded reluctantly. "I knew going into this it would be risky. I'm not gonna back down now."

Pulling away, I looked at both girls. "The moment you guys covered for Henri when Victor interrogated us was the moment you ensured luck will favour us. I know it. We'll get out. We'll get everyone out. You'll see. And if we don't? Well, I'm going to fight the whole damn way."

Chapter Sixteen

Henri

THE CURSE OF BLOOD & DARKNESS
by
Henri Mercer

I've always liked to read.
I can still remember my first book as if it were yesterday. A boy, who sat in the desk next to me at school, forgot his thick fantasy book as he chucked everything into his backpack the moment the bell rang on Friday afternoon. All the kids bolted toward the weekend. Most of them ran home to families and friends, their days full of adventure and fun.
Me...I didn't rush.
I hated weekends.
I hated my quiet house and silent mother. I'd amble around the village when the silence got too much and usually ended up at the beach till way past bedtime.
She never grounded me.
Didn't even care to ask where I'd been when I finally walked through the door.
But all of that changed the day I borrowed that book and took it home.
I vanished into the pages and traded my life for that of a man who didn't know he was a Seeker. I struggled with some of the English words, my mind slowly trading French for a different language. Even at my snail's pace, I finished by Monday and returned it to the boy despite wanting very much to keep it. He thanked me profusely for finding it, letting slip that he'd stolen it from his older brother because he'd

overheard him saying some woman called a Confessor was hot. I look back now and see what I missed when I was thirteen. The strangest pang in my body when he mentioned an older brother. The quickest memory of siblings that felt familiar before vanishing just as quick.

Thanks to him, I found a way to cope with my weekends and spent every hour in the local library from then on. I read every book in The Sword of Truth series by Terry Goodkind and fell in love with words because they were never silent or cold. They were messy and chaotic, giving me pages full of friends, enemies, lovers, and homes.

Reaching for the ice-cold beer an inconspicuous staff member had left for me on the side table where I wrote in the library, I swallowed a tart mouthful.

Even this short break.

Even this micro-pause where I returned to reality—everything inside me howled and snarled and left me in the eye of the hurricane that hadn't stopped blowing.

Every time I slipped back into the present, the darkness snatched me quickly.

My skin broke out with chills.

The abyss opened wide inside me.

I felt like I was falling, falling—

Finishing my mouthful, I stretched my fingers back on the keyboard and did my best to sink back into a different time, different place.

I hadn't wanted this story to become an autobiography, but somehow...all the words I couldn't say to Ily poured out on the page.

The blackness inside me crushed me into the chair.

Bookshelves towered over me, whispering that perhaps it was the darkness in their pages that'd tainted me. Books full of black magic and dark wizards. Pain and suffering of fantastical and historical characters—

But...the truth blared far too bright.

This endless filth inside me was caused by one thing and one thing only.

Genetics.

A curse that flowed from father to son even though I'd never been around him.

But that isn't true...

I sighed.

My fingers flew as if possessed, accessing archived memories, the keyboard unlocking far too many flashbacks from my past.

> The monster called him Quincy.
>
> I'd met him before.
>
> Spied him as I was dragged through the mansion and past priceless things I wasn't allowed to touch. The man growled at the young teenager lounging in the doorway. "Scram, you worthless child. I'm busy."
>
> My ears rang with his barked French, so different to the quietly spoken women in pinafores who brought us food and told us to behave.
>
> Quincy glanced at me, his light green eyes cold and unreadable. "Where are you taking him?"
>
> "To do what you refuse to do."
>
> "What? Learn the family trade?" His cold voice could've cut stone.
>
> "At least he's willing to sit and watch without trying to scurry away like a terrified rat."
>
> Quincy sniffed.
>
> It looked as if he'd reply, but with a curl of his upper lip, he pushed off the door, shoved his hands into his jeans pockets, and strolled away.
>
> I watched him go like always.
>
> I kept my eyes on him even as the older man dragged me into a room where a woman hung in the centre with her mouth gagged and wrists bound.
>
> "Sit and learn and maybe I won't kill you with the rest." He threw me to the side. I collapsed against a sideboard.
>
> And the same thing that happened each time he came for me played out in awful clarity.
>
> Her every scream. Her every sob. Her every drop of blood. Little by little, those afternoons contaminated me. Day by day, those horrors found their way into my dreams.
>
> And I did the only thing I could.

> *I boxed up those days.*
> *I deleted all those nights.*
> *I removed myself from my brothers and sisters in the hope I wouldn't infect them too...*

Exhaling heavily, I glanced up and noticed my beer was gone. Dusk had fallen.

Another night was coming for me.

Where the hell is Ily?

Every afternoon, she visited Peter and the jewels, and I was grateful.

Grateful for the space to suffer the overwhelming despair and misery that only grew worse.

I couldn't breathe anymore.

Couldn't exist without fighting, fighting, *always goddamn fighting* my true nature whenever she was around.

All those black, awful urges that'd been instilled inside me when I was a kid. All those diabolical traits that I'd smothered and deleted, giving myself amnesia where I forgot the siblings I'd lived with, all so I didn't have to remember what happened in that room with our mothers.

Tearing my hands through my hair, I trembled.

That amnesia was cracking.

The more the darkness claimed me, the faster my past came back.

It'd been two weeks since Victor left, and I remembered something new every day. The manuscript had become a channelling medium. Snippets of moments when I'd spied my older brother as I was dragged to witness yet another rape now haunted me in my sleep.

I didn't *want* to remember.

I didn't want to be this way.

I didn't want to lie awake in the dark, gagging on the same darkness inside me.

One night last week, I'd dreamed of bathing in blood. The silky slippery sensation of red, red, red. Instead of waking up and rushing to the bathroom to heave my rotten guts up, I'd been rock fucking hard and moments away from rolling Ily onto her stomach and taking her.

Shit...I'd been close.

So *damn close* to letting out all the pressuring filth inside me.

I fucking *hated* myself.

I loathed every thought in my head.

I might've been bred by a monster and had him pour his curse into me one day at a time, but I didn't want it.

I thought I did after playing Ruby Tears.

I thought I could trample on other people's lives so I could finally be free, but the truth was?

Fuck, the truth was I'd had it right the night I'd tried to end it.

The scar on my leg taunted me to try again.

The hatred inside me spilled out to include my older brother.

I knew now why I hated him so badly. Why he conjured such rage. Why I'd taken such perverse satisfaction in disowning him.

It wasn't because I'd turned into our father.

It was because I blamed my brother for failing me.

All those days when he'd left me at that creature's mercy.

All those moments where he turned his back and walked away.

Back then, I was trapped.

Right now, I was trapped.

I couldn't leave.

I couldn't stay.

Death truly was the only answer.

Chapter Seventeen

DOING MY BEST TO KEEP MY attention on Faiza, I listened with Mollie and Rachel. Three weeks had passed, and we'd managed to meet most days. The guards didn't care, the cooks just rolled their eyes, and we'd made headway…but not as much as we needed to.

I rubbed at the persistent bruise in my heart. A bruise that refused to heal like the others had on my body.

Three weeks and Henri hadn't said a damn word to me.

Each time we made eye contact, he tore his stare away.

Each time he climbed into bed, he grabbed a book with shaky hands and threw himself into the pages with feral desperation, hinting he wasn't coping.

I'd tried to talk to him.

I'd tried to give him pieces of my past. I whispered about my dream of working with the Crown Jewels. Of my job at the Tower of London. I even told him a little about Krish and his unique, wonderful way of viewing the world.

And…nothing.

Not a peep.

He showered alone.

Dressed quickly.

And visibly exhaled in relief when afternoon rolled around, and I left to visit the jewels.

By the time I returned to him in the evening, his face held so many shadows and his eyes so many ghosts, I didn't know how to bring him back.

He's dying right in front of me.

"—but I did manage to get Willem to give me some slow-release fertilizer pellets so that should help, right?"

Shaking my head, I scattered the fears over Henri and focused on Faiza again.

Rachel gave me an odd look before nodding with Mollie. "That's amazing, Faiza. I can't believe he agreed to help after catching you stealing the indoor plant food."

Faiza grinned. "He was brought here as a fourteen-year-old boy. Snatched at a local fete where he showed off his home-grown vegetables. He'll do anything to get back home."

Short and petite with glossy black hair, bright ebony eyes, and gorgeous caramel skin, she could've been a social media superstar if she hadn't been targeted and trafficked. Dressed in a prim maid's uniform, a silver choker glimmered beneath the starched white collar of her shirt.

The first time I'd seen that collar, I'd felt so angry. Absolutely livid that she wore a ticking time bomb around her throat, knowing that any day Victor could swap the silver for gold and her job description would end up like us.

The torment of that had ensured she'd not only agreed to help but went above and beyond to the point she'd become our linchpin in this whole attempt.

Faiza stepped a little closer. "I know you've made a couple of presents with the bleach and vinegar I gave you, but…if we're truly doing this, you're going to have to target all the guard posts, most of the Master's bedrooms, and as many large common areas as you can."

Dismay trickled through me. "H-How many is that?"

Faiza pursed her lips before huffing, "About fifty. Give or take."

"*Fifty?*" I whisper-hissed, shooting a glance at the camera. The lens pointed toward the row of knives and pots hanging against the stone wall.

"They don't all have to be huge," Mollie whispered. "The ones in the Master chambers could consist of smaller explosions…just enough to create confusion and smoke. But the ones near the guard posts and communal areas will need to cause a decent amount of destruction. Do you think you could get your hands on any petrol or diesel, Faiza?" Mollie quirked an eyebrow. "If we can get some Styrofoam, I could make—"

"No way," Rachel hissed. "You want to make foo gas? Homemade napalm? Have you completely lost the plot?"

"I know it's highly unstable and dangerous, but—"

"But nothing. You'd kill yourself before we could hide it and set it off. It's lethal, Mols." Rachel crossed her arms. "We'll make fifty smaller ones and hope for the best."

"Can you make fifty?" My heart raced, amazed at their scientific knowledge of turning simple ingredients into such mayhem. "How long will that take? Will you have enough containers and supplies? How will we place them in the rooms?"

I'd thought three weeks would be enough time.

Turned out, it'd been nothing.

Rachel cupped her belly without thinking. I wanted to ask how she was. Morning sickness had started, so meeting in the kitchens sometimes sent her rushing to the bathroom.

Catching my stare, she winced and dropped her hand. "May has raided the recycling shed again. She's selected all the bottles that will work. The shed only gets emptied once a month, so it holds more than enough containers for us to make that many."

"You just need to sneak us as many chemicals as possible, Faiza," Mollie said quietly. "You've done amazing on the bleach, and I tend to agree that napalm might be pushing it, but if you could get other things like ammonia, pesticides, oven cleaners, hydrogen peroxide, paint thinners, solvents, chlorine, and mold removers. With a few additions and tweaks, I can make some substantial weapons." She smiled and dropped her voice even lower. "The bleach-and-vinegar mix will create a noxious gas that can kill. If we trapped a few Masters and guards in their rooms, we'd whittle down the numbers quite well. I can make mustard gas too. If we manage to make enough of them and ensure they all go off at the same time, it'll be chaos."

Rachel hugged herself, a violent tint to her stare. "While the castle burns and everyone runs around with damaged lungs and stinging eyes, we can race in here, grab all the knives, and start slashing."

I flinched at the mental image. Of stabbing someone as viciously as Henri stabbed Kyle.

"How do we get everything to go off at the same time?" I asked.

"I'll make fuses out of cotton, potassium, and sugar," Mollie answered. "If we make the wicks long enough, and if Faiza can recruit more cleaners, we could have her team light them when doing their cleaning rounds in the morning and an hour or so later…*boom*."

My mind raced, trying and failing to see how this would work. "What about our collars? I doubt they're still inactive after running around the island?"

"Yeah, Vic came and turned all ours back on before he left." Mollie bared her teeth. "But we figure they can't shock all of us at the same time. We'll be okay as long as we stay separate and don't congregate. We'll also have to get out of the castle once the gas goes off. Otherwise, we'll just poison ourselves with them, but…if one jewel is being electrified, then another can hopefully get close enough to kill the Master doing it."

"So…some will be used as bait while others turn into assassins?" I rocked back on my heels.

"You got a better idea?" Rachel asked.

I paused, thinking. "No one's turned my collar on. At least…I don't think so. Perhaps if I'm still free, I could use that to my advantage."

Everyone went very, very still. "Has Master H had any reason to zap you? You need to test it…if you're right, then *wow*." Mollie's eyes lit up. "This could be the break we were looking for. You could sneak out and get past the electric boundary line. You could—"

"Where's she going to go?" Faiza whispered. "When I was flown in, all I could see for miles and miles was ocean."

"Wait." I narrowed my eyes. "You saw where we are? Victor didn't block the windows?"

Faiza shook her head. "No, they were wide open." She shivered. "I was still a little loopy from the drugs he gave me, but I saw enough."

"Can you describe what else you saw?" I asked. "The layout of the island, the shape of the castle from a bird's-eye view…I might be able to figure out where we are and…" My shoulders slouched. "It probably won't help, but…all information is good information."

"Sure, I'll remember as much as I can tonight and do my best to give you as clear of a description as possible."

I gave her a weary smile. "We get one shot at this." I didn't want to be pessimistic, but….

"Agreed." Mollie nodded. "It's why, even though we need approximately fifty bombs to make even a dent in this damn place, I'm going to aim for sixty, seventy, eighty…I want spares. I want some hidden in the gardens. I want some where no one will expect them." Her eyes lit up. "If we can enlist more gardeners and get more fert, I could really make something worthwhile. Something large enough to draw all the guards off the battlement and give us a chance to steal a few sniper weapons."

Rachel sucked in a breath. "Can you shoot one of those?"

"No, but I'm willing to have a crack. You?"

I balled my hands. "I'm willing to do anything."

"Same." Rachel nodded.

"Me too," Faiza whispered.

Seriousness fell over our little group.

"So...we're still forging ahead, then?" Mollie asked. "Victor is due back any day now."

"I know." Rachel cradled her stomach again. "We need to get as much done as possible."

We all nodded.

I stiffened, hating that I didn't have the science degrees or other know-how to help. "I'm sorry I haven't been able to contribute as much as you have. I hate that I'm not allowed to sleep in the slave quarters with you. This would be so much easier if we could—"

"There is *something* you can do," Rachel muttered, flicking a cagey look at Mollie. "Something that none of us can achieve. Only you."

"Of course." I swayed closer. "Anything."

"Rach." Mollie winced. "Are we sure we want to do this? I know we said he has potential, but he's still—"

"He protected us that night. He killed—"

"Wait...you're talking about Henri?" I whispered, my heart skipping.

Rachel pursed her lips. "The way he lost his shit on Kyle for hurting you. The way he kept us safe—"

"He's still a Master, Rach." Mollie crossed her arms. "He's still the enemy."

"Yes, but...what if he truly *was* acting like he said in those videos that day Victor almost shot him?" Rachel shivered. "What if he's like a triple-crosser, you know? A cop, turned baddie, but really still a cop?"

"You've watched way too many action movies." Mollie rolled her eyes.

"And you've turned into a cynic." Rachel shot back.

"Being raped by a necrophiliac will do that to a person," Mollie snapped.

I held up my hand. "You...you want me to ask Henri to join

us?"

Both girls slouched. "Want is a strong word. But…we might need someone who's above every rule. He can go anywhere he pleases. He can explain away his presence far easier than we can if he gets caught in certain areas—"

"Victor is still suspicious of him." I tensed. "He might not be as inconspicuous as you think."

"Then you tell us." Mollie looked me up and down. "You live with him. You sleep with him. How has he been since his mentor flew away? Has he taken to whispering to you again? Asking you to go along with him?"

My heart seized, hating that her question was so close to my own hope and reminding me all over again that Henri hadn't said yes.

"Has he hurt you in the past three weeks?" Rachel asked softly.

I caught her eyes. "He hasn't laid a single finger on me."

Rachel grabbed my hand. "That's a good thing, don't you see? The moment Victor left, he stopped. That has to mean he's still on your side. That he's still a—"

I clamped a hand over her mouth. "Don't say that word again. Twice is already too much." I shuddered, remembering my own voice echoing the word 'cop' thanks to Victor's show-and-tell with the video recordings. "He's not one. He's never been one. And I think…" I swallowed hard. "I think it's a risk to include him."

"You do?" Rachel pulled away from my hand.

I wished it were different.

I wished Henri would return to goodness and light before it was too late, but…I had to be smart about this. I wouldn't let my heart get in the way of my mind. My heart might be an idiot, but my mind had decided to get these jewels out.

They came before me.

They came before my scrambled feelings for Henri.

I wouldn't jeopardise them for anything or anyone.

I dropped my arms and nodded. "He's different. Ever since the night he carried Peter back here, he can barely look at me. He has the worst nightmares. He can't cope unless he's reading or typing. He…he isn't the same man who targeted and claimed me."

Mollie nodded. "See, Rach? It's a risk that even Ily doesn't want to take, and we both know she's caught feelings she shouldn't."

I flinched but didn't try to deny it.

Mollie continued. "He could tattle on us. We could all be killed by morning—"

"But what he did in that cave," Rachel murmured, cutting Mollie off. "The way he looked at you, Ily. Victor has *never* looked at me that way. In fact, I've never seen any Master become completely unhinged at someone else touching their jewel. Most of the time they just laugh and watch. He's possessive of you, and I think...I think if you could convince him that he could keep you, even if we managed to make a dramatic escape...he might help."

"Keep me?"

"You know...if you agree to stay his no matter where you guys end up."

I scowled and tapped my collar. "The minute this comes off, I won't *belong* to anyone ever again."

"I'm not saying you will." Rachel scowled. "I'm saying just make him believe it."

"Even if he did believe it. Even if I was the best actress in the world and convinced him we have a future together outside of here, he won't buy it and he won't go for it." I shook my head. Hating that truth stung my tongue.

"Why? You're the only one he wants. He hasn't touched another jewel—"

"You heard him that day. If he leaves here, his brother will hunt him down. He won't trade his life for ours. There's just no way."

"Maybe not our lives but yours..." Rachel whispered.

My heart skipped.

"And besides," —she continued— "he and his brother are family, whether they like it or not. And family forgives each other. If you convinced Henri that you'd fallen in love with him—that you'd stand by him no matter what. That you'd protect him from his brother...he might help. Not to help *us* but to keep you all to himself. He hates the other Masters. He slaughtered two of them that day without even batting an eye. He shot us, not because he was thinking about winning a game and earning a few more jewels for his twisted pleasure, but so others wouldn't lay a finger on us."

Pressing one of the faded bruises on her arm where Henri had layered both of them in red paint, she added, "Peter was right when he said he saw something good in him. I saw it too. It might've only been for a second, but...no other Master would've carried

Peter back for treatment." Rachel took my hand with a warm squeeze. "No other Master would've gone to the lengths he did to protect you. He loves you, Ily—"

"He what?" I stumbled back. "No, he—"

"I don't think he realises it himself yet, and I'm pretty sure he'd do whatever it took to prove otherwise, but…I think we could use him to get free…if *you* think he's trustworthy."

Loves me?

Ha!

My insides tangled at the thought.

Henri was many things. Kind in a dangerous way. Protective in a monstrous way. Messed up in *every* way. He couldn't even say my name anymore. Couldn't look at me, talk to me, touch me…

They're wrong.

If anything, his unwillingness to have anything to do with love was the reason he was here in the first place. Even the offer of staying with him in the outside world wouldn't be enough to make him rejoin it.

"What if he doesn't agree?" I asked quietly. "What if he's loyal to Victor and merely waiting for him to return?"

Rachel shook her head. "I think he's loyal to you."

"That's a lot of thinking, Rach." Mollie sighed heavily. "Know what I think? *I* think you've read too many romance novels."

"No. I just have eyes." Rachel sniffed. "I haven't been immune to feelings in this place. Crap, a year into being Victor's favourite, I truly thought I was falling for him. So yes, I admit I might not be the best judge of character. And bringing Henri into our little operation could backfire, but…you both said we need as many hands as possible. And I agree. The workload is immense. I want out of here before I'm seventy-five, so…we have to be prepared to use everything and *everyone* we can."

Goosebumps scattered down my arms.

I hung my head, a confession springing free. "I admit it's crossed my mind to ask him. It's on the tip of my tongue every night when he looks so tormented and tragic, but…he hasn't said much of anything to me since the night of Emerald Bruises. Each time I try to talk to him, he ignores me and acts as if he can't stand me. Whatever you think you saw between us is over and—"

My throat closed up.

God, that hurt.

Admitting that all the cold rebuffs and lack of intimacy hadn't been because he was sinking into places I couldn't go but perhaps because he no longer felt anything for me.

"Test him out tonight," Rachel murmured.

"Test him out?" I squeaked. "How?"

"Seduce him." Rachel leaned closer. "Give him whatever he likes and make him confess how he feels about you. Depending on his answer, tell him what we're planning or don't. We trust you to make the call."

I shivered. "And what if he doesn't react the way we hope? What if the man who tried to protect us no longer exists?"

Mollie shrugged. "Then he'll die with the rest of them."

My entire body flinched.

We all paused for a long moment, mulling over our separate tasks.

Finally, I whispered, "I know we said we'd try to blow this place up while Victor and the Masters are gone, but...we're nowhere near ready...are we?"

Mollie shook her head. "Unfortunately, no." Her eyes glinted. "But...Christmas is always quiet here. Most of the Masters go back to spend the holidays with families and oblivious little children. Victor will probably be in residence, and I would very, very much like to kill him so...if we plan our siege for around then, we'll stand the best chance."

My mind raced.

I'd been here a month.

It'd been the end of June when I'd gone to Paris with Sam.

That means it's August.

"So we have four months?" My throat closed up at the thought of enduring another *four months* in this place.

Then again, Peter had endured five years. Rachel three. Mollie who knew how long.

I could handle four months.

As long as we don't get caught.

If everything goes to plan, we'll be free in sixteen weeks.

And if you're not?

I shut off that thought immediately.

Failure was not an option.

This Christmas, Victor would receive a present he never saw coming. A firework display explosive enough to burn his entire island down. And if luck was on our side and karma kept us safe, he'd never go hunting for jewels again.

"Have you asked him yet?" Peter murmured.

I nibbled on a piece of apricot shortcake May had given us when we'd huddled in the larder's shadow four days later. Just Rachel, Peter, and me today. Mollie was busy making wicks in the slave quarters, hidden under her covers. Faiza had managed to sneak in three bottles of bleach, some pool chlorine, two bottles of pesticide, and even a bag of fertilizer pellets, courtesy of Willem, the gardener.

Our supplies were carefully tucked behind all the pasta, flour, and sugar boxes in the larder.

Peter leaned against the wall, his bandage-wrapped hands not as thick as that first day but still a nuisance. Passing him a napkin to protect his bandages, I gave him the rest of my shortcake.

He gave me a soft smile.

My heart surged with warmth, grateful for the friendship after the chilly few days I'd spent in Henri's company.

I'd tried to seduce him.

I'd deliberately stepped out of the bathroom and dropped my towel by 'accident'.

He choked and looked away.

I'd lain beside him and watched him type on that blasted laptop. I'd even touched his arm and sat up, leaning toward him like I had the night I'd been high on GHB.

He gritted his teeth and leapt out of bed.

He'd cradled his laptop and sat in the throne chair, resuming his frantic typing.

His grey eyes almost manic.

His skin etched with fine lines from lack of sleep.

For four awful days, I'd tried to get him to see me again.

To talk to me.

Touch me.

Fuck me.

And nothing.

He'd shut me out.

Cut me off.

Died right in front of me.

If he wasn't typing, he had his nose in a book or his gaze on far-off places. He often woke me in the night, tossing and turning, muttering in his sleep before violently waking as if ready to attack some phantom.

The nights he shot awake covered in sweat, he slipped out the door and didn't return until morning.

I'd followed him last night, my heart pinching as he made his way to the library and grabbed another book at random, diving into the pages as if it were an antidote to whatever poisoned his mind.

Pushing my worries away, I shook my head. "No, I haven't asked him."

"Why not?" Peter polished off the shortcake, his skin glowing a little healthier now that his fever had broken, and healing had progressed. Rachel stood beside him, her own skin glowing with pregnancy hormones, her dark hair extra luscious. The difference between being tortured every day and having three weeks of normalcy was blinding.

Looking back at Peter, I sighed heavily. "He doesn't even notice me anymore."

While Henri lost weight, Peter put it on. His eyes lost the desperate need to look after everyone. He still hobbled around with crutches and was confined to a chair or bed as much as possible—doctor's orders as his feet continued to heal—but I'd been there the last time his bandages had been changed, and the difference in his soles and palms from the day in the cave to now couldn't be compared.

"Oh he notices you, I can promise you that," Peter whispered, careful of the cameras despite their lack of hearing. "You said he hasn't touched you in weeks and it's obvious. He looks like a man on death row every time I see him."

Rachel added to Peter's list. "You say he's having nightmares and barely talks to you. Those are all signs of guilt, Ily."

Peter interrupted, "He's ashamed of what he's done because he's woken up and seen the light." Lowering his voice, he muttered, "You need to give him a reason to fight again. To fight on the right side."

"Peter's right," Rachel said. "It's the shame that's killing him. He needs a way to feel worthy."

"Give him a way to redeem himself." Peter crossed his arms.

I looked between the two of them and their seemingly planned attack. "I can't believe you're suddenly the president of his fan club." I met Peter's dark stare. "You said he's the worst of the worst."

"He is." Peter nodded. "And we need the worst on our side. Besides…" He shrugged. "I can't explain what I saw. But I know I saw *something*. Kyle helped Victor burn me. Kyle's the reason Suri and Dane chose to be shot and why so many of us have been carved and are missing pieces. I would've been grateful to anyone who stopped that fucker, but waking up just as Henri was stabbing him? I thought he was a goddamn angel."

I forced a smile even though my insides felt heavy. "You were on death's door, Paavak. I'm not surprised you saw angels."

He nodded. "I agree I hallucinated quite a bit at the end there. I thought you were burying me alive at one point—"

"We told you, Pete. We were dragging you *out* of the earth not pushing you into it." Rachel rolled her eyes with a grin.

Peter glanced at his bandaged hands. "I'm sorry I didn't wake to help you."

Rachel smirked. "It would've been a help, not gonna lie. You're skinny, but man, you're heavy."

He snickered.

My heart tangled with utter gratitude that my friends were okay even as I sank into a sea of confusion that Henri wasn't.

Well, most of my friends were okay.

Five jewels had lost their lives.

The knowledge of that refused to soak into my brain, almost as if my system protected me from the sheer horror of their deaths.

When we were free, then we could mourn.

For now…we needed to focus on the living, not the dead.

At least the seven slaves that'd been healing were now back in the dormitory with the rest. Peter had resumed his position as shepherd, and each day the Masters stayed away, the jewels grew a little braver in tiptoeing into the kitchens looking for food.

Peter didn't stop them as it covered our clandestine meetings. May and a few other cooks happily stuffed freshly baked croissants and delicious morsels into eager hands.

The guards got lazy and never stopped anyone. They watched. They followed sometimes. But no one told us no. No one electrified us if we went for a walk in the gardens or kept busy by helping other staff. I'd even heard Nancy and Rebecca had taken over looking after the chickens, spending all day out there.

The only one who seemed determined to die was Kirk.

His fight had ended with Suri.

He didn't speak a word to any of us.

He stayed on his own, sleeping or sitting on the balcony with its black barred birdcage trapping him, denying him the chance to jump and join Suri.

He had the same hollow look in his eyes that Henri did.

I froze.

Henri...

Was that what the broken-hearted look was? A reflection of all the shattered pieces within?

Does he want to die?

He'd tried once before.

The scar on his leg revealed evidence of that desperation.

Could he...could he do it again?

Urgent fear. Terrible premonition.

God, how had I not seen it?

Before, this place was a playground for demons. Now, it was a heavenly holiday for the jewels.

Henri was the only demon left in their midst, and it showed.

Everyone ignored him.

The guards didn't go near him, the staff stayed clear, and the jewels darted away if he came close. He acted as if it didn't bother him to be so blatantly unwanted, but...every day, he retreated a little more, sank a little more, became a little less alive than before.

"I-I have to go." I backed away.

Panic fizzled in my blood.

What if he'd done it?

What if he'd hurt himself all while I'd been too focused on escape to notice he'd fallen so far into his own imprisonment?

"You're going to ask him?" Rachel arched an eyebrow.

"We're running out of time," Peter whispered. "We won't be able to keep meeting like this when the Masters are back in residence. We'll probably have hell to pay once Victor sits down and sees how often we've come into the kitchens. Hopefully, he'll just think we're being pigs and indulging in food while he's not here to enforce his smoothie rule, but...we need to get everything locked away so we all know our jobs and can keep working without checking in with each other."

I nodded. "I know."

Stepping into me, Peter murmured, "Don't be afraid of using him for your own ends, *jaanu*. You have to know how he feels about you. Use that to your advantage. Don't let your goodness get in the way of manipulating him."

I hid my shiver at the thought of being cruel enough to wield someone's emotions for my own gain.

But…it wasn't just about me.

My shoulders rolled and honesty spilled free despite myself. "I think whatever you saw the night he killed Kyle might've died in that cave too. He can barely look at me anymore and…and the truth is." I looked down, unable to keep eye contact. "I asked him to play along with me the night of Emerald Bruises. I was as high as a kite and let my guard down. I practically begged him to choose me. I said if the guy who asked me to play along with him was still in there to play with me now."

Peter sucked in a breath. "What did he say?"

"He didn't say anything." I looked up and stepped back. "And that's the problem."

Peter studied my eyes. His own gave too much away. Asking me to seduce Henri hurt him. His love for me exceeded the bounds of friendship. And every day he grew stronger, I feared he'd step over the line between us and force me to admit that I loved him as deeply as I did my brother, but…the tormented beast I slept with conjured a different sort of—

Not love.

Never that.

What I felt for Henri had no title, no definition.

It was just…*ugh*.

Kissing Peter's cheek, I smiled at the girls and backed away. "Look, I'll try again tonight. I'll do whatever it takes to find out if Henri can be trusted. I'll see you later."

Slipping out of the kitchens, I broke into a run.

Henri would most likely be in the library working.

That would give me time to figure out how the hell I could get through to him…before it was too late.

Chapter Eighteen

Henri

THE CURSE OF BLOOD & DARKNESS
by
Henri Mercer

THE BOY WHO WOULD NEVER be my brother, despite the shared blood in our veins, appeared in the wing of the house where we were kept.

He emerged covered in blood. A gun in his hand and murder in his eyes. He looked at us as if we were something he'd scraped off his shoe. A hoard of children sired by his father, a harem of women who'd been his chattel.

Two of my little sisters crawled into my arms, breaking into wails as Quincy strode amongst our midst. Counting us, he nodded, then spun on his heel and left.

A day later, the locks on the doors and the bars on the windows were removed. Our mothers were interviewed and given rooms. Their children going with them.

By the time my mother and I were dragged before the new lord and master, my mother had pissed herself in fear and I prepared to kill him if he laid a single finger on her like our father had.

Instead, he'd handed her an envelope and offered to send her home.

We'd been flown far, far away.

I didn't get to say goodbye to my half-blooded siblings.

And that was when the loneliness set in.

Amnesia wrapped my memories in forgetfulness far stronger

than the blackouts of before.
I'd deliberately forgotten what my father did to those women so I didn't pass on the curse to my sisters and brothers.
But now I deleted those siblings from my mind so I didn't have to suffer heartbreak every time I remembered I'd once had a family, and now I had none—

Digging my fingers into my eyes, I highlighted every fucking word I'd written so far and deleted them. Every comma, paragraph, and memory. Hours upon hours' worth of transcribing all gone.

Pointless.

Ridiculous.

Agonising.

I didn't want to remember anymore.

I wanted peace.

The longer I stayed here with Ily trying to seduce me and the castle whispering I was sane instead of twisted, the more I sank deeper and deeper.

Every part of me was heavy.

Lethargy turned into quicksand, clinging to my limbs every time I tried to move, to think, to talk. I couldn't remember the last time I'd spoken out loud. I'd let my fingers do all my speaking and my mind—

I've had enough.

Slamming the laptop closed, I swooped to my feet and stalked out of the library.

I was done with the past.

Done with everything.

I wanted out.

I needed to run before I lost my fucking mind.

Stalking up the stairs, I ignored the opulence surrounding me. My fingers almost dented the laptop as I took the steps two at a time and practically ran down the corridor.

Exploding into my chamber, Ily squeaked and leapt back from where she'd been rummaging in the wardrobe. Hugging a baggy beige jumper that seemed to be the only thing of substance Victor had ordered for her, she backed up with eyes wide. The sight of her clothes hanging with mine. The fact that we'd been living together for weeks. That I still wanted to hurt her even now…

Christ!

Throwing the laptop onto the bed, I bolted into the bathroom and slammed the door.

Grabbing the sink, I breathed hard.

The screams as my father molested his current woman.

The whippings, the bleedings, the rapes—

Panic latched around my throat.

My vision went hazy.

That's inside me.

That curse would never stop.

Until the day I died, the madness that'd lived within him would live within me, and the only way to stop it was to kill the host. Just like Q did back then. He'd shot our father in cold blood, then turfed us out of his inherited estate all because he knew.

He *knew* he'd end up having to kill us if we stayed because we were all infected—

I gagged.

That damn fucking nausea was back.

"Henri?" A tentative knock on the door.

My head tipped down.

Guilt festered with the putridness inside me.

Go away, little nightmare.

I beg you.

"Are you…are you okay?" The door opened a crack.

I bared my teeth and spun to face her. "*Get out!*"

She blanched and backed up.

The fear in her eyes.

The hate beneath all her sweet obedience.

Ah shit.

My lunch reappeared as I crashed to my knees by the toilet. Closing my eyes, I rode through the wracking heaves and flushed my shame the moment my body had purged.

Staggering to my feet, I grabbed my toothbrush, scrubbed away all the shit I could never say, then spat minty froth into the sink.

By the time I'd splashed ice-cold water on my face, the attack had faded, leaving me jittery and guilty and *fuck*…

I yelled at her.

My first words to her in weeks, and they'd been delivered with violence.

I flinched.

She'd asked me why I'd scolded her. Asked why I'd said such cutting things to her when Victor interrogated me all while I stood dripping in Kyle's cold blood.

I'd snapped because she stood up to Victor even then.

I'd put her in her place because she was so much braver than me, so much *better* than me, and if Victor grew to know her resilience like I had, he'd do his utmost to break it.

It was the one thing I couldn't protect her from in here.

The one man I wouldn't be able to stop from taking her.

My only weapon was to belittle Ily to the point she became completely undesirable in his eyes. If I could reduce her to nothing and demean her to the point she lost all intrigue, then…*she'll be safe*.

Smoothing back my longer hair, I sucked in a deep breath and prepared to go back out there. To apologise. To do my best to explain the unexplainable shit inside me.

Only…

A heavy drone.

The telltale growl of an aircraft engine coming in to land.

No…

Bursting out of the bathroom, I spied Ily by the window.

Her face gilded in metallic pigments of red and gold from the setting sun, her eyes never straying from Victor's private plane as it touched down beyond the wall.

I moved to her side, but we didn't say a word as the plane came back into view as it taxied on thick grass, its engines screaming in the dusk.

Sighing heavily, Ily hugged her beige knit jumper. Her skin broke out in goosebumps beneath her skimpy black dress. I didn't think the early autumn chill caused her to shiver but the arrival of monsters.

Masters had returned to indulge in sin and sadism—leaving behind naïve spouses and transforming into animals the moment they arrived.

I shuddered as the drawbridge slowly clanked open, forming a pathway over the moat.

The final spiels of sunset shone through, welcoming the men to step inside and undergo their metamorphosis of evil.

"They're a few days early," Ily whispered, her golden eyes full of worry. Flicking me a glance, she forgot the month-long silence between us and murmured, "Do you think Victor will summon you tonight?"

I backed up.

Another clutch of panic fisted my heart.

I couldn't answer her.

If he requested my presence, I didn't know if I'd have the strength to perform like last time.

He'd see right through me.

See me breaking…

She sighed and turned to follow me. Gathering her jumper tighter against her, she whispered, "Henri, I…there's something I need to ask you—"

A soft plop on the carpet by her feet.

Something dull and plasticy, shaped just like the gems from that godawful treasure hunt.

It rolled to a stop by her foot.

Glancing down, she frowned, blinked, then gasped in absolute horror.

"Oh no…God, no." Dropping to her knees, she tossed her jumper away and snatched the cloudy gem. "Please don't be what I think this is." Her hands shook as she cracked open the faceted container as if it was a grenade.

My heart pounded as if she'd pulled out its pin and it would explode at any moment.

"Wh-Where did you get this?" She ripped out the piece of paper inside. "Did you hide it? Do you know what it says? Why didn't you *say* anything?"

I frowned, my ears ringing.

In all honesty, I'd forgotten about it.

A maid must've placed it in the wardrobe because I didn't recall what I did with it once I'd carried Ily into the shower and touched her all over, ensuring she was intact after what those bastards had done to her.

When I didn't reply, she unfurled the chit, staggered to her feet, and tripped sideways.

I caught her elbow on instinct, keeping her standing.

She didn't even notice me touching her.

Her face shock-white, entire body trembling.

Reading over her, I scanned the small scroll.

This entitles one of Victor's illustrious guests a rare and exclusive right to a Diamond Kiss. (Terms and conditions to be discussed on what jewel is chosen and time of kiss given.)

With a sharp cry, she grabbed it with both hands and went to tear—

I clamped my fingers around her cuffed wrist, stopping her. "What are you doing?"

Her gaze landed on my lips as if shocked I'd spoken.

She struggled in my grasp. "I have to destroy this. He can't know you have it."

"Victor?"

"Yes!" Fighting me, she cried out as I snatched the piece of paper out of her hand. "Henri…don't. You can't. You have to get rid of it. Right now."

"Why?"

Why had this tiny thing sent her into such a tailspin?

Her panic interrupted mine for once, giving me a quick reprieve from the deep, dark depression I couldn't shed.

"It's the prize Peter was trying to find in the storm," she whisper-hissed as if the cameras hadn't already heard. "If Victor finds out you have this…" She shook her head, flicking a look at the always recording red dot.

Too late…

Her shoulders slouched as she came to the same conclusion. Tears glossed her golden stare. "Is that why you kept it?" She swayed. "Do you…do you plan on using it…with me?"

My heart kicked at her fear, her hatred. "I literally have no idea what you're talking about." Rubbing my mouth, I shrugged. "I've heard Victor mention a Diamond Kiss before but don't know what twisted game it involves."

"It's murder, you fool," she hissed, snatching back the chit and trying to hide it. "A Diamond Kiss is *murder*."

"*Murder*?" I tripped back.

A hot tear ran down her cheek.

The inhuman urge to drink it down crippled me.

I stepped toward her without control, my tongue desperate to lick.

Her eyes widened. Her tears stopped. She went to dash past me, but I grabbed her around the middle, pressed my lips to her soft cheek, and captured that salty droplet.

She inhaled sharply.

I used her shock to grab the chit and wrench it from her hold.

Letting her go, I marched away. My blood singing from her

taste.

"Henri…" She charged after me, following me into the bathroom where I'd flushed one lot of shame already tonight.

She skidded to a stop beside me just as I tore up the piece of paper until it resembled a million tiny squares. Without a word, I flushed it.

Together, we watched the scraps swirl around and around before vanishing.

Neither of us spoke for the longest moment.

Ily made a choked noise, wrenching my gaze to her as she tripped backward and crashed into the towel rail. "Even with it gone, the cameras…"

I nodded. "He knows."

I'd seen this woman argue with Victor, stand up to Masters, and endure a hundred awful things, but I'd never seen pure terror on her face.

Until now.

Clawing at her collared throat as if she couldn't breathe, her knees buckled—

Darting forward, I caught her.

In a moment of insanity, I scooped her into my arms and cradled her ever so close.

My world righted.

My darkness paused.

Christ, she felt good.

So, *so* good.

I could barely breathe as I carried her into the bedroom and tucked her into bed.

Her chest rose and fell, her eyes glazed with panic.

For a moment, I forgot she hated me, forgot she feared me as she looked at me for comfort and safety.

Tucking black hair behind her ear, I bent over her and whispered, "You've walked on eggshells around me all month. You've kneeled for me when I didn't ask you to. You've tried to seduce me when I've done my utmost to give you space. You've turned into one of *them*—a broken obedient jewel—and now…now you think I would happily cash in a voucher that gives me the right to murder you." Inhaling her perfect scent, I sighed, "I knew you hated me, nightmare, but I had no idea how deep that hatred goes."

Grabbing my hand, she shook her head. "It's not like that. I—

"

"Go to sleep." Wrenching my fingers from her hold, I swallowed back another wave of darkness. "Don't touch me, don't fear me. I'm the winner of that prize, and I'm not going to use it, okay? That's the end of it."

Before she could say anything I couldn't survive, I turned on my heel and left.

The knife dripped black with blood.
My blood.
I dropped it, and it tumbled into shadow.
The wound in my leg kept growing, growing.
The shadows kept creeping, creeping from my puddling lifeforce on the floor. Every heartbeat, the shadows grew thicker and taller, sucking all the light from the room.
A chasm, not a room.
Rock all around me, cold and entombing like a crypt.
My crypt.
Someone walked toward me.
Someone with light for blood and sunshine glowing eyes.
"Ily…" I stepped toward her, yanked to a stop by shackles made of shadow.
Luminous tears rolled down her cheeks, glowing brighter and brighter. "You have to set me free, Henri. Let me go before you're completely swallowed."
I kicked at the shadows restraining me and marched toward her.
Fingers of black jerked me back before I could touch her.
"Help me," I whispered. "Kiss me."
She cried harder. "You wish to kiss me? That's all you have to offer me after everything you've already taken?"
"A kiss is worth far more to me than anything else."
"A kiss from you is death." She hung her head. "But perhaps…that's the only freedom I'll earn from you." Her skin kept glowing—a perfect star lighting up all my blackness. She stepped into me and tipped up her chin. "Go on then. Kiss me. Kill me."
Darkness swamped both of us. If it wasn't for her light, we'd be blinded by my night.
"I'd never kill you, Ily."
I.L.Y.
I love you.

"You already have." *Another iridescent tear rolled; I longed to drink it down.*

My neck bent.
Our noses brushed.
So close.
So fucking close.
Stop!
I jerked back.
Kissing her wouldn't kill her, but it would kill me.
I'd die from the want, the need, the heartbreaking desperation that made everything so damn hard. "Wait—"
"No." Catching my cheeks with her luminous hands, she tugged my head down. "Do us both a favour and end it."
"Ily, don't—"
She kissed me.
A thunderbolt crashed.
She screamed.
She dropped to my feet, open-eyed and...dead.
Pain I'd never felt before crushed me.
Every memory. Every horror. Every loneliness.
Shadows shot down my throat.
Love broke me into pieces.
Ily's corpse broke into light-bright fractures, shattering into stardust.
I dropped to my knees.
My heart turned to coal.
I howled—

"Henri! Henri!"

My eyes snapped wide.

Ily sat on top of me, her thighs straddling my waist, her hands shaking my shoulders.

S-She's still alive.

I wasn't responsible for my actions.

For the blistering thankfulness and motherfucking tears stabbing behind my eyes.

Just a nightmare.
Thank fuck, just a nightmare.

Jack-knifing up, I grabbed her around the waist and tossed her onto the bed. I rolled over her. Trapped her beneath me. Imprisoned her where she belonged. Where she would *always* belong.

With my mind completely gone and my heart utterly broken, I nuzzled her neck, kissed her cheek, then smashed my mouth to hers.

She froze.

She cried out.

She couldn't stop me.

Another kiss.

Another stolen moment where I didn't know which one of us would die.

My arms coiled around her until she gasped in pain.

Her slenderness, her heat, her strength—everything about her shattered the forcefield around my depressed-crippled heart, and I couldn't do it.

Couldn't handle loving this woman all while she hated me.

Couldn't kiss this woman all while she accepted my abuse instead of fought me off.

As suddenly as I'd covered her, I ripped myself away.

Breathing hard, I shot out of bed and rubbed sleep and nightmares from my eyes. With trembling hands, I wrenched open the bedside table.

There.

Just where I'd left them.

Two birdcage cufflinks.

Snatching them into my fist, I charged for the door.

I ignored Ily's sharp question about where I was going.

I did my best to shut down the sickness inside me.

As I bolted down the stairs, the evening came spooling back.

I'd ripped up the Diamond Kiss chit.

I'd left Ily before I could shatter and prowled around the castle all while a few early Masters reacquainted themselves with their chambers.

Victor hadn't returned.

I hadn't been summoned.

I'd waited until two a.m. before going back to her, grateful to find Ily asleep in our bed.

She'd faced my side.

Hugged my pillow to her chest.

I'd slipped under the covers and stared at her. I'd memorised every eyelash, then fallen asleep…

I shuddered.

My other nightmares had been of sisters I couldn't save.

Mothers I'd abused.

They'd been absolutely agonising, but this one? This one tore me into motherfucking pieces.

She chose death over me.

She hates me.

I sucked in air.

I gagged on oxygen.

Smashing my way out of the fortress, I broke into a sprint toward the battlement wall. Moonlight splashed so bright, it lit up the gardens like a silver midday. Pewter shadows and monochrome grass blurred as I ran faster, faster.

She hates me.

Hates me.

Said my mind.

You love her.

Love her.

Said my heart.

Make it stop.

Make it stop.

Begged my soul.

Only one person could do that.

Only one brother who'd promised to end me.

I was ready for peace.

I wanted it over.

Reaching the wall, I sucked in huge heaves of oxygen and searched for the cameras.

No blinking red lights.

No guards and their snipers.

With all my strength, I hurled the cufflinks over the wall.

Victor's satellite probably covered this entire island.

The cufflinks would most likely never send out their coordinates.

But if there was a chance.

A minuscule, microscopic chance.

I needed to try.

Because…*I'm done.*

Come find us, brother.

Save her.

Kill me.

Find us both…

Dropping to my knees, I sucked in gulps of moonlight.

My final act on this earth would be to get Ily the fuck out of here.

And then…I could die and finally be free.

Chapter Nineteen

Ily

VICTOR ARRIVED FOUR DAYS LATER.

The friends he'd permitted to return flew in before him—as if they couldn't tolerate being away for so long. They behaved themselves and didn't cause any issues. They didn't even play with any jewels, preferring to decompress by the pools and drink long into the night.

I managed to meet Peter, Faiza, Mollie, and Rachel one more time before we all decided it would be too risky with a full house once again.

We had our tasks. We had our timeframe.

We would continue gathering supplies, making presents, and hiding them around the castle where no one would find them until it was too late. Faiza had recruited three other cleaners who helped smuggle Mollie's gifts under loads of laundry and trolleys full of fresh sheets and towels. They had instructions to ensure every Master's room had at least one explosive hidden inside.

Everything seemed to be going as smoothly as it could.

Apart from Henri.

I touched my lips where I sat by our bedroom window, looking down at the gardens below.

That nightmare a few nights ago had been the worst one yet. He'd often woken me thrashing and tossing, but this was the first time he'd screamed.

His voice had cracked.

His hands had grabbed at shadows.

Pure despair poured from him, and I couldn't let him stay in such misery.

I'd woken him.

He'd kissed me.

And then he'd bolted off and hadn't come back.

Goosebumps erupted, recalling the way he'd ripped up the

Diamond Kiss chit. The gesture had sent my heart flying. The clench of his jaw lit me up with hope.

I'd wanted to ask him there and then.

To finally test to see if he would be on our side, but…he'd avoided me ever since.

He never seemed to sleep.

He'd lost more weight.

His grey eyes always black with nightmares.

Each time I reached out to him, he shrank away as if my touch physically hurt him. Each time I tried to speak, he shut down.

The helplessness as he faded before my eyes drove me mad.

If I didn't manage to break through to him soon…

My eyes strayed to the switchblade he'd smuggled here in the lining of his jacket.

It sat smugly on his bedside table, the blade tucked away, the handle metallic and smooth.

He'd returned with it yesterday.

At some point, he'd gone up to Victor's dead zoo where he'd drawn my blood and taken me on the cross. He'd reclaimed that sharp little knife…for what?

For protection from the Masters roaming the halls again?

To slay the monsters in his mind when he woke up screaming in the dark?

Or for something else?

He needs to talk to me.

He'd bottled up far too many things.

Every feeling had noosed around his throat until he hung on that rope, slowly choking.

But how could I get him to talk in a place where talking was so treacherous?

It wasn't a simple matter of sitting down and clearing the air between us.

I'd often gotten so frustrated at couples who never talked through their problems. So many issues could be solved with a frank and accepting conversation.

But here, under the constant watch of cameras?

Everything I needed to say was treasonous and everything he had to say was probably far too personal for an audience.

Didn't stop the words lingering on the tip of my tongue.

Assurances that I didn't hate him, that I cared, that I trusted him despite the mess between us—

The door crashed open.

As if I'd summoned him by thinking about him, Henri appeared.

Dressed in black jeans and a black t-shirt, he looked like a man who'd already been hung from the gallows, and now only his ghost haunted me.

"He's here," he muttered.

My ears rang, so used to his silence by day and screams by night.

It took a while for those two words to compute. "He's here?"

"He's summoned all of us. We're to gather in the ballroom."

"Victor." I shuddered and crossed my arms.

"Victor." He nodded.

Marching into the bathroom, he closed the door.

Victor was back.

Yippee.

Sunshine streamed through the ballroom's stained-glass windows, determined to give no places for shadows and evil to hide, forcing them out into the open.

Unlike all the other times Henri had fed me in here—all the nights I'd kneeled at his feet and done my best to stay quiet while jewels acted out pornos and Masters stuffed their faces, there were no scents of dinner or slaves dressed up for a show.

The stage was empty.

The aura of the room tense with expectation.

My ears pricked as two Masters a table away shot us a look. Their whispers couldn't be deciphered, but the way they gawked at Henri hinted at what they spoke about.

They still thought he was either a cop or a killer.

Weeks had passed, and still, their suspicions fogged the room.

Drinks were served, and Henri sat fisting his beer glass, his eyes skimming the crowd of men, some with a jewel at their feet and others sitting together, quietly chatting. A few awful rounds of laughter. A quick squeak from a slave getting reprimanded.

I flinched as I caught the jewel's eye. Corinne. Bowing her head, she used her hair to curtain her face.

Sucking in a breath, I scanned the room.

Twenty-two guests.

I'd hoped Victor would see fit to revoke more memberships than he had. Seemed the month long abstinence from this place ensured an eager crowd.

I counted the guards next.

Twelve ringed the doorways dotted around the ballroom.

Mollie was right.

We were severely outnumbered. Hopefully in four months, when we'd done all we could and Christmas rolled around, there'd be half this number of patrons. A quarter. We'd need all our strength to fight the guards without fearing the Masters and their electricity remotes.

My heart rabbited as I stroked my collar.

I hadn't had the opportunity to test to see if it was still inactive. Even if it was…it didn't suddenly open doors that'd once been closed. I couldn't waltz over the drawbridge and hail a taxi. I couldn't send telepathic messages to my brother and give him our address.

Telepathic.

I stiffened as I recalled a few more twin flame notes that Krish and I had researched: *The intensity between you and your twin flame can sometimes cause phenomena like telepathy and psychic connections. An intense connection of belonging and yearning. An inner pull that can't be ignored or stopped. Your bond can be so profound, you begin to feel the other's pain, desire, and stress.*

Was that why I could sense Henri's unravelling?

Were we that connected even when we both struggled against it?

Sighing heavily, I dropped my fingers from my collar.

My eyes snapped to Peter across the ballroom.

My heart instantly squeezed.

He kneeled like the rest of us next to a Master with a bushy brown beard. The man's large belly sat on his thighs as he chuckled at something another Master said.

Peter gave me half a smile as our eyes met. The shadow of a bruise on his cheekbone made my hands ball with fury.

He wasn't even out of bandages yet, and someone had already struck him.

My heart didn't just ache. It tore.

Fucking bastards.

All of them.

They'll die.

We'll make sure of—

A loud bang and a shrill scream sounded beyond the double doors to the ballroom, capturing everyone's attention. Masters quietened. Jewels flinched.

Peter winced and shook his head.

He mouthed something I didn't catch, then sighed and looked away.

"Good afternoon, my dear friends!" Victor suddenly appeared, arms aloft like a returning conqueror, black suit impeccable, his stride eating up the dance floor with eager, powerful strides. "I can't tell you how good it is to be home."

A murmur of welcomes.

A few men stood to shake his hand.

Henri stiffened, his knee touching my shoulder. He smiled when Victor nodded in his direction, but he didn't wave or clap like some of the others. Throwing his beer down his throat, he slammed his glass onto the table and snapped his fingers for another.

A server placed another ice-dewy glass before him just as Victor finished his parade to the podium and leapt up the steps.

Trim and toned, he didn't look his age, despite the grey tinsel in his hair. His navy eyes glinted and his skin glowed as if he'd just stepped off a plane after the best holiday of his life.

Sick bastard.

Smirking at the Masters and jewels scattered around different tables, he bowed with a flourish. "Welcome back, everyone. Welcome home."

"Thanks for the invite, Vic!" A few Masters toasted him.

"Appreciate the second chance." Another tipped his chin.

"Yes, yes, you're quite welcome." Victor straightened and clasped his hands in front of him. "I'm sure you've all taken my instructions to heart, and we will have no more mishaps, yes?"

"Definitely." Two Masters nodded.

"We'll play within the guidelines from now on, never fear." Another laughed.

"Good, I'm glad." Victor bounced on the balls of his feet, brimming with energy. "In that case…I have gifts for you. But first…how has everyone been?"

"Better now we're all back, Vic!" someone said.

"Come on, show us the new stock, mate!" Another snickered. "I caught a glimpse of them when you arrived, and a couple looked right up my alley!"

Oh God.

My skin pebbled with frost and fire.

How many?

How many had been trafficked into this hellhole this time?

How many more do we need to save?

Another bang in the foyer followed by a pitiful cry.

Sickness crawled up my throat.

Henri stiffened.

Peter rolled his shoulders across the room, knowing better than I did what was coming.

I'm no longer the new girl...

"So impatient." Victor laughed. "But...seeing as you're all so keen to see what I've brought you, fine. We can catch up over dinner later." Clicking his fingers, he raised his voice. "Bring them in."

The floor beneath my knees turned into an arctic tundra as two guards shepherded eight new faces into the ballroom.

Eight?

The room swam.

God, *eight?*

Peter sucked in a breath, his stare snagging mine with matching horror.

The past month of preparing for a jail break seemed utterly pointless as six girls and two boys were prodded at gunpoint toward the stage.

Even if we managed to claim our freedom in four months, the amount of abuse these poor souls would endure. The terror they'd feel. The pain—

A sharp gasp ripped my gaze to Mollie. She knelt beside Roland's polished shoes, her hands balled on her bare thighs. We just nodded at each other. Our plan had to work. There was no other option.

I couldn't exist in a world where men like Victor got away with using people like throwaway toys. Even if we got out, I would never stop hunting others like him, doing my best to prevent anyone else from living this awful, *awful* nightmare.

Henri inhaled sharply, his knee digging harder against my shoulder as if he needed to touch me. Needed that connection so he didn't do something ill-advised.

Glancing up at him, I flinched.

His jaw clenched so tightly, the tendons in his throat popped like ropes beneath his skin. Sweat glittered on his temples. His slightly longer hair curled a little over his forehead, making his hollow cheeks all the more severe.

"And here they are, gentlemen. It has been a successful hunt, I must say." Victor chuckled as the eight new jewels all shuffled and sniffled, herded at gunpoint through the ballroom.

Jittery steps, wet cheeks, wild eyes.

The flash of newly fastened collars and cuffs.

The stench of terror and dismay.

All naked.

Clapping his hands again, Victor waited until the sounds of appreciation and wolf whistles had silenced before beckoning the guards to march the new jewels onto the stage.

"Aren't they precious?" Victor ran his fingers through the blonde hair of the closest girl. "So pretty. So young."

"Where did you find them, Vic?" asked the brown-bearded guy currently running his fingers over Peter's hunched shoulder.

"Oh, I've been all over, *mon ami*," Victor replied, eyeing up each new jewel as the guards ushered them into a trembly line. "I do hope you like them."

"Pass one here, and I'll tell you if I like them or not." An untoned, dark-skinned man laughed.

The cold in my bones turned glacial.

My heart riddled with frostbite.

He'll die.

And him.

And him.

And him.

All of them.

"Yes, yes, you're all at liberty to play, of course. But first." Victor grinned. "Allow me to introduce you to our newest members of my Jewelry Box. I do hope you will make them feel welcome."

A few men chuckled. "Hell yeah, we'll make them feel welcome. *Very* welcome."

Victor gave the man a tight smile, then prowled along the line and planted his hands on the smallest girl's shoulders. Looming over her from behind, he looked like the worst kind of predator. "First up, this is…what was your name again, my sweetling?" He squeezed her until she winced and dropped her eyes. With black hair and a gaunt frame, she didn't look old enough to graduate high-school, let alone be trafficked into this place.

Horror filled me.

Despair followed.

Henri shifted on his chair as my insides crawled.

"Are you squirmin' because you want a piece, or are you uncomfortable, Henri?"

My eyes shot to the table next to ours.

Henri grunted and swallowed hard. "What?"

An older red-headed man who'd lurked around since the beginning smirked. Patting Nancy on her head where she knelt next to him, he grinned. "I've seen you around. I watched you fuck your little tidbit the night of the storm. Despite the minor misunderstanding of your profession as a cop, I thought you'd slotted right in."

Henri gave him a tight smile. "Then what's your problem?"

The man leaned closer, his eyes mean. "My point is you're very tightly wound. I would've expected the opposite, seeing as you were the only one allowed to stay. You're not the one who had to tame himself back in society. You've been here the whole time, fucking your jewel, being who you truly are." He waved a limp wrist in Henri's direction. "So why are you so...*jumpy*?"

Henri stiffened. "Forgive me if I still have a shred of empathy. They're new. This will be overwhelming. I remember how my first day felt, and I was on the opposite side of the collar."

"Could always shackle one around your neck too, hey? Let you feel firsthand what they're going through?" He snickered. "Perhaps you're a cop after all, and that's why you're curling your lip at the new merchandise."

"Can't help it if they're not my type."

"No." The man narrowed his eyes on me. "Turns out *she's* your type, and you're not the sharing kind."

Henri went terrifyingly still. "You're right. I'm not."

"Pity." The Master chuckled. "But oh well. Eight new treats to sample. Tell me." He rubbed his chin and looked at the jewels on the stage. "Have *any* caught your eye because I have first dibs on the blonde and would hate to find you being annoying and paying yet another fortune to keep her out of our reach."

"Nope. She's all yours," Henri muttered.

"You bloody bastard," I hissed under my breath, my rage pouring free.

Peter's head snapped up across the ballroom. Rachel shot me a wide-eyed look as she kneeled by the stage waiting for Victor.

Oops.

I hadn't meant to say that.

Henri wasn't the one I was furious with.

It was this.

This sick energy percolating in here. The rancid lust from horrible men and petrified fear from captives.

Rolling my shoulders, I whispered, "Sorry, I didn't mean—"

"Yes, you did." Henri sighed with stark weariness, not reacting to my fire.

I hated that he didn't react. If he snapped. If he snarled. If he burned with me...there'd still be a chance. A chance he was still in there...still the one person I couldn't stand to want and the one man I needed above all others.

"I am a bastard." He nodded.

I hated the monotone, the dead tone.

Twisting to look at him, my temper sparked again, driven by loss and loneliness. "You know what? You *are* a bastard."

He froze.

His grey eyes flared.

The other Master huffed and looked back at the stage.

God, Ily...now what have you done?

But something pushed me, needled me.

He had to snap somehow. He had to wake from whatever misery had drugged him.

Slowly, incredibly, a flare of silver light appeared in his shutdown stare. "You're agreeing with me now? After trying to come onto me all month?" Bending over me, he breathed into my ear, "I might be a bastard, but I'm the only one ensuring you stay alive."

"How? By ignoring me?"

"By staying the fuck away from you," he snarled.

Finally.

Passion.

Pain and passion and spark.

I raised my chin. "So you're not a bastard...you're just an asshole."

God, Ily!

It didn't even make sense.

I had no idea what I was doing yet...

Henri shifted and speared his fingers through my loose hair. Dragging me closer, he groaned, "*Fuck*, I've missed you calling me names."

The way he trembled.

The way my heart *pounded*.

Everything erupted with life.

His eyes dropped to my mouth.

And I let stupidity and instinct rule me. "Fuck you."

He shuddered. His eyes snapped shut. When they opened again, they blazed. "You have no idea how badly I—"

"Ah, Henri." Victor chuckled, cutting through our flaming chemistry like a garotte. "Back to your whispers, hmm?"

As if he remembered where he was. As if the weight and blackness of the past month leapt on him in one move, Henri sagged in his chair and let me go. "*Je suis désolé*, Vic." He forced a grin. "Please…continue."

"Do you wish to share with the rest of the class?" Victor smiled at me. "Ilyana…what did he say to you?"

Ignoring Peter's, Rachel's, and Mollie's fearful eyes, I sneered. "Only that he plans on fucking me the moment you finish waffling on."

For a moment, Victor didn't say anything. His eyes gleamed as if he knew more than he let on. Finally, he laughed delicately and glanced at Henri. "We'll catch up tonight, *mon ami*. We have much to discuss."

Henri jerked a nod as Victor turned his attention back to the blonde beside him.

"Your name, sweetling. I won't ask again."

The poor girl rattled with shakes. "L-Laura." Tears spilled down her cheeks.

Victor stroked her shoulders. "Good girl. See? That wasn't so hard, was it?"

Clasping her hand, he raised it in his. "Everyone, please give a very warm welcome to the lovely Laura."

"Please!" Laura begged, tugging where Victor held her. "This must be some mistake. I-I'm not meant to be here. I only left my boyfriend for five minutes. H-He'll be looking for me. This is a mistake. Please, *please* take me back."

"Sweetling, there is no mistake." Victor let her go. "You're home, whether you like it or not."

Striding past her, he touched the next girl—a curvy dark

blonde with large nipples. "Gentlemen, this is Chloe." He smiled kindly. "I remember you as it's such a pretty name to go with your very pretty face."

Chloe shied away, but Victor didn't reprimand her.

Striding to the third girl, he ran his hands over her corkscrew brown curls. "And this is Tanya." He glanced down. "It is Tanya, correct? My memory is starting to go on me, I'm afraid."

"I-It's Talia." She flinched back from his caress.

"Another pretty name." Victor pressed a fatherly kiss on her forehead. Turning to face the crowd, he beamed. "Say hello to Talia, my dear friends!"

"Wait. Please. I-I don't want to be here," Talia begged. "I was only supposed to sleep with one guy. That's what the escort service said. I-I have a daughter back at home—"

"Ahh, Vic." A grumble of voices sounded from Victor's despicable guests. "A mother? Fuck that. What the hell?"

"I've been assured she's tight, gentlemen." Victor held up his hand. "Don't begrudge the gifts I'm giving you before you've had a play, yes?"

Glancing down the line, he commanded, "Start from the end. Please give us your name, and then you'll be permitted to rest. It's been a long trip, and I'm aware you'll all be tired."

The two newly collared men who looked in their late teens glowered at Victor with hatred.

"I'm Carlos," the Spanish-looking one spat.

"Jayden." The dark-skinned one bared his teeth.

"And now you four, if you would." Victor smiled at the remaining girls. Two exotic beauties and two mousy English roses.

"I-I'm Devi," the smaller one whispered.

"I'm Jin." The Korean stunner sniffed.

"I'm Ava and that's Sadie. We…we're sisters." They looked at each other. "We only snuck out to go to that party because our dad was being such a bore. It was our last night in Santorini."

The taller one started crying. "We only wanted to have some fun before we flew home. Please…this can't be happening. We just want to go home."

The second sister hugged her, tears rolling. "We won't tell anyone, we promise. Just let us go and—"

"Fuck this." Laura bolted.

Dashing off the stage, she darted around the tables only to fall flat on her face as one Master stuck out his leg, tripping her.

Victor sighed and rolled his eyes as the two boys joined her.

They exploded in a fit of speed, their bare feet slapping on the oak floor as they leapt off the stage.

Victor ran a finger over his eyebrow. "There's really no point in running. You're just harming yourselves by trying."

"Screw you." Talia grabbed Chloe's hand and jumped down the steps. They almost made it to the double doors before they dropped to their stomachs, jerking with savage electricity.

Striding off the stage, Victor kept his thumb stabbed into his black device as he marched toward the thrashing jewels. The guards rounded up the others, poking them back into place with their guns.

Talia and Chloe twitched at his feet.

Victor never stopped pressing that damn button.

"First lesson, my new pets. Don't speak if you're not given permission. Don't fight unless you're told. Don't run unless you're made to. Don't scream unless you're being fucked."

A few Masters laughed all while the girls learned firsthand what their collars were capable of. The other six just watched, yanking at their own collars, desperation clawing at their souls.

Hot, blistering tears scalded my eyes.

I couldn't look away.

Couldn't breathe.

My own veins sliced with memories of what that felt like.

I rolled into myself as phantom pains rippled down my body.

Henri touched my shoulder. "It's okay, little nightmare."

The first willing pet from him. The first kind word in so long.

I couldn't look at him.

Across the room, Peter vibrated with uncontrollable rage. Every jewel present at dinner pulsed with violent energy. Waves of it wafted from the floor where we knelt. Our matching hate and hopelessness itched in my teeth and pressed against my skull.

The surge of despair and revulsion coming from all my fellow prisoners cut through every illusion of training and obedience.

There was still life in us.

Still courage in us.

Still *fight* in us.

We have to get the fuck out of here.

Peter raised his eyes and met mine.

In a terribly bold move, he raised his bandaged fist and thumped it over his heart.

A single tear swelled and spilled down my cheek.

I raised my hand and thumped my heart too.

Henri's chair fell back as he shot to his feet.

His suddenness cut Victor's punishment short.

The new girls gasped and cried as their bodies jerked with exhaustion.

Bowing his head in respect at Victor, Henri grabbed me around the bicep and dragged me toward the doors leading to the deck outside. Smashing one open, he yanked me over the threshold, then broke into a run, dragging me beside him.

Chapter Twenty

Henri

WHAT THE FUCK WAS THAT?
Code?
Commiseration?
Peter couldn't hide his rebellion even while wearing bandages, and Ily…
Fuck.
Blackness poured over my mind as I glanced at her jog-tripping beside me.
What was she trying to do? Get herself killed?
Her arm was so slight and cool in my pinching fingers. Her body exquisitely beautiful beneath the beige jumper she'd slipped into. The same jumper where the Diamond Kiss chit had waited. The hem kissed her upper thighs as I pulled her faster, the flash of a white G-string visible as I hauled her over the grass.
The minute she'd spoken back after a month of pandering to me.
The *second* she told me to fuck myself, my entire body roared to life.
The desperation to throw her on the table again and repeat what'd happened the night of the treasure hunt splintered my bones.
It'd been too long. Far, far too long since I'd been inside her.
Despite the misery of the new jewels and the horror that I couldn't do a damn thing to save them, all I could think about was kissing her. The moment our eyes met, and all her fire tangled with mine—the second her slur burned my blood…all my self-control sizzled into rusty dust.
Only her.
Just her.
No one else had the power to invoke such heat inside me. Such an uncontrollable combustion that seared around my despair,

set alight all my blackness, and gave me a reprieve...just for a moment.

And that tear?

Are you fucking kidding me?

I went past blazing and straight to conflagration.

I didn't stop jogging until we reached the castle's east corner. Ily slowed beside me as I eyed up the large portico with potted manicured trees flanking yet another door. Unlike the modern sliding doors leading from the ballroom and dining hall, this one looked ancient. The heavy wood pockmarked and chipped as if some long-ago invader tried to hack at it with an axe.

I had no idea where it led, but I wanted privacy.

I needed Ily alone.

Now.

She didn't say a word as I yanked open the door, and we stumbled into a room.

Vaulted ceilings, swept-back bronze curtains, metallic threaded tapestries, and a giant amethyst geode all glittered in the soft glow of two huge chandeliers.

And the best part...it was empty.

Pulling Ily deeper into the room, the outside door banged shut, wrapping us up in the silence of stone, plush tan leather couches, a huge fireplace with stone foxes, and rugs thick enough to sleep on.

Guiding her to one of the couches, I pushed her down and sat close enough for our knees to touch.

I went to speak, but she tipped up her chin, and her eyes flashed with gold. "Do you know this is the first time you've sat me on a chair like a normal person instead of making me sit by your feet like a dog?"

I frowned, ready to argue.

I *needed* to argue.

Arguing could be the lifeline to pull myself out of the swamp I'd fallen into.

I choked on all the things I wanted to say, but the shackles of shadow slowly came back, trickling through my mind, gifting me yet more memories that I'd blocked out.

I'd accepted her kneeling by my feet—not because Victor expected his jewels to assume such a subservient position but because...I'd been raised that way.

I'd watched my father snap his fingers and witnessed how our mothers would crawl for him. I'd often filled up a dog bowl at his command, cutting up pieces of decadent food that they had to eat face first and ass up.

I groaned and rubbed my eyes.

How could I tell her that those memories were no longer forgotten thanks to trauma-amnesia protecting me? That they were now brightly lit and centre stage in my head? How could I confess that the longer I stayed here, the more my past knitted with my present and made all this so *normal* for me?

So fucking normal, which only made my grief so much worse.

Because I didn't *want* this normal.

I didn't want Ily on the floor.

I didn't want her jumping at my every command.

I might want to rule her, but I wanted her to rule me right back. I wanted her to leash the despicable darkness inside me by being stubborn and brave and wonderfully unafraid.

And then I'd do my best to make her cry—

Ah, Jesus Christ.

Dragging my fingers through my hair, I rested my elbows on my knees and looked away.

Had the cufflinks managed to alert my brother yet?

Was he coming, or did I need to throw them farther than just over the wall?

Maybe I should retrieve them and find a way to strap them to the leg of one of the pigeons that roosted on the carved gargoyles outside our bedroom. They could fly above the net of no internet and send an SOS because I couldn't exist this way much longer.

And I couldn't die until Ily was safe.

If you're coming, brother, you need to hurry.

Squeezing my skull, I shook as the urge to crack open my brain and systematically slice out all the pieces of my past became overwhelming.

"Henri…" Ily's fragile hand landed on my thigh. "Are you…do you have a headache? I can get you something—"

"You're asking me if I'm unwell?" I dropped my hands and caught her worried stare.

Biting her lip, she pulled her hand back. "Yes, well, you look like death warmed over."

I flinched at that word.

Was it normal for someone to crave such a thing? To long for death like one longed for a good night's sleep or a holiday? The peace that would come from being free of this body, this mind, this soul. I just wanted to dissolve into the darkness and be done with it.

A slithery, sinning part of me wrapped around my voice box. I sounded flippant and cruel when every damn molecule begged for help. "Don't worry. I'm fine."

"Could've fooled me."

God, what would I give to just *talk* to her. To blurt it all out there. Probably sob like a pussy as I recounted why I was the way I was and that there was no cure.

I'd hoped *she* was my cure.

That the moment I understood what the scratchy, searing mess in my heart meant that I'd be miraculously freed from this black-tinged disease.

But no.

I still wanted to hurt her despite my despair.

I still wanted her blood on my tongue regardless of my nightmares from my father doing the same damn thing to countless screaming, sobbing women.

I wasn't just fucked up.

There wasn't a word for what I was.

I needed to be exterminated before it was too late.

Reclining against the settee, I sucked in air. I still tasted the toxic terror from the new jewels. Fresh marks glowing on previously un-scarred skin—faces that couldn't quite believe what'd happened, quickly shutting down to become empty shells.

An image of Ily breaking that way haunted me.

None of the other jewels made eye contact with me. Not even Rachel or Mollie.

Peter dared look at me, but his stare reeked of judgement and something I couldn't quite decipher.

"You did come for us. You're going to free us. I know it—"

Fuck!

Pushing that awful echo out of my mind, I leapt to my feet and paced in front of the fireplace.

Ily stayed on the couch, watching.

The tension between us dragged out until it twanged like a screeching violin string.

"Why did you bring me in here, Henri?" she finally asked.

I stopped dead and balled my hands.

My eyes zeroed in on her dry cheek. "You cried."

Her shoulders swooped back. "And you figured you'd what? Bring me here and see if you could make me cry harder?"

I groaned at the thought. I hardened at the image.

I'd made the choice to bring her to this hellhole.

I wore the crime of my past.

Yet I couldn't stop the idiotic boy inside me getting on his knees and pleading with her to *fix* me. To give me her tears so I might find salvation in this storm. To cry for me and scream at me. To kneel for me and curse me.

Fucking hell.

My stomach clenched.

Familiar sourness tainted my tongue.

Was a bathroom close by because the beer turned rancid in my gut.

I hated that the Masters were back.

I despised that Victor had returned, and instead of feeling fear, I actually felt a smidgen of relief. While he lurked around every corner, I had to keep my wits. Had to remember how to act. Had to actually speak instead of giving every word to my useless manuscript. But the real reason was…while he groomed me and pushed me, I could give myself grace because I wasn't the worst one in the room anymore.

He was.

The internal double doors leading to yet another dayroom suddenly sprang wide and in he walked, summoned by my thoughts.

"Ah!" Victor opened his arms, a black and silver bag dangling from his left hand and a familiar leather leash in his right. Rachel trailed docilely behind him, her collar clipped to her beaming, well-rested Master. "There you are! Why did you run off, my dear Henri? Was it something I said? You're missing the canapés and entertainment."

I flicked a look at Ily.

Her face turned unreadable; eyes narrowed.

I searched her gaze for that spark of fire that always singed me. I wished I could rewind time and actually give her an answer when she asked me to play along with her. I wished I could make her feel anything but hate.

I didn't want Victor in the same room as her, but I was tired. So motherfucking tired of swimming against this black undertow and it took every effort. All my self-control to swallow down the misery and mayhem and step back into my expected role.

"Vic. Sorry, I…I needed to reprimand Il—"

I cut myself off.

I hadn't said her name since she'd told me what it meant.

I still couldn't say it.

Had Victor watched the camera feed while he'd been away? Would he watch them now like some bad daytime soap opera? I wasn't stupid enough to think he wouldn't check on me. A month with no chaperone? He'd be curious, and I already knew he'd find me lacking.

"Come. Sit, sit." He moved to the second settee facing the one Ily sat on.

Narrowing his eyes at her sitting on the couch instead of on the floor, he grinned slyly. "I wasn't aware you'd had a promotion, Ily sweetling." He cocked his head. "Tell me, are you still defying your Master, or did he give you permission to perch on my furniture?"

Marching back to her, I sat down, planted my hand on her thigh, and forced a grin. "I sat her there. It's, eh…easier access."

"Oh, yes. I see what you mean." Victor patted the tan leather beside him and smiled at Rachel. "Come here, my little incubator. Henri is right. I'll be able to touch you better with you beside me, and…I suppose you will require certain concessions, seeing as you're currently cooking my heir."

"Yes, Sir V. Thank you." Rachel shot Ily a look as she sat elegantly beside Victor. Folding her hands primly in her lap, she cupped her lower belly. The see-through white teddy she wore couldn't hide the faintest shadow of her bump.

Victor undid the button of his blazer and groaned. "*Mon dieu*, it's good to be home." With a yawn, he cupped Rachel's breast and ran a thumb over her nipple. It pebbled instantly.

He sighed with a happy smirk. "Have you missed me as much as I've missed you, my darling?"

Rachel blushed and fluttered her eyelashes, seduction all over her. "Every day has been miserable without you, Sir V. I'm so glad you've come home to me."

With a sharp twist of his fingers, Victor pinched her breast until she flinched. "You're putting it on a little thick, my pet." Grabbing her chin, he whispered loud enough for all of us to hear. "I'm aware you have days where you genuinely care for me. Once, I would've sworn you loved me, but…you can't hide the truth in your eyes, and that truth will one day get you killed."

Keeping her lashes lowered, she licked her lips. "Yes, Sir V. I'm sorry. And…and you're right that I do have feelings for you. I…I'm grateful you let me live."

"Yes, well…there's always tomorrow to change my mind, isn't there." He kissed her cheek, then let her go. Kicking out his long legs, he smiled in my direction. "So tell me, Henri. Have you enjoyed having my home all to yourself? Have you been a good boy? Haven't killed anyone or gone behind my back with yet more secrets?"

My pulse skipped. "Nope." I reclined against the soft leather. "I've been impeccably well behaved."

"And Ilyana?" Victor looked at her, a glint appearing in his blue eyes. "Have you behaved yourself?"

Without looking at Victor, she shot Rachel a smile and didn't reply.

She bristled with defiance.

Yearning snarled through my blood.

Merde, I'd missed this part of her.

I'd forgotten how hard her strength made me.

My palm twitched.

The thought of punishing her all while begging her to continue being rebellious…

Fuck, you're twisted.

Clearing my throat, I said, "She's not much of a talker these days, I'm afraid."

"Oh?" His eyes skated to Ily. "Why is that? Have you finally made headway on those obedience trainings? How far along have you gotten with her discipline?"

The urge to lie came thick.

But he'd see the truth on the cameras.

"To be honest, I've been rather busy. I've been writing a lot, and time tends to slip away when I'm in that zone, you know?"

A pinch appeared between his eyebrows. "You're saying you chose work over fucking? Oh no, no, Henri, that won't do at all. All work and no play is not conducive to a happy environment. I myself work hard but still carve out time to play. It's sacrilegious not to give in to our urges."

Ily didn't say a word.

Victor sniffed. "Of course, I'm happy you've had a chance to pursue other interests, but it pains me that you haven't made better progress with our jewel or looked after yourself."

Our?

I stiffened.

He wouldn't...would he?

Icy water shot down my back at the thought of him asking for a turn with Ily now that he was home.

When I didn't—couldn't—reply, he added, "What happened to the ownership levels we spoke about? Are you ever going to instil good behaviour, or do I have to do it?"

I tried to come up with an answer that would satisfy him.

I couldn't tell him the thought of her broken scared the living shit out of me.

How was I supposed to discipline and dominate her when I wanted to keep her as vibrant and violent as possible?

You don't.

It would be an open pass to shatter her.

Glancing at the fading shades of yellow and green on her skin, I muttered, "It took a while for her to heal." I shrugged. "Her bruises were extensive. My bicep also took a while to knit together, and my ribs still hurt. I figured a small time of abstinence would be a good thing." Smiling, I squeezed her knee, making her jump. "But now that you're back, the urge to play is returning quicker than I anticipated."

I hated that was true.

It'd been a long month of no sex.

And now...my body had a hunger growling deep within it. Heat throbbed between my legs, and my stomach twisted with other sensations, not just sickness.

"That's because you still don't trust yourself." Victor clucked his tongue. "I represent the freedom you're still not brave enough to take. Come now, Henri. I would've expected you to be over that little obstacle of your subconscious." He sighed almost sadly. "I don't like the thought of you struggling. I don't like the idea of you being lonely all on your own. Tell you what. We will spend the evening together, just the four of us. What do you say?" He smiled kindly. "We can catch up, have a few drinks, maybe a few fucks. I'm happy to be home but I'm not in any rush to hang out with those ingrates. I'm still annoyed at them, but you..." He bowed his chin. "You—the brother of my greatest enemy—have somehow become my friend."

My eyebrows shot up. "Your friend?"

"I know. Shocking to me too." He chuckled. "While I was away, I had time to think, and…my conclusions took me by surprise. I thought I was beyond the need of a genuine friend. Those with that label surround me. I have many acquaintances all around the world and some in very powerful positions that enable me to live the life I do, but…" He sighed. "Until you came along, I wasn't aware how empty those relationships were."

I blinked.

I had nothing to say.

My mind completely shut down, unsure how to play this.

"Here." Victor snatched the black and silver bag he'd placed by his thigh. "I bought this for you." He tossed it in my direction.

Catching it, I cocked my head. "Been shopping while hunting, Vic?" Catching his eyes and ignoring Ily beside me, I forced myself to ask, "Where have you been? Where did you find your new jewels?"

He shrugged with a secretive smile. "I will admit business has been good. And not just in my safari for new gems. It's been a good month all round."

"Care to share?"

He chuckled. "Always so curious."

I did my best to remember how to play this game. I forced a chuckle. "I think you mean nosy."

He laughed louder. "Yes, your nose is definitely rather large."

"It seems your guests missed you." I forced more small talk. "I overheard them taking bets last night on how many jewels you'd return with."

"Oh? And what figure did you wager on?"

"I didn't."

"Shame." He swiped a finger over his bottom lip. "You say my guests missed me, but did you?"

"Like one misses a root canal," Ily quipped under her breath.

She flinched as if she hadn't meant to say anything.

Rachel made a strangled noise.

Ily's shock coupled with my brittle mood made a half grunt, half chuckle escape my lips.

Not funny, you idiot.

Fuck.

Ily shot me a look.

Something blistering, *burning* passed between us.

Victor sniffed. "If you missed me that much, Ilyana, perhaps I should reward your affection with a ride, hmm?"

She sucked in a breath.

My heart stopped.

Victor didn't move, but his smile turned sharp. "I think you both got a tad too comfortable in my absence. All work and no play equals unruly, naughty jewels."

Balling my hands, I growled with far too much truth. "She's exactly how I want her."

Ily threw me a bewildered look before dropping her gaze to her knees.

Victor scowled. "I see your argumentative self is still flourishing, *mon ami*. You're like two peas in a pod."

That damn sickness rushed up my gullet. "Sorry, Vic. I just mean she's—"

"As spicy as ever." Victor shrugged away whatever he'd been thinking. "No matter. I've grown rather used to her audacity. It'll be a sad day when you finally whip that flagrant rudeness out of her. I admit…I do enjoy her spirit."

Once again, my voice deserted me.

"Go on, Henri." He arched his chin at the forgotten bag in my hands. "Open it. It's merely a trifle for my favourites."

"Favourites?"

"Of course. You and your little nightmare make this place highly entertaining." Shifting his smile to Rachel, he commanded softly. "You may kneel now, my pet."

"Yes, Sir V." Rachel instantly folded off the couch, her breasts bouncing a little beneath her teddy. She was a stunning woman, but everything about her subservience turned me off.

I hated that Ily had adopted such traits.

That she'd thought the way to seduce me was to be like them when the opposite was true. If she'd slapped me instead of kneeled for me? Kicked me instead of 'accidentally' dropped her towel? Fuck, the past month would've been a very different story.

Ily and Rachel shared another look, and without a word, Ily dropped elegantly to the carpet and bowed her chin. She went without my command. She went because Rachel did.

The urge to drag her onto the couch was unbearable.

The desire to slap her awake from whatever submission she thought I wanted had my teeth clenching and cock twitching in my jeans.

I wished I could reverse time and never hug her the night she was high. Never kiss her. Never meet her at the club because every day I spent in her company, I died a little more. I died because I couldn't breathe. I couldn't breathe because she'd stolen everything.

Victor eyed Ily kneeling demurely, her slouchy jumper puddling around her thighs. He huffed. "For a woman as beautiful as you, you're always so determined to hide. Pity."

I needed his attention off her, but Ily continued to dig her own grave. "For a man as sick as you, you somehow remain alive. Pity."

Rachel coughed.

Victor scowled.

And lightning bolts of savage lust shot right between my legs.

There she was again.

The girl who blazed.

The jewel who burned me alive.

Fuck, she was otherworldly when she let her temper free.

I felt so connected to her—dragged into her scalding energy as it tattooed embers on my heart.

"I see your tongue has not been tamed in my absence." Victor sighed as a staff member entered, carrying a tray with two beers, two waters, and a big bowl of french fries. Doling out the beer to me and Victor and the water to Rachel and Ily, the guy placed the fries on the coffee table and slipped out the door again, leaving us to a tense silence.

Ily broke it with a sneer. "And like I said, I see you're still breathing...unfortunately."

Victor snickered around a mouthful of fries. Chasing it with some beer, he smirked. "Oh, Ilyana...are you so sure you wish to spar with me?" His pupils dilated in interest.

I made the mistake of sipping the cold, crisp IPA.

I choked.

Fuck.

This was exactly what I'd hoped to avoid.

Out of all the moments I wanted her to be submissive, this was it.

With trembling hands, I placed the beer on the table and ripped open the bag. Anything to change the subject or stop his intrigue. "I wasn't expecting a gift, Vic."

Almost reluctantly, Victor shifted his stare to me. His posture softened, and he sipped his beer again. "Like I said, it's merely a trifle. I keep suggesting we have a session in the snuffbox, and now that I'm home, we'll make it happen. How about tomorrow? You can use your new friend."

"New friend?"

"Open it."

Rachel suddenly looked up and caught my stare. Her icy-blue eyes blazed, narrowing with things I couldn't unravel. Her gaze slipped from mine to Ily. The two girls shared a glance before they stared at the carpet.

What the hell was that?

What was I missing because I was sure as hell missing something.

Whatever it was, Peter was in on it too.

The way he thumped his fist over his heart had to be some sort of acknowledgement.

What the fuck are they up to?

Ily stayed stiff on her knees as I fisted the bag and looked inside.

Instinct made me jerk away.

Snake.

Peering closer, I rolled my eyes at my stupidity.

No, not a snake.

A whip.

Holding my breath, I reached in and wrapped my fingers around the leather braided handle. So soft. So smooth. The perfect width and length for my hand as if Victor took measurements of my palm and had this especially made for me.

Pulling it out, the tight coil stayed in a neat circle thanks to the black ribbon knotted around its length. The dark brown tannins released an oaky, earthy scent. It filled my nose with a thousand urges to swing it and hear it sing.

Stroking the tip where it ended in a nasty forked lash, I hefted the weight and despised that, once again, Victor had seen a weakness and toyed with it. "Thank you." I cleared my throat. "It's stunning."

"And it will deliver stunning results too." He smiled at Ily. "Now you. Reach into the bag and take out your gift."

I tensed for her to say something derogatory in return, but she merely soared higher on her knees, dove her hand into the bag on my lap, and pulled out a box with a glass lid and two items nestled in black velvet.

Her eyes narrowed on the present before shooting hate at Victor. "Yet again, you've found a way to take something I love and ruin it."

"I admit…it's a talent." Victor chuckled.

"May I?" I quirked an eyebrow, reaching for the box.

She offered it up to me. "Why even bother asking? It's meant for you more than me."

"On the contrary." Victor grinned. "It's for both of you."

Opening the glass lid, I ran my fingertips over two long, thick crystals. Carved into the shapes of veiny phalluses, both of them were garishly obscene.

"Rose quartz and obsidian," Victor said. "I suggest you use the smaller one in her ass to stretch her, *mon ami*." He threw me a conspiratorial look. "Preparation is key, yes?"

Images of pinning Ily down and taking her in that way exploded in my mind.

Once I thought it, fuck me, I *wanted* it.

Badly.

"Why two?" I swallowed hard.

"To stretch both holes at once, of course. Fuck her with both or fuck her with one. The choice is, as always, yours."

Standing suddenly, Victor grabbed another handful of fries. "Right, that's enough of chit-chat. I'm going to shower away my travels, have a quick massage by my lovely Rachel, and then…I'll send my butler to find you. I'm tired but horny so we'll share a private dinner in my personal chambers before I retire." He huffed happily. "I never let anyone up there, so I hope you appreciate the invitation. If I'm honest, I'm feeling all round very content. My business went well. The energy in my home is balanced. And I have a true friend who needs some fatherly guidance." Tugging Rachel's leash, he smiled. "I look forward to tonight, Henri. We both need a good fuck so tomorrow we can play all day in the snuffbox."

"See you soon." I gave him the best smile I could as he left with Rachel in tow.

The moment the door closed behind him, Ily let out a breath.

Our eyes met.

And the dark depression grabbed me all over again.

Chapter Twenty-One

STEPPING INTO VICTOR'S PERSONAL SUITE on the top floor felt as if I'd stepped into the bedroom of the devil. Not because the walls melted with flames or the floor fell away into a bubbling volcano for wretched souls to burn in eternity but because of his sheer presence.

He slept here.

Showered here.

He was vulnerable here, and if we could somehow smuggle a bomb beneath his huge four-poster bed and blow it into rubble, we'd free a million spirits trapped within the walls. Jewels he'd hurt in here. Women and men he'd abused and tortured.

Twice the size of his gold-carpeted office, his bedroom was vast. A sitting area complete with a stripper pole stabbed out of the glass-topped coffee table to the right, a patio with a Jacuzzi waited beneath the moon, and giraffe skins littered the floor leading to another circular lounge. On the walls hung yet more mythical monstrous artwork. Cupids slaughtered on the spears of demons. Men with forked tongues licking out virgins and a huge canvas where soldiers lay like a carpet of corpses, all while some vanquisher rode over them with his blood-splattered white horse.

Was that how Victor saw himself?

The mayor of his own country? The victor of his own battleground?

"Impressive," Henri muttered, striding forward with long-legged steps.

To me, his voice sounded raspy and off. I'd caught him scrubbing his tongue with his toothbrush as I'd slipped into the bathroom to take a shower earlier this evening. He'd glanced away, but I knew.

I'd heard him throwing up before.

I'd learned what the black shadows beneath his eyes meant.

Nausea tormented him often.

Just like in that video Victor made us all watch the day he almost killed Henri—his tummy had been delicate then, and it seemed to punish him still.

I didn't know why he suffered such a debilitating condition, but it'd gotten worse.

Is that why he's lost weight?

Because he couldn't keep anything down or because unsaid things kept eating him alive?

Victor didn't seem to care or notice that Henri vibrated with a million different things. Pouring crystal-clear liquid into three glass tumblers, he strode from the private bar by the doors leading to the patio with a grin. Dressed in black silk pyjamas bottoms, bare lean chest, and a long, slackly sashed red silk dressing gown, he either watched far too many pornos or fancied himself as some Mafia boss.

His hair gleamed from his shower, and his steps were loose and languid. Was Rachel the reason for that? He'd mentioned he wanted a massage from her.

My eyes shot to Rachel where she kneeled in another sitting area to the left. The long beige couch curled into a semi-circle, the white round carpet in the centre so perfect, so pure, it looked like a portal into heaven.

She gave me a flickering smile.

I returned it.

Dropping my eyes, I watched with my peripheral vision as Victor passed one of the glasses to Henri, then patted him encouragingly on the back. "Welcome. Make yourself comfortable." With a mocking bow, Victor took my hand and wrapped my fingers around the second glass. "You too, Ilyana. Tonight is for all of us, so drink up. We can all indulge together. Apart from Rachel, of course. She can't drink for obvious reasons." He blew her a kiss, his flippant joy almost infectious if it wasn't for the aura of evil. "While I was away, I came around to the idea of having a child. I'm rather excited now."

Henri didn't reply, sipping a scant mouthful of whatever clear alcohol had been given.

Chuckling, Victor swallowed his own sip. "Actually, I never thought I'd see the day that I'd have a screaming baby in my home. However, it has opened my eyes to other business ventures."

Henri went stiff beside me.

My heart stopped.

No...don't say it...

Henri stayed deathly quiet, making Victor's happy voice all the more obscene. "You know, *mon ami*. I've dabbled in the skin trade for over three decades. I've lost count of how many girls and boys I've trafficked, but...I've always stayed clear of children because they're messy and loud and not worth the trouble but..." Kicking off his lambskin slippers, Victor padded barefoot toward Rachel and fell backward onto the couch. "Come, come. Sit. I've taken the liberty of ordering some dishes to be brought up, so there's nothing more to do than to relax while we wait."

Swallowing another mouthful of his drink, Henri forced a smile and marched toward Victor. His black loafers, black slacks, and black shirt were far too dressy compared to Victor's slinky bedwear. Sitting opposite Victor, Henri cocked his head in my direction, summoning me to his side.

I went without a word, keeping my chin tipped low and eyes on the carpet.

No one moved as I sank to my knees beside him. My skimpy black negligee with its gauzy lace and ribbony straps showed my pebbled nipples and matching black G-string.

Rachel still wore her white see-through teddy, marking both of us as something to be studied, mauled, and claimed.

"Ah, this is nice." Victor toasted us from the other side of the couch, his fingers straying through Rachel's dark hair. "What was I saying? Oh, yes." Sipping his drink, he smacked his lips. "Do you remember me mentioning the dark web, Henri? Where you can buy all nationalities, ages, and creeds?"

"I remember." Henri smiled, his outward appearance unruffled all while I sensed his energy as a jagged, jittery mess. "What about it?"

"Well, I had my eyes opened thanks to a friend in Vietnam. I was there checking on my sapphire mine, you see. I happened to mention the next time I visited, I might bring my heir with me. That got us onto the topic of babies." His eyes narrowed as he leaned forward. "Apparently, I'm a bit of a dinosaur with the dark web and covertly trading skin in very exclusive circles. There's a new breed of trafficker. So bold and uncaring, they openly trade on mainstream platforms."

Snow dusted my shoulders.

Rachel hunched over her knees.

And Henri kept his tone insolently bored, all while his energy crackled with rapidly rising disgust. "Oh?"

"It's all about emoji and code language." Victor leaned back, gloating at his wisdom. "Triangles and spirals and a bunch of others. These codes are well-known, apparently. I need to study their meanings, but what really intrigued me was the use of popular selling sites."

Henri coughed on a mouthful of liquor. My own untouched glass sagged, forgotten in my hand.

"What do you mean?" Henri spluttered. "They're uploading people and taking online bids now?"

"Exactly!" Victor snickered and shook his head. "Unbelievable, isn't it? In plain view, no less. Right there, beneath people's noses!"

"How?" Henri scowled. "I don't understand how they don't get caught the moment they upload a fucking *person*. Surely, those sites are monitored. Police would be notified immediately if a missing person suddenly appeared with a price tag."

"It's because they don't upload a person." Victor tapped his nose. "They upload—"

"Sir?" A soft knock as the door to Victor's bedroom opened. "Your dinner is here. Shall I have the staff bring it in?"

"Yes, thank you, Tim." Victor nodded. With a twinkle in his eye, eager to spill such horrendous information, he waited patiently for a few servers to march in, each carrying large trays full of plates and dishes.

I recognised a few of them from being in the kitchens so much. One of the men had smiled at me last week as he dashed out with a trolley full of food.

Silence fell over our group as the staff unloaded the trays and lifted off the silver lids. The glass coffee table went from empty to groaning beneath delicious-looking morsels. Steam curled from platters of vegetable kebabs, saffron rice, perfectly filleted steak, pan-seared fish, chunky homemade fries, and so much more.

Once napkins, plates, and cutlery had been positioned, the staff swept out, and a butler stepped forward. He poured more liquor into Victor's and Henri's glasses. The huge crystal decanter trapped rainbows thanks to the chandelier dripping above.

Only once we were alone again and Victor had piled his plate with something from every dish did he sit back, cross his legs, and grin. "They upload clothing."

"Clothing?" Henri's forehead furrowed as he gathered some food and reclined. He didn't take much, and I had a feeling what he did take he wouldn't eat, and even if he did, it wouldn't stay down.

My stomach rumbled a little, and I caught Rachel gazing at the food wistfully, but no one offered us the opportunity to join the feast.

Sighing heavily, I placed my untouched glass on the table and balled my hands on my lap.

This will be a long night.

"Yes." Victor nodded, his words garbled with food. "I saw it with my own eyes. They list a pretty dress and use a header like 'Stunning Gracie Birthday Dress,' then in the drop-down box, they have ages instead of sizes. Age six, age eight." He waved his fork. "Etcetera."

"And your friend thinks those are links to purchase children?"

"Oh, he doesn't think, he knows. He's the one who uploads them. Or at least, one of them. That particular link was for a blonde, slim girl. He said the word Gracie depicts slim and small, whereas other names are different nationalities and shapes. Like I said…it's all in code."

Swallowing hard, Henri asked, "But how is a simple girl's dress suddenly code to buying the actual girl who would wear it?"

"Simple." Victor passed a chunky fry to Rachel.

She took it and ate it, her appetite not diminished by the abhorrent dinner conversation.

Henri copied Victor but went one step further. Gifting me his entire plate, he muttered, "Eat what you want. I'm not hungry."

Victor sniffed. "Food not to your liking, Mercer?"

Henri rubbed his palms on his knees. "Had a late lunch. You feed us too well in here. I have to be careful not to indulge." He chuckled and patted his flat, carved belly. "If I keep eating the way I have, I'll end up as round as Roland."

Victor kept staring for a moment, but Henri didn't flinch.

If Victor looked at the camera footage, he'd see Henri eating a club sandwich in our chambers this afternoon while I'd enjoyed a sweet potato and mushroom wrap. What he wouldn't see was Henri vomiting it all back up again, thanks to Victor admitting the only place he didn't put cameras was on the toilet.

For Henri's sake, I hoped Victor had no idea how often his stomach punished him because even I knew the more his system broke, the more his thoughts unravelled.

Stabbing a piece of succulent fish, Victor accepted Henri's answer. "Tomorrow, I'll show you what I mean. These sites are riddled with sales like this. The only difference that makes them stand out is the price."

"The price?" Henri asked coldly.

"Well, you can't very well sell a blonde eight-year-old girl for the same price as an ugly dress, now can you? The auction usually starts around thirty thousand, but one of my friend's listings ended the night I was there, and the final price was fifty-four thousand."

"Fifty-four *thousand*?" Henri shook his head, his energy once again coiling and clotting. "Surely these sites would flag those transactions. No one in their right mind would spend that much on a dress."

"I'm not sure how he gets away with it. But he does." He winked. "Makes bank too. All he needs is a warehouse to keep merchandise and a way to ship them to their new homes." He winked. "And here I was thinking I earned a good living mining my jewels once they'd passed their use-by date."

Rachel stiffened.

My heart stopped.

What?

Henri leaned forward, repeating my horrified silent question. "*What?* You don't mean…"

"Organ trade?" Victor stuffed another forkful into his mouth. "Of course! Lucrative. Very lucrative."

Pinching the bridge of his nose, Henri sucked in a breath before dropping his hand and asking, "You're saying you carve out the organs of your jewels and *sell* them?"

"Oops. Cover your ears, Rachel. Ily." Snickering, Victor tore through a piece of steak with perfect white teeth. "Waste not, want not." He chuckled at Henri's slack face. "Oh, I'm sorry. I thought you were ready to hear all aspects of my operation, my friend. My overseer told me that you've been diligent in learning how my estate works while I've been away."

"Your overseer?" Henri forced himself to relax again but his energy tangled and snarled. "I mean, I inspected a few of your processes." He flicked me a look. "And I spoke to a few staff. I also visited your orchards and maintenance areas of your castle. I'm impressed with how well it's all run."

"*Merci.*" Victor grinned. "I appreciate your acknowledgement of the time and effort that goes into running a place such as this.

But my apologies." Chewing another strip of steak, he chuckled. "I thought you might be ready to hear the rest of my business endeavours, but perhaps it's a tad too soon. Don't worry, Henri, I won't expect you to cut out the organs of those I request you to exterminate. I have a man who carefully does that for me. For now…let's just enjoy our meal and return to other subjects, yes?"

Henri tossed back his entire glass of alcohol before raking a hand through his hair and nodding. "Sure."

Finishing his meal in contented silence, Victor passed a few morsels to Rachel before reaching for his glass and sighing. Watching her closely as she ate the food he'd given her, Victor leaned forward and kissed her forehead. "It pleases me to see you eating so well, my pet. I'll ensure you receive three meals a day while carrying my child so my son is born as healthy as can be."

Licking her lips and lowering her eyelashes, Rachel played a far better slave than I ever could. "Thank you so much, Sir V. Your kindness is much appreciated."

"Good girl." Scratching his bare belly, Victor yawned. "Tell me, Henri. Have you ever had the urge to propagate?"

Henri flicked me a horrified look before his face shut down. He shrugged. "Never really crossed my mind."

"You could knock up your precious jewel. Between the two of you, you'd create a stunning child. It could sell for far more than a measly fifty grand, I'm sure."

I swayed.

Dark spots danced in my vision.

He couldn't be serious.

He was a monster, but *this*? No one could be this extreme. My mind literally couldn't accept it. Couldn't fathom that men like him existed. Men who clapped their hands at the thought of selling *children*.

Our children.

Men who saw nothing wrong with cutting out organs or making a profit from things that ought to be untouchable.

Henri couldn't hide his temper this time. "You're saying you've gone from a strict no-children policy to suddenly wanting to—"

"Breed my gems like livestock to pad my retirement?" Victor laughed loudly. "Yes, I'm contemplating it. Of course, my guests wouldn't be open to fucking anything but perfection. However, I'm sure they could be encouraged to impregnate a few. When those chosen jewels get too weathered to be pleasurable, and their bodies have popped out one or two bank deposits, then they'll be dispatched, and I'll earn more income with their remains on the black market." He scratched his jaw. "It really is a smart business decision if you think about it. After all, I'm not getting any younger, and I would really like to buy another island or possibly one of those doomsday fancy bunkers. All the billionaires are building them. Of course, you'd be welcome. We're family now, you and I."

A flash of Henri's loathing appeared. "Family wouldn't ask each other to sell their own flesh and blood, Vic."

"Meh. Each family has their own dynamics. Humans are nasty creatures, especially to their loved ones." He smiled slyly. "You should know. Look at what your brother did to you."

Shifting to the edge of the couch, Henri bared his teeth. "I'm telling you now, if you think I'd happily hand over a son or daughter, then we're going to have a big fucking problem. To even suggest such a thing hints you don't know me as well as you think you do."

He just smiled. "So you're not open to knocking Ily up?"

Henri didn't look in my direction. "She said she'd jump off the roof if I ever got her close to being pregnant, so no, I'm not. I like her alive. I like her in my bed. And if it's all the same to you, I just want to live a simple life of fucking, writing, reading, and eating—probably in that order. I have no intention of passing on what I am to another or having a fucking kid running underfoot."

Victor laughed again. "You really are a hoot. You might change your mind one day."

Balling his hands, Henri didn't shut himself down as he snarled, "Do whatever you want, Vic. I can't and won't stop you. But I remind you that I bought Il—I mean, I bought my little nightmare, fair and fucking square. She's mine. She isn't some breeding mare for whatever sideline venture you start. Got it?"

Holding up his hands, Victor snickered. "Heard loud and clear." Dropping his arms, he curled his fingers into Rachel's hair. "But you know…if you don't have a child, your bloodline will end with you. The Mercer line will die out, which would be such a pity."

Rachel pursed her lips as we shared a look.

Tension crackled in the room.

Henri sat straight, his motions deliberately slow. "That's wrong. You know my brother has a son. You heard on the phone, same as me."

"Oh yes, I heard. Lino. It's true, but…it won't be for long."

My heart skipped a beat.

No…

I didn't even know these people, but the thought of Victor going after them. Going after Henri's nephew.

God, I'm going to be sick.

When Henri didn't reply, Victor grinned. "Your brother managed to keep that piece of information quiet. He knew it would paint the biggest target on his back." His eyes glinted. "At least Q won't be an issue for you soon."

Henri stopped breathing. His voice came out like dry ice. "What do you mean?"

"I mean I used his ultimate weakness against him. I heard his wife was stolen early on in their relationship, and it almost destroyed him." His smile was utterly inhuman. "So…I went after his child."

The plate of untouched food slid off my lap and tumbled all over the white carpet.

Victor sniffed with annoyance. "God's sake, clean that up. If that carpet stains, I'll skin you to replace it."

My pulse roared in my ears.

I couldn't move.

"*Now, Ilyana!*" Victor roared, bypassing my shock and electrifying my limbs.

Darting to my feet, I charged into the marble-tiled bathroom, grabbed an armful of towels, dumped one into the sink to soak with water, then raced back to the mess on the floor.

Henri scooped up the food and placed the plate on the coffee table. Without a word, he wiped his hands on the wet towel and then sat back on the couch.

His entire system had shut down.

No energy bled through.

No hint of what he felt.

Scrubbing at the carpet, I kept my eyes on him. He shrugged as if he didn't care. "You've killed his son?"

"Not yet." Victor sighed. "My team has finally tracked down where he goes to school. They're on their way to grab him now, actually. Once Q goes after them, well…let's just say his wife will be a childless widow, and in all fairness, you should inherit the Mercer estate. I can see if my lawyers could arrange that if you'd like? Last I heard, he was worth over a billion euros."

My hands stilled.

Victor cocked his eyebrow in warning.

I kept scrubbing.

Finally, Henri reclined and exhaled as if he'd given up every last piece of himself. He looked exhausted—as if he couldn't keep doing this dance. The vacantness in his grey eyes terrified me. The coldness wafting from his body dusted the air with frost. "It's fine. Let his wife have the estate."

"You're far too good a brother, even now." Victor pouted. "You know, *mon ami*. It hurts me to see you ostracised even amongst your own kind. You're desperately lonely, and I understand now that I shouldn't have left you alone for so long. You're unhappy, and seeing as you're quickly becoming my only true friend in this world, I did this for you, don't you see? I figured out a way to prevent your brother from killing you the moment you're off my island. Next time I travel, you can come with me. Won't that be nice? In fact, Rachel and Ilyana can join us. Just the four of us…or five, depending on due dates."

He gave Rachel a doting look before glancing at Henri. "I know you'll feel guilty that your brother and nephew will soon be dead, but you shouldn't. He failed you, and you deserve better. You have my word that I'll always look out for you. As long as you are loyal and honest with me, we can have differing opinions and agree to disagree. I want you to be yourself, Henri. How many of your past acquaintances can say that? How many people have you had to hide from? Do you even know how to be yourself?" He shook his head kindly. "Even now. Even after the opportunity to become who you truly are, you continue to fight it. You're not well, my friend, and it's an honour to be the one to help you because you need looking after."

Victor's voice tinged with passion, not giving room for anyone else to speak. "Before you came along, I had no such nurturing instincts. To be honest, I despise most people—my guests included—but you…you remind me so much of me at your age that I catch myself remembering those days when I too had no one. The days when I could barely get out of bed because the heavy weight of depression refused to let me breathe. I've skimmed enough of the camera footage to see those same sufferings in you. It doesn't seem as if you've indulged in pleasure since I left. You've barely eaten. You write feverishly, yet there's nothing to show for it on your computer. You're breaking beneath what you think you should be and what you truly are, and I need you to listen to me because I've been there. I was you. I hated myself for the longest time. I even feared myself and yes, I made myself sick with the urges in my blood. It wasn't until I became accepting of my truth that I found happiness."

"Wait." Henri held up his hand, stilling Victor's speech. "You read my manuscript? How?"

Victor ducked his chin, guilt tinging his cheekbones. "Ah, yes, I know I shouldn't have, but...I have a big nose too." He tapped it with a laugh. "I told you I was eager to read your book, so I was disappointed to find only blank pages."

"Ever heard of asking first?" Henri sniffed.

"Does it look like I ask for consent?" He chuckled. "Besides, if I'd asked you, you might've said no—"

"I would've definitely said no. It was personal."

"Is that why you deleted it?"

Henri's eyes tightened. "Amongst other reasons."

"What reasons?"

Rachel and I looked between the two men as if we were watching a tennis match. The rising testosterone, the tension.

I didn't think Henri would answer him, but he strangled, "I've been remembering my childhood. It turns out I repressed everything. Writing unfortunately unlocked that repression."

"Interesting." Victor topped up both their glasses. Glancing at my untouched one, he commanded. "Drink that, Ilyana. I won't ask again."

Henri glanced at me; he gave me the slightest nod.

With gritted teeth, I grabbed the glass, shot it back, and grimaced.

Vodka.

Victor refilled it, then turned his attention back to Henri on the couch. "So...what have you been remembering? Tell me. I wonder if our childhoods were the same, and that's why we're so similar."

My nose wrinkled.

Henri might want dark things, but he was *nothing* like Victor. I couldn't picture him hacking up a body to sell the heart or a kidney of someone he used to know—

Then again, he'd filleted Kyle pretty good.

He stabbed him so many times I'd lost count.

Different…
That was different.
Is it?
Murder was murder.
A life was a life.

"I seem to have been one of my father's favourites," Henri finally muttered. "He made me…help."

"Ah! That explains your needs, then. I can imagine—from what I heard about him and his harem—that my island must feel familiar. A coming home of sorts."

"You could say that." Henri flicked me an unreadable glance.

Victor clapped his hands, making me jump. "I want to hear all about your memories, *mon ami*. Not because I wish to upset you by dragging up a childhood you refused to recall but because it has become my own personal task to make you happy. I will teach you how to shed the parts of yourself holding you back. I will give you the same joy you touched the night you finished Ruby Tears. That freedom can be yours again. You only need to reach out and claim it."

Henri didn't say anything as Victor stood and stretched, his satin pyjama pants revealing every part of him.

He was hard.

And not wearing any underwear, judging by the grotesque outline.

"But right now, I'm hungry for a different sort of delicacy." Bending over Rachel, he cupped her cheek. "I'm going to be rather possessive of you now I've accepted the gift you're giving me. For the next year, you will serve no one but me. However…" His navy eyes flickered to Henri. "There is a matter of a small debt, and I don't like IOU's hanging over me. So…for tonight only, I will share."

Every bone in my body locked.

Rachel sucked in a breath. "Sir V?"

Pressing a soft, chaste kiss to her mouth, Victor stood and crossed his arms. "Master H won you in Emerald Bruises. You wear his fading marks even now. Please allow him to claim his prize and make him as happy as you make me."

Rachel shot me a horrified look but bowed her chin and nodded. "Yes, Sir V. Forgive me, Sir V, but…are you asking me to present to Master H?"

Victor nodded with a chill. "I am. Allow my friend to fuck

you. Accept a part of his darkness so he can breathe a little easier. And if you please him, I'll order your favourite caramel crème cheesecake and draw you a bath so you can soak away his cum before those swimmers get anywhere near my baby."

My heart literally splashed onto the dirty stain on the carpet.

Raw, stinging tears cut my eyes.

I loved Rachel as much as I loved Peter.

She was my friend.

She was a prisoner.

But the thought of her sleeping with Henri?

She...she can't.

He's mine.

He's...

My lungs stuck together.

A panic attack hotter and darker than the one that'd smothered me in the library that first day threatened to make me hyperventilate.

Henri.

Henri with Rachel.

Rachel with Henri.

Henri inside Rachel.

Henri...

It took forever and a million broken hearts before Henri slowly raised his chin and swallowed hard.

His eyes sought mine.

Torment carved deep crags in his face.

With a quiet shift, he planted a hand on my quaking shoulder. "It's fine, Vic. I relinquish my right of winning. She's the mother of your heir and—"

"You will, and I'll tell you why." Victor clasped his fingers in front of his red silk robe. "You're boxing yourself into yet another black hole. This one might be different to the black hole you existed in out there in society, but in here, you've found a way to imprison yourself all over again. It seems as if you haven't touched Ilyana in weeks. You have urges. You have needs. By ignoring those needs, you compound your suffering, and I'm sick of it. Do you hear me? You're doing exactly what you did to your childhood and repressing yourself all over again. I won't let you mope around my home. I won't let you fade away all because you're too afraid to be free. So..."

Victor marched toward me, snatched me around the elbow,

and yanked me to my feet. "Take the gift I'm so generously giving you. Fuck my favourite jewel all while I fuck yours. A trade. An exchange. We'll agree that all other types of play are off the table. I won't hurt Ilyana, and you won't hurt Rachel. Tonight is just a simple fuck and—"

"So that's what this is about?" Henri soared to his feet. "You think you could distract me so you could take what's mine?"

"No, I'm being courteous by offering to break the rut you're obviously in. You need to fuck other jewels, *mon ami*. Monogamy does not work for men like us. *Feelings* do not work for men like us. They only trap us and make us suffer."

Grabbing my other elbow, Henri tugged me. "Let her go. I'm open to a night of pleasure, Vic, but if it's all the same to you, I'll stick my dick in what belongs to me."

Victor yanked me back, treating me like a toy two boys wanted. "I'm aware you haven't had an authority figure for most of your life, Henri, so you're not used to receiving instructions, but I must warn you, rather carefully, that this is *not* a negotiation."

Ripping me out of Henri's hold, Victor shoved me behind him.

I crashed to my knees beside Rachel.

Grabbing my hand, Rachel hissed into my ear, "I'm sorry. So sorry. I don't want to. I would do anything to—"

"*Enough!*" Henri roared. "This isn't happening. I've changed my mind, Victor. I'll give you whatever you want, but the option of fucking Il—*her*—is no longer—"

"My dear friend." Stepping into Henri, Victor grabbed his cheeks.

The shock of Victor holding him so intimately made Henri speechless.

"I know you don't see it yet, but I'm doing this for your own good." Kissing Henri on the cheek, Victor whispered, "This is happening. There is absolutely nothing you can do to stop it. You need a gentle little push, and I'm more than happy to push you. In fact, if the next words out of your mouth are something along the lines of not being able to get it up for anyone other than Ilyana, then I will force a little blue pill down your throat and prove to you that you can and *will* fuck other people, despite your broken little conscience telling you that you can't."

Henri grabbed Victor's wrists, ready to yank his hold away, but Victor dug his fingernails into his cheekbones. "Don't make me summon my guards, Mercer. You're going to do this. You're going to fuck another all so you can break out of this self-imposed prison, or…I'll get my guards to beat you to a pulp. A good thrashing would do you the world of good. It might even help you snap."

Trembling with rage, Henri snarled, "I'm telling you as the winner of that stupid game, I'll claim the girl I shot the most. Il…fuck…" He swallowed hard and spat, "*Ily*. I shot *Ily*. You saw how many bruises she wore. She's the one I want. The one I'm owed."

Letting Henri go, Victor splayed his hands. "And I'm not taking away what is rightfully yours. I'm merely sharing. We're big boys. We can share, can we not? I assure you Rachel is a good fuck. Probably even better than Ilyana. She actually tries to please instead of shutting down and enduring it."

Inhaling deeply as if Henri still tested his patience, Victor shrugged. "Your choice. Your choice to take the gift I'm so generously giving you and then grant me the same courtesy by offering up what's yours, or…you can spend the next few weeks nursing a few more bruises. What's it going to be?"

Henri shot me a look.

I had no idea what went through his head, but he looked as if he was seconds away from either slaughtering Victor or going into cardiac arrest. Balling his hands, he hissed, "Ily's education is mine. You said it so yourself. As her teacher, I'm not comfortable trading her yet. She's not obedient enough for you. I fear…" His face twisted with loathing. "I fear she won't live up to your expectations, and I'll let you down."

Victor snickered. "Your concern for my pleasure is touching but never fear." Stalking toward me, he scooped me from the carpet and dragged me into his arms. "Like I said, tonight we won't do anything else apart from a quick fuck. I'm tired. I'm jet-lagged. Tomorrow, we'll play in the snuffbox where I can help guide you with her education. For now, I just want to come so I can sleep soundly." He pouted as he nuzzled me close. "You won't deny me a quick release, will you?"

I couldn't look at Henri.

Couldn't look at Rachel.

My head filled with static. My heart transformed into a rabbit.

Images of Mollie with Roland down below. Peter with that brown-bearded guy, and all the other jewels currently serving out monsters' fantasies.

All of us existed in different nightmares.

The new jewels would be petrified.

Their arms sore from injections and blood tests. Their entire souls screaming that there had to have been some mistake.

I locked onto their misery instead of mine.

The empathy for them threatened to cripple me, but I would be strong for them.

I *had* to be strong for them.

Whatever they went through downstairs was far worse than this.

This was just sex.

Victor wouldn't hit me, strike me, or hurt me.

A simple transaction of bodily fluids, and it would all be over.

It's fine.

I can do this.

You knew this would happen one day…

My teeth chattered as I pictured him inside me. My insides revolted at the thought of him ejaculating—

Oh God.

Swallowing hard, I met Henri's gaze, and something happened.

Something unexplainable and mystifying.

The world fell away as I sank into his hurting silver stare.

I didn't feel Victor's touch. Didn't sense Rachel's warmth against my leg.

Just him.

And in some puzzling, incomprehensible heartbeat, I *felt* him.

I'm sorry. His eyes screamed.

I can't stop this. His entire soul howled.

For the first time since we met, I saw him. Felt him. *Heard* him.

God, did I hear him.

His anguish.

His heartbreak.

His horror.

How had I not heard him up till now? How had I not seen behind his mask and mirrors and found the missing piece of…me?

Every illusion fell away.

He was no longer the handsome demigod who defied all facets of male beauty. No longer the man I hated or the man I lusted for.

I saw him.

My twin soul.

Twin flame.

Everything the Vedic astrologer told me that fateful day collided with a heart-shattering implosion.

We would one day destroy each other.

But that day was not today.

Today, we were one, and I could survive this as long as he was near.

He could survive this as long as I was near.

Him with Rachel.

Me with Victor.

Both unwanted but…they didn't matter.

The only thing that mattered was this. Our connection. Our bond that'd grown like weeds through concrete, tenacious and insidious.

And that? God, that was blisteringly profound.

It's okay. I half smiled.

I won't watch. I arched my chin.

It'll be over soon…

I didn't know if he could catch my silent words, but he staggered to the side and groaned.

The silence of our stare screeched to a stop, and the world rushed back in.

Victor's aftershave of musk and tart citrus.

Rachel's soft presence on the floor.

And the sickening fear in my veins.

"Y-You know what, Vic…" Henri stuttered. "I'm not in the mood to fuck, so Rachel can have a night off." Squeezing his eyes shut, he opened them again and raked a shaking hand through his hair. "I accept I can't stop you from claiming Ily. We made a bargain and…fuck. I'm not gonna lie and say I'm okay with it, but…" Wiping his mouth, he sat heavily on the couch. "Just fucking get it over with."

His eyes met mine.

They glimmered sterling as if he was moments away from tears.

The memory of my vow came back to haunt me.

The day I'd given him a blowjob by the pond, I'd promised to make him weep. To sob.

Was this the catalyst that would break him?

He can't.

If Victor knew I'd somehow become Henri's ultimate weakness…

He'll make him use that Diamond Kiss chit—

Huffing with disappointment, Victor let me go. "Well, that isn't part of the plan, Mercer. Forgive me if I don't fancy you looming over me, watching my every thrust."

Without Victor holding me, I dropped to my knees beside Rachel. Our fingers instantly entwined. I wanted to tell her it was okay. None of us had a choice. I wouldn't allow jealousy to coat the very real notion that as much as I enjoyed sleeping with Henri…to her, it would still be rape.

And perhaps, just perhaps—because this place screwed up even the most sane of people—a small part of her would be jealous of me with Victor.

"All things pass," I whispered under my breath. "Whatever happens…in an hour, this will all be over."

She sniffed and squeezed my fingers so hard they hurt. "Together. We're in this together."

I squeezed back.

I grabbed the second glass of vodka and tossed it back.

And together, we waited for what came next.

Chapter Twenty-Two

Henri

COULD EMOTIONAL PAIN KILL A person?

Because I felt seconds away from death.

I couldn't breathe, blink, think, or swallow.

My eyes locked on Ily, where she huddled next to Rachel. Their hands entwined, their thighs kissing. Two stunning women but only one of them had the power to reach into my chest and wrench out my godforsaken heart.

I swore I heard her in my head before.

The quietest whisper that she was okay.

Which was fucking *ridiculous* because she wasn't okay. Rachel wasn't okay. I definitely wasn't okay.

None of this is okay!

I gagged on the thought that Q wasn't coming. His life was over because of me. I'd killed him all because I'd confessed who I was instead of letting Victor shoot me. His maid had stupidly signed her signature next to mine on his death warrant the moment she let his biggest secret slip while on the phone to his greatest enemy.

No one is coming.

I can't save her.

Can't stop this.

Fuck!

Sweat poured down my back; my shirt stuck to my skin.

I was hot and cold, calm and crazy.

Not only had I gone mad thinking I could sense Ily without words, but I literally wouldn't be able to get it up, even if Victor held a gun to my head.

Every urge and need sucked deep, deep in my belly, leaving me flaccid, limp, and sick.

The vodka in my stomach did nothing to take the edge off.

If I wasn't responsible for Ily, I'd probably do what she

suggested and leap off the patio. Then again, if I'd never met her, I wouldn't be in this unwinnable situation. I wouldn't have a rebelling heart or a mutinous body. My soul wouldn't be dying the slowest, blackest death.

Victor padded closer and sat beside me.

He rested his hand on my thigh.

I shook with dripping, feral violence to take his hand and rip it the fuck off me.

"I'm sorry you're still suffering," he murmured, squeezing my kneecap. "And I'm sorry if you feel like I'm pushing you too hard, but…I mean it when I say it's for your own good." He stroked his palm up my leg.

I turned to stone.

His touch…

His closeness.

Flashbacks of him enjoying a blowjob from Peter crowded my head.

Leaping to my feet, I paced with my hands buried in my hair.

Did he just come on to me?

And if he did…how far would I be willing to go to protect Ily from him?

Offer myself up instead?

Get on my knees and—

"Enough, Henri. Jesus, calm down." He tracked me as I paced. "You say you don't need a fuck? I hate to tell you, but you're beyond need. It's a matter of survival." Clicking his fingers, he ordered, "Rachel, come here, please."

Immediately, his pregnant jewel—*fuck, she's pregnant. He wants me to sleep with a pregnant slave*—crawled to us and rested on her knees.

Keeping her chin down and hands loose on her lap, she glowed like an angel in white lingerie. I did my best to see her like the old me would've. I would've appreciated the fall of her dark hair, the ice of her blue eyes, full breasts, and sultry pink lips.

But nothing.

My cock barely twitched. If anything, it crawled even deeper inside me.

Ily sucked in a breath, wrenching my gaze to her golden ones.

And there it was again.

The heat, the crackle, the profound knowingness and calm.

Just do it. Her eyes narrowed.

I'm okay. Her lips thinned.

I shook my head. I wanted to clean out my ears because no fucking way could those thoughts be real. She wouldn't give me permission to screw another because no way in hell could I survive the thought of her being with someone else.

That part of the night is already a done deal.

As if Victor snatched that thought out of my head, he huffed and crossed his arms. "I'm getting a little tired of your dramatics, *mon ami*. In fact, I'm well on my way to becoming offended that you're not accepting my offer of Rachel. Is she not beautiful to you? Don't you see the honour I'm giving you?" He canted his head. "Would you prefer Mollie? You won her too, but I'm afraid she's otherwise disposed with Roland tonight—"

"I told you, Vic." My voice came out black and thin. "I can't help how I'm wired. I'm loyal…" My stare snagged with Ily's again. "I have a crush—"

"A crush?" He burst out laughing. "Oh, dearie me." Turning on the ball of his foot, he studied me, then Ily, then back to me. "You think you merely have a crush?" Laughing again, he marched into me and grabbed me right between the fucking legs.

"What the actual fuck, Vic?" I shot backward, cursing the sensation of his hand on my cock.

He rubbed his fingertips together. "You're softer than a slug. Figured as much. Stay there." Stalking barefoot into his bathroom, he came back a few seconds later. Taking my hand, he smacked a little blue pill into it. "Take this, or I'll force it down your throat."

I scowled. "Viagra? No chance—"

"You have three seconds." Grabbing my abandoned vodka on the coffee table, he forced my fingers around the cool crystal. "Swallow it because I'm not letting you out of my chambers until you've fucked Rachel, and I've fucked Ilyana." His smile turned soft and dreamy. "We will enjoy a mutual evening of pleasure, yes? I told you I wouldn't hurt yours, and you won't hurt mine. I'll even let you watch. In fact, we'll do it together. How about that?" Turning around, he pushed the food-laden coffee table to the edge of the huge circular carpet, leaving the centre free. "We'll share in our lust right here. No secrets between us. Only fun." His eyes narrowed. "I won't ask you again to take that pill, Henri, and I know you're probably cursing my strictness, but allow me to tell you why you need to do this."

Giving me a sad smile as if he truly cared about the fucked-up state of my soul, he murmured, "I hate to tell you this, Henri, but you don't have a crush." He clucked his tongue. "You're so past a crush it's a disease at this point."

"A disease?"

"In our lives? Yes. Love is a disease that needs to be cut out, eradicated, and cured."

"*Love?*"

"Oh, come now. You can't be that naïve. You're in love with her."

My legs threatened to buckle.

I wanted to deny it.

I needed to.

But...hadn't I had the same thoughts lately?

Hadn't I felt it taunting me beneath the black blanket of depression?

I watched her when she slept, my heart ballooning out of my chest with tenderness.

I hung on her every word, desperate to hear more.

I begged for a single tear, grateful when she was too strong to cry.

Fuck.

"The fact that you're not denying it proves I'm right," Victor said quietly.

Ily made a noise behind him, wrenching my stare to her. Even Rachel looked over her shoulder, studying Ily's reaction.

My entire heart felt like it was on fire. A never-ending fire growing wilder, hotter, and far, far too destructive.

Victor tapped my chin, bringing my gaze back to his. "We are monsters. We're at the top of the food chain and that's why you're struggling so much. Every atom in your body is telling you to let go and be free, but your heart—that stupid human heart—has latched onto the final thing holding you back."

Fisting my wrist, he pushed my hand toward my mouth.

The blue pill rocked on my palm.

"This will stop all that pain inside you." He nodded encouragingly as my strength wavered. "All that second-guessing? All that suffering? Poof." He smiled as my palm touched my lips. "I promise you, Henri...if you cut those ropes and break out of that prison that love has bound you in, you'll be free...once and for all."

I hated my weakness.

That my despair perked up at the very notion of no longer feeling this way.

She said it was okay…

I sighed and hung my head.

Nothing was okay.

But nothing about my life or childhood had *ever* been okay.

Perhaps…maybe…I could be okay if I did this. If I allowed Vic to free me, maybe I wouldn't have to use my switchblade to reopen my scar and end it.

I didn't have long.

The misery and melancholy were winning, crushing.

I honestly didn't know how much longer I could fight the urge to rest, to sleep, to die.

Q isn't coming…

If I died, Ily would be alone.

But if I cured my affliction of loving her, then perhaps…just perhaps, I could learn how to be better at this. I could still be her Master. We could still have a life together. Just without the mess and agony of feelings.

With a groan, I allowed Victor to tip the pill onto my tongue.

I didn't fight as he took my glass from my shaking hand and pressed the drink to my lips like I was a child.

The wet stabbing pain behind my eyes came again.

He cared.

He truly cared.

I swallowed.

He hugged me, and I sagged into his embrace.

The wretchedness inside me crashed too hard, too deep.

I sank into it.

Darkness tugged me down and down.

Guiding me to the couch, he sat me down, then padded toward Ily.

My fists balled to stop him.

My body fought the sluggish riptide inside me, making everything so slow and stilted and sad. Just so fucking sad.

I'd never felt such pain.

Such heartache.

Such despair.

I didn't know what was wrong with me.

Why I could barely move.

Why I felt utterly spaced and seedy.

Closing my eyes, I tried to get a better grip on my rapidly fraying sanity.

Surely, I could come up with a way to prevent Victor from fucking Ily. Didn't matter I'd agreed to it. Didn't matter he'd probably try to kill me if I forbade him. I just couldn't put her through that. Couldn't run the risk of him breaking her like she'd broken me.

He expects you to fuck Rachel.

I swallowed hard as nausea clutched my throat.

The thought of being *inside* her. The thought of feeling another woman's heat around me.

Jesus.

Every inch of me recoiled. I shrivelled inside.

The room swam; white noise hissed in my ears.

Stand up.

Tell him no.

Grab Ily and leave.

Do it!

Before it's too late.

Shifting on the couch, I went to stand, but my heart didn't beat right.

I groaned as I collapsed backward, weighted down in every possible way.

The blackness inside me—the thick, impenetrable depression—buried me alive, handcuffing me, gagging me, throwing a hood over my head, and blinding me.

Forcing my eyelids up, I fought against the current and blinked back the dreadful despair.

Victor pushed Ily onto all fours.

He pulled down her G-string.

No...

My heart cracked as Victor landed on his knees behind her and smiled in my direction.

Do something!

Shimmying out of his pyjama bottoms, he said something I couldn't catch. Words warbled and echoed like pecking crows at my broken brain.

I felt drugged.

Woozy.

His voice came again down a long, thin tunnel.

Fractals of black and white scrambled my eyesight.

Time skipped.

My breathing quickened.

My lower belly grew hotter. The clock on the wall ticked louder. My trousers grew tighter.

"—aren't you?" Victor's voice cut through my daze.

What did he say?

I blinked and lurched forward. The room turned upside down.

Was this panic?

Could a person snap and lose all their faculties?

Wedging my elbows on my knees, I rubbed my eyes, trying to make sense of why I was so lethargic, so goddamn tired. I felt utterly drunk, drowned by the fermenting depression that just wouldn't leave me the fuck alone.

I winced as my cock speared upright, trying to break through my pants.

Adjusting myself, the tip crawled out of my waistband, hard as stone but without any of the usual sensitivity.

Everything about me felt dead.

Dull.

Bloodless.

Lifeless.

Not panic then.

Death.

So this is what it feels like to die…

A fading.

A falling.

A perishing beneath hopelessness.

"You're acting as if I roofied you." Victor laughed. "Come on. I'm being patient, but I can only wait so long." He flicked a look at the clock hanging by his bathroom door. "It's been fourteen minutes. You should be good to go."

Fourteen minutes?

What?!

I scowled and begged my eyes to focus on the clock.

He had to be lying.

It wavered and wobbled, the hands flickering with every heavy thud of my very heavy heart.

"Come on, Henri." Arching his chin at Rachel, he ordered, "Present on all fours, my pet. That's it. Remove your underwear. There's a good girl. Come a little closer to Ily. You can hold hands if you like, I know you jewels get comfort from one another. Good, now face me. I want to watch you as he rides you." He grinned. "You better not enjoy it too much."

"No, Sir V." Rachel shook her head. "I only ever get pleasure from you."

"That better be the truth." He chuckled.

The room spun as Victor raised his voice. "Henri, hurry the fuck up."

His command.

So similar to my father's.

Memories opened a trapdoor.

I tripped—

"Onn Ree, whip her, there's a good boy. Onn Ree, taste her tears, aren't they sweet? Onn Ree, touch her there. Go on, I won't tell. Onn Ree, cut her and maybe you'll be the one to inherit everything instead of my legitimate son."

With my father's voice in my head and my mind back there, I couldn't reach dry land. I drowned beneath the kid who'd had no choice. The prisoner who couldn't say no. The man who thought he wanted this but now would rather die.

"Henri!" Victor barked. "Don't make me show you how to fuck her. Just do it."

"Onn Ree, feel her. Squeeze her. That's it. Now…put your cock in, it's alright. She likes it…see? Onn Ree, are you not enjoying yourself? Move faster, boy. Go on—"

My teeth clenched as another gush of nausea threatened to evict every recollection I'd ever repressed. I wished I'd never unlocked them through writing. Wished I could go back to that amnesiac existence where I had no idea why I was the way I was. At least I could've survived then. Could've pretended I was happy.

But now?

Knowing what I'd done?

Remembering how much I'd hurt our mothers—

Fuck.

I fell off the couch as my stomach roiled.

"Henri, if you don't appreciate my gift and fuck Rachel immediately, I'll call the guards and have them help you."

"Good." I groaned, pushing to my knees. "Maybe they can beat this out of me."

A few seconds ticked past. Victor's heavy huff sounded like a cyclone in my ears. Finally, he muttered, "I told you, you're sick. I'm helping you, don't you see? Tell you what, if you don't accept my generosity, I'll call the guards in and give *them* a gift instead. I believe there are four in the corridor at present. I'll let each of them have a piece of Ily. I'm sure they'll be more than happy to—"

"No." I crawled toward the woman kneeling on all fours. "I'll do it," I slurred.

Victor might've gotten me drunk before Ruby Tears, but tonight…my own grief had done that.

"Finally." Victor sniffed. "I feel as if I've aged five years waiting for you to hurry it along."

"Finally, Onn Ree, took you long enough to get hard. What's wrong with you? Why can't you come? Have you never had a wet dream before? Go on, try again."

"Sorry." I hung my head, unsure if I apologised to my father or Victor.

Rachel looked over her shoulder as I slowed behind her.

Her ice-blue eyes widened at whatever she saw on my face.

I couldn't look at Ily.

Couldn't breathe.

All I wanted to do was die.

"Tick-tock, Henri."

"Time's ticking, Onn Ree."

A childhood of despicable instruction took over. Parts of my psyche that were so damaged, so dark that I'd done my utmost to forget them, rose and took charge.

In a fugue, my hands reached for Rachel's hips.

They were a stranger's hands.

An enemy's hands.

A splicing vision settled over my eyes, replaying a piece of my past.

I'd seen this before.

Seen my boyish hand landing on the bare ass of one of our mothers. It blended with my own larger one as I reached for Rachel against my will.

I'd never been able to say no.

I'd screamed the first few times.

I'd fought his hold as he made me abuse them.

I'd tried to shut down, but he soon learned how to keep me present.

Kind words, nice praise, sweet encouragements.

Love.

Motherfucking love had shackled me to such atrocities.

"That's it, Onn Ree. She's all yours. They're all yours. Do you like it?"

"That's it, *mon ami*." Victor's voice rearranged my memories, inserting himself into them, replacing the role of my sadistic father. "Get your cock out and stick it in her."

The noise of my zipper as I shoved my pants down merged with the sobs I'd made as a little boy, forced by his father to do such unspeakable things.

The similarities. The sickening déjà vu.

"*Good boy, Onn Ree.*"

I fisted myself with a quaking hand.

"Do it, Mercer."

I choked as I notched inside a woman I didn't want.

"All the way now."

"*You're doing so well, my son…*"

"Thrust, Henri."

"*Thrust, Onn Ree.*"

My chin sank onto my chest as I pushed.

I didn't feel a damn thing.

I checked out.

Went numb.

I'd forgotten for a reason.

I'd forgotten because I couldn't survive.

The nausea in my stomach as I threw up the rich chocolate cake my father had given me the first time I'd drawn blood. The trembles and shakes as he came for me again and again. The horrors as he tried to make my prepubescent body come. The absolute despair as he taught me how to swing a flogger—

"My turn." Victor let out a roar as he mounted Ily in front of me.

She cried out.

Her eyes snapped closed.

And that was the moment my entire existence shattered.

I didn't help her.

I failed her.

Trapped in the past.

Shackled by the boy I'd been.

A boy who'd watched so many women being raped.

A boy who'd been forced to watch and never interfere until it was his turn.

And I couldn't do it.

Couldn't cope.

Not anymore.

Not now.
Not again.
My body and heart didn't break, but my mind?
It snapped like a rubber band.
I flatlined—

Chapter Twenty-Three

Ily

I FLOATED ABOVE THE CASTLE.

The stars twinkled in all their might. The Milky Way splashed across the sky like a pathway to better days. And the moon played peek-a-boo behind wispy silvery clouds.

So beautiful.

So perfect.

So pure.

I lay on my back beneath all of the night's glory and didn't watch.

Didn't watch.

Back there in reality, my body rocked with his every thrust.

Back there in hell, I felt him sliding inside me, deeper and harder, rocking me forward and back, forward and back, all while I fought to stay on all fours.

It didn't hurt.

But it did destroy me.

But I didn't watch, so it didn't matter.

It didn't matter as he picked up his pace and fisted my hips to pump harder.

It didn't matter he took my body against my will.

I was free of him.

Free of Victor. Of Henri. Of nightmares.

My fingers might be entwined with Rachel's as we faced each other. Our breath might mingle with every vicious thrust, our lips near enough to kiss. She might rock in the same primal rhythm, driven forward and back by my twin flame as he made love to her.

But it wasn't real.

It wasn't love.

It was rape on both their accounts.

Every facet of Henri was dead. His face, his eyes, his energy. He thrust like a robot, blank stare, and hollow heart.

The man I'd accepted as mine no longer lived inside that shell. He was free like me...detached and dissociated from reality.

But what was reality?

Could the freedom and light I floated in be our true reality, while down there, where everything was evil and hardship, the illusion?

A dream.

Nothing but a hologram, a hallucination, something that would end and fade.

I floated around the gargoyles and angels of Victor's parapets as he used me. I disassociated all over again and sank into a mediative calmness unlike anything I'd ever experienced.

Golden light enveloped me, blocking out all sights and sounds and senses.

It cradled me until I lost all touch with my mortal body; I hovered in ultimate freedom.

A part of me knew it couldn't last.

Beauty and wonder such as this could never exist forever.

But while it did, I was grateful.

So grateful to find a way to be untouchable all while being touched. Protected all while being used. I no longer sensed Henri or Rachel. No longer suffered hate or fear or pain.

Wisdom that didn't come from me blanketed my entire soul, wrapping me up in protection full of forgiveness, courage, and truth.

Time drifted without me under its influence.

Days could've passed.

Weeks.

And my golden light didn't falter.

But then...finally, a feathering tug from my body to my soul.

A fishing hook digging into my spirit, reeling me back on a nylon line I couldn't escape.

What would happen if I cut that line?

What if I refused to go back?

Would I float to the next life and leave my body to rot?

Would I be free of living in a place I didn't want, struggling with feelings I couldn't stop, and enduring things I wasn't strong enough to survive?

You are strong enough.

You have to be.

You made a promise.

To Peter.
To them.
Get them out...

My golden light faded a little, allowing mortal sensations to enter my serenity.

Hands on my hips. Grunts in my ears. The faintest pressure as the beast who raped me reached his end.

Not yet.

Not yet.

I would go back.

I would finish what I started.

But not yet.

I flew higher into the stars as he spilled inside me. I stayed in the cosmos as his body withdrew from mine.

I didn't know what happened for a while after that.

I stayed up there where it was quiet and safe.

Where no one else could reach me.

I wasn't aware of Rachel whispering in my ear or someone picking me up.

The detachment grew stronger as I sank from the heavens and hovered near the ceiling of Victor's bedroom.

I'd never experienced such a thing.

The projection of my consciousness as a separate entity.

My body draped like a broken bride's in Henri's arms.

Sweat glimmered on his temples.

His trousers done up, his shirt neatly tucked, his face carved from stone. He might stand like a man and smile like a friend, but nothing was inside him.

Broken.

Empty.

Gone.

Bowing his head, shifting me higher in his arms, Henri said softly, "Thank you for allowing me the honour of Rachel's company, Victor."

Just like his body, his voice held no life, no spark.

I studied my face, where I hung in his embrace.

No life, no spark.

My eyes might be open, but they didn't focus.

Lips slack.

I looked dead.

But that couldn't be.

I floated a little closer, my light-ball heart skipping at the torment on Henri's face. Beneath his emptiness, the faintest shards of agony gleamed. The longer I stared and saw past his brokenness, the more my heart flurried faster.

I'd never seen a man so...shattered. So damaged.

Lines bracketed his mouth. His eyes aged a million years. A glossiness coated his stare as if every inch of him had filled up with tears he couldn't spill.

The longer he stood holding me, the more his energy swelled from dread to despair. It billowed in every corner. It howled in every bone. A ferocity kept building, curdling, until the cold draft of his misery sucked me close.

I tried to fight it.

But he was too strong. His soul summoned mine, pleading with me, begging me—

I snapped back into my body.

The floaty, airy feeling of drifting by the ceiling vanished.

I jerked as I settled back into blood and bone.

Heavy and solid, sticky and used.

Henri looked down at me.

The ticking of time stopped.

I bit my lip as the memories my physical body had recorded replayed in crystal clarity.

Henri on his knees behind Rachel.

Henri mounting her with a grunt that sounded as if he'd stabbed himself in the heart.

Henri moving stiffly, unwillingly.

Rachel whispering in my ear that it meant nothing. Henri meant nothing. Victor meant nothing. It was just us. Me and her. Just us. Just *us*. She'd kept whispering such a thing as Victor orgasmed inside me. His shuddering pulses despicable and his kiss on my shoulder utterly vile.

Henri had torn himself free the moment Victor finished.

Rachel had sagged and pushed her white teddy back into place.

I wanted to console her.

Hug her.

Make sure she was okay after years of abuse.

"You're leaving?" Victor strolled toward us, tying the string of his pyjama bottoms and raking a hand through his hair. "But you haven't come."

"I'm sorry. My body…I'm tired." He didn't look up from the carpet. "I fucked her. That's all you asked me to do." He sounded as if he'd swallowed a canyon, and his soul echoed back.

"It was supposed to relax you, not…" Victor waved at Henri's condition. "Whatever this is."

Henri chuckled. "I'm fine. Truly."

The edge of insanity sharpened his tone.

He's not fine.

So far from fine.

His pain overshadowed mine like the biggest thundercloud. I couldn't think about what'd happened to me. Couldn't look at Victor and know his DNA was inside me.

For now, it never happened.

And really, it hadn't.

Not in my world.

Not in my meditative freedom where no one could touch me.

But Henri?

God…I didn't know how to help him.

I hung in his arms and witnessed a slow car crash. I could see the flames about to erupt. Hear the smash. Watch the carnage. But I couldn't do a damn thing to stop it.

Pouring a glass of water from the carafe on the table, Victor padded toward Rachel and passed it to her. "Here, my sweetling. Go start a bath and take a soak. I'll order up some cheesecake, hmm?"

Rachel blinked, wary of Victor's kindness. Climbing to her feet, she drank the water and nodded. "Thank you, Sir V. You're so good to me."

"I'm proud of you, my pet. If you continue being so obedient and appreciative, I might allow you to sleep in my chambers every night until the baby comes. Would you like that?"

Rachel resisted the urge to look at me, but I felt her horror. Matched it with my own.

If the two of us weren't able to sleep in the jewel's quarters, our resistance might struggle to hold meetings. Mollie would have to keep things going without us. Peter would have to take over the leadership role all while he dealt with bastards.

"That's very kind of you, Sir V. I-I'd like that…but I wouldn't want to be any trouble."

"No trouble at all. You're rather precious to me now." Kissing her on the forehead, he motioned toward the bathroom. "Run along now. I might join you in a bit. I'll just see Henri out."

"Yes, Sir V." With a snatched look in my direction, she scurried into the bathroom and vanished.

The moment she was gone, Henri marched toward the exit. "Thanks for having us. I hope you have a restful sleep."

Rote phrases. Programmed delivery.

All the sharp, savage emotions within him stayed bottled up.

Pressurising, amplifying, pressing against the brokenness inside him.

Victor padded after us. "And you, *mon ami*." Cutting in front of us, he eyed me lying silently in Henri's arms and curled his upper lip. "I thought she'd be more…lively." Poking me in the breast, he shrugged. "Frankly, she was a bit of a letdown."

In a horrifying full-circle moment, he reminded me of Samuel. His disappointment of me in the bedroom. His slurs that I couldn't match a blow-up doll. And just like I'd been grateful for Sam's comments, I was thankful for Victor's because—

"So once was enough for you?" Henri paused as Victor opened the door.

Victor huffed. "I'll never say never, but…I've had a better release with a half-hearted blowjob from Kirk."

"I'm sorry she didn't live up to your expectations," Henri said, barren and bereft.

Victor didn't see how close Henri was to the cliff.

A cliff that tugged him closer, closer…

"Until you've instilled some willingness to participate, then I've had my fill." Victor sniffed. "I honestly don't know what you see in her."

Henri sagged as he stepped over the threshold.

He didn't reply.

His teeth sank into his bottom lip as if holding back all those feelings mushroom clouding inside him.

"Never fear," Victor said, completely oblivious. "We'll work on that tomorrow." Patting Henri on the shoulder, he grinned. "Shall we say midday? We'll meet on the deck, and I'll show you my favourite place on my island. You can christen your new whip. In fact…" He snapped his fingers as if he'd had a brilliant idea. "I'll introduce you to my favourite game. I don't let many guests play as I don't like my jewels too marked, but…it can be our little secret. It's called Sapphire Scars, and well…I'm sure you can guess what it entails."

Henri nodded, his eyes blank. "I'm guessing high tea and sandwiches?"

Victor chuckled. "You and your dry sense of humour." Stepping back into his bedroom, he waved. "Ta-ra, then. I must admit, I'm enjoying this little group of ours. Sleep well, and we'll play again tomorrow."

He shut the door.

The moment the lock snicked into place, Henri staggered back and slammed into the wall.

His arms trembled. Every part of him began to shake. And shake. And *shake*.

I squirmed to get down.

I needed to be on my feet before he dropped me.

But he sucked in a guttural groan, then swayed toward the stairs.

My heart leapt into my mouth as he tripped and stumbled down them. I didn't know how he stayed upright as his breath came fast, his face turned white, and he broke into a run the moment we reached our floor.

Down the corridor, over our threshold, and straight into the bathroom.

With exquisite gentleness, he placed me on my feet.

With heavy, gasping inhales, he tripped to the sink and clutched the vanity with white-knuckled hands. His eyes squeezed closed. His fingers dug into porcelain. Dropping his head, he panted, "Shower. Now."

I didn't know what to do.

I'd seen Krish suffer a few episodes. Been witness to my poor brother as he reached critical mass and tipped over into despair. But I'd never seen a man shatter into splintering pieces before me.

Swaying toward him, I went to touch—

I stopped.

My own pain wrapped around me.

Memories of Victor.

The stickiness between my legs.

The imprint of his kiss on my shoulder.

Henri's energy was overpowering, all-consuming.

But mine billowed too.

Hot and stinging, sharp and cutting.

I might not have watched, but my body held remnants.

I couldn't help him.

Not yet.

Not until Victor's horrid touch was gone.

Keeping a careful eye on Henri as he folded over the vanity, dug his elbows into the bench, and buried his face into quaking hands, I stripped out of my black lingerie and stepped into the shower.

As cold water became hot and the bliss of cleanliness helped soothe my jagged pieces, I never took my gaze off Henri.

The more seconds that ticked past, the more he shook.

The entire bathroom filled with his pain.

By the time I finished and wrapped myself in a towel, he crashed past me fully clothed and stood beneath burning water.

Holding his face to the gushing shower, he tore off his sodden shirt, unzipped his drenched pants, and coated every inch of his body in soap.

And then, he scrubbed.

And scrubbed.

His fingernails left tracks over his skin, welts and lashes as if he could scratch out the horrors inside him.

He pumped his Viagra-forced erection as if he could delete all traces of tonight.

He washed every inch.

Again and again.

Crazed and jerky.

Backing away, I hugged my towel as his motions turned manic. Desperate.

Closer and closer to that edge.

Nearer and nearer to the end.

Until finally, with a gasp and a grunt, he fell to his knees...

...and broke.

Chapter Twenty-Four

Henri

HER EYES.
Her stare.
Empty.
Vacant.
Gone.
I'd done that.
I killed her.
The agonising wrongness of being inside another woman.
The guttering despair of another man inside her.
The godawful horror of being hard against my will.
Even now.
Hard and heartbroken and *fuck*!
My mind didn't just break. It demolished.
I kneeled in the burning shower and begged the water to wash away every sin. Every failure.
I killed her.
The floppy way she'd hung in my arms when I'd first grabbed her from the floor.
The loss of her fight, her soul, her heart.
My eyes stung.
My lungs ached.
Every piece of me trembled and tangled until I wasn't a man but a mess of vibrating molecules ready to shatter in every direction.
Glowering at the scar on my leg, I scratched at it.
I needed to finish the job.
She was dead.
I killed her.
I'd brought her here and subjected her to these horrors.
There was nothing left for me now.
Nothing.

The stinging in my eyes grew worse.
The aching in my chest crushing, crushing—
Blood pooled in my mouth as I bit my bottom lip, doing my best to trap the screams inside me.
I scratched harder.
I-I killed her.
I—
Hands on mine.
Gentle and so, so kind.
I paused my scratching, scrubbing.
I looked up.
Into golden beautiful eyes.
Alive eyes.
No longer vacant or dead.
And every part of me cracked.
I'm sorry.
So sorry.
"Henri..."
Her voice.
Christ, her voice.
I swayed toward her.
I crashed against her.
Her arms wrapped around me and held tight.
The stinging in my eyes became caustic.
The searing in my lungs so vicious.
I wanted to tell her so many things. All of it. Everything. But I couldn't because the devil wrapped his hand around my throat and *strangled.*
I gasped.
I can't breathe.
My heart bucked.
I can't breathe!
Pushing the angel away from me, I crawled out of the shower.
My bones jangled.
My blood jumped.
Nausea tore through me, and I needed—
I'm going to—
With a lurch, I reached the toilet, flipped up the lid, and purged.
A lifetime of horrors. Of memories. Of imprinting.
Every moment my father made me hit a woman. Every drop

of blood he'd forced me to drink. Every tear, every scream, every cry.

My ribs bellowed.

My head pounded.

A soft hand landed between my drenched shoulder blades.

"It's okay," she whispered. "You're okay."

The stinging behind my eyes became daggers.

My ribs broke one by one as pressure swelled bigger, blacker—

Slamming the lid down on my shame, I fumbled with the flush, then landed in a painful, naked heap on top of the toilet.

Icy shivers merged with my shakes.

I was hot and cold, grieving and guilt-ridden.

Golden eyes looked up at me where she rested between my legs. Her fragile hands landed on my knees.

My kneecaps jittered and jumped.

I couldn't stay still.

Too much.

Too hard.

Too painful.

My legs danced up and down on their own accord as every emotion I couldn't shed bled out the only way it could.

She shuffled closer, stroked her hands higher until they landed on my quaking thighs.

She.

Her.

Ily.

I.L.Y.

I love you.

I do.

God, I do.

I love you.

I'm sorry.

So, so fucking sorry.

Grabbing her cheeks, I pressed my forehead to hers.

The stinging in my eyes grew worse. So, so much worse.

I choked.

I gagged.

With her so close, so alive, so pure, I couldn't fight it anymore.

A sob broke free.

Followed by a single tear.

She cooed under her breath and rose on her knees. "Ah, Hen…"

Hen…

My arms lashed around her, dragging her from the floor and onto my lap.

The moment her weight landed on me.

The *second* her heat sank into me.

It was over.

An ocean of tears poured free.

A torrent of them.

A river of them.

Shame and disgrace, self-disgust and remorse.

I painted her in wetness as I nuzzled into her neck and let go.

The noises I made.

The sobs I couldn't hold back.

I was that little boy again.

The boy who could never cry because he had sisters and brothers to protect. Lies to say and horrors to forget.

A lifetime of misery chose that moment to destroy me.

I couldn't catch my breath.

Couldn't stay alive.

I'd hurt so many.

So, so many.

I hurt her.

So, so badly.

Crushing her to me, I wept into her perfect skin and laid every rotten piece at her feet.

Time ticked onward. But I wasn't aware.

Ice settled into my bones. But her warmth kept me alive.

I couldn't stop.

It just kept pouring, pouring—

At some point in my breaking, Ily shifted on my lap. Wrapping her arms around my head, she hugged me to her breasts. She held me to her, cradled me, protected me.

I cried harder.

I should've been the one to protect her.

Guard her.

Avenge her.

Because of me, he'd taken her.

Because of me, she was a slave.

Because of me.

Because of me.

Always because of me.

God—

My head cracked from the pressure. I bled out all over the floor.

"I'm sorry." My voice broke. "I—" I couldn't finish.

Another feral noise tumbled from my mouth; I held her far too tight.

She moaned in my arms, but I couldn't stop.

How could I ever make it up to her?

How could I ever repair this?

How could she ever forgive me?

The thought of her hating me for eternity was too much.

Too painful.

Fresh tears stung.

Horror that I'd lost her.

Acceptance that I deserved it.

"I'm sorry…" I tried again. "So, so fucking sorry."

"Hush." She kissed the top of my head. "It's okay. You're okay…"

Jesus Christ, how was this woman so goddamn strong?

Her strength put mine to shame.

He'd raped her.

Hurt her.

Yet I was the one who broke.

I clung to her like a drowning man.

I rocked and sobbed and begged, fucking *begged* her to fix me. To erase my past, delete my sins, and somehow heal me from everything my father had made me become.

The pressure in my eyes slipped down onto my tongue.

Just like I couldn't stop the tears, I couldn't stop the confessions.

"H-He made me lose my virginity at seven years old." I cringed at the words. I wanted to snatch them back. I hated that more flowed free. "He made me cut them…fuck them…"

The sobs came back.

Fresh tears washed away words and secrets I'd kept hidden even from myself.

What was I doing?

Dumping that shit on her?

I should be the one cradling her.

Letting her cry and heal.

Raising my head, I tried to be better. To be the man I should've always been.

But the moment our eyes locked, I forgot everything.

A quaking cavernous silence filled me; I sucked in my first breath in so long.

No more noises or sorrow…just aching quietness after the storm. A blanketing lull that felt both peaceful and terrifying.

Shifting on my lap, she draped her legs on either side of my hips.

Her towel rode up, exposing her.

The hard-on that wouldn't fade for hours thanks to that awful fucking pill speared between us, and I *hated* it. Hated that part of myself. Hated how much pain it'd caused me and all those I'd abused.

Sickness rose again, but Ily kept me stable. The dizziness couldn't find me. The horrors blocked out thanks to her touch.

"Tell me," she whispered. "Let it out."

With a groan, I clung to her.

I couldn't.

I had no right.

But the despair inside me bled out anyway. "I remember. All of it. I know now why my mother absolutely despised me. She knew. She knew what he made me do. What I did to those women. And…and I don't think I can live with what I've done. With what I am."

She hugged me back, so kind, so wonderfully, horribly kind. She didn't speak. Didn't offer absolution. She just held me in my pain.

Tears welled all over again.

For my brother.

His son.

His wife.

Were they still alive?

How could I warn them that Victor was coming?

How could I stop all of this because I couldn't stay here. She couldn't stay here. None of those jewels, new or old, could stay anywhere near this nightmare.

My body quaked and rattled.

My mind refractured and reformed.

I'd been searching for validation in all the wrong places, in all the worst people, but now...I knew what I had to do.

I knew what was worth fighting for, dying for...her.

Always, forever *her*.

Pressing my lips to her ear so the cameras couldn't hear, I whispered, "That's the last time he'll ever lay a finger on you. You have my absolute vow."

Sucking in a breath, she pulled back and caught my eyes.

Cupping her cheeks, I tucked blue-black hair behind her ears. *"Ce qui reste de ma vie sans valeur est à toi et tu peux en faire ce que tu veux. Je ne m'attends pas à ce que tu me pardonnes. Je sais que tu ne feras jamais plus que me détester mais... j'en ai fini."* (What's left of my worthless life is yours to do with as you please. I don't expect you to forgive me. I know you'll never do more than hate me, but...I'm done.)

The final dregs of the ocean inside me ebbed and sloshed as I hugged her again.

A simple hug.

My ultimate undoing.

I didn't know if I wanted to live or die, but I did know this woman now owned me.

I would lay down my life for her.

I would do whatever it took to get her free.

Sucking in a haggard breath, I pulled back.

Tears tracked her cheeks.

Her sadness merged with mine.

For once in my life, I had no desire to drink her grief. No sick urge to taste.

Our despair splashed together, binding, baptising.

I couldn't look away.

My heart didn't just burst wide open; it threw itself onto a pyre and *burned*.

"Ily..." I shook my head at the weight of it. "Ily..."

Her tears dripped faster. A smile tugged her lips. "So you do remember how to say my name."

"I love you," I breathed.

She stiffened. "Yes, that's what it means—"

"No." Reaching into the vanity drawer, I grabbed the mouthwash and swilled away the awful taste of sadness and shame. Spitting the minty mouthful into the sink, I cradled her close, brushed my nose against hers, and said the most honest, petrifying truth of my life, "I meant...*I love you*."

I felt as heavy as the world.

As wrung out as a dirty towel.

But…lighter too. Sunshine spearing through the cracks in the black clouds, giving me just enough light to stay alive.

Her lips pressed together. Her body stiffened on my lap.

The old me would've closed himself off, backed up, pretended he hadn't said such things because he couldn't handle the thought of being so vulnerable. But…this was no longer about me. It'd *never* been about me.

It's always been about her, and I was just too much of an idiot to see it.

"I love you, Ilyana Sharma, and I know you'll never say it back. But I need to tell you anyway. I love you. Christ, I love you. Loving you is the worst pain I've ever felt but I'm grateful because…I deserve it. I deserve to be in agony for what I've done. Deserve to be in pieces for how much I've failed you."

"Henri, I—"

"It's fine. Don't say anything. I'm…" I sagged and forced a wet chuckle. "I didn't mean to break that badly. I'm sorry—"

"It's okay—"

"I shouldn't be sobbing all over you. I should be the one holding—"

"Why? So I can cry over what Victor did?" She rolled her eyes as if he meant nothing. "I accepted that it would happen, and I didn't watch when it did."

"Didn't watch?" Fresh tears stung my eyes. What did that mean? Why wasn't she a mess over this? Had she snapped like I had and refused to come back?

It's true then…I-I broke her.

Here I was pouring my fucking heart out, and she wasn't sane enough to understand me.

Gathering her closer, I rocked her on my lap. "Please, Ily. Don't let him take you from me. Don't let him win—"

"Win?"

"I know I didn't stop him. I know I didn't protect you, but please, I won't survive if you leave me—"

"Leave, wh—?"

"It's okay. I'm gonna fix this. I promise. I swear I'll find a way and—"

"Henri—"

"Just come back to me and—"

"*Henri!*"

I froze, terror spiralling in my chest. I blinked as she cupped my cheeks, her fingers strong and sure. "Stop talking over me and *listen*."

I swallowed hard, captivated and confused. The way her golden eyes blazed. The way her body sat so proud and defiant. She looked the opposite of broken. She looked...untouched.

I frowned. "How are you okay with this? How are you not in pieces?"

She shook her head, her damp hair sticking to bare shoulders, her towel gaping around her breasts. "I'm fine."

"*Fine?*" I reclined against the cistern, the cold porcelain biting into my naked skin. "You shut down completely. You weren't aware when I picked you up. Your eyes were vacant, your soul gone. You were a goddamn corpse."

She gave me a soft smile. "I wasn't gone. I just wasn't watching."

My nose wrinkled. "I-I don't understand."

"I went somewhere he couldn't touch me."

"Where?"

"Not sure. All I know is, Victor happened. Rachel happened. I'll have to deal with everything eventually, but right now...right now, I need to be strong to keep my promise to Pete—" She smashed her lips together. Her eyes widened as if she hadn't meant to say such things. For a moment, she looked as if she'd push away and leave.

"What promise?" I asked quietly.

Her shoulders braced but then...her face softened, her hand reached up, and she brushed away my tears with a gentle thumb. "Did you mean it?"

Goosebumps darted down my back at her caress. My cock throbbed with need—lust so honest and raw compared to the pharmaceutical chemicals keeping me stiff. "Mean what?"

"That you're done playing his games?"

Her whisper was just the same as any other, yet...

Every part of me had changed.

It was as if the boy inside me who couldn't protect his siblings had finally taken control and would do absolutely *anything* to right his wrongs.

Smiling gently, falling deeper into love with her, I pressed a chaste kiss to her lips. We sat entwined on the fucking toilet, the still-falling shower muting our whispers, our skin chilled from droplets, and our connection unseen by the cameras. "You asked me a month ago to play along with you." Kissing my way along her jaw to her ear, I murmured, "I should've said this back then, but...I'm ready. I'm ready to do whatever it takes to finish what I started. I came here to free all those trapped. So...I'll free them. Or I'll die trying."

It was her turn to sob.

My arms twined around her; I held her exquisitely close.

I gave myself this moment of absolute surrender.

Victor wouldn't know.

The one spot he couldn't watch.

For a few stolen seconds, we were free.

And as Ily cried in my arms and purged this awful night onto my shoulder, I scattered kisses all over her, then signed my life over to hers. Sunshine filled my heart. The path I should've followed all along unravelled in blinding light.

I was ready to walk it.

Ready to repent.

Ready to be worthy.

"I'm yours, Ily. Every piece. Today, tomorrow, and always. Let's play..."

Chapter Twenty-Five

Ily

I DIDN'T WANT TO CRY.

I'd done everything I could to avoid such a thing.

I'd allowed Henri's despair to nullify my own, grateful to be strong enough to put another before me. After a lifetime of looking after Krish and placing his needs before mine, I had a good crutch to lean on, convincing me I was okay.

Of course I wasn't affected by Victor raping me.

It was just sex. Just a body. Just whatever…

Of course I wasn't dying beneath constant fear of living in this place.

It was just a castle. Just monsters. Just another day…

Of course I wasn't living in constant stress or misery or panic or horror or pain or worry or, or, or…

Of *course not*.

Of course—

Lies.

Pretend.

Coping mechanisms.

As Henri slowly climbed out of his ashes and the deadness in his eyes transformed into vicious life, he stole all my distractions. Tore apart all my careful lies and forced me to see just how much I *wasn't* okay.

It'd been so long since I felt safe.

So long since I could take off my mask and be honest.

And as his arms came around me, cocooning me in a safe harbour, I folded inward, gave in, and let go.

Victor raped me.

I felt him. Even now. Inside me. *Moving*.

I cringed away.

I tried to run.

But my mind popped the corks of every moment I'd bottled

up. Every horror I'd shrugged off and every sleepless night I'd shoved away.

It was too much.

I wasn't alright.

I wasn't.

I was afraid and lonely, lost and dying day by day.

My brave face for Peter and the jewels.

My determination not to let evil win.

I was exhausted.

Barely hanging on.

Drowning…

I hated Henri for showing me that.

Hated that I'd been so alone.

Hated how wonderful it was to suddenly *have* someone. Someone who threw up a shield between me and horror and kept me hidden just for a moment.

The past weeks unravelled, crushing me into tears.

Victor.

H-He raped me.

I didn't watch.

But I'd *felt* it.

My body *endured* it.

He'd sullied me.

Defiled me.

Fucked me—

Nausea brewed hot in my stomach.

The urge to purge clutched around my throat.

I had a sudden commiseration for Henri and all the moments his system forced him to retch. It made sense. He had a lifetime of nightmares haunting him.

I only had one and it was enough to make me want to scream and scream and scream!

I cried harder.

I couldn't stop.

God, I couldn't stop.

"Ah, Ily…I'm sorry. So, so fucking sorry." He rocked me, cradled me, treated me like spun sugar and gave me the sweetest kisses. He didn't try to lick my tears. Didn't growl at me to cease.

His strong arms wrapped tighter. His hard body supported mine.

Never in all my life had I felt so accepted, so cherished, so *seen.*

Never trusted someone enough to be so ugly and sad.

Just him.

This enemy turned twin flame.

My missing piece of my soul.

Victor's grunts.

Victor's thrusts.

Victor—

I couldn't do it anymore.

Pulling away from Henri's embrace, I tripped and grabbed his hand.

He arched an eyebrow as I dropped my towel and dragged him back into the shower. Hot water rained as I plastered myself to his perfectly trimmed chest and whispered around my tears. "I need you to erase him. Tonight. Right now."

He cupped my cheek in worship. "I'll do anything you want."

I might love others.

I might need others.

But what I felt for him?

It was different. Just more. Just…everything.

"Tell me what you need." He kissed me ever so softly.

The moment his lips touched mine, I flung my arms around his shoulders.

How could he make me feel so fragile and fearless at the same time?

How could I forgive him for everything just because he'd trusted me enough to break in front of me?

We'd allowed each other to see past all our defences, peer deep into our truths, and nothing frightened me anymore.

Not his past.

Not his needs.

Nothing.

Because I knew him.

I'd *always* known him.

And it'd taken me this long to recognise what he meant to me.

"Help me forget, Hen."

He groaned into my mouth. "Having you call me that…goddammit, Ily." Picking me up, he pressed me against the tiles and shuddered as I wrapped my legs around his hips.

I didn't know if his erection was from wanting me or the Viagra, but the little voice in my head forced me to check I wasn't doing to him what his father had done. "Wait..."

God, my heart *ached* for him.

For all those evenings when he'd been taken by the hand and delivered into absolute evil. No wonder he was so hung up on monogamy. He'd been forced to love countless women when all he ever wanted was one.

One mother. One lover. One heart.

He paused, his chest rising and falling, the knitted wound on his bicep from Kyle's stabbing extra bright from the hot water. "I'm sorry. I didn't mean to trap you. I'll put you down—"

"It's not that. I...I want you. I need all traces of him gone. But...only if you want me too. I won't take from you. I won't be like him."

His face scrunched up with absolute awe. Fresh tears clung to his eyelashes. "You think you're taking me against my will?"

"I'm making sure I don't."

He sighed heavily. "Fuck, Ilyana."

New sadness tracked down my cheeks. I felt so sorry for Rachel. For everything she'd endured. I hated that she'd been forced to sleep with so many men. Despised that Henri had the same experience. Just because he hadn't been violated in that way, he *had* been violated.

He'd been raped, over and over again.

Peter and the jewels were slaves here.

They were used and abused on a daily basis, but Henri?

He'd been a child when it started.

A baby of seven years old when he'd been forced to be with a woman in that way.

What did that do to him? How had he survived? All his urges and fetishes were nothing compared to the mess inside him.

A surge of protectiveness rose.

I wanted to slay every nightmare he'd endured.

I wanted to go back in time and slaughter his father.

I wanted to hug that little boy and promise him that eventually, he would be free of that life...only for him to step back into it as an adult.

I brushed his hair back as the shower continued to pummel us. "Do you think your memories came back because of this place? Being here? Reliving the past you repressed?"

He pursed his lips. "Pretty sure it was writing. I started off wanting to write about you and all the things I wanted to do to you.

Instead, I ended up falling down a fucked-up rabbit hole."

"That's why you deleted everything? You didn't want Victor to read it?"

"*I* didn't want to read it. Or remember." He huffed, widening his legs. "Pity I now remember everything."

I slipped a little in his arms. I wriggled closer, trapping his cock between us.

He groaned, his forehead furrowing. "You keep doing that, and I won't have the ability to talk for much longer."

My stomach flipped. "Does the Viagra feel different? Less sensitive?"

"You're still worried that I don't want to do this?" He kissed me softly. "That I don't want to do *you*?"

I kissed him back. "I will never take advantage of you. Regardless of what I need."

"And that's why you're the most incredible person I've ever met." His voice roughened. "I love you, Ily. So fucking much."

Wrapping my arms around him, I hugged him.

He trapped me against the wall, quaking in my hold.

The same words danced on my tongue.

Pulling away, I asked quietly, "Did your brother know? What your father made you do?"

He flinched.

I worried he wouldn't answer, but then he dropped his eyes and shrugged. "I don't know. I only saw him a few times when I was dragged through the house. He was never there while it happened. I think…I hope he wasn't aware. I do know he killed the bastard. I remember that too. I remember him appearing in the quarters where we were kept, holding a gun. The next day, we were all freed."

"Do you think he would've sent you here if he'd known what you endured?"

"I don't know." He winced. "Unfortunately, I've probably killed him, so the chances of asking him are gone."

Life seemed to narrow, knotting us together.

All the conversations in the kitchens. Peter's urging; Rachel's advice. They'd told me to see if Henri would fight on our side.

After tonight, I had no doubts.

His nostrils flared as he studied my face. "What? What is it?"

Heat throbbed between us, sex hung in the air, but our connection burned hotter.

My mind raced with a new plan.

One that'd begun the moment Victor thought he was helping by making Henri rape Rachel. "You said you were ready to play....You said you're done with this place and your past, and...if that's true, I have an idea."

He wrenched back. Flicking a look at the camera in the corner of the bathroom pointing directly at the shower, he ducked his head by my ear. "We've already talked for too long. It'll start to look suspicious if we don't either fuck or I do something cruel." His face scrunched up. "And I can't hurt you again. Not tonight. To be honest, I'll probably struggle for the rest of my life—"

"And that's why you have to. Don't you see?" I reached between us and grabbed his hard cock.

He hissed between his teeth as I jerked him off. "You want me to hurt you? After everything?"

"Victor thinks he's helping free you. He expects you to be 'cured' from your little love disease. So...let him cure you."

"*What?*" He stilled my hand, wrapping his fingers around mine. "You expect me to forget tonight? Forget this? Forget how I feel about you?"

"Not forget...pretend." I squeezed him.

His eyes snapped shut.

Biting the shell of his ear, I whispered, "Play with me, Hen. Be the worst Master you can be so Victor trusts you. Do whatever it takes to convince him that you're his."

His entire body turned to stone. "What are you saying?" He yanked my hand off his erection. "Stop that. I can't think with you touching me."

"I'm saying you need to be the Master Victor wants you to be. Distract him. Mislead him. Keep his eyes on you instead of on...other things."

"Other things?"

"He obviously cares for you. Even Rachel said she's never seen him be this friendly with another."

He groaned and closed his eyes. "Please don't mention her name. I feel sick to my stomach for hurting her. Yet another woman I was forced to—" He pressed his lips together as if fighting his natural inclination to purge. "I—" His lashes flashed up. "I need you, Ily. Promise me. Promise me that it's just us from now on." Nuzzling into my neck, he pushed me higher up the wall and notched his cock against my entrance. "Tonight never happened, alright? Victor didn't happen. Rachel didn't happen. Only this." He pushed slowly, carefully. "Only us."

My lips parted as he filled me.

My eyes rolled back at the exquisite sensation of penetration.

Clinging to him, I panted as he slid all the way in.

We moaned in unison.

So much, so full, so *right*.

I clenched around him.

He groaned and pressed his forehead to mine, but he didn't move. He just stayed deep and still, letting our bodies adjust, remember, and reaffirm that this was it.

No one else.

Just us.

Tears trickled over my cheeks as I held his stare. "You're wrong, you know."

He scowled. "Wrong about what?"

"That I hate you."

He froze, his eyes filling with panic. "I don't expect you to tell me things you don't mean. Don't lie to me. I won't be able to stand it—"

"*Mujhe tumase pyaar hai.*" Leaning forward, I kissed him. "It means…I love you."

His legs buckled. He almost dropped me. Slamming a hand against the wall, he staggered sideways before pinning me against the tiles again. His voice cracked. "*What?*"

I clung to his shoulders. "*Je t'aime*, Hen."

"I-It's not possible." Fresh tears glossed his eyes; the violence I was used to from him rippled down his arms.

Snatching me close, keeping his cock deep, deep inside me, he wrenched off the shower and tripped onto the bathmat. Dripping wet, he carried me into the bedroom and fell onto the bed, wedging me beneath him, his cock still locked right where it belonged.

"Say it again." His panic turned to desperation.

"I love you," I whispered, kissing the tip of his nose.

A tortured noise fell out of him. "Are you sure? I mean…why? Fuck, *how*—"

"How?"

"God knows I've done nothing to deserve it. You should hate me. A large part of me *needs* you to hate me. I can't handle anything else. I…I'm not *worthy* of anything else."

My heart tore into pieces. "It's because of your lack of self-worth that I do." Arching my hips, I rocked against him. "You *are* worthy. I wouldn't love you if you weren't."

He groaned. "Ily—"

Dragging his head down, I whispered too quietly for the cameras, "Tomorrow, when Victor forces us to do whatever sick game he has planned, we play together, okay? Promise me you'll hurt me if he makes you. Vow to me you won't make him suspicious."

"God, I can't." He pressed his lips to my throat. "The thought of ever harming you again turns me into fucking knots. I wouldn't survive if you broke."

"But…" My nose wrinkled as I figured out the best way to say something so delicate. "But that's who you are. You know it yourself. You need to deliver pain—"

"No." He shook his head. "I'll change. I'll stop. I don't want—"

"It's who you *are*, Hen. Either because of what you lived through as a boy or what you need as a man…you can't change something so ingrained. Not now. Not that quickly."

"I can. Watch me."

"Don't hate yourself for what you need." I ran my fingers down his damp back, making him break out in goosebumps. "You'll destroy yourself if you do."

"What I *need* is you."

"And what *I* need is for you to play along with me."

We were running out of time.

If we were going to hoodwink Victor, it had to seem as if Henri had snapped thanks to Victor's tutelage tonight.

Dropping my legs and going meek beneath him, it looked as if Henri took me against my will. The moment I surrendered, the truth I still hadn't accepted shivered through me. Just the act of playing his captive made me wet and needy.

God, it felt so scandalous and dirty and…safe.

Safe now that I trusted him.

Safe now that I knew him.

Safe.

He sucked in a breath as he felt my shift, felt the flush of wetness inside me. "W-What are you doing?"

"Being honest with myself." I licked my lips and stared at his mouth. "What if…what if I need you to hurt me? What if I'm exactly what you said I was…"

He went very, very still. "You're not a masochist, Ily. I was seeing what I wanted to see. Trying to convince myself what I was doing wasn't wrong."

"It wasn't wrong...not all of it."

"You don't mean that."

I melted beneath him. "You asked what parts of me react at the thought of you punishing me. You asked if I would bow for you—"

"Stop it." He clamped a hand over my mouth. "Don't say something that isn't true."

Nipping at his palm, I smirked as he ripped his hand away. "The night of Emerald Bruises. When I was high and used you for sex—"

"Fuck." His cock jerked inside me. "Don't remind me. And you didn't use me. Far from it. I felt like a monster for taking you in that condition."

"I asked you to bite me. I couldn't come until you did."

"That doesn't mean anything."

"It does." I smiled, so grateful I still could after what'd happened tonight. "I'm a Mercerchist. I'm *your* Mercerchist."

His forehead furrowed. "I have no idea what that means."

"It means...I hate pain from others. But with you? I...I like it. I *like* when you bruise me. When you treat me with violence, I feel your love beneath. Your love is painful. And now I know why."

"*Merde*, you're trying to kill me." His hips jabbed into mine.

I gasped. "No. I'm just being honest."

His eyes flashed. "You want honesty? Fine." His hips rocked again, feeding me his throbbing hardness. "The taste of your tears. The moans of your pleasure. The knowledge that I hold your life in my hands? It turns me the fuck on, and...if you truly want to know the sick monster you've let into your bed, I probably wouldn't be able to keep it up right now without the Viagra." His kissed me hard, forcing me to choke on his words. "Being inside you this way is far too gentle and sweet. It's scrambling my mind. I'm in love with you. You come first in everything, yet this..." He thrust, sharp and savage. "This wouldn't be enough to satisfy me and that...fuck, that destroys me because you deserve gentle. You deserve sweet."

"Isn't that up to me to decide?"

"No. I can't risk it. I...Christ, I can't lose you. I refuse to do anything that might break you. I'd never forgive myself."

"I won't break, Henri." I kissed him back. "I trust you not to go that far."

"But that's the thing." He gave me a heartbreaking shrug. "I don't trust myself."

My mind scrambled for a way to give him what he needed.

We had to put on a performance for Victor, all while keeping our sanities intact. "You said the connection you felt when we played along when we first arrived frustrated you. That you didn't like me obeying you, even though I'd agreed not to fight."

His eyes narrowed. "Where are you going with this?"

"Let's play a different game." I shifted beneath him, my body humming for him to move, to take, to thrust. "I'll fight you back. I'll give you that fire. I'll be unbroken all while you do your best to break me."

"That sounds incredibly dangerous."

"Khushi."

"What?"

"It's the nickname my brother calls me. It means happiness." I kissed his ear. "I vow I'll say it if you ever go too far. A safe word only we know. As long as I don't say it, you need to trust me…just like I trust you. Trust that I can handle what you give me. Trust that I'm with you. Trust that I'm strong enough to play the games Victor expects you to play, and hopefully, if you distract him for long enough, then our plan will work, and we can go home."

He didn't say a damn thing.

Time ticked past before he cupped my cheek and stared deep into my eyes. "Vow on your life you will never, *ever* let me destroy you."

The warnings came back from the astrologer.

"Destined to destroy each other."

I nodded. "I vow it."

"Fine." He dropped his head and kissed me. His tongue slipped past my lips just as he withdrew and drove punishingly hard inside me.

I moaned into his mouth.

He thrust again, tortuously slow and sweet.

Threading his fingers through my hair, he held me down and took me.

Long, slow, deep, *deep* thrusts.

I couldn't fight it.

Each rock wrapped me in warmth and comfort, making my

blood sing with gentle arousal instead of burning lust.

Breaking the kiss, he whispered, "I'll play along, Ily. I'll do whatever it takes, but for now…I don't care what the cameras record. I don't care what Victor thinks. This might be the only time in my life I can have simple, innocent missionary, and I'm going to enjoy it. I'm going to make love to you, not fuck you. And I'm going to show you just how much you mean to me instead of making you scream."

I cried out as his mouth claimed mine again.

He thrust with a worshipping rhythm—relentless and ruthless, full of respect and benediction.

If Victor asked why Henri made love to me like a husband instead of fucked me like a monster, we'd tell him this was goodbye.

Goodbye to the feelings between us.

Goodbye to the love Victor said was such a disease.

Wrapping my legs around his rocking hips, I hugged him ever so close.

We kissed, we moaned, we rocked, and writhed.

And when his lips pulled back and his cock thickened to an unbearable size inside me, he set my heart on fire.

"Come with me." His hand burrowed between us, finding my clit and stroking me.

I gasped as his length stroked my G-spot, but I didn't reach those soul-scratching heights. Didn't tangle fear with lust or drown beneath right and wrong.

For the first time, sex between us was simple instead of savage, and it made me fall in so many other ways.

He rubbed me and made love to me, and when I came, the wakes and ripples felt exactly like a hazy summer's day.

"I love you," he groaned, his spine rolling, breath catching, cock rippling with his own summer-sweet release.

This man had driven me to the depths of despair and revealed parts of myself I would never have been brave enough to explore.

But in that bedroom, on that night, I knew we would win.

We would get free.

We would save Peter and Rachel and every jewel.

It was destined.

I stroked his back as he collapsed on top of me. His cock continued to twitch inside me as he whispered, "Are you going to tell me what you, Peter, and Rachel have been up to now?"

I twisted my head, catching his soft grey eyes. "How…?"

He smirked. "I knew you three were up to something."

"And you didn't tattle?"

He sighed, rolled onto his side, and ripped the blankets up and over our heads.

In a tent fort hidden from the cameras, he cupped my cheek and ran his thumb beneath my eye. "I told you, little nightmare, I'm loyal. I think I loved you the moment I saw you, so no, I didn't tattle." He glowered at my collar. "You might wear that damn thing, but you put an invisible one on me in that club. You've made me feel things I'm definitely not strong enough to feel." He shrugged sadly. "There's a weight inside me that I can't shed. A darkness that keeps clawing me back, but I have a purpose now. I have you…somehow."

Cradling me with his protective arms, he whispered, "I accept your safe word, Ily. Whatever you're planning with the jewels, I'm in. Tomorrow, I'll be the worst of the worst all in order to save them. I won't hold back. I'll trust that you're with me. And when the day comes that we can walk the fuck out of here, I'm ripping that damn collar off your throat, then spending a lifetime trying to deserve you."

Chapter Twenty-Six

Henri

VICTOR GRINNED AS HE MARCHED toward our table.

No sun today, the sky overcast and miserable.

Ily kneeled beside my chair, her beautiful body hidden beneath a black silk dressing gown that barely skimmed her ass. I'd eaten as much as I could. My stomach revolted against anything more than one scrambled egg and toasted ciabatta. I'd hoped now that Ily and I had talked, my appetite would come roaring back.

If anything, it made it worse.

Not because I wanted to vomit at the thought of hurting her but because the fear of losing her now tore me in two.

You won't lose her as long as you play.

Our script was rewritten.

Our pantomime in its second season.

As long as we remembered our lines and places, we could win.

We have to.

I flicked her a look where she finished off a small plate of honeydew melon and dragon fruit.

Ready? I arched an eyebrow.

Together. She smiled softly.

Once again, I had the strangest sensation of hearing her subliminally. It didn't make sense. It couldn't be real. But the level of connection I felt to her transcended everything I'd ever felt. Maybe the depth of our bond *could* create fantastical abilities. Maybe the wand tattooed onto her back gave her real magic.

All I knew was…I'd actually slept last night without being tormented by nightmares.

I'd woken to her snuggled in my arms, our legs entwined, my front spooning her back and I'd tripped even harder.

I'd yanked the covers over our heads, hiding us from the bastard cameras and made use of the residual hardness from the

Viagra along with my usual morning wood.

I'd woken her as I'd nudged against her soft, wet warmth.

She'd moaned as she parted her legs and welcomed me.

I meant what I said that vanilla affection had never done it for me.

But with her?

Damn, it felt so fucking good.

"Bonjour." Victor spread his arms. "Isn't it a fabulous morning?"

I stood and shook his hand. "The weather could be better, but yes, not bad considering."

His navy eyes twinkled as two female staff darted forward. One carrying a fresh coffee, the other his usual plate of pastries.

Bowing, the two girls placed his breakfast on my table then scurried away to serve another Master snapping his fingers for attention. I scanned how many Masters and jewels surrounded us. My eyes snagged on Roland and Mollie at the next table. Just like I felt responsible for Rachel after what'd happened, I felt responsible for Mollie too.

I just hoped she'd survive long enough for me to free her.

My hands balled as Roland kicked her, laughing as she flinched and kept her face down.

Fucking bastard.

Ily sucked in a breath as she looked in the other direction, her gaze locked on Peter as he led the brand-new slaves to breakfast. His face was dark as thunder, his hands and feet encased in white thin bandages. The flashes of golden collars as he dispersed the new gems around eager Masters fisted my heart with rage.

Shifting in my chair, doing my best to hide that rage, I pasted a smile on my face as Victor sat down and smoothed his white knitted jumper and grey slacks. Taking his coffee, he sniffed it and shuddered dramatically. "I tell you, Henri, there's nothing better than a good brew before an afternoon of pleasure." He sipped it, leaving a milky moustache. "By the way, how are you feeling this morning? I take it that was your first time using Viagra? No heart palpitations? No jitters?"

Taking Ily's empty plate, I placed it beside mine and reclined. Ignoring the sneers and jests of the Masters as they poked and squeezed the new jewels, I focused entirely on being the best friend Victor had ever had. I winked. "I made use of the effects, if that's what you're asking."

"Yes, I skimmed the footage this morning." He nodded, licking away the milk on his upper lip. "A shower fuck and missionary. How very old-fashioned of you."

I laughed, doing my best to remember how it felt to be so light-hearted after Ruby Tears. How happy I'd been to be free. "You know what? I've never actually fucked in missionary before. Couldn't seem to keep it up." I tipped my chin. "Thanks to you, I got to see what all the fuss was about."

"And?"

"Meh." I shrugged with a chuckle. "I think I prefer them bound and bleeding."

"That's my boy." He saluted me with his coffee cup.

Deep in my memories, my father's voice echoed too. The same line. Gifted to me for raping one of his harem.

"Well, I can tell you right now, missionary will definitely not be on today's menu. However…" He canted his head. "I must ask, what on earth were you talking about for so long last night? You and those whispers, *mon ami*." His gaze flickered to Ily. "I have no idea why she fascinates you so. It's certainly not her ability in bed. I had to indulge in Rachel after you two left. I was feeling wholly unsatisfied."

"She's your favourite for a reason." I swallowed hard, hating I now had intimate knowledge of that favourite. Just like it'd taken Victor to point out I was in love with Ily, I wondered if anyone had pointed out to him that he had strong feelings for Rachel.

He might've been willing to kill her but somewhere deep, deep inside him, he might still have a human heart. Rotten and decayed but still there.

I'd felt nothing but shame and regret while being with Rachel, yet with Ily? Fuck, my entire being hummed with electricity.

My fingers strayed to Ily's shoulder, needing to stroke. The satin of her black dressing gown felt so soft, so feminine.

I snatched my hand back.

We hadn't spoken this morning—not daring to with the cameras but…we both had our lines and curtain calls and if we were going to play…*there's no time like the present*.

How the fuck do I do this again?

"To be honest, Vic…" I raked a hand through my hair, my thoughts a mess on how to lay the ground rules to protect Ily, all while distracting him from whatever her and Peter were planning.

It would fucking help if I knew what those plans were.

Swallowing hard, I shot him a smile. "I do have something I want to say, and I hope you can accept it. I hope you can accept *me* because thanks to you, I'm finally ready to admit what I need."

His eyes narrowed with interest. "Oh? I do love a bit of intrigue in the morning." Finishing his coffee, he placed it back on the saucer. "Go on then. You should know by now I never judge. I only want you to be happy, Henri." He reached across the table and patted my shoulder.

It took everything not to cringe but the longer I let this roleplay evolve, the more I shut down the parts of myself full of nervousness and fear.

Victor might be the scariest son of a bitch I'd ever met but…he *did* have a heart. He might happily carve out the hearts of others and sell them on the black market, but with me…*for now*…he'd willingly stepped into the role of my mentor. What better way to distract him than to appeal to that mentoring father-figure? After all, I had experience in that. I'd learned how to keep my father happy by doing exactly what he wanted.

"You're right that I've been low the past month. I've been in a bit of a black place actually, but…thanks to you pushing me last night, I think I know how to be happy. I've fought it for a while, but I'm done. I like what I like. It's time I start enjoying myself."

"Ah, I'm so glad." Victor smiled. "I did wonder if I'd annoyed you last night. I know you probably weren't ready to fuck another, and it probably made you jealous seeing me fuck yours, but…I admit." He leaned back and waved a hand in my direction. "You seem different this morning. Calmer."

Studying Ily out the corner of my eye, I waited for her to react at the mention of her rape.

Would those memories set her back? Hurt her? Rattle her?

She didn't even flinch.

Two parts of me battled.

The monster who was so in awe of her resilience and rebellion and the man who worried she'd break at any moment.

Breathing deeply, she closed her eyes as if she was meditating.

I still didn't understand what she meant about not watching when Victor took her but…I'd learned firsthand what sort of power concentration and centring could do.

Looking away from her was a struggle but I forced myself to grin. "You showed me, once and for all, what I need to get off. You asked what I talk about when I'm in the midst of a fuck with

Ily? I told you at the start of our friendship and I'll tell you again." Leaning forward, I linked my fingers on the table. "I tell her what I want to do to her. Last night, I told her in explicit detail what I plan on doing when we visit the snuffbox this afternoon. Words have power. They can deliver tomorrow's fear and yesterday's pain. A simple reminder or a cruel promise can burrow its way into someone's psyche so deeply that by the time you come to do the act, they're already broken."

Victor shivered as if I'd actually touched a nerve. "You truly could be remarkable if you let yourself go, Mercer." Holding out his arm, he shoved up his cable knit jumper. "See? Chills. You just gave me chills." He grinned. "I love it." Dropping his hand, he nodded. "Fine. Talk away to your jewel. Who am I to say what fetishes are better than others."

"Thanks." Bending down, I pulled the black and silver bag from the floor and dumped it on the table. "You ask me what fascinates me so much about Ilyana? I'll tell you. It's her strength. I tell her what I plan on doing to her and instead of cowering and spoiling all the fun, she stands up to me. You see that as a flaw in her obedience, but I see it as a motherfucking aphrodisiac."

Victor curled his upper lip. "You enjoy it when she fights back."

"I do." I let the truth of that darken my voice. "Like I said, you see bad behaviour and something to be beaten, I see it as a red flag to give in."

"Yes, I'm beginning to realise that. I, too, enjoy the journey from unruly to ruled but…surely you don't want her to stay that way forever? There's just so much enjoyment in knowing you're the one to silence them. You're the one to mould them. If she never learns to submit, then where is the peace for you? You'll never have the joy of a jewel who obeys your every whim, no matter how dark or painful. You'll have a war on your hands every time."

"It's that war that turns me on."

"Yes but—"

"I need her to fight with me, Vic. Always. You saw how I reacted when she kicked me in the nose the night I snapped. I couldn't help it. Give me a woman who screams and tells me to fuck myself and I can't stop what I do in response. Give me a girl who just bends over and takes it? Well…." I splayed my hands. "You get what happened last night. A cock that won't work and the administering of a blue pill that's just plain embarrassing."

Sighing, he nodded along. "You make a decent point. I'd just hate for you to miss out on all the ways a subservient jewel can make you feel."

Grabbing the brand-new whip from the bag, I tossed it by my plate. "I won't be missing out on anything. You gave me this to use. I'm grateful and I'm looking forward to it, but I'll only agree to go into the snuffbox with you if you agree to let me do this my way. You want me to be happy? Give me full rein of Ily's education. You've had her now. I honoured that part of our deal. While she's in your home, she will obey and be polite to you. I'll ensure she doesn't speak back to anyone but me. She will be the perfect jewel you expect. However, when she's under my rule and about to take my cock, she has my permission to call me whatever the fuck she wants. She can fight me. She can try to hurt me. I need you to agree that you won't interfere because this is what I want, got it?"

For the longest moment, he didn't speak.

Shit, what are you doing?

I'd shared too much. Given too much away.

But…if Ily and I were going to do this. If we were going to pretend? If we willing engaged in all the depravity on offer in this place, I needed constant fucking feedback that she was still with me. Still playing with me. Still strong. If she turned into Rachel or the others…

It can't happen.

If she broke, *truly* broke, I'd use my switchblade to end both of us because freedom or no freedom, if her mind didn't stay intact there was nothing left for either of us.

Steepling his fingers, he pursed his lips and studied me then Ily. He looked as if he could smell a rat without being able to see it. Perhaps he'd seen what happened on the toilet last night. Maybe he'd heard our pact. Maybe he knew far more than I feared but finally, he stood and held out his hand.

I stood too, placing my fingers in his.

Squeezing hard, he dragged me forward. "I accept your requirements, and I look forward to seeing you step into your rightful place as Master. Shall we get started?" Letting me go, he looked at the sky. "I know we said this afternoon but I'm suddenly eager to see you in action. What do you say, pretty Ily? Fancy being whipped before lunch?"

Her eyes snapped open.

A flash of light in her gaze.

Behave. I glowered.

I'd agreed to hurt her while we had sex, but I didn't want to ever raise a hand to her without it.

For a second, rebellion twitched her lips, but then she nodded like a perfect jewel. "Yes, Sir V."

He swooned dramatically, pressing his knuckles to his forehead. "Be still my heart, it's a miracle. Polite *and* demure. Wonders will never cease." He waggled his finger in my face with a chuckle. "Seems you might be onto something. Right…I'll just go collect Rachel from her appointment with Dr Belford, and we'll go have some fun."

Striding off, he gave me a wave.

I waved back.

The minute he was gone, my legs gave out, and I fell back onto the chair.

Ily shifted closer. Her hand touched my ankle beneath my jeans.

I looked down and caught her stare and prayed to every fucking entity that still listened to help us.

I won't break. Her eyes shouted.

I might. I shrugged.

Together, we waited silently for Victor's return.

The snuffbox was pretty much everything I expected.

Tucked down in the eastern most corner of the gardens, past the vegetable patch, behind the glass-fronted orangery, and hidden in the shadow of the battlement wall, the brick and ivy-covered tower looked like a small observatory.

Or a jail…depending on the viewer.

"Here we are." Giving me a beaming smile, Victor withdrew an old-fashioned key from his pocket and opened the heavy, creaking metal door. It swung inward, sensor lights sprang on, and he led us inside like a sadistic prince.

Unclipping his leash from Rachel, he pointed at a spot on the floor in the centre of the room. "Wait there for me, my pet. I'll just show Henri the ropes."

Her blue eyes skated to me, then to Ily.

Something passed between them.

Ily tipped her chin.

Rachel nodded and braced her shoulders.

What had they communicated?

The fact that I'd slept with both women last night repeated over and over again, amplifying my shame and regret. Rachel carried Victor's baby. He'd so flippantly ordered me to kill her. She'd lived a life of horrors, and now I was going to save her.

Save both of them.

Somehow.

"Run along," Victor repeated, annoyance on his face for her delay.

"Yes, Sir V." Rachel dropped her eyes then stepped down the four stone steps and into the pit below. With a barely-there shiver, she kneeled on the hard damp rock and bowed her head. Her teal silk dressing gown splayed around her bare legs like turquoise puddles.

I didn't dare look at Ily.

I didn't know if my monster would take charge or my damn humanness would make this impossible for me. The darkness I couldn't shed slithered on the outskirts of my mind. The bag holding my new whip grew extra heavy.

What if I can't do this?

What if I lose myself while hurting Ily, and she breaks, after all?

She has a safe word.

As long as I kept listening for it, I would stop.

Khushi.

Happiness.

Fuck, that word mocked me.

Why did she have to be named after two things I'd never earned and so desperately wanted?

Sighing heavily, I glanced around at the high rotund walls.

My eyes widened as I found out why Victor called it the snuffbox.

His theme of gemstones repeated itself. Giant artwork surrounded us at least two stories high, sweeping toward the domed roof above. A never-ending pattern of sparkling, priceless jewels. Sapphires blended with rubies; diamonds scattered on emeralds.

It felt as if we'd be buried under an avalanche of gems at any moment.

"Exquisite, is it not?" Victor puffed with pride. "One of my first jewels was a world-renowned painter. I managed to acquire her when she accepted a hefty commission to paint for a private collector on his yacht. Unfortunately for her, this collector owed me a few debts, and when I went to collect, I couldn't take my eyes off her. So…I took her with me." He pointed at the outstanding art. "I allowed her to paint these before I ever laid a finger on her. She lived in here for almost two years. When it was done, I gave her the option of becoming my personal favourite or…I could free her for the work she'd so skilfully done."

"Free her?" I raised an eyebrow. "You actually let her go?"

Victor chuckled. "Don't be ridiculous. But I did let her go somewhere else."

"Somewhere else?" I played dumb, stroking his ego, all while my mind raced with the ramifications of how many people he'd killed and butchered.

Just how many body parts had he sold over the years?

"You'll soon learn, Henri, that sometimes, the only fate available to a jewel is to kill them. I tried for a year to make Beth behave. I tried all manner of things, but alas. She would rather get hurt trying to kill me than fuck me, so…I gave her what she wanted and killed her instead. Let's hope a similar fate for Ilyana is still far, far away, hmm?"

My heart fisted.

Ily didn't rise to his bait. She gave none of her usual retorts or barely hidden slurs.

I wanted to hug her for that.

Get on my knees and thank her for staying in character.

Tapping his polished shoe on the echoey floor, Victor muttered, "So…you've told me what you want to happen, and I've agreed to let you play your way, but…I still expect you to work on the levels of ownership. I refuse to let her cause discord amongst the other jewels again, especially now my home is rebalanced."

I stiffened. "You said it yourself that the purpose of those levels was to break a jewel. I don't want her broken, Vic. As long as she never speaks back to you, then what's the harm if she speaks back to me?"

Victor sniffed. "You're proposing to let her keep her backbone, which never works—as I've just shown with Beth. If Beth had submitted, I would still have an incredible artist. My home could be brimming with stunning art, but I saw her for the infection that she was. She would've stirred unrest in my other gems, just like Ily attempted to do." He crossed his arms. "While she's obedient, it's fine. But what about the day she shows flagrant disregard and disrespect again? What about the day she tries to turn Peter against me again? I might be forced to step in. And I'd hate to have to pick up the pieces once I was done."

Ily sucked in a breath.

I sighed and raked a hand over my face.

Getting my shit together, I snapped, "You have my word she'll behave. And I have your word that you won't interfere."

"Ugh, fine. *Oui, oui.*" He threw up his hands. "It's on your head."

A wild, *stupid* idea popped into my mind.

He wanted proof she'd behave?

I'll give him proof.

"Ilyana," I said softly. "Please assure Victor that you've finally accepted your place and will behave."

She flinched.

Shit.

What the fuck am I doing?

"Yes, Master H." Swallowing hard, her eyes tightened. "I've accepted my place, Sir V." The words literally looked as if they choked her. "I promise to behave from now on."

Victor snickered, enjoying her little show. "And..." He arched an eyebrow.

Bastard.

Cunt.

Fuck, this is hard.

Inhaling deeply, condemning myself to hell all over again, I murmured, "Apologise to him, little nightmare."

Fuck, I'm sorry.

So, so sorry.

Making her apologise to her rapist?

I'd hit my absolute lowest.

She dropped her gaze to the floor, her shoulders bunching. "And I'm sorry for my behaviour, Sir V."

"*Aaaand...*" He dragged out the word.

"What else do you want her to say?" I barked.

He gave me a sharp look. "I merely want—"

"I won't disrupt the balance again, Sir V." With balled hands, Ily dropped to her knees as elegantly as a falling feather. "I won't turn Peter against you. I belong to Master H and exist by your magnanimity."

"Magnanimity, huh?" He smiled with an evil glint. "That's a big word for a little jewel."

Bowing her head, she committed to her role in ways that churned my guts. "I'm yours, Sir V."

He sniffed. "Quite right." Stepping into her, he rested his hand on her head.

She couldn't stop a tortured moan escaping.

To let him touch her after what he did to her?

Jesus Christ.

It took all my fucking strength not to kill him.

Images of him thrusting into her from behind.

Foggy memories of him grabbing her hips and—

"I'm enjoying your obedience, my sweetling, but I do have to wonder if it's because Henri has shackled your mind like he did when you thought he was a cop." He grabbed her chin and yanked her face up. "What else has he been whispering to you, hmm? What other promises has he vowed?"

She blinked with blank eyes. "It wasn't him, Sir V. It was…I saw the cave where…" Closing her lashes, she sighed. "I know what will happen if I don't obey."

He chuckled and let her go. Wiping his hand on his trousers, he smirked. "I knew Peter would lead my jewels there. I suppose he told you what extra activities I have him do for me, too?"

Extra activities?

What?

Crowding closer, I did my best not to rip Ily into my arms. "As you can see, Vic, she's learned. Shall we—"

"No, Sir V," Ily said quietly. "T-The altar spoke for itself."

Altar?

The cave with the carved seats and a stone table shot back into memory.

The whole energy in that place had been sick.

Victor laughed and clapped his hands. "Oh, this is going to be fun. Perhaps I should invite all of you down for the next Diamond Kiss. If it instils this level of compliance, it might save me a lot of headaches. I do have eight new jewels to train. Perhaps a quick field trip to the Temple of Facets could fast-forward their education considerably."

Diamond Kiss…*shit.*

Ily froze.

I turned into stone.

That damn fucking chit.

The back of my neck grew hot as Victor pinned his blue eyes on me. "You don't happen to know who won that gift in the treasure hunt, do you? No one has come forward and it's usually the first prize to be cashed in."

Sweat rolled down my back.

If only Ily hadn't found it in the wardrobe. If only I hadn't asked what it meant. If only I'd found it first and torn it quietly into shreds.

No one would know what I'd flushed.

No footage would exist of me winning it.

"I'm sorry." I shrugged. "No idea."

"No matter. It'll turn up eventually. And if it doesn't, I'll have my guards go through the recordings to see if it was lost or misplaced. I like to skim the footage to keep abreast of what my guests are doing, but I don't have the time to watch every little moment—especially now that you're not nearly as entertaining with your mystery and secrets."

I laughed around the boulder in my throat. "Sorry I'm not giving you viewing pleasure anymore."

"Me too. It was fun playing detective and figuring out who you are."

"Who I am is grateful." I lowered my chin, playing right into his hand. "I don't know who I'd be without you guiding me, Vic."

His eyes softened. He looked genuinely pleased. "And you're so welcome, my friend. Right." He clapped his hands. "Enough standing around talking. Let's have some fun." Marching into the centre of the pit, he clicked his fingers. "Come here if you please."

Drained beyond belief and we hadn't even started yet, I left Ily kneeling by the doorway and joined him.

My damn legs trembled. The bag holding my new whip dangled in my fingers.

I stopped beside him. The room ringed out like a perfect clock. Beneath my feet, a drain with rusty grates allowed an icy breeze to escape, hinting it wasn't dirt beneath our feet but another room, another torture chamber. At each time marks where clock hands would go, certain *apparatus* existed.

At twelve o'clock, a giant cross waited for its next martyr.

Two o'clock, a strange looking chair with no bottom and a

sling.

Five o'clock, a rack full of whips and paddles.

Seven o'clock, a device covered in cuffs and chains to trap the limbs of its victim.

Nine o'clock, a table, stained and pockmarked with unmentionable things.

Eleven o'clock, a bed with black silk sheets and four posts with hooks for collars and cuffs.

The rest of the room blurred as I spun a full circle and caught eyes with Ily still kneeling by the closed door.

My heart picked up speed, growing sicker by the moment.

I love you. I balled my hands.

She half smiled, fear tiptoeing through her golden gaze.

Tearing her eyes away, she looked at something at four o'clock. A round mirrored ball—large enough to splay someone over, glittered with shackles and chains.

Images of Ily tied down in whatever position I wanted shot into my head.

Parts of me rebelled.

Parts of me woke up.

My monster prowled with its shadows of depressing darkness, twisting me the fuck up for wanting any of this.

Victor beamed at his playground. "What do you think?"

I locked my quaking knees, ignored my aching cock. "Looks fun."

"Oh it is." He winked. "*Beaucoup* fun. I look forward to teaching you how to use each one."

My heart stopped.

"I think you should start with the St Andrew's cross, seeing as you enjoyed Ily on a cross in my trophy room. This one can be tilted, flipped upside down, and widened...depending on your preference and access to what hole you require."

I wanted to be sick.

I laughed instead. "Sounds good."

"Let's get the games going, shall we?" Victor strode toward the cross and quirked his finger. "Come here, Ilyana. Allow me to give your Master a quick demonstration."

She flicked me a panicked look.

I shutdown all my terror.

Every molecule wanted to forbid her, but I nodded. "Go to him."

I coughed.

Those three words gagged me.

Stuck like glass shards in my throat.

With a heartbreaking inhale, Ily obeyed.

With more poise and elegance than I could stand, she climbed to her feet, padded barefoot down the stone steps, and cut across the large pit.

Rachel looked up and gave her a quick smile.

Ily gave her one back.

With tight fists, she stopped before Victor.

She didn't speak. She merely stood there…brilliant and brave, serene and submissive.

"You're learning, my pet." Grabbing her by the shoulders, Victor spun her around and pushed her against the cross.

She grunted as her back slammed against the hard wood.

I saw red.

I drowned in black.

I stalked forward, ready to tear his motherfucking head off.

And…stopped myself with agonising self-control.

Play along.

Distract him.

Do your part.

"Oh, I apologise, Ilyana. Did that hurt?" Victor smirked.

Keeping all her hate hidden, Ily bowed her head. "No, Sir V."

He chuckled. "I have to say, I'm liking this improved version of you." Pawing at the sash of her black dressing gown, he spread it wide and revealed her perfect body. She didn't look at me as he tore it off her shoulders, leaving her bare.

He cupped one of her breasts, grazing his thumb over a nipple.

My restraint snapped. "Victor."

"Yes, I know. Yours." Letting her breast go, he grabbed her wrist and slammed it above her head.

Guilt and grief and godawful fury churned toxic in my stomach.

With a happy huff, Victor fastened her golden cuff onto a hook, then repeated the process with her right arm. Once both hands were trapped above her head, he toed the leather buckles dangling near her ankles. "It's up to you how tightly she's bound. Personally? I just confine the wrists. It's easier to do this." Grabbing her by the hips, he flipped her around. She moaned as her cheek and breasts wedged against the cross, her wrists criss-crossing with the hook twisting on its length of chain above.

Tears shot to my eyes.

Followed by the hottest, sickest gush of lust.

Fuck, I grew hard.

Achingly hard.

With a heady groan, Victor ran his hand down her waist and cupped her ass.

"*Victor*," I snarled.

God, what was this doing to her?

Being touched by the man who raped her last night?

Having me stand by and *allow* him?

Jesus Christ.

He chuckled and let her go. "With their ankles unbound, it gives them a bit of leeway to dance under the whip's sting."

My head rushed with static.

I couldn't breathe.

Stay in the role!

Wiping my mouth, I choked, "I can imagine."

"Oh, no need to imagine, *mon ami*. You're about to do it."

I shivered with equal parts desire and despair.

"Have you ever whipped someone, Henri?"

"That's it, Onn Ree. See how they welt for you? You're very good at this, my boy."

Swallowing my past, I shook my head.

No way would I admit I could swing a flogger at seven years old. That my education in this filth started well before I could read.

No wonder my mind blocked it out so completely.

Flipping Ily back to face us, Victor ran his knuckles over her cheek. "Let's see how much you're willing to fight when my friend paints you in lashes, hmm? Henri seems to think you'll stay belligerent. Me? I think you'll start begging. Shall we take a bet?"

Letting her go, he came toward me and stole the bag dangling forgotten on my fingers. Pulling the whip out, he tossed the bag to the side then yanked off the black ribbon. The oaky tannin smell grew stronger as the long length unspooled and landed across my loafers.

My cock thickened to painful levels.

I'd worn jeans and a black t-shirt; I sweated right through them.

This is bad.

Very, very bad.

Pressing the whip into my palm, he grinned. "Ten thousand euros if you go too far and make her sob instead of swear. Deal?"

Wrapping my fingers around the leather braided handle, my head swam as I did my best to cling to sanity. "Fine."

"Excellent. I do love a good wager. That reminds me, we still need to transfer those funds." Stroking the whip, he smiled. "No matter, I have a feeling you'll be undergoing your initiation sooner rather than later, and we can get the nasty business of money over and done with, but for now…seeing as you're new to this, this is called a bullwhip, and it's a personal favourite. It leaves the most delightful lashes."

"Use the bullwhip, Onn Ree. No, not that one. That's a tigress whip. No, that's a cane. God's sake, boy. That one. Yes. Now…hit her."

My heart pounded through my ribs. "Awesome." My hand trembled as I stroked my thumb along the handle. It looked similar to the one in my fucked-up childhood. Only difference? This was dark brown and my father's had been tan. A colour light enough to turn rusty with layers of shed blood.

Feeling sick to my stomach, I made the mistake of looking at Ily.

Everything screeched to a halt.

Every moment of last night.

Everything we'd said.

Every promise we'd whispered.

They seemed utterly stupid now.

Were we really going to fucking do this?

Do we have a choice?

Victor manhandled me until I stood at a good striking distance. The pit enveloped me with its icy draft and cold stone. "Now, I'm being lenient with your requests for her to fight back. But I hope you realise I won't tolerate you being in love with her. You need to do whatever it takes to break that little disease. Your loyalties are to me and only to me, and love will only—"

"*Love?*" I laughed mockingly. "Yeah, about that. You're wrong, Vic. You completely got the wrong end of the stick last night." I shook my head with another chuckle. "I'm not in love with her. I don't care about her apart from how hard she can make me blow."

I didn't look anywhere near Ily.

I wouldn't be able to hide the truth if I did.

"Oh?" He raised an eyebrow. "How would you explain your feelings for her, then?"

"I dunno. You tell me. I was under the impression it was an obsession. A fascination maybe? Definitely possession." I smirked. "Could even be a delusion at this point."

He cocked his head. "I fear you doth protest too much, my friend."

"Nah." I shrugged. "Just trying to figure it out for myself. I'm hardwired to fixate on one person. The thought of sharing that one person makes me aggressive. But if I find a better person, then…" I splayed my hands. "I'm open."

He studied me carefully. A bit too carefully. Finally, he pursed his lips and nodded. "I suppose time will tell. For now, I'll permit your closeness as it seems to be helping your evolution but the day I suspect you're lying, well…I have a particular game in mind. For both of you."

I ignored the urge to gulp. "Sounds good."

"Okay then…" He smiled widely and stepped back. "In your own time, Henri. I trust you'll figure out how to whip your jewel while I play with mine. By the way…" Tapping my chin, he pushed up.

I fought him, but he just clucked his tongue and forced my eyes to rise to the domed, gemstone-painted ceiling.

I stiffened.

Lounging on metal walkways above, two guards with sniper rifles resting by their feet waved.

Whispering in my ear, Victor said, "I value our friendship and no longer doubt you, but…I never said I trust you. For future reference—so we can continue to play with ease—just know we're never alone. I hope that isn't a problem for you."

He let me go, and I acted my fucking ass off. "Not a problem at all. I think you're wise to protect yourself. From what I witnessed in Emerald Bruises, your other guests are deranged."

He laughed loudly. "Yes, you're quite right. They are. And that's what makes you so special." Smacking a kiss on my cheek, he backed away. "Right, I'll let you have your fun. Don't hesitate to— ah! I almost forgot!"

Ah fucking hell, now what?

"Rachel, come here, my sweetling," he called.

Climbing elegantly to her feet, Rachel padded toward us, her teal dressing gown swaying. "Yes, Sir V?"

"Show Henri your scars from the last time we played this game."

Without a word, she untied her sash and spread her legs.

I gritted my teeth as memories of last night came back all over again.

"See?" Victor grabbed her knee and opened her legs a little wider. On the creamiest part of her inner thigh, hidden from view and rather close to her pussy, five thick lines glittered blue in the low light.

What the fuck?

Pulling a small vial out of his pocket, Victor tossed it to me.

I caught it by instinct, narrowing my eyes at the sparkly powder. "What's this?"

"I told you." He let Rachel go. "It's my personal favourite of all the games we play here. I only let a few indulge because frankly, the dust is expensive, and I don't like others marking my property." Tapping the tiny bottle, he added, "First you cut them, then you scar them. This is the pigment that makes those scars shimmer."

Shaking the vial, I scowled. "That's why you call it Sapphire Scars?"

"Precisely. The body is miraculous in its healing. I appreciate the silver lines left behind after a wound has healed, but sometimes, I want to see my hard work, don't you agree?"

"So you tattoo them?"

"In a manner of speaking."

I held the vial up to the watery daylight coming from the high windows. An iridescent blue glimmered. "You're saying I'm holding a jar of microscopic sapphires?"

"Not microscopic. Crushed. Each time I go to my sapphire mines in Vietnam, I ensure a few of the very best stones are crushed into powder."

"Why?"

"Because sapphires are my favourite stone and just happen to match my eyes." He fluttered his lashes with a laugh. "And also, because it makes such pretty markings."

I didn't want to know why or how he knew that. Why he'd even come up with the idea or how many times he'd experimented.

"What do you want me to do with it?" I asked.

"Tattoo Ily of course."

"Excuse me?"

"After you've whipped her, taste her blood like you so enjoy, then sprinkle some of this in the wounds. Don't worry, it won't hurt her. Gemstones are naturally antibacterial. Did you know that? Ily would being a gemmologist. I'm sure she'd love the opportunity to wear the very thing she's studied permanently on her skin."

I shook my head. "She's already tattooed. Her wand—"

"I know." He grinned. "But you're about to whip her. Beginners never get the whip's pressure right. You'll end up cutting her. And when you do, I want you to pour some sapphire dust into the wounds. Within a week, her body will heal around the tiny particles and forever glitter in the sun."

I hated the longing springing inside me. To have her wear my mark? To brand her?

I shook my head, dispelling such darkness. "It'll ruin her ink."

He shrugged with a sick smirk. "Don't tell me you didn't enjoy her wounds as they healed after Ruby Tears, *mon ami*. I saw you looking at them. I saw the pride on your face. Wounds heal. This scars. She'll always wear your signature after today. Won't that be nice?"

He prowled away before I could argue or convince myself I didn't want this.

Going to Rachel's side, he whispered something to her, then guided her to the four-poster bed with its shackles and chains.

My eyes met Ily's.

Our connection flared.

She gave me the softest, saddest smile.

Fuck, how many times would we have to play these twisted games? How long would Ily have to endure such unacceptable things? And how much could I resist before I lost myself all over again?

Fisting the vial, I placed it into the back pocket of my jeans.

When you've got her free, then you can have an existential crisis.
For now…keep him happy.

Victor wouldn't let me leave here without doing what he wanted.

I'd have to scar her. But at least I wouldn't damage the drawing her brother did or destroy a part of her past.

Victor thought I was a novice at this.

Sure, a couple of decades had passed since my education in these arts, but…I'd been taught by the best. I knew the noise of a perfect swing. I remembered the slice of miscalculation. I might have muscle memory in a boy's body, but I recalled enough to be confident I wouldn't hurt her…too badly.

Fuck.

Pinching the bridge of my nose, I allowed myself to accept what I was about to do.

I was about to whip a woman I'd fallen stupidly in love with.

My life was about to come full circle, and…the chances of me snapping were sky-fucking-high.

But…she'd agreed to fight me back.

As long as she gave me her fire, I could remember where I was.

But her fight will draw out all that darkness.

The beast inside me would take over.

I'd enjoy this far more than I should.

Merde.

Today might truly be the worst and best fucking day of my life.

The bullwhip warmed in my hand.

My black blood sang.

This was happening.

For better or for worse.

And I suppose I better get started…

Chapter Twenty-Seven

NEITHER OF US MOVED FOR AN eternity.
Hearts pounded.
Energy flowed.
Adrenaline drenched my system.
It'd taken absolutely everything not to scream when Victor touched me. My entire body recoiled and rejected him. I felt psychically sick and horribly vulnerable.
Just because I hadn't watched him abuse me last night didn't mean my body wasn't highly, *highly* aware that this was the man who'd done it. This was the monster that hurt me.
And Henri made me apologise to him.
For show.
I'd seen how much it cut him to do it.
How much his pain matched mine.
That was the only reason I wasn't a mess.
Why I could hold my chin high and not cry.
He loves me.
My heart squeezed.
We'd found love in hell.
We'd made a pact against the devil.
I can do this.
He won't hurt me.
Not really.
And if he did…well…
I swallowed hard, still not comfortable with the admission.
I'll…probably enjoy it.
Standing taller in my binds, I found Henri's eyes and lost myself in his churning grey-dark depths.
Victor had left to join Rachel on the bed. His attention only on her.
It was just me and Henri.

Just us in this despicable world.

We stared for far too long, both of us waiting for the other to make the first move.

With a grimace, Henri shook his head and looked down at the whip in his hands.

I shifted where I stood, bound to the cross. The chain and its hook jangled, sending a wash of the same delicious, dangerous awareness through me. I'd felt it last night when I'd gone pliant beneath him.

Playing the captive.

Relinquishing my power.

It'd done something to me.

It'd done something to him.

He'd infected me with his dark disease, and I couldn't hate him for it. How could I hate him when he made me feel so alive, so in-tune, so sensitive?

His face darkened as time ticked past.

His chest rose and fell, his breathing shallow and harsh.

His knuckles whitened around the whip as he fell back into memories.

No...

Stay with me.

You have to stay with me.

I cleared my throat loudly; the noise wrenched his eyes back to mine.

He froze.

I shrugged. *It's okay...*

Rocking backward on his heels, he reacted as if he'd heard me.

All those warnings I'd read of twin flames being graced with almost telepathic abilities didn't seem so crazy anymore.

You need to do this. I arched my chin at Rachel, making Henri look over his shoulder. Victor had stripped and shackled her, spread-eagled on the bed.

Henri tore his eyes away, his throat flexing as he swallowed hard.

I felt no jealousy that he'd slept with her. No complicated possession or pain. Just needling determination to get through today so I could take him to the kitchens and tell him everything.

Henri... I jangled my cuffs, getting his attention. *Do it. Do it now.*

Sighing heavily, he wiped his face with a shaking hand.

I knew why he struggled.

Why he hesitated.

He probably thought I was mad to suggest doing this. To willingly taunt the darkness in him, but…he was the only one who could ensure Victor stayed lazy and content. We couldn't have him scouring the video feeds. Couldn't have him being suspicious.

Our entire plan hinged on Victor not questioning why maids suddenly hid things under beds or why the orders for cleaning supplies had increased or why the recycling shed didn't hold as many bottles.

Henri was the key to keeping Victor happy.

So…please *make him happy*.

Dropping his hand, he gave me the saddest smile.

Then his jaw clenched, his face hardened, and he spread his legs as if he was about to go to war.

Oh God.

This is it.

My ass heated, remembering the punishment of his palm as he spanked me by the pond.

I hadn't been prepared for the aching desire his hand had caused.

Would this be the same or—

My core clenched as Henri suddenly flicked his wrist and sent the whip and its nasty forked tongue licking through the air. He didn't aim at me.

Practicing.

Most likely remembering.

His first swat looked a little shaky, his second a bit stronger, his third smoother, and his fourth—the sharp *snap* as it cracked—echoed loudly in the torture chamber.

Well, fuck me…

Dressed all in black with unreadable eyes and perfect mastery over such a violent weapon…he was stunning.

Beyond stunning.

Diabolical.

I melted.

My insides turned to liquid.

My adrenaline switched to arousal.

Terrible, tempting, *treacherous* arousal.

Victor glanced over. "Nice crack, *mon ami*." His eyes narrowed. "You said you've never used a whip before?"

Henri had a hard time looking away from me. His voice sounded like smouldering volcanic ash. "Pure novice, but…I watch things."

Victor's forehead furrowed. "Just like you watch MMA and somehow became a killing machine?"

"Something like that."

"Hmm." Victor sniffed. "It took me weeks to master the art of cracking a whip. Either you're very humble or you're lying."

Henri stiffened. "You know I'm descended from Quincy Mercer the First. I witnessed him playing. One of his favourite toys was a bullwhip." He swallowed hard before admitting, "And I may have had a few swats myself, now and again."

"He taught you?" Victor lost all his tension, a slow smile crossing his face. "In that case…carry on. I've always thought Mercer the First and I would've gotten on quite well. It's fun watching you step into his shoes."

Henri didn't respond.

Victor returned to Rachel, stripping off his jumper and grabbing a few silver clamps from a nearby rack.

Henri turned back to me; the whip coiled like a sleeping serpent on the floor. With a flick, he cracked it again.

Another droplet of need.

A heavy emptiness needing to be filled.

I feared him and wanted him.

I hated that he had to share a past he obviously detested. I pitied him that his mind had protected him from all of this, yet his present dragged every dirty memory to the surface.

My thoughts raced and collided for ever agreeing to this.

For making him *become* this.

I grew wetter and hotter, and God…

I *wanted* this.

I wanted *him*.

I-I couldn't help it.

I wanted to save him, submit to him…

I felt ashamed and embarrassed and so turned-on that tears prickled up my spine.

I couldn't look.

Closing my eyes, I did my best to remember who I was.

I was strong. I was smart. I—

Henri suddenly crowded me against the cross. His heat, his hardness, his power.

I moaned as he grabbed my chin and forced my eyes up.

His skin blazed with wildfire. His lips wet from his tongue. Tipping my head to the side, he whispered, "Don't be afraid of me. You promised you wouldn't be afraid—"

"I'm not." I sagged against him, humming under his touch. "I'm afraid of myself. Of how much I need you."

"I can see how wet you are. It's taking everything I have not to fuck you and forgo all this shit." His hand holding the whip grazed along my hipbone. His thumb stroked those maddening little Morse code swirls, sending me messages of love and togetherness. "I'm jumping out of my skin, Ily."

Behind him, Victor kissed Rachel as he finished clamping silver things to her breasts. She didn't utter a single word to her Master, yet I had a million I wanted to say to mine.

Henri sensed the racing alphabet of my thoughts as he nipped the shell of my ear. "If you've changed your mind about doing this—"

"No." I shook my head. "It's not that…"

He groaned and pressed his hips against mine. His cock branded me through his jeans, hinting I wasn't the only one struggling with right and wrong. "Feel that? I could climax right now. One touch from you and I'd cover you in cum."

I shuddered.

I bit my bottom lip as his voice entered me, stroked me, made my entire body quiver.

How could I have this reaction with Victor in the room?

How could I even think about sex after what'd happened last night?

For a second, I feared my mind *had* snapped, and this was just another coping mechanism, but then Henri kissed his way along my jaw and captured my lips with his.

Everything fell away.

All of it.

My heart ached with a thousand bruises as he licked me.

The kiss wasn't just a kiss but everything we couldn't say and everything we would always mean.

I'm yours.
You're mine.
I love you.
I'll free you.

Teeth and tongue, breath and bliss.

He groaned as I nipped at his bottom lip. I moaned as he grabbed my bare breast.

For a moment, I let romance carry us away. Enchantment and passion blocked out the entire island, but as Henri's hand skated from my hips and dove between my legs—as two fingers slipped exquisitely deep inside me and he stumbled as if my wetness completely undid him, I pulled away from his mouth and provoked the sinner he was.

He wouldn't do this without trusting me. And he couldn't trust me unless I played.

So…I played.

"Don't fucking *touch me*." I spat on the floor.

In my lust-hazy stare, Victor smirked across the room.

The more Victor thought I hated this—that I obeyed merely because of what I'd seen in the caves—the less he'd see the truth.

The truth that I was absurdly, alarmingly, absolutely in love with Henri freaking Mercer.

"Get away from me," I hissed, committing to this ruse. "I hate you."

Henri didn't just freeze, he died.

Perished right before me.

Blackness hooded his eyes.

For a moment, he looked as if he'd throw up—the good parts forbidding him from enjoying this—but then the bad parts…all those parts cultivated in those formative years. The parts that'd evolved from sheer terror and survival sprang into being.

I didn't need psilocybin to see the devil before me.

Didn't need bat wings or hallucinations to witness his transformation.

Slowly, ever so slowly, he withdrew his fingers and brought them to his kiss-swollen lips.

Not looking away, he inserted both into his mouth and sucked. Hard.

His moan was pure eroticism. His flicking tongue as he cleaned my flavour from his fingers deliciously perverse.

Finishing the last drop, he grabbed my chin with his wet hand and descended into all that black. "You tell me not to touch you, little nightmare, yet your body fucking *drips* for me."

"Go to hell."

Oh God.

I was prepared to fight him back. To show him I was still here and not broken.

But I wasn't prepared for the addictive rush of filthy, greedy *yearning.*

His entire body shuddered. "Only if I can take you with me."

Victor chuckled as he ran a soft flogger over Rachel's barely-there baby bump. His eyes flickered to us as if amused by our show.

We couldn't talk freely. We could barely talk at all on this fucked-up island, but…I trusted Henri.

I trusted in our vow.

And I let go.

I dove into that black.

I let the twisted creature who'd been born the night of the treasure hunt take control. To embrace her fury, her lust, her violence.

"Touch me again, and I'll make you wish you were dead."

A gush.

Not a droplet this time but a river of hot, slick, ravenous need.

"Ah, Ily…" Falling on me, he bit my neck above my collar. "Are you sure you want to threaten me?"

"Get *off* me."

He chuckled.

The softest hiss of the whip on stone echoed as he flicked it left and right.

An orgasm kindled in my core.

Already?

How?

God, why?

Why did this turn me on so much?

How much more could I stand before I shattered without a single touch?

He grabbed my jaw. His fingers scalded; body heat seared.

I gulped as electricity crackled between us.

"Tell me again what will happen if I touch you? Because…" He licked my cheek, his tongue pointed and cruel. "I'm touching you."

I moaned.

My heart flurried.

My fault.

My choice.

I'd allowed my synapses to accept this.

Encouraged my system to crave his.

And damn…I craved and craved and *craved*.

Grasping at sanity's shore that seemed so far away, I bared my teeth. "You're sick."

"Tell me something I don't know." He shuddered as if he couldn't control the hungry beast snarling in his eyes. Wedging his hips against mine, he thrust. The iron rod in his jeans stabbed against my belly. "Feel that? See how much your fire turns me on? See how badly I want to snuff it out?"

Words flew away.

All I could see was his smoky-grey eyes. Heavy lidded, magnetic, hypnotic, demonic.

His hands feathered into my hair, the whip dangling from his right and branding my shoulder. Pulling me forward until my shoulders threatened to pop from the hook holding me in place, he hovered his mouth over mine.

My lips stung for his kiss.

I grew drunk and dizzy, waiting, needing—

Without warning, he flipped me as nastily as Victor had.

I moaned as my breasts wedged against the cross. My stomach and cheek smashing against the wood. My criss-crossed wrists kept me trapped. "Henri—"

"Master H, if you don't mind." His slightly calloused hands roamed over my back and ass. Squeezing hard, he spread my cheeks and wedged his hips against me. "Fuck, I want to take you here."

True fear returned, amplifying my out-of-control need into something heart-fistingly potent.

The gemstone dildos Victor had given us. Would Henri use them? Did he truly plan to take me there?

I'd never…

I didn't want—

"Christ, you're soaking." His fingers drove from behind, spearing inside my core, sending me soaring onto my tiptoes.

I didn't just moan this time, I cried out—tortured and tormented, desperate and dark.

Running his nose along my tattooed spine, he murmured, "I honestly have no idea how I'm going to react when I start whipping you, Ily, so…I suggest you hold on."

My heart skipped. "Wait…don't—"

"You look fucking amazing strung up like this." Two fingers

became three. My mind blacked out. "Ride my hand. Come for me like a good little girl, then maybe I won't whip you after all."

His command soaked into my blood.

Any normal person would obey. They'd choose a release over pain and do whatever it took, but today…I wasn't normal. *He* wasn't normal. In this place, we were *ab*normal.

And so…my response was the only one I could give.

Clamping my legs together, I tried to bruise his wrist. "Stop touching me, you bastard."

Hissing between his teeth, he yanked his hand away.

I mourned the loss of being filled, but then…his body heat vanished too. His footfalls tripped unevenly away. And the slither of that terrifying whip ratcheted up my pulse until I breathed with quick little pants. True terror shoved aside my script. "Henri…wait…"

"Master H is my title. Use it."

"Don't—"

"Too late." He made a guttural noise that made my hair stand on end. "I tried to warn you and even gave you an out. You didn't take it."

The quiet hiss of leather flying through the air landed with the sting of a thousand angry bees.

"Ah *fuck*." I jolted. My cuffs jingled. My back *burned*.

Never.

I'd never felt anything so sharp, so stinging, so savage.

The whip snapped over my left shoulder blade, burning me with a million fires. The ink down my spine seemed to throb, the tip of my wand pulsing with heinous magic.

"Jesus fucking Christ." Henri groaned.

I scrambled against the cross. The hook clanged against its chain. And I screamed as the whip sang again—

"*Ahhh!*" The second lash burrowed deep into my skin, blazing on my other shoulder blade.

"Your tanned skin makes me work harder for those red welts," he groaned. "You should see what I see. See how drenched you are. See how you arch into the whip's kiss."

He struck again.

I collapsed against the cross, my shackles holding me upright.

Just a game.

Just a game.

Playing.

Faking.

So why did it feel so *real?*

Why did my mind fracture, and my body shatter, and everything I'd ever known tear itself into silly little pieces?

He struck a fourth time.

Fire.

Liquid, luminous fire.

Everywhere.

"Your tattoo is glowing red, little nightmare," he grunted. "The wand looks alive. A curse just for me."

The pain billowed and cycloned. It soaked into my blood and travelled straight to my soul. With fingers made of light and whispers made of night, it shut down my thoughts one by one. Snuffed them out. Turned them off.

I was no longer human with feelings and fears. I was pure energy and vibration.

I sank into the trance.

A fifth lick, this one tattooing my very heart.

I screamed.

I convulsed.

My insides contracted on emptiness, needing, needing, *needing…*

"You were made for this," he snarled. "Made for me to mark."

I sagged. I tensed.

The synergy between us became carnal.

His energy wrapped around mine. My energy bled out to join his.

Crowding me against the cross, he pressed his front to my blazing back. His sweaty, scorching skin plastered to mine. He must've ripped off his t-shirt and, good *God*, it felt too good. Far, far too good.

I moaned as his hand speared between my thighs, penetrating me with three thick fingers. My legs spread of their own accord, delivering myself up to him. My ass backed up, begging him.

He groaned as he grabbed my hip with his other hand, rocking me over his hand.

Stars in my eyes.

Galaxies in my heart.

"Tell me again not to touch you," he grunted. "I dare you."

I almost swallowed my own tongue as he pumped into me,

rough and primal.

An orgasm spindled from nowhere.

So close.

So near.

Up and up and—

"I feel you." He pressed his forehead right on the tip of my wand. "Feel your greedy pussy milking my fingers with those hot little pulses." He bit my ear, his breath tattered. "It makes me want to fuck you so bad."

Do it.

Yes.

Please!

"I hate you," I groaned, falling deeper into love.

Just words at this point. Just scrambled-up lines that meant the absolute opposite.

"You hate me, huh?" With a soft, sensual chuckle, Henri removed his fingers.

I moaned as my core rippled with frustration.

I needed him to fill me.

Complete me.

A cold draft prickled down my back as he stumbled away. The warning hiss of the whip and its dangerous song slicked through the air.

Another lash cracked right on my ass.

"Ah fuck!" My hips shot forward, bruising me against the cross.

I had no words for what happened.

No explanation for how the corporeal part of me suddenly existed on a spiritual plane of sensuality. I'd touched such a metaphysical place yesterday when I'd hidden from Victor. I'd fallen into sublime quietness for only a few seconds every time I meditated, but this…

God *this*…

"Beg me to stop," Henri gasped. "Tell me how much you hate me."

I couldn't breathe, let alone speak.

Another lash.

A waspish sting.

Meditative calmness.

Intense mindfulness.

I burned alive.

Because of him.

My other half.

My *missing* half.

My blood turned to light as every molecule shivered for more.

"I want to do such bad things to you, Ily…" He struck again, this time on my other ass cheek.

I snapped forward against the cross again. My knees trembled. My legs threatened to give out. Another wave of hot fire cascaded down my back and into my blood.

It pushed me headfirst into a deeper realm.

An awful detonation.

It wasn't his darkness that shoved me into pleasure but the innocence beneath his mastery. The pain tangled in his power. The vulnerability and love and kindness.

A kindness that hadn't been eradicated despite what his father had done to him.

A commitment that came from a lifetime of needing to belong. To belong to one person. Just one. Just me.

Another lash directly on my spine.

I went completely blind as all my heat soaked into my clit.

I hovered on the edge of an orgasm.

I panted and sweated, moaned and mewled.

All I wanted was for him to finish. To fill me. Instead, I clung to our play and forced, "Fuck you."

"Such a filthy word from your pretty little mouth."

"Get away from me."

"Nope." His heavy footsteps stepped into me. The prickle of his energy coated my entire back. "I have just the thing to tame that mouth of yours."

My hovering orgasm teased.

If he touched me, I'd fall.

I held my breath and—

With brutal hands, he flipped me to face him.

My wrists uncrossed.

Our eyes locked.

And all our games fell away.

His gaze held no light, just pitch blackness. His lips thin, temples glittering with sweat. He'd stripped to his tight navy boxer-briefs, his erection popping out.

Whatever intensity we existed in lashed us together.

I felt him.

Heard him.

You're perfect. His eyes glowed.

"You're drenched," his lips murmured.

I love you, his heart whispered.

"You're going to pay." His mouth smiled.

I strained for him to kiss me, but he dropped to his haunches, and with swift fingers, he buckled leather straps around my ankles. His touch felt like a million needles dipped in velvet.

I moaned and shivered. "Stop."

He didn't reply. Standing upright, he grabbed a lever to the left, and I screamed as the cross flipped upside down.

Blood rushed to my head as my view switched.

Upside down, gravity grabbed my hair, my breasts, my mind.

The shackles around my ankles kept me upright, cutting into my skin.

He groaned as his gaze locked onto my spread and exposed centre. "Damn. I'd hope your mouth would line up with my cock. Sucking me would've definitely shut you up." He sighed. "Ah well, I have other ways."

I'd never felt so vulnerable as he ran his nose along the trimmed black hair between my legs then stuck his tongue inside me from above.

Not a lick.

Not a lave.

A takeover.

I didn't scream this time, I choked.

My entire body went to explode—

He stopped.

Tears rolled from my eyes, falling the wrong way, soaking into my hair. "Hen…"

"*Don't,*" he barked. "Until you say my name correctly, you don't get to come."

Breathing hard, Henri left me upside down as he strode across the snuffbox and grabbed a sharp little knife from the rack housing all manner of awful implements.

I hovered in that nondescript magical place, hyper aware of his every move.

I lost all track of where we were and why and how and became nothing more than a river of need.

He returned with a tiny jewel-handled dagger. Flicking a look at Victor, he grabbed his discarded jeans on the floor and grabbed the vial from his pocket. "How many scars am I allowed?"

Victor paused mid-thrust, his hips plastered against Rachel's. It took a moment for his mind to catch up. "However many you want. Now shut the fuck up. I'm busy." He resumed his rock.

Henri fisted his two toys.

I trembled as he marched back toward me.

I waited for him to flip me the right way up.

To whisper to stay calm. That he hadn't lost himself.

But he merely latched his mouth on my pussy again.

Every nerve ending arrowed right where he punished me.

My entire system fritzed and fried.

The lashes on my back braided with the pleasure between my legs, and I lost myself completely.

Overwhelming.

Encompassing.

Tears sprang.

I sobbed as he ate me out. I shuddered as his teeth scraped my clit. I scrambled and screamed as he drove me straight toward that lacerating climax only to stop as the first ripple of release worked its way through my entire body.

He laughed cruelly and pressed the sweetest kiss on the paper-thin skin of my inner thigh. "Not yet, little nightmare. I mean to make you bleed first."

His left hand landed on my thigh, stroking me in the exact spot where his own leg wore the permanent reminder of where he'd tried to take his own life.

I shivered as he pressed a kiss there, then replaced his lips with the dagger. "Don't move."

Every part of me tensed as he added pressure to the blade.

My skin resisted.

Pain intensified.

The dagger won.

I cried out as he cut me.

Too many feelings at once.

Too many sensations.

I couldn't keep track of them all.

They all spiralled into one ball of fire, and blood, and *need*.

"Three lines. Just three." Dragging the dagger over my skin, he sliced me with a steady, focused hand. Blood trickled, rolling hotly toward my hipbone. The first line scrambled my every thought. The second shoved me straight into spiritual salvation.

And the third…it scribed me with everything I shouldn't want…building, building, *building*.

I strained in my bonds, scratchy and achy and going out of my *mind*.

Henri let out a savage snarl as he licked up my blood. His tongue flat and heavy, licking me clean with every long swipe.

I pulsed in time to the blood throbbing in my punishments.

I trembled.

I ached.

I'd never felt this way. This unbound. This honest. This free.

Tossing the knife away, he fisted the vial and yanked out the small cork.

Without a word, he sprinkled sapphire dust on the three lines—two vertical, one horizontal—sealing up the wound with glimmering blue, coagulating with the red of my blood.

Victor wasn't the first to do such a thing.

In my studies, I'd come across many indigenous people who used gemstone dust to harness the properties of the stone and alter their physical capabilities. Victor was right that gemstones were antibacterial, antiseptic, and often used in healing modalities.

The thought of forever having sapphires in my skin? It intrigued me. Perhaps I'd inherit the metaphysical properties of the blue stone and gain wisdom, intuition, and spiritual insight.

Or maybe it would do nothing more than brand me with Henri's mark—

Sudden wetness.

Aggressive heat.

My thoughts scrambled as Henri's tongue dipped inside me again.

The three stinging lines on my thigh faded. The punishment from the whip meant nothing.

His tongue was *everything*. Deep and worshipping, addictive and all-consuming.

I groaned as a flush of sick, sick desire made my entire body contract.

"Christ, you have no idea what this is doing to me." His voice sounded utterly inhuman. "Your blood. Your taste. I can't wait any longer. I can't fucking *do this*."

Breathing hard, he flipped the lever.

With a wooden groan, the cross righted itself, taking me with it. My head swam as I went from down to up.

Dizziness added to my desire.

Out-of-control hunger only magnified as he grabbed my hips and stroked his thumbs in those maddening little swirls.

I was too far gone to sense him beneath the game we played. Too deep into lust to care about anything but coming. "*Please…*" I whimpered.

Tracing his thumb over the sore sapphire-branded wounds, he sighed in absolute awe. "It looks like you got mauled by a beast with blue claws. A beast that can spell…"

I looked down.

H.

A crude, primitive H marked my skin forever.

"You…" My words slurred. "Autographed me."

His eyes snapped closed; he swayed on the spot. When he opened them again, I no longer existed in this world. I was his. Just his. My every thought, breath, and whimper…*his*.

"So you never forget." He licked his lips. "Now…tell me, little nightmare. Do you need me? Tell me you need me, and I'll put you out of your misery."

It took every ounce of control. Every drop of discipline. But I shook my heavy head and mumbled, "Fuck…you."

He grinned.

A boyish, blinding grin.

Leaning close, he breathed, "*Mon Dieu, je t'aime.*" (My God, I love you.)

Pulling away, he laughed for our audience. "Ah, Ilyana, I think you'll find I'm about to fuck *you*." Without warning, he spun me around again. My front whacked against the cross, sending agonising shockwaves through my breasts.

"No," I panted. "No more."

"No more? You should know by now not to tell me what to do." His voice was gravelly with sin as he tripped away from me. "For that, I'll give you *more*. Three more before I fuck you. Hold on."

"No—" I screamed as he flicked his wrist.

The whip sang. Connected. *Pain.*

This one thinner, crueller—a single bite of torture.

"I need you to suffer," he groaned. "I need you to know how it feels."

A faint ringing noise was my only warning as he whipped me again.

Tight and tangy, tormenting and torturous.

I moaned as pain became pleasure. Life became death. And he became the only thing that could save me.

My body took control, preparing to come without any other touch.

I'd never been so sensitive that the very air fondled me.

My insides weren't just liquid anymore they were molten and glowing and on *fire*.

The slither of the whip over stone became its signature song as he flicked it one last time and kissed me with leathery, lashing pain.

It bit into my left hip.

I didn't know who I was anymore.

So desperate.

So—

"Shit, you're bleeding." I convulsed as Henri cursed. "Fuck." With a savage groan, he threw the whip to the side and crashed into me. Grabbing the vial forgotten on the floor and dropping to his knees, he latched his mouth over my new cut and sucked.

His hot mouth.

His silent worship.

I cried out as the first coil of a release unravelled.

Yes.

God, yes—

"Wait," he seethed.

I squirmed as he cleaned the red mark, then shivered as he scattered sapphires like blue snow on my side. With a gentle thumb, he smoothed away the loose grains and sucked in a tattered breath.

I wanted to see what it looked like.

The smallest sapphire scratch.

But he shot to his feet and pressed his entire body against mine.

His entire *naked* body.

The world narrowed to a pinprick.

The second his chest kissed my back. The *moment* his heat and hardness covered me, my body fell and—

"I said *wait*," he panted.

With a guttural snarl, he yanked my hips back, arched my spine, and kicked my shackled legs apart. Bending his knees, he notched his crown exactly where I needed him…

"Now scream," he growled.
And slammed home inside me.
To the hilt.
To the heart.
I did what he commanded.
I screamed.

Chapter Twenty-Eight

Henri

I LOST MYSELF.
To her. To sin.
Nothing else existed.
Just her scalding, sopping heat.
Her body milked mine as I impaled her, forcing my way in as a vicious orgasm tore through her, making her entire body seize.
God, she was beautiful.
So, *so* fucking beautiful.
The metallic sharpness of her blood on my tongue. The smell of her need on my skin. The slipperiness of her sweat and welts on her back and the sapphire scars—
Fuck, the scars.
I roared as she fisted me, rhythmical clenches as she came.
Her head tipped back as she surrendered entirely to me. Her body completely mine to use and abuse and worship.
Everything about her burned.
Everything inside me answered.
I fucked her.
Harder, faster, deeper than I'd ever taken anyone.
I willingly tried to hurt her.
I thrust and pumped, forcing her to feel every ridge and rock.
My head clouded with memories of the whip. My past tangled with my present. I felt sick and ecstatic. Lost and found.
My spine rolled as I fed her everything. Stabbing again and again, going out of my fucking mind as she kept coming, her whimpers getting louder, her back arching for more and more and *more*.
I gave her more.
Fuck, I gave her everything.
I jack-knifed and pounded, and the longer I took her, the

deeper my mind fell.

We *burned*.

Not just our bodies.

But our spirits too.

We writhed together like demonic creatures.

Our hearts smoked and minds melded.

She screamed as I hit a thick, tight part of her.

She shuddered and gasped.

I kept fucking her. Over and over, driving her straight into hell.

Killing her with pleasure. Killing myself with everything I'd tried to forget and everything I didn't want to be.

I hated that this felt so *good*.

I despised that her blood made me throb.

I would never forgive myself for committing violence toward the one person I loved, even as it drove me into such delicious, despicable darkness.

But in that darkness, as her whimpers became pleas, and her legs gave out—as I impaled myself deeper and deeper—we somehow became one.

Just one.

No longer my body and her body but *ours*.

Us.

All the good, the bad, the sick, the twisted, and the wrong.

I took her and fucked her and with no space between us, no secrets to hide, no curses to utter, light cracked in the blackness.

A transcendental light. Luminous and iridescent, soaking into my very essence, knotting me to her for eternity.

I *felt* her as she reached her pinnacle.

I *was* her as she stopped breathing and gave everything she was to that final crest of pleasure.

A gush of wetness around me. A rush of searing heat. Her body didn't just come, it erupted, coating my pounding cock in her orgasm and shoving me face first into mine.

My climax started in my toes and shot all the way up my spine and into my heart.

We rode each other as the waves of her release consumed me. We became the same ocean where those waves crashed. The same tragic sea where sex somehow shifted from physical into profound.

I felt her in my *soul*.

I had no idea what was happening.

No idea how to stop it.

Stop the pull of her. The call of her.

I gasped as the first pulse of my orgasm spilled.

Blinding, blistering.

I couldn't breathe as every synapse arrowed between my legs and exploded.

I came.

God*dammit*, I came.

I filled her up.

I coated every inch.

Our shared releases oozed down her legs, making our connection sinfully slippery.

I roared as pleasure became pain, and pain became pleasure, and I couldn't survive the intensity anymore.

It kept going.

Kept pulsing.

And when I reached the end, I collapsed against her, panting, sweating, fucking changed and completely broken.

We stayed like that for the longest moment.

Gasping and shaking.

Our breathing in sync and hearts colliding.

In the distance, Victor reached his own release, tainting this moment—this profound, crazy moment. I needed to play the part of a Master who just got his dick wet with his jewel, but for now, I was completely enslaved by her.

Nuzzling my way through her sweat-misty hair, I murmured, "Four scars for four things you now own."

She shuddered.

"You own me, Ily. Body and mind, heart and soul. Forever."

Chapter Twenty-Nine

Ily

I SIGHED AND SNUGGLED CLOSER to Henri.

Hidden beneath the blankets, tucked away from the world and cameras, we knotted each other up in arms and legs and lay still.

I'd never felt so cosy, so comfortable.

Never thought I'd find my place in the arms of someone who battled such demons and won.

His lips skated along my shoulder blade where he hugged me from behind, making my lash marks twinge.

Hug wasn't the right word. Smothering was better. The way he held me so tightly ought to be claustrophobic, but it only granted safety.

I sighed again, sleep tugging on my eyelashes.

It'd been a long day.

After we'd finally disengaged in the snuffbox and Victor finished with Rachel, all of us were surprisingly quiet. Victor inspected the cuts Henri had given me, then snapped his fingers for Rachel to follow him.

They'd left, and we'd followed.

Henri had taken me to see Dr Belford.

She'd treated the whip welts and cuts but admitted she couldn't clean out the sapphire dust thanks to Victor's many rules. Instead, she'd applied a salve to speed up healing and placed a small bandage over my hip and thigh.

We'd returned to our room.

I'd expected to talk or shower or relive the most heightened sexual experience of my life. Only, Henri laid me down, applied more arnica to my lashes, then bundled me beneath the blankets and just held me.

"I'm sorry for hurting you," he breathed drowsily against my skin. "I'm sorry for what I am."

I shivered as he kissed my ear.

"You don't owe me an apology, Hen. You saw how much I enjoyed it." My cheeks flushed hot.

"Yes, I did see. I felt it too." A rumbling chuckle vibrated in his chest, tickling my smarting back. "Has that…ever happened to you before?"

I knew what he meant.

The savagery of my climax.

The gush of embarrassing liquid…

For a moment, I tried to figure out a way to deny what'd happened, but he murmured, "You squirted on me, Ily."

I gasped. "I did nothing of the sort."

He chuckled again. "The mess we left behind hinted it wasn't just me who created that puddle."

"You sound rather proud of yourself." I sniffed. "Rather cocky actually."

"Exceedingly." He sucked the top of my shoulder, his mouth wet and hot. "To know I can give you that level of pleasure?" He groaned. "It helps redeem some of the filth inside me."

I arched my chin, giving him greater access to my neck.

"I could barely climb inside you, you were coming so hard," he whispered. "You started coming without me even touching you."

"Oh, you touched me alright. You touched me in far too many ways."

"So you're not usually that sensitive? You've never reached the level of squir—"

"If you say squirted one more time—"

"You did."

"Did not."

"Pretty sure you ejaculated all over me."

"Oh God, will you stop." I buried my face into the pillow.

He laughed.

A laugh I didn't think I'd ever hear from him. Loose and languid, untainted with stress or shame.

It made my heart glow; my chagrin fell away.

I wanted to make him laugh every day for the rest of his life so he never had to be sad again.

With my face flaming, I whispered, "What you made me do was…definitely a first."

He sighed and hugged me bone-breakingly hard.

He didn't speak, almost as if knowing he affected me that

intensely made him speechless.

"The things you make me feel, Hen…" I shrugged in his embrace. "It's out of this world. Literally."

He chuckled against my hair. "Probably shouldn't tell me that if you don't want me cocky."

I snuggled closer. "In that case, I definitely shouldn't say I've never experienced pleasure like I have with you. Never knew it was possible. Your anatomy is so perfect, it should be illegal."

"My *anatomy*?" He snickered.

"Yep." I grinned beneath our blankets. "You have this uncanny ability to hit my G-spot. A mythical spot before you came along, by the way." I kissed his forearm wrapped around my chest. "If a sex toy company made dildos off your size and shape, then women might finally learn how to—"

"Squirt?"

"No!" I giggled, absolutely shocked that this moment was so normal, so…sweet. "I mean…find pleasure from other parts and not just her clit."

"I'll see if Victor has some plaster of paris lying around." He chuckled. "We could ship replicas of my dick to every frustrated housewife around the world."

A rush of jealous possession ripped through me. "I hate to tell you, Henri, but the only one who will ever feel you inside her is me. Real or toy."

He fell silent.

Our light-hearted energy solidified into seriousness.

I didn't want it to.

Everything had been far too serious for far too long, but we weren't free. Eight new jewels were here. Peter was being tormented. Mollie was being abused. Rachel was pregnant.

Compared to them, I was so lucky.

I'd been given a man I'd never expected, and we'd experienced something soul-changing, but…this moment of reprieve was just that…a moment.

"I know I have a thousand messed-up feelings, but hearing you being possessive over me?" He yanked me tighter against him. "I can't tell you how that makes me feel." His voice turned achingly quiet. "That's all I've ever wanted. To be *wanted*. To be loved despite all the shit inside me."

Squirming in his arms, I turned to face him and cupped his cheek. His grey eyes glowed silver in the dark, the sheets hiding us in our own fabric world. His sheer size. His immense presence. He oozed power and masculinity, but beneath those muscles and all that darkness, he was painfully vulnerable and innocent.

It was that innocence I'd sensed all along. A wide-eyed naivety when it came to love and all its facets. My heart ached as I kept my voice too low for the cameras. "You're mine, Henri Mercer. Got it?"

He sighed heavily. "I'm yours until my last breath, Ily." Shifting a little, he added, "I'm yours, yet I barely know you. We haven't had the chance to talk about such simple things, but...I *know* you. I do. I know all the important things."

"Important things?"

"You have to have felt it." He shrugged self-consciously. "Today, when I entered you? Something clutched me around the heart and forged me with you. I-I can't explain it, but—"

"It felt like we were one?"

He flinched. "Yeah..." His gaze locked on my mouth. "You felt it too?"

"I did." I ran my thumb over the hollowness of his severe cheeks. "And I think I know why."

"You do?"

I dropped my eyes. "Umm...it'll probably sound silly, but...someone once told me that I'd meet a man who would turn out to be my twin flame and—"

"Twin flame?" Henri whispered. "What does that mean?"

I twitched, not really ready to share my mystical hypnosis. "Eh, well...a soulmate is a separate soul you've known before. Someone you've loved in every lifetime and are connected to in many ways, but a twin flame...it's the missing *piece* of your soul."

He went very still. "How...how do you know when you find this missing piece?"

"There's a few ways but the main one would be, um, the sensation that you've met before."

"The recognition." He froze. "The familiarity. You feel so familiar to me. You always have."

"You too." I smiled softly.

"So there's an explanation for all of this? A black-and-white reason you've become every-fucking-thing to me, yet...I don't even know your favourite colour, favourite fruit, favourite memory?"

"Gold, dragon fruit, and my brother finding me on the steps of the hospital—not that that's a memory but a story my family has told me over and over again. And yes...I'm sure there's a reason we met. An explanation for why it's so strong between us. Why I feel safe with you even though we're surrounded by danger."

A few moments ticked past before he murmured, "I'd like to meet your brother." He nuzzled my nose with his. "He's the reason you have the worst/best name I've ever heard."

Tears shot up my spine at the thought of Henri going home with me. Of walking into my family's house. Of saying hello to Krish. "One day." I swallowed back stinging hope. "Hopefully, you can meet them one day. My parents are the most wonderful people. Our community so caring. I come from a large group of families—some related, some not, yet we all look out for one another. You'd probably be overwhelmed if I'm honest."

He huffed. "Your dad will probably take one look at me and kill me on the spot."

"Lucky for you, my dad is Buddhist, and killing is against our philosophy." I toyed with the sprigs of black hair between his pecs. "He won't even kill the tiniest bug. He gives water to the smallest cricket. He's the wisest, kindest man I know."

"And I've killed four men, so what does that make me?"

"Protective." I ran my finger over his bottom lip. "Prepared to do whatever it takes to keep me safe."

He licked my fingertip. "And I failed you in so many ways. Failed Peter and all the others...I'll never be able to change that."

"No, you can't. But you can help us now."

The air grew static with unsaid things.

Were we safe to do this?

Hidden from the cameras with our voices as low as possible?

The best privacy we were going to get but still so, so dangerous.

"Are you finally going to tell me?" he asked ever so quietly. "Tell me what you're planning?"

"Not here." I shook my head, fear creeping through me. "But...tomorrow. I'll go to the jewel quarters at dawn before the Masters start summoning and speak to Peter. I'll arrange a meeting for you two. He can tell you. He'll have the most up-to-date information."

"Where?"

"The kitchens."

His eyebrows shot up. "The kitchens?"

My mind raced with what tomorrow would bring. Excitement.

Dread. Fear. Hope.

"It has a dead spot in the recording," I whispered. "It's the safest place to talk."

"Is that where you've been running off to while I was writing?"

"Yep."

Silence for a moment before he said, "I went to check on the jewels a few times while Victor was away."

"You did?"

He scowled. "Victor liked me enquiring about how he ran his home. I figured he'd like it if I cared about his jewels too."

"So you did it for appearance's sake?"

"I told myself I did, but…that's not entirely the truth. I failed to save my own flesh and blood. I need to get the jewels free so I don't repeat my past. I need to help…for selfish reasons."

"Selfish?"

"I need to find a way to redeem myself."

Snuggling into his arms, my whip marks twinged, and the sapphire scars on my thigh and hip already itched with healing. "Don't beat yourself up for doing the right thing for shadowy reasons, Hen. You want to save them. That's all that matters."

"I want to scar you again even though I know it's wrong. What matters in that scenario? That I want to do it or that I know I shouldn't?"

"I…don't know."

"I can't stop thinking about cutting you. I'm hard just thinking about the blue lines on your thigh branding you as mine. I…I didn't mean to cut you with the whip. I miscalculated. I thought I had it. I—"

"Henri." I kissed him softly. "It's alright. Dark thoughts are okay."

He groaned. "No, they're not. Not when I act on them."

Shadows crept under our blanket with us. The familiar depression I'd seen him suffocate beneath settled in his eyes.

"Listen to me." I grabbed his chin. "You are not your thoughts or your past. You are your actions and your present, okay? You cut me…yes. It hurt, I won't lie. But…you're not the only one turned on by the thought that you've branded me."

"I'm not?"

"I love you," I said simply. "The marks you've left on me will always remind me of that. When we're out of here and living a normal life far, far away, I'll look at that glittery H on my thigh and remember how much we overcame together, how much we fought side by side. It will be a talisman of everything we did and every game we played to win."

His eyes snapped closed; he hugged me so, so hard. "I really don't fucking deserve you."

"Yet I'm yours, so doesn't that tell you that you're worthy? Regardless if you believe it or not?"

He shuddered. "Ily, I—"

"I know." I yawned, the intensity of the day catching up with me.

"If anything ever happens to you…" He suffocated me in another hug. "My heart would stop alongside yours. If this twin flame thing is real and you are my missing piece…then I don't want to exist without you."

I stroked his chest and did my best to lighten the heavy darkness. "You know…most girls would go running if a man said such things so early in their relationship."

"You run, and I'll chase you."

"Tempting." I giggled.

"Fuck, isn't it," he groaned. "I'd pin you down. Take you on all fours. Christ…"

My insides clenched. I waited for him to shove off the blankets and put on a show for the cameras, but…his melancholy returned, and he hugged me right against his heart. "I've always known you were the one." Fractures of grey appeared in his gaze, fighting back the black. "Also…say that again."

"Say what again?"

"The part where we're in a relationship."

"Oh." I grinned. "Well…I don't know if we are. You haven't exactly asked me."

"You're right." Pinning me onto my back, he settled his legs between mine. His lips quirked with a boyish, blinding smile. "Ilyana Sharma…I saw you, and I knew you. You're brave enough to face up to me. Kind enough to forgive me. And wise enough to see things in me that even I don't see. If you run, I will chase. I will always chase you even if you don't want me because I need to protect you. I'm loyal to you and only you, and I'll do whatever it takes to deserve you, all while knowing I never will. And so…I need to ask you…beg you really. Please put me out of my misery and say you'll go steady with me."

Tears pressed against the back of my eyes as my body cradled his and our pulse thudded to the same beat. Somehow, I'd found a monster with the most devoted heart. A heart riddled with darkness but also aglow with light.

I had no idea if we would ever get out of here or for how long we would belong to one another, but right there, in that moment, I felt the world shift and realign, snapping us together. "Jeez, okay then." I grinned. "I'll go steady with you."

"Thank God." He kissed me.

Deeply.

Madly.

Our tongues stroked, our breath caught, and when he finally pulled away, drowsiness pounced, and he rearranged me on my side. Settling closer, he spooned me again. "Get some sleep…wife."

My eyes flew open, my heart skipped. "Eh, Henri?"

"Hmm?"

"I agreed to be your girlfriend, not your wife."

"Same thing."

"Eh, not quite."

"In my eyes?" He squeezed me. "The moment I met you, I put an invisible ring on your finger. It's there, Ily. It's always been there."

It shouldn't.

My heart really shouldn't jive and skip.

No other man could say what Henri did and ever be called sane. But…I couldn't help it. I fell for his chattiness, his eagerness, his absolutely depraved and damaged heart.

Wife was just a title.

Girlfriend was just a word.

And what we had transcended both of them.

I closed my eyes as sleep crept closer. "If I'm agreeing to be your wife, I hope it's a huge invisible diamond on my finger."

"Ah, about that. Unfortunately, it's small. Positively tiny, actually." He chuckled behind me. "I'm penniless, after all."

"You know what? I've changed my mind. I don't want a diamond. This place has cured me of my love of gems. A simple string knotted into a circle would be enough."

"And that's why I.L.Y.," he breathed.

Tears shot to my eyes. My memory of Krish saying those three little letters before he went to bed each night. Knowledge that

Henri was no longer afraid of such things.

"I.L.Y. too," I whispered.

He exhaled and snuggled closer.

Sleep kept creeping but before it towed me into dreams, I murmured, "Tomorrow, after I've met with Peter and we've had breakfast, I'll go to the kitchens alone. If you follow me twenty minutes later, no one should get suspicious. We'll be able to tell you everything."

His arms banded tighter around me. He pressed a kiss to the top of my head. He didn't speak for a while, our breathing syncing and slowing. Ever so quietly, he said, "I tossed the cufflinks over the wall. I doubt the signal scrambler suddenly stops working outside the castle, but…I had to try."

"You called your brother even knowing he'll try to kill you?"

"I called my brother because if I don't get you out of here, I *want* him to kill me."

The truth of that punched me in the chest. The honesty of his affection and the depth of our connection. Our bond couldn't die in here. Whatever this was. Whatever we'd become. Neither of us could die.

We can't destroy each other.

Twin flames or not.

Real or fantasy.

Neither of us could die.

Because if one died, the other would suffer…for eternity.

Chapter Thirty

Henri

I RESISTED THE URGE TO look over my shoulder as I made my way down the service corridors of Victor's castle. Guards loitered along the journey, some alert, others bored. At least no one stopped me as I counted off the excruciatingly long minutes since Ily had left my side. I'd lasted eighteen of those damn minutes before stalking after her.

Luckily, Victor hadn't been around this morning.

The Masters at breakfast were far too interested in playing with their new jewels.

And Peter had given Ily a pointed look as we'd entered the ballroom at nine this morning, confirming whatever appointment they'd made.

Yanking at the collar of my grey t-shirt, I second-guessed the colour. I should've worn black to hide the pit stains if I started sweating. I prickled with sickening nerves.

I had no idea where I was going, but I followed the clamouring noises of pots and pans and the whiff of tasty things. Stepping into the kitchens shot me back to medieval times with soot-stained ceilings, coal ranges, and harried servants.

The bricked walls formed a circular shape, reminding me of the caves beneath our feet. The huge slab of beef popping and sizzling in a gigantic hearth turned by itself on an automatic rotisserie. Cooks and sous chefs, pastry artisans, and scullery maids; the entire place bustled with activity.

A short, curvy woman with greying hair and a food-stained apron noticed me first.

Abandoning a bubbling pot and wiping her hands on a tea towel hooked into her apron strings, she hustled toward me and tugged on my wrist for me to duck to her short height.

Scowling, I shot a look at the guard watching the mayhem and the other standing by the open door to the outside. A few chickens squawked beyond, kicked at by a young man as he carried in an armful of greens.

I ducked at the knees and tipped forward.

"They're by the larder," she whispered. "The camera only has a narrow dead spot. Send the three girls to me. They've been talking for long enough. Ensure your back is to the room and be quick about it."

Before I could ask anything, she pushed me toward the shadowy left corner.

Ily beckoned from where she stood with Rachel, Mollie, and Peter.

My gut churned as I strode toward them.

Shoving my hands into my jeans pockets, I hoped to God I wouldn't reach for her, kiss her, or try to snatch her away from Peter. Every instinct surged to keep her close. I hated that she'd been away from my side twice this morning.

Twice too many.

Peter never took his dark eyes off me as I ducked around a girl carrying a large tray of sliced fruit. Skin-coloured fingerless gloves and socks covered his hands and feet. His bare chest didn't seem too bruised, and his linen pants were free from blood.

He looked a damn sight better than he had when I'd carried him back from the caves. That night, his skin had been grey. Now, it glowed with the same honey tan as Ily. Taller than her but just as lean, he could've been her brother.

A cousin.

Family.

Gritting my teeth, I gave myself a stern talking to.

You will forgive him for wanting her.

He isn't competition. He's her friend. We are on the same side.

Did Ily know she had two men in love with her?

Did she suspect the depth of his feelings?

My heart fisted with a surge of pity for him.

I was the luckiest motherfucker in the world because she'd chosen me. The threads of fate had given her to me. I had no idea what this twin flame thing meant or if it even existed, but I did know Ily was special. Ily was *mine*. And I would do whatever it goddamn took to get her free.

Including being kind to the man who would never have her.

Stopping in the shadows of a walk-in pantry, I made eye contact with all of them.

Rachel blushed and dropped her gaze.

All the sickness, depression, and horror of that night in Victor's chambers came back. I had no control as I stepped into her and whispered, "I am so, *so* sorry for what I did."

She froze. Her lips parted in shock. "I-It's…fine."

"It's not fine." I balled my hands. "And I don't expect you to forgive me. But…it happened. I hurt you. And I'm forever in your debt." I glanced at Mollie. "I'm in both your debts for not ratting me out to Victor about Ky—"

"Ah, the less spoken about that, the better," Peter interrupted, throwing a look at the camera angled away from us. "Just in case."

Nodding, I shrugged. "I owe all of you the biggest apology."

Ily squeezed Mollie's hand.

Mollie flinched, pain etching her face. I skimmed her body and the skimpy blue lingerie she wore. Bright red handprints painted her belly and thighs.

Roland.

Fury howled. My temper exploded. "I promise I'll kill him for you. Somehow."

She gave me a conspiratorial glance. "Definitely not a cop if you're willing to kill for us."

"Better than a cop," Ily whispered, smiling at me softly. "He's a Mercer."

My heart skipped.

I practically fucking swooned toward her, drawn in by the leash of her love.

Peter looked at both of us as if his favourite puppy had just died.

The moment stretched until Ily shook herself and glanced behind me.

I turned to look, spying the older woman waving at us with her tea towel.

Releasing Mollie's hand, Ily caught my eyes. "We have to go. I'll return to the jewel quarters with Mols and Rach."

I opened my mouth to stop that idea. She might not be safe wandering around the fortress with Masters high on testosterone, but she held up her hand and proved our thoughts were in sync just like our heartbeats and souls.

"I'll be safe, I swear. We'll go straight there. I won't leave until you come to get me."

Genuine fear cut through me at the thought of her being so

far away.

"I'll talk to you soon then," Peter murmured, his eyes flicking to Ily's. "We need to find a way to catch up properly." His gaze shot to mine, narrowed and cold. "Maybe you can give her more time with us. We can't liaise properly if you keep her shackled to your bed."

"Paavak," Ily grumbled.

"I know. I know." Giving me a wary look, Peter stepped into her and wrapped his arms around her. "Just be safe, *jaanu*."

Ily gave me a guilty wince all while her arms went around him.

Jaanu?

What the hell did that mean?

It took all my willpower to stand by and let Peter hug my reason for existence.

Rachel gave me a sad shrug and Mollie a wry smile before the two jewels broke apart and Peter pushed his luck by kissing Ily on her cheek. He whispered a string of Hindi into her ear.

It was so fucking hard not to grab her.

Breaking apart from him, Ily stepped into me, squeezed my shaking fingers, then darted out of the busy kitchens.

Mollie followed her, but Rachel lingered.

Cupping her lower belly, she struggled for words. "W-We're trusting you with our lives, Master H."

"Henri."

She ducked her chin. She looked so frail and young and afraid.

Sleeping with her meant nothing. It'd been forced on both our accounts. Yet I couldn't deny a tenderness bloomed inside me. A protectiveness full of despair for how long she'd been Victor's plaything.

Stepping into me, she kept her voice low. "I see the way you look at her. I know how much it broke you to have to…to have to be with me. But I hope you know I'm grateful it was you he shared me with. You didn't hurt me. You're willing to help us. And you're doing something no one else has done. Ily's very lucky to have you."

She scurried away before I could reply.

I exhaled heavily.

My nape prickled as I braced myself and looked at Peter.

Standing with his back against the pantry wall and arms crossed, he arched his chin. "You better come closer so the cameras can't see you."

Sucking in a breath and all my restraint, I stepped deeper into the shadows and fought back the shadows within me.

I had no idea how or where to start.

This was his show. His plan.

We didn't speak for ages, animosity crackling loudly between us.

His fingers dug into his biceps as he crossed his arms tighter. "I'm going to say a few things, and once I've said them, that's it, okay? Bygones."

I nodded warily. "Okay…"

"Thank you for carrying me back to the castle." His cheeks pinked. "I hate that it happened but…thank you."

I reared back, not expecting that. "Eh…you're welcome?"

"Don't think that one act of kindness means I suddenly like you. I don't." He sniffed with his chin in the air. "In fact, I can't stand you because I know what you are and this tame front you're putting on doesn't fool me. I've always told Ily you were the worst of the lot, and I stand by that, even now."

"You what?" My knuckles cracked as I balled my hands. "You told her I was the worst?"

"I did and I'm right. The way you stabbed…" He shook his head. "The way you shut down your humanity that night. Only a psychopath can do that, and I'm still not convinced that isn't what you are. This could be some kind of ploy to make us trust you, only for you to deliver us up to Vic."

I glowered at him. "Then what the fuck am I doing here?"

"Because we don't have any other choice."

"So you figured you'd get me on your side by calling me a psychopath and kissing Ily in front of me?" I chuckled blackly. "You're lucky I don't punch you."

"Ily is my friend."

"Bullshit." I coughed.

"*Excuse me?*"

Fine.

He wanted to do this?

Okay then.

I hadn't come here to hurt him. In fact, I clung to my best behaviour because I felt sorry for the bastard. But…if he wanted to play…*I'll fucking play.*

Stepping into him, crowding him against the wall, I smirked from my taller height. "Alright…you asked for this. You say you know me? Well, I know *you*. I know that you're in love with her. I know that you want her. You think she'll choose you over me because you're the good guy in all of this, and the good guy always wins."

His eyes flashed, true fury appearing. "You're right. I *am* the good guy. So what does that make you?"

"The devil." I nodded. "I'm fully aware."

"You've hurt her. She'll never forgive you for that."

"I've already told her I'll do everything in my power to repent. Including helping get you free."

"Whatever. You won't stop. You'll keep hurting her because that's who you are."

"She knows who I am. I haven't hid a damn thing from her. Unlike you—"

"*Me?* I've hid nothing."

"Liar." I squeezed my nape. "Keep telling yourself that. Doesn't change the fact that we're both in love with her. Only difference is, I had the guts to tell her. What's the matter, Pete? Afraid she'll tell you point blank that she doesn't feel the same way?"

"Whatever." He rolled his eyes. "You're not in love with her. You don't know a damn thing about her. You're just in love with the *idea* of her. You're like a kid who has a toy for the first time and can't share."

"I just shared her with you, didn't I? I let you hug her. Kiss her. Whisper whatever pet name you used in her ear."

He smirked. "Jealous?"

"Of you?" I shrugged. "Nope. Actually, you know what? You want the truth? Fine. You're the only man who has ever threatened me in that way, so yes. You made me jealous. But…" I smiled. "That was before I realised that she loved me back. Before I realised there is no way in hell she wasn't born to be mine when every cell in my body belongs to her. So…" I stabbed him in the chest with my finger. "Be my guest. Love her without telling her. Believe in your little fantasies that one day she'll be in your bed, not mine. I won't stop you. I won't even hate you for trying to steal her. I know Ily is mine and I know what it's like to want something you can't have. It hurts. It hurts so fucking much. So no, I don't hate you anymore, Peter. I just pity you because I *was* you."

He winced and rubbed at where I'd poked him.

Our verbal fight swirled around us.

I braced for more.

A myriad of emotions flashed over his face. Loathing, loss, pain. So, so much pain.

My heart twisted; I backed up a step.

Ah shit.

I hadn't meant to do that.

For all my conviction, he *still* threatened me. Still made me worry that despite all the love I had for Ily, it might not be enough. He *was* the good guy. He was the hero to all the jewels in here. He deserved her. Not me. He was worthy. I wasn't.

My issue with him went far deeper than just his ability to steal Ily from me. My issue was that I'd actually *let* him. If Ily one day admitted she'd made a mistake and loved him over me…I—

Fuck, I'd let her go.

I'd stalk the shit out of her to make sure she was safe but…I would let her be his because her happiness was far, far more important than mine, and in the outside world, Peter could make her far happier than I ever could. He'd be good to her. Kind to her. He wouldn't crave her blood or dream of making her scream.

An image of Ily taking Peter home to meet her parents instead of me caught me around the back of the throat. He probably practiced the same faith. Spoke the same language. Had a good and pure heart.

He would be accepted. *Acceptable.*

But me? I would always have to hide the depth of what I was when face to face with the wonderful people Ily had descended from.

My chin tipped down.

I pinched the bridge of my nose.

This was pointless.

I'd get the details from Ily.

Just run.

Looking up, I dropped my hand. "I'm gonna go. This…this isn't gonna work."

His jaw clenched.

He nodded.

I turned to leave.

His hand latched around my bicep. "Fuck…wait." Letting me go, he raked his fingerless gloved hands through his thick brown hair. Looking up at the sooty ceiling, he closed his eyes as if begging the Almighty for strength.

When he finally looked at me again, he said stiffly, "I...you threaten me too. And you might be right."

"That you're in love with her."

He just shrugged so fucking sadly, I had the crazy urge to pat him on the shoulder.

Sniffing back whatever emotions he refused to share, he braced himself. "Look, I'm sorry. This is asking a lot of me. To trust a Master? To trust *you*? I know what I saw in that cave and know that Ily sees the good in you, but...it's hard."

"I get it." I crossed my arms. "More than you know."

He huffed. "I...I've always been sceptical and have a habit of trusting the wrong people. That's how I ended up here so...I can't really claim I have good instincts. So...fuck it. I'm going to ignore those instincts and trust what I see instead."

"And what do you see?"

He gave me a twisted smile. "I wished I didn't...believe me. But I see a man who is so fucking in love with Ilyana he'd carve out his heart and slap it onto a plate for her to eat if she told him she was even slightly peckish."

I stiffened.

Not what I expected him to say.

"I see a man who killed out of pure passion not psychopathic joy. I see a man who's made mistakes and definitely has a shit ton of issues but...a man who wants to be good despite every part of him being dark."

My spine tingled. "I didn't come here for the shrink special—"

"You don't understand how much it meant to me that Kyle got what he deserved. He's cut so many of us. He's burned us, brutalised us, and has torn my body in two each time he fucked me." His limbs started to shake as he dug his hands into his linen pockets. "I wanted to die that day. Pretty sure I would've if it wasn't for Ily, Rach, Mollie...and you. I'm kinda mad at all of you if I'm honest. I could've been free by now, and...seeing as I can't say this to them, I'll say it to you." He snickered. "Isn't that fucking hilarious? Can't be honest with the people I love the most, yet I'll confess all this shit to the man who has everything I want."

He looked at the floor.

I waited.

I'd been where he was so many fucking times.

The least I could do was be patient.

Finally, he choked, "I'm so close to being done, man. I-I'm

barely holding on."

I rocked back on my heels.

Yet another thing I definitely hadn't expected.

But...I probably should have.

Peter came across as flippant and bold, but wasn't everyone hiding something in this godforsaken place? All of them just hanging on, surviving, hiding, hoping?

Standing there in a busy kitchen with steam and sugar and salt, I saw everything he'd done his best to hide.

Everything Ily probably saw. Everything mirrored in me.

And all that tenderness inside me welled up to include him.

The guy in love with my girl.

The one man who had the power to rip out my heart if Ily ever chose him.

"You're not allowed to give up yet," I whispered, my voice rough.

He laughed under his breath, trying to hide his despair. His brown eyes met mine as he flashed his gloved palms in a sad shrug. "When?"

Fuck.

That one word.

It cut me.

Stepping into him, all those urges to protect my siblings when I was younger surged. I fought the very real need to hug the bastard. "I don't know. But not yet."

He sniffed and nodded.

It took him a moment, but his shoulders straightened. "I did not mean to say any of that. What the hell?"

"It's fine."

He narrowed his eyes with a flash of rage. "You're good, I'll give you that."

"Good at what?"

"Making people hope."

I flinched.

"You tortured Ily with that hope when you first arrived. I hated you for that. I still do. Hope is the worst fucking emotion in here and I was perfectly fine before Ily infected me with that disease. She gave me *hope*. And God, it's *ruined* me." A deeper flush of anger on his face. "You know, I was coping just fine before she came along. Of course, for the first year, I fought. I got my ass handed to me over and over again. But by the time I realised I couldn't win, Victor started rewarding me. Trusting me. Making me do things I can never undo."

He shook his head, unable to stop now he'd started. "But the thing about hope is…it's too fucking powerful to stop once someone dangles it in front of you. It spreads like the flu. It kills the weak and weakens the strong. So I hope to fucking God you're going to see this through with us, because if you don't? If you decide the darkness is easier and keeping Ily collared is better than all the other shit that might follow, then you might as well just kill us now because we won't survive. Not after this."

His words hovered in the air between us.

I swallowed hard.

I had no idea what to say.

For a moment, I wanted to run again but then I found myself saying, "I get that asking you to trust me when I'm a Master and you're a slave isn't easy. But we're more similar than you think."

"Yeah, okay." His rolled his eyes. "Sure."

"I have shit in my past that I can't undo as well. The things I've participated in…" I shuddered. "I'll take most of them to my grave."

"What could you have possibly done to say we're similar?"

I stiffened. I didn't want to tell him, but words tumbled anyway. "There was no one to protect me either. No one to stop him. I cried as I hurt women who'd only ever been nice to me. I had to live with those same women afterward and rightly deserved their hate. Not one of them dared look in my direction. No one talked to me, hugged me. The loneliness of being ostracised—" I cut myself off with a sneer. "Fuck. That's not important. What is important is—"

"You were raised in a place like this?" Peter sniffed, his face guarded.

"Not as grand or with lots of guests, but yes."

"So you admit it's not just a desire but in your fucking genes? And you think you can ride off into the sunset with Ily and what? Forget who you are? Put aside all that shit? All this power?"

"I know enough of my needs that I never want to break her. I need her to fight back—"

"Wow, you truly are sick." He almost spat on my feet. "I hope she leaves you. She deserves better."

"I agree. She does deserve better." A wash of remorse chilled me. I snorted with disbelief as I confessed. "And if she chose you over me, I wouldn't stop her."

"*What?*" He eyes popped wide. "Y-You're saying you'd step aside?"

"I am." I fought the jittery mess of my pulse. "But I would also fight like hell because what you saw is true. I would cut out my heart if she wanted to dine on it. I would cut out the heart of all those she asked me to. I'm twisted, I won't deny that. But what you didn't see is...when I love someone, I become the most faithful son of a bitch. And Ily loves you. Therefore, I'll do whatever it takes to help you."

He staggered a little. "She said that? That she loves me?"

I sighed.

I really, really didn't want to hurt him.

I tried not to say it.

I said it anyway. "As a friend. A cousin perhaps."

"A cousin?" He winced. "She said she loves me like a cousin?"

"Fuck's sake." Raking both hands through my hair, I glowered. "No, you fool. We don't exactly lie around talking about you. I have no idea how she feels about you. I just...I saw the way she looked at you before Emerald Bruises started. You were high and hurting and her heart fucking broke for you."

"Because she loves me..."

"Because she *cares* about you. Look, I have to go. I don't trust anyone in this godforsaken place and can't think straight when she isn't near me. Are we doing this or not?"

"You think a sob story of you as a kid is gonna earn my trust?"

"*Merde*, you're hard work." Crowding him, I held out my hand. "You need a vow? Fine. I'm in. I'm all fucking in. I'm doing this—not for you or for her—but for my brothers and sisters who I failed when I was younger. I'm *in*, alright?"

Peter never broke eye contact.

His worry and fear faded a little as he looked at my outstretched hand.

"Come on, Peter..." Ticking time scratched against my nerves. "Do we have a deal or not?"

Swallowing hard, he studied me.

He saw me.

Judged me.

And then, he softened.

His hate turned to hope.

His loathing to trust.

And for the first time in my pitiful life, I felt a brotherly bond. The same bond I'd tried to cultivate with Q.

I hated that it was with the man who wanted what I had, but...it also made sense.

We were the same in that respect.

Slowly, he inserted his gloved hand into mine.

We both winced at the contact.

Both cringed away from the sensation of signing our lives over to each other.

"It's Paavak," he said with a proud edge, shaking my hand. "Paavak Chauhan."

"Henri Mercer."

His lips twitched. "And you're not a cop."

"Better." I grinned and broke the shake. "I have no laws I need to follow and already have blood on my hands. What's a little more?"

Stepping into me, his voice dropped to a quieter whisper. "When the time comes to kill Victor...I-I want that right."

My eyes flared. "Fine."

"In that case..." Stepping back, he nodded at the cook beckoning us to hurry. "So far, we've made twenty-three small bombs and hidden them in the bedrooms that aren't used. We're on track to making eighty of the damn things, including a few sketchy ones that Mollie doesn't want to make but Rachel says are needed if we want to cause structural damage. We have a few cleaners on our side and most of the jewels. We haven't told the new slaves yet for obvious reasons. We have two gardeners working for us and most of the kitchen staff. And are currently trying to figure out what guards could be turned. If you can get a guard or two on our side, then it would mean we had a few guns for when the time comes."

He gave me a weary look. "That reminds me. The night of the treasure hunt, Ily and I overheard Master L—Larry—say that he has a guard on retainer and plans on killing you with their gun."

"Wait, what?"

"Keep your wits about you and stay alert. Not sure who he's bribed, but...I'll let you know if I find out anything more."

"Gee thanks."

His eyes got shifty as he glanced around the kitchens. "Joyero will be busy until Christmas, especially now that Victor has allowed his guests back. We need you to keep him distracted. Listen if he starts making noises about anything we're doing. If he sounds suspicious or gives you any reason to think he's onto us, let us know immediately."

My heart thudded painfully. "You're planning on blowing the place up?"

He nodded. "Christmas Day Victor will be here, mostly alone. A few stragglers will be here too—those without a family or kids to entertain on the big day. We'll have all the presents go off at noon. And then…we just have to hope."

Shit.

I didn't speak, absorbing the mess he'd just described.

Fidgeting, Peter asked quietly, "So…what do you think of the plan?"

Yes, the plan.

I had a fuck ton of issues with it.

I'd read enough books to know that the grand plans of attack and surprise never went like the characters expected them to.

Especially a ragtag bunch of people who had no experience in war.

I exhaled hard. "Want my honest opinion?"

"I don't know…do I?"

"I'm assuming by bombs you mean smoky things that have to be lit by hand? Little fire starters that are more of a nuisance than catastrophic?"

"We've got all the usual household cleaning supplies. Diesel and petrol from the different generators and Styrofoam that Rachel says will make—"

"Homemade napalm."

His eyebrows knitted together. "You know how to make it too?"

"I read. And if you intend on setting yourself on fire along with the entire island, then sure, make that. Napalm spreads in a second, melts even stone, and cannot be put out." I struggled with another wash of despair. The waves weren't as thick now that Ily and I had talked, but I still suffered beneath the crushing, miserable weight.

Especially now.

Especially now that I'd heard their plan and came face to face with the very real notion that…there was no plan.

Not one that would work anyway.

"Even if you do manage to fly under Victor's radar long enough to make your little 'presents', hide them, and find a way to light them all at the right time, unless you have weapons, you're just as dead."

"Well, you're a bag of fucking positivity."

"I'm only trying to help. Even if you succeeded and pulled off the impossible—because it is impossible unless you have proper ignition, fuses, fuel, correct placement, structural blueprints, etcetera—it's a waste of bloody time."

"You got a better idea?" Peter scowled.

"Nope, but I'll think about it. I need to know every little detail. How are you keeping the chemicals separate before detonation? What fuses are you using? Do you have checkpoints and timeframes mapped out? Who lights what? What if one doesn't go off and—?"

"Rachel is a chemist. Mollie is a quantum physicist. I'm leaving the finer details to them."

"Still won't work." I checked my watch.

Too long.

Time to go.

Peter looked as if he'd punch me, but then he groaned and scrubbed his face. Thick depression rose up and choked him. "So you're saying to give up before we've even begun? What the fuck sort of advice is that? I told you…I won't survive. I'm done. I'm so fucking done that I'm ready to do anything, even if I die while doing it."

I fought the urge to leave. "Want to know what I'd do? What all the successful breakouts in the books I've read have done?"

"I'm dying with suspense."

"Keep it simple. If this was an old castle with old wiring, that would be your ticket. Short-circuit the switchboard and start an electrical fire. Maybe try to blow up the generator tanks. Diesel doesn't ignite easily, though, so you'd have to consider that. But this place isn't old, and Victor is far too sly for you to underestimate him. He's always one step ahead, and you know as well as I do that it will be a fucking miracle if you manage to get a fart past him, let alone a fucking coup."

Peter hung his head and didn't say anything.

I'd hurt him again.

I didn't like it…but it was necessary.

If they continued running around thinking they were all James fucking Bond, someone would slip up and we'd all die.

"Stop making the bombs. Focus more on what's going to happen on Christmas Day. Where will the guards be? How many jewels per guard are needed to overwhelm him and grab his gun? You don't need bombs if you plan it right."

"We're out-numbered. Of course we need bombs."

"No, you need distractions. Set some fires. Splash some petrol around to make it spread. Distract and disorient. Get as many weapons as you can and be prepared to actually use them—"

"Peter. *Peter.*" One of the girls working at the stainless-steel bench threw a peeled onion at us.

His eyes shot behind me. "Ah, *shit.*" Bolting away from the larder, he skidded to a stop beside the pretty cook seasoning a huge tray of vegetables. The girl gave him a worried look. He shook his head.

I spun on my heel just as the other cook collided with me and shoved a shiny green apple into my hands. "*Here.*"

I went to ask—

The guard by the door stood to full attention.

And in walked Victor.

A surge of fear swamped me, followed by an ice-cold blanket of detachment. Perhaps I was a psychopath after all, because the dissociation between planning a war with Peter and my current snowy calm couldn't exist in the same person.

"Victor!" I strolled toward him, tossing my apple into the air before catching it and taking a big juicy bite. "You hungry too?"

He scowled, looking me up and down. "Henri. What on earth are you doing down here?" He eyed my apple. "Didn't you find enough to eat at breakfast?"

I took another bite, smacking obnoxiously. "Of course I did. Your staff put on a fabulous spread. I was just craving some fruit is all."

"Humpf." His gaze left mine, distracted and not interested.

His face slipped into a snide, cruel smile the minute he found who he was looking for. "Peter. There you are."

Peter had enough acting ability to look up in pure, perfected shock. "Me, Sir V?"

"Branson said he sent you on an errand thirty minutes ago and you haven't returned to him. There better be a good reason for the delay."

"Sorry, Sir V." Ducking around the bench, he stopped in front of Victor. "I...Master B asked me to grab some of his favourite tartlets. I didn't see them at breakfast, so I came here to see if any had been made."

"Tartlets? What tartlets?"

"These, Sir." The short cook bustled forward with a steamy tray of lemon custard things. "Guest Branson asked me to make them when he arrived yesterday morning. I've only just had time." She bowed over the tray. "Forgive me, Sir. We're just so busy with how many guests are here and—"

"Yes, yes. That's quite enough." Victor snagged a tart for himself and pointed at Peter. "Take a plate to him immediately. How dare you fucking dilly-dally as if you own the place." He looked past him to the pretty girl who kept seasoning the vegetables. They'd be inedible with the amount of salt she'd sprinkled. "I might think you came down here because you've decided to tup the scullery maid."

Peter shook his head. "No, Sir V. Never."

Victor studied him carefully. "Remember what happened when you kissed Ily in the vault?" He clucked his tongue and tapped Peter on the cheek. "Do you want to be reminded that fraternizing with any jewel or staff upsets me?"

"No, Sir V."

"Well then. Run along."

"Yes, Sir V."

Peter grabbed a few tarts and took off.

He didn't look in my direction.

I took another bite of my apple all while my stomach snarled and my old friend nausea came thick.

Sighing heavily as if he was sick of unruly jewels, Victor rolled his eyes in my direction. "Honestly, how am I supposed to provide a good fuck to my guests when my jewels are running around like cockroaches?"

"I hear you." I nodded. "Hard to find good slaves these days."

Victor snickered. "That it is, my friend. That it is. No matter." Clapping his hands, he twisted his wrist and looked at his sparkly Rolex. "Damn, I have a phone conference I need to attend. No time to play for me today, but...if you're interested. We could maybe catch up tonight? A few drinks? Another evening with just the four of us?"

"Sounds great." I toasted him with my apple.

"*Fantastique.*" Squeezing my elbow, he grinned. "See you later then, Mercer. Don't have too much fun without me."

I watched him go.

I didn't move until the guard stopped puffing out his chest and slouched again.

And then I moved as slowly and as inconspicuously as possible toward the jewel quarters and Ily.

Chapter Thirty-One

Ily

AUGUST

TIME HAD THE TERRIBLE ABILITY at changing the length of its minutes.

One day, hours sped past in a blink. The next, seconds crawled by with an age.

Our mornings were spent on the deck or in the ballroom sharing breakfast with so many other Masters and kneeling, unhappy jewels. Afterward, Henri would leash me and take me for a walk in the gardens. In the afternoons, he'd write or read, and I'd do yoga and meditate.

And our evenings…well.

Those became the bane and highlight of my existence.

Not because of the things we did.

But because those things destroyed us.

Piece by piece.

Heart by heart.

Until we were nothing more than creatures of the same twisted longing.

"Ah good swat, *mon ami*!" Victor slapped Henri on the shoulder as he delivered another shot of cognac to him. Henri took the glass with a shaking hand, wiping the sweat off his upper lip.

My eyesight faded in and out.

My blood positively burned.

My entire body *scorched* with fire.

The fourth lash of a tan-and-white flogger that Victor had

bare belly.

The meditative intensity that used to be so elusive now found me every time we played. It uncoiled slowly, insidiously wrapping me in its blanketing sensitivity, quietening my mind and making my entire body feel *everything*.

I felt Henri's stare as he glowered at the welts left on my belly and breasts from his flogger.

I saw his desire, his despair, desperation, and darkness.

I heard the heavy thud of his thundering heart as if our pulse pounded to the same beat.

You doing okay? His silver gaze asked.

I'm with you. I ducked my chin. *I trust you.*

The more we played, the stronger our bond became.

It'd been three weeks since Peter and Henri met in the kitchens, and almost every night, Victor had summoned us to his chambers.

Returning here and being forced to kneel on the same carpet where Victor had raped me was one of the hardest things I'd ever done. I'd fought the very real urge to dissociate so I didn't run screaming into memories.

But...Rachel had been there. Henri had been there. And in some twist of normalcy, Victor had indulged in one too many whiskeys and fallen asleep on the couch before he ever laid a finger on Rach or ordered Henri and I to perform.

The next night, Rach and I had been allowed to actually sit on the furniture and eat off plates instead of our Master's fingers. Victor treated Rachel like his own life-size doll. One currently fragile and in need of smothering so she delivered the healthiest heir.

That was until he tied her to his four-poster bed and whipped her the same way Henri had whipped me in the snuffbox.

While Rachel swallowed her soft screams, Henri had ordered me to blow him on the couch—neither of us watching Victor welting Rachel's pretty skin. We'd fallen into our own world of depravity and learned to tune out those around us so it remained only us.

The next night, more of the same.

And the next.

And the next.

"Your ability to create a criss-cross pattern over her breasts is rather impressive." Victor sipped his drink, his awful eyes slithering over me.

"Thanks." Slashing the flogger through the air, Henri grinned. "I rather like this gift. Where did you say you got it from?"

"A little shop in Hungary."

"Kinky Hungarians." Henri smirked.

"I agree." Victor laughed. "I have a couple who visit, and they're definitely rather ingenious with what they get up to." Finishing his drink, he ordered, "Now, finish whipping her and fuck her if you must. I need to kick you out. I've had a long day of meetings and need to get some rest."

Strolling to where Rachel knelt by his bed, Victor snapped his fingers. "Actually, you know what?" He grinned. "I think a quick nightcap would help me sleep. Don't you agree, my pet?"

Rachel kept her chin low. "Yes, Sir V."

"Good girl." Placing his glass on his side table, he unbuckled his slacks and let them drop to the floor. Victor never seemed to wear underwear, his cock long and hard. Lying on top of the bedding, he fluffed up a pillow behind his head, then grabbed the base of himself. "Ride me, my sweetling. I'm feeling rather lazy tonight."

"Yes, Sir V." Climbing to her feet, Rachel gave me a quick look before getting on the bed and settling herself over Victor's hips.

Henri stiffened. His hands throttled the flogger as we both watched Rachel position herself over Victor's erection and sink down.

Victor gave a thick groan, his hands landing on her hips. Looking at me bound to his four-poster, he licked his lips. "Actually, do fuck her before you go, Henri. I want to watch."

My stomach plummeted.

Henri sighed heavily.

And the flogger caught me a final time as if Henri struck without control, his frustration at having to perform like circus animals bleeding through.

The pain and heat of the swat feathered over my abused skin until my nipples turned into diamonds, and the trickle of desire slipped farther down my inner thigh.

I no longer tried to stop myself from reacting this way.

No longer argued with what my body wanted and desired.

Henri was what I desired. And the pain he gave me was always bittersweet.

"Of course, Vic." Henri tossed the flogger onto the bed and stepped into me. Grabbing my jaw, he tipped my head back. The hook holding my shackled wrists jangled as he pressed his body against mine. His fingers pinched into my cheeks, holding me violently and possessively, yet his eyes glowed just for me.

I need you. His heart whispered to mine. *I need you to show me you're okay.*

Every night before he took me.

Every scene we played and every nightmare he delivered, he always asked before he fucked me.

Surrendering into his savage hold, I sucked in a breath and hissed, "Fuck you for ever making me think you were different."

His eyes snapped closed; his nostrils flared.

When his gaze opened again, his utmost gratitude flared with absolute corruption.

"Aw, don't be like that, little nightmare." With trembling hands, he unbuttoned and unzipped his jeans. "I never hid who I was. In fact, I remember telling you that I'd be the worst friend you'd ever had."

"One day, I'll make you pay for this." I did my best to hide how my heart flurried as his hands landed on his hips and shoved his boxer-briefs to mid-thigh.

His body.

His beautiful, perfect body.

So hard for me.

So bad for me.

Grabbing me around the waist, he hoisted me high. His fingers activated a particularly deep lash from the flogger all while stroking those maddening little coded circles on my skin.

Our own language.

A way of communicating right beneath Victor's nose.

God, I love you. His thumbs swirled over the blue H marking my thigh.

I need you. I arched into his touch. *Now.*

"You're soaking for me." He chuckled. "Tell me again how you intend to make me pay."

"Put me down." I snapped my teeth. "Don't touch me." Squirming in my binds, I couldn't hide my tattered moan as his hips lodged against mine and the heavenly nudge of his hot, hard cock found me.

My heart unravelled.

My blood prepared to detonate.

"Don't touch you?" He smirked, rocking his hips between my legs, coating himself in my arousal. "But where would be the fun in that?"

His teeth found my ear and bit hard, all while his quietest whisper licked against my soul. "You own me, Ily. Body and soul."

And then, he thrust.

Hard.

Vicious.

A spearing, pillaging penetration as he claimed me as spoils of his war.

I screamed.

I didn't fake that.

It felt too good as our two bodies became one.

With a feral snarl, Henri's control snapped.

His hips pistoned.

His cock slammed into me, again and again, pinning me against the wooden pole.

I gave up trying to act.

I sank into every thrust and spun into tighter knots.

Who would've thought I'd find freedom in captivity?

Who would've guessed when my Master used me like he hated me that I would feel such overwhelming love?

"I hate you!" I tried to bite his neck as he rode me harder.

"Hate me all you want," he grunted, driving deeper, faster. "It won't stop me from fucking you."

Victor chuckled.

Henri bit my neck.

And the rest became a supernova.

I shielded my eyes as we stepped into Victor's private nightclub.

The rainbow flashing strobe lights, hazy air, and scents of sharp alcohol reminded me so much of the night I was stolen that my heart stopped.

My feet stopped too.

Henri turned to face me.

His gaze held matching memories.

The way our eyes had met across the bar.

The way I'd known right there and then that he was different and unique and *mine*.

Reaching out, he grabbed my hand. Taking a gamble that Victor wouldn't see as our host and capturer strolled through the elegant chaos, he squeezed my fingers and pressed a fleeting kiss to my lips. "It's okay. It's just another night."

We'd gotten good at 'just another night'. We dabbled with the toys Victor gave us and sometimes put on a different show, doing our best to prove that Henri felt nothing for me each time he abused me.

So far, we'd won.

Victor continued to be gallant and generous.

We'd headed back to the snuffbox as a foursome two days ago and regularly shared breakfast with him and Rachel in the mornings.

Victor had well and truly bought Henri's act, and if a trafficking psychopath could be capable of favourites and fondness, he seemed well and truly smitten with Henri.

If I didn't know any better, I'd say he even had a crush.

The way he watched Henri sometimes. The pride in his eyes as Henri drew my blood. The joy on his lips as Henri made me beg. Each time my Master whipped me, punished me, or chained me to fuck me, Victor praised his protégé as if he was personally responsible for Henri's change of heart.

I didn't care if he thought he was the reason.

I knew the truth.

I knew he was mine and no one else's.

Henri flashed a look at the circular black velvet couches ringing the dance floor. Red light turned the entire place into a hell realm, crimson illumination falling from chandeliers dripping over each table, making the Masters' eyes ghoulish and their skin as sickly as the dead.

"Peter mentioned Faiza and the cleaners managed to place a few small bombs in vases in the foyer today," I said. The pumping music offered a perfect chance to talk.

I kept a careful eye on Victor as he patted the shoulders of his guests on the small dance floor, gossiping with those who'd flown in this weekend.

Another week.

Seven days tiptoeing us closer to Christmas.

"I really wish Peter would stop encouraging that foolish

enterprise." Henri cupped my throat and dragged me into him. Fisting my breast, he painted an image of a Master groping his jewel all while we plotted anarchy. "I told him to stay simple. Fuel and fire. That's it. He should be focusing on weapon collection."

"Mollie and Rachel know their stuff. If they say it's worth making them…then I don't see the harm."

He huffed and bent me backward, latching his teeth on my throat. "The harm will come if Victor catches one of them red-handed."

I scrambled in his hold, giving off the impression of a jewel fighting her Master's bite. "The kitchen staff have already placed a few knives around Joyero." I struggled harder as he dropped his hand between my legs and shoved me high onto my tiptoes. The purple negligée and G-string I wore were no match for his questing fingers.

"Christ, Ily." He groaned as he penetrated me, half for show, half because we always lost ourselves. "Do you always have to be so fucking wet for me?"

Whatever black magic existed on this island had well and truly cursed both of us.

My insides clenched around his touch, hypnotised and wanting, all while I snapped my legs together. A sudden flash of fear spilled from my tongue. "Do you…do you think we're losing our minds?"

Henri froze, his finger deep inside me, his arm lashed tight around my back. "Losing our minds?"

I wanted to take those words back but…now I'd thought them, I worried.

Like…really worried.

"What if…" I sighed and kept pushing his shoulders for show. "What if we get out of here and we still need…"

"Need what?"

"*This*." I beckoned to the mayhem and Masters. "What if we're pretending too much? What if we're infected like they are and—"

"I *am* infected. I've been infected my entire life." He let me go and withdrew his touch. Pulling a leash out of his pocket, he snapped it onto my collar. "I know we're playing a really dangerous game. And I'm aware that once we get out of here, we'll need to stop. But…" He shrugged and pulled me onto the music-blaring dance floor. "You don't need to worry that you're infected too. I know you're doing this for me, and—"

"Hang on." I slammed to a halt, keeping my head down so none of the other Masters thought I'd been the one to rule Henri. "You think I'm still doing this because of you? Not because I've grown addicted to it too?"

He stepped into me, grabbing my chin to tip my head back. His gaze flicked from my mouth to my eyes, his face flashing with colour from the strobes. He looked as if he wanted to argue, but he finally sighed. "You want the truth? The fact that you get off on telling me no? The fact that you drip for me and come for me—despite being surrounded by bastards? That says you're either an angel willing to do whatever it takes to free her friends or…"

"Or?" I shivered.

"You *are* as sick as me." He licked his lips and rushed, "But when I get you out of here, I promise you, Ily, I'll find a way to cure you so you don't have to spend the rest of your life struggling like I do."

I wanted so, so badly to hug him.

To soothe him.

Breaking his hold on my chin, I kissed his palm as quickly as I could before he pulled his hand away. "What if I don't want to be cured?"

His eyebrows shot into his hair. "You're saying even when you're back with your family. Back in your sleepy little village. Back with your brother and life that you'll want to remind yourself of this horror by playing slave with me?"

I shuddered.

The dark infection in me answered with a flush of desire. "If it's consensual, then—"

"It's still me hurting you when you don't deserve any kind of pain. Especially after enduring this place." He hung his head. "I'm sorry, little nightmare, but…once we're free, I never intend to hurt you again. Needs or no needs."

Yanking me deeper onto the dance floor, he deliberately kept enough distance to avoid talking again.

I followed, the leash our only contact.

My mind raced as I studied his powerful back, his white shirt glowing pink, then green, then blue.

I longed to be in our room, hidden beneath our blankets, plotting war.

Last week, Henri had commanded the cleaning staff to teach

us the schematics of this citadel. He regularly dropped me off at the jewel quarters before heading to the library under the guise of writing, leaving me an hour or two to go over the mental blueprints each of us were learning. With every whispered room, nook, and portico, Joyero slowly came alive in our minds, dotted with the bombs already hidden.

Some days, Peter would arrange dance lessons, using the talent he'd learned from a Latin exchange student at school to hide the fact that we needed to whisper so closely.

As each of us took turns dipping and swaying, we'd trade information on which guard seemed particularly disgruntled and those who looked like they could be turned.

Mollie also worked with one of the new boys, Carlos. Peter had told the new jewels about our ticking countdown a fortnight ago. A few had agreed to help. Others had huddled deeper into their terror. But Carlos—who'd been studying engineering—worked closely with Mollie, highlighting what walls and corners were load bearing and where best to place the next lot of presents.

Jerking me to a stop, Henri grabbed me around the nape and made me trip into him. "Remember…you say Khushi if I go too far, okay?"

My eyes flared before I nodded. "Do you think tonight might be bad?"

"I have no idea, but—"

"Ah, Henri!" Victor strolled toward us, gifting Henri a flute of champagne. Another man kept pace at Victor's side. A younger, handsome blond who looked more at home in the surf than in a rapist's nightclub on a hidden island.

Vic waved a hand at the man. "Travis here was just saying how I haven't played Topaz Torment in a while. He's keen. Are you?"

Henri stiffened and let me go.

I tripped a little, dropping my eyes like a good little jewel.

What the hell did Topaz Torment entail?

And just how badly would I be bleeding by the end of it?

"Sure." Henri accepted the champagne and tossed it back in a single mouthful. "Sounds fun."

"You don't even know what the rules are yet, mate." Travis smirked, his accent heavily Australian.

"I've learned that each of Vic's games are well worth playing." Henri pointed at the blue braille scar on my thigh. The sapphire dust glittered in the H branding me as his.

"Ah, you lucky duck. I've heard about Sapphire Scars." Travis toasted Henri with his beer bottle. "Can't say I've had the pleasure." Nudging Vic with his shoulder, he grinned. "Fancy letting me scar Talia?"

Victor sipped his champagne. "Perhaps. For now, don't be greedy. I've agreed to play Topaz Torment. How about be grateful for that, hmm?" Before Travis could reply, Victor smiled slyly. "Henri? If you'd be so kind and allow your jewel to come with me. We'll get started."

Henri's energy pulled shadows from the nightclub, coiling around him like a typhoon. "Why do you need to take her?"

"You're about to find out, aren't you?" Victor reached for me.

Henri jerked my leash, making me trip into him. "I'd rather know before—"

"Henri." Victor clucked his tongue. "Haven't I been exceedingly accommodating to you? I've tolerated your little whispers and enjoyed watching you fuck her. But the matter still remains, I believe you're in love with her. This little game will help—"

"I'm not fucking *in love* with her." Henri crossed his arms, the leash in his hands cutting my collar into my neck. "I'm just obsessed with her." His voice turned crude and crass. "She milks my dick real good, Vic. Is that a crime?"

"No of course not. But…I'm doing this for your benefit. I told you, my dear friend, you won't be truly free until you're cast from such human emotions. This might be the beginning of that freedom." Tapping Henri on the cheek, Victor winked. "You're still too close to that line of caring. Tonight, it's time to give you another teeny, tiny push."

Chapter Thirty-Two

Henri

SEPTEMBER

THE GAMES ALL BLURRED TOGETHER.
Topaz Torment pushed both our limits.
But we survived.
But then there was Moonstone Marks. Then Amber Lashes. Citrine Cuts, Opal Welts, and Quartz Scream.
On and on and *on*.
Victor had an endless amount of sick and twisted entertainment. On top of the porn put on every night and another treasure hunt he organised on the night of a full moon, he kept us all very busy.
Luckily, Ily and I had already discussed what we'd do if we had to play that particular game again. We didn't speak as Victor chased the jewels out of his castle with a loaded pistol then gave the Masters permission to hunt.
Ily went straight to the recycling shed by the kitchens.
She took Mollie and Rachel with her.
Peter refused.
He preferred to run with the others, doing his best to put himself in danger over them.
As the silvery cast of the moon revealed Masters darting around in the dark, some getting lucky and catching unfortunate jewels, I stood guard on the threshold of the shed and protected my heart, a pregnant girl, and a friend.
The next day, Peter came to breakfast hobbling on feet that'd healed, covered in fresh bruises that had not.
My chest had grown tight.
I'd had the unbearable urge to leash him to me so no one else

could hurt him.

By the end of September, Victor had to go away for a week on business, leaving our nights to ourselves once again.

I'd prepared to leave Ily alone—now that we weren't forced to fuck in front of the man who pulled our strings, we didn't have to put on a show.

But the first night Victor was gone, Ily broke into a run after dinner.

She darted into the gardens.

I'd caught her in the maze.

She'd cursed me.

I'd forced her to her knees.

She screamed as I fingered her.

And begged as I fucked her.

With no one watching our performance, we didn't *have* to be so reckless or so feral.

We could've been sweet. Soft. Gentle.

But…Ily was right.

The longer we played these twisted games, the sicker we became.

We were lost.

Well and truly corrupted.

And I had no idea what would become of us if we kept doing this.

THE CURSE OF BLOOD & DARKNESS
by
Henri Mercer

I truly am my father's son.
The things I've done to my jewel.
The things I want to do to my jewel.
I've drawn her blood, marked her, whipped her, flogged her, fucked her, and last night…I completely consumed her.
One rose quartz dildo in her ass.
One obsidian phallus in her pussy.
My hard cock in her mouth.
She looked fucking spectacular.

> *Skewered in three ways.*
> *Teary eyed, body pleading, whimpering, and quivering.*
> *The blackness doesn't just welcome me anymore, it has become me.*
> *I'm polluted by it.*
> *Defiled by it.*
> *I no longer fear the black because I am the black.*
> *And she is my—*

"Oh, I'm so happy to hear you used the gifts I gave you." Victor reached around the back of the wingback where I sat in the library. His hands landed on my shoulders, giving me a quick massage.

Slamming the laptop closed, I spun in the chair and dislodged his hold. "Do you fucking mind?"

He smirked. "Still not ready to share your manuscript, *mon ami?*"

"I'll share when and *if* I'm ever ready, Vic."

"Fine. Fine." He held up his hands and strolled around the library. The soaring shelves of literature wrapped us in paper motes and history. "I'll let you keep writing your secrets. Just, I'm curious. Tell me, Henri. Tell me what she is…"

"What she is?"

"You said you've become the darkness. Which makes me so incredibly happy to hear. I admit you seem far more content these days. But…how do you see her? *'And she is my…'?*" He raised an eyebrow. "What were you going to write before I stupidly interrupted?"

Placing the laptop onto the side table complete with a figurine of a hedgehog, I shrugged. "Guess you'll never know. That's the price you pay for reading over my shoulder."

"Spoilsport." He chuckled and ran his fingers along one of the dust-free shelves.

My heart kicked as I flicked a look at a section of books where I'd planted one of Rachel's and Mollie's presents in the limited-edition shadows last month.

I hadn't wanted to do it.

Frankly, I thought they were still wasting their time and playing with fire (literally), but…I was all in on our war, and if they wanted me to help plant useless bottles with homemade wicks and dodgy chemistry, I wouldn't argue.

As long as I kept distracting Victor and gave him no reason to look at the security feed, they would go unnoticed. Even if the bombs didn't go off, we could use the substances to splash over the carpets and curtains, adding fuel to the fires I intended to set on D-day.

"Do you celebrate Halloween, Henri?" Victor finally stopped pacing and faced me.

"Never. Why?"

"I'm hosting a soiree that night. Only intimate, of course. Nothing too grand. A few of my favourite guests is all. Luckily, events off my island detain many of my friends with their own families, and each year I host a special ceremony for the trusted few I actually like."

"Sounds fun." I smirked, ignoring the warning prickles down my spine.

"Oh, it is. Most enjoyable." He smiled. "However, I'm undecided on a theme. Past years I've dabbled with witches and warlocks. The trope of vampire and maiden has been done far too often. As has the devil and his sacrifice. I want to do something different this year. Do you have any suggestions?"

Climbing to my feet, I snagged the laptop and tucked it under my arm. "None, sorry. I don't really have the imagination for party events."

"You have plenty of imagination, my friend." Victor snickered. "I've only read a few paragraphs of your book, but I must say, I'm very intrigued to read more."

I drifted toward the door.

I needed Ily.

Being in the library with Vic reminded me of our very first day here. The hope in her eyes as she asked if I was a cop. The heat in her skin as I spanked her with a copy of *The Count of Monte Cristo*.

My cock swelled.

I subtly rearranged it.

I'd intended to leave her in the jewel quarters for the afternoon, but fuck it.

I couldn't relax unless she was near.

Victor followed me as I strode in black flip flops, jeans, and a grey cable-knit jumper through the archway and into the chilly stone corridor. "No suggestions at all? Come now. You're far better at this than I am."

"Told you." I threw him a look. "Not a party planner."

"I know. But…" He bumped his shoulder with mine as we walked toward the heart of his citadel. "How about Lycans and…something? Or fae and…?" He snickered. "Some sort of monster perhaps? We could order in some more toys to play with. Perhaps even put on a show?"

Fighting my reaction to get away from him, I forced myself to be friendly. Stopping as we entered the large airy foyer, I smiled. "Do you even need a theme? All your games are epic, Vic. You're the one with the great imagination for this sort of stuff, not me. I mean…" I whistled under my breath. "Amethyst Anguish that we played last week? Fuck me, that was hot."

"Oh you liked that, did you?" He tapped his nose with a conspiratorial smirk. "I must admit, I came up with that playing with one of my previous favourites about eight years ago. A beautiful little submissive called Skye. She was so timid, so shy. I think a part of me fell for her—I'm a sucker for the fragile. One night, she seemed a little…tired from our previous excursions, so I decided to be nice for once. I teased her with feathers, flower petals, that sort of thing. She slowly grew so relaxed and dreamy, she no longer even knew I was there."

His eyes flashed. "I didn't like that, of course. I wanted her to be aware *I* was the one giving her pleasure instead of drifting off. So…I hit her with a cane." He laughed. "She came back to earth with a bang, let me tell you."

I nodded along, eyes wide with fake respect and awe. "It was definitely a power trip. Ily did the same thing."

"I was watching you while I played with Rachel. I did notice your little nightmare was a sobbing, soaking mess by the end of it." He grinned. "What did you use again?"

"For soft, I used my fingertips. For hard, I used the tawse."

"Ah, one of my favourites. Did you know that split leather strap was still used in classrooms when I was a boy? I got swatted a few times in my youth."

I laughed. "I didn't know what it was until that night." Lowering my voice, making it seem as if I confided a secret, I added, "I loved that Ily's anguish came from not knowing what I'd deliver. It was genius to blindfold and ear-plug the jewels before playing. Ily had no idea if my fingers would pet or the tawse would punish. It turned me the fuck on watching her body sway toward mine hoping for soft only to flinch when I chose pain instead."

"Ah, Henri." He patted my cheek. "If only I didn't have a son on the way. It would've been an honour to have you as my heir." He dropped his hand, his face almost wistful. "Tell you what…I'm not getting any younger. If I don't live to educate my son in all the ways he will rule, would you be open to it?"

I froze. "Y-You want me to teach your son?"

"As his guardian…yes. His godfather if you will." His eyes grew serious and tinged with sadness. "You have no one. I have no one. No one else I'd rather ask anyway. So…what do you say?"

A pang in my chest.

A complex mixture of loathing and…loss.

I was a monster's bastard.

I'd been raised far different than most children.

I suffered the ramifications of that curse daily.

And the thought of Victor's child going through what I did?

Becoming what I am…

Swallowing hard, I said, "You never told me. Did you do it?"

"Do what?" He quirked an eyebrow.

"Kill my brother."

His face turned dark. "Alas, there have been minor complications, but I've been assured he'll be dead within the month. Perhaps after our Halloween celebrations, we can go on a trip together? Just us? I can take you to one of my mines. I've had some renovations done to house merchandise to sell online."

Nausea splashed onto my tongue. "You've started doing what your colleague suggested? The one from Vietnam?"

"I have." He nodded. "It's not as easy as I thought. There are still glitches and techniques I need to learn to get around the pesky flags of such large transactions. I'm even considering hosting my own shop on an encrypted network, but…it's all very promising."

Clapping his hands, he looked past me to his butler subtly trying to get his attention. "Oh dear, I'm late for a meeting. Have a think about the theme for Halloween, and you never answered me." He caught my eyes. "Will you be godfather to my son?"

The thought of being responsible for Victor's kid?

Agreeing to raise his offspring, even while I planned on killing him?

Even hypothetically agreeing to something like that felt like the biggest commitment of my life.

I rubbed my mouth, delaying one last time before adding yet another stain on my soul. "You're so sure it's a son, Vic.

But...what if it's a daughter?"

His mood instantly soured. "I've ordered an ultrasound for Dr Belford. Our surgery wasn't equipped for birthing, but soon, it will be. She'll tell me what it is in a month when the machine arrives."

"And?" I needled. "If it's a girl?"

His gaze turned deadly, his infamous temper appearing. "Then I guess I'll be a hundred grand richer. I've heard rumours that's what female babies fetch."

The urge to be sick surged through me.

In a single sentence, he reminded me, all over again, that for all his friendliness and suavity, he was the vilest son of a bitch and deserved to die.

Laughing, I slapped him on the shoulder. "You truly are something, you know that?"

He grinned, but his eyes remained black. "Oh I know." Striding toward his butler, he gave me a look over his shoulder. "And you're exactly like me, Mercer, whether you can admit that yet or not. Ta-ra."

Two weeks since Victor asked me to be his child's godfather, and I still hadn't shed the slimy shadow inside me.

I'd returned to my room and purged before I went to get Ily.

The nasty habit of throwing up had faded thanks to having Ily's heart and support. But every now and again, the darkness in this place became too much. My system churned. My guts revolted. And I had no choice but to get it out of me before I either accepted what occurred here as normal or remembered everything about this place was repugnant.

And now it was another day.

Yet another night.

Sucking in deep lungfuls of cool air, I tipped my face to the stars.

I'd kicked off my shoes as I'd plucked Ily from where she'd kneeled by my feet during dinner and dragged her into the gardens. No one stopped me. No one even looked in my direction anymore.

I was merely one of them.

A Master who'd enjoyed a four-course dinner, watched a porno put on by trafficked slaves, and then dragged his jewel into the gardens for a fuck.

All in a day's agenda on Victor's island.

Ily didn't speak beside me, sucking in her own breath.

The half-moon shone its silver light over us, painting her beautiful face in pearly luminance.

I wanted so fucking much to sink to the grass and just hug her. Kiss her. Whisper about our dreams. Be gentle and loving before I pinned her beneath me and delivered pleasure that drove us straight into hell.

But we did our best to never touch sweetly.

If I stroked her without thinking, I made sure I made her squeak for an audience.

If I caught myself staring at her with my heart in my fucking throat, I ensured I cursed her, demeaned her, and said things I didn't mean so the cameras portrayed a Master who might have a soft spot for his jewel but definitely wasn't a man in love.

"Do you want to take a stroll?" Ily finally asked after ten minutes of moon bathing.

I nodded and broke into a slow amble.

Soft grass tickled my toes. The dew already damp and cold.

Autumn colours transformed Victor's gardens, turning greens into oranges and flowers into corpses.

We headed toward the battlement walls, following box hedges, drifting around fountains, and finding peace after a busy ballroom full of Masters and their jewels.

Fuck, I was exhausted.

I just wanted this over.

I wanted to go to sleep and not wake in a cold sweat fearing Ily had been stolen.

I wanted to write without fearing someone reading over my shoulder and have sex without someone watching.

But most of all, I wanted to get Ily safe.

I needed her back with her family so if I died sooner rather than later, I could rest peacefully, knowing she was far, far away from Victor and his horrors.

Two Masters and two jewels appeared to our left, striding quickly in our direction. The citadel glowed behind them. Arrow slits and windows glowed bright yellow, looking like a thousand judging eyes.

"Ah shit," I muttered under my breath. "I have no desire to perform tonight. Let's go into the maze." Grabbing Ily's hand, I cut across the courtyard where vines crawled up a trellis and a small sala waited for lovers. The familiar hum of energy and awareness sparked between us, making my heart pound faster.

I let her hand go the moment we entered the huge, manicured maze.

I didn't know if Victor had cameras in here, but I wouldn't risk it.

I would never risk Ily, even though my fingers craved hers and my heart hurt and my bones throbbed with madness.

Ily remained silent.

She huddled deeper into her beige jumper—the only warm thing she had—her nose pink with cold.

Left then right, right then left, we travelled deeper into the maze, heading toward the centre where another sala and a wishing well had been built. We'd spent enough time wandering that we'd learned the maze's dead ends and tricks and often came in here to get away from the other Masters.

A month ago, I'd fucked Ily against one of the posts of the wishing well, putting on a show just in case. Our show had turned into truth, and I'd made her come hard enough to reward me with one of her G-spot orgasms.

My stomach clenched as we stepped into the centre of the maze.

"Should've brought a few drinks with us." I smiled at my twin flame. "Gotten tipsy and enjoyed our own celebration."

"What celebration?" Her adorable nose wrinkled.

"Our four-month anniversary is coming up."

She cracked a smile all while her eyes pooled with sadness. "So it is."

Stepping into her, I whispered, "I don't know if I have the strength to last till Christmas."

"Ugh, me either." She pressed her forehead against my chest before stepping back. "But...we will."

I sighed. "I know. We don't have a choice."

Her hands went to her jumper hem, her lashes flirting. "Want to put on another show for anyone watching?"

My cock twitched.

Despite the lifestyle of this place—full of daily sex and games of pain—I never lost the urge for more. Apart from the month where Victor was gone and I'd drowned beneath depression, I took Ily often. I fucked her every night because being inside her gave me just enough strength to survive another day.

"Fine." I gave her a black smile. "Strip and lean over the picnic table." Unbuckling my belt, I pulled the leather from the loops of my slacks. "Five strikes before I fuck you."

She shuddered.

Her eyes glowed as bright as two suns.

Our chill vanished thanks to our blood burning.

"Yes, *Master H*." Giving me a sinful smirk, she padded toward the table and went to lift her jumper only—

"Umm, before you play, can we talk?"

She spun around.

I fisted my belt.

The two Masters and their jewels who I'd spied across the lawn, stepped into our sanctuary.

It took me a moment to recognise them.

I hadn't seen them since Emerald Bruises when I'd interrupted their little game in the first cave.

"*You.*" I bared my teeth. "Just like you told me to fuck off that day, allow me to repeat the sentiment. Fuck off."

The bald Master, Ben, if my memory served, held up his hands. "Give us three minutes. That's all we ask."

"It's important," the other one, Stewart maybe, muttered.

Ily shot a look at the two girls. A strawberry-blonde and an auburn beauty. Both jewels stared back with intensity.

Yet…they didn't look like they wanted to run from their Masters.

They stayed by the men's side, at ease and comfortable.

If I didn't know any better, I'd say they looked like a couple.

Like…me and Ily.

"What is it?" I threaded my belt back through the loops and did it tight. "Three minutes."

Striding closer, the two men gave each other a glance then snapped their fingers. "Pen. Abby. If you'd be so kind."

Without a word, the two jewels shifted to stand in front of their Masters. They dropped to their knees and reached for their Master's trousers, unzipping them and—

"Whoa. What the hell? You tell me to stop, yet expect me to stand here while you get a fucking blowjob?"

"Have yours kneel too," Ben ordered. "It'll look like we're enjoying a suck off."

I struggled for words. "Leave."

"Just…you'll want to hear what we have to—"

"I said *leave*—"

"Ily." The strawberry-blonde looked toward my jewel all while her hands fumbled into Ben's pants and withdrew his cock. He wasn't hard. His face was all business, not pleasure. "Please hear us out. It's important."

For a second, Ily didn't move. Her gaze locked on the auburn girl as she exposed Stewart's cock and hovered her mouth over him.

Neither of the girls sucked, though, rocking back and forth, faking it.

Scowling, I looked into the hedgerows.

"There's a camera above and to my left," Ben whispered. "It's not infrared and will only show a grainy picture of three Masters getting sucked. Come on, Mercer. We don't have all fucking night."

Ily made the decision for me.

Marching into me, she dropped to her knees, unzipped my slacks, and went to pull me free.

I stopped her.

"Just…pretend." I swallowed hard. "I don't need my dick out."

I'd lost any shyness I might've had about group fucking after living here for four months, but I didn't want to be the only one hard in this little get together.

Ily slipped into the same sort of slow rock as the other jewels.

Having her mouth anywhere near that part of my anatomy made it really fucking hard to concentrate. Scrubbing my face with my hands, I glowered at the two men. "Go on then. Three minutes."

"We'll be fast," Ben said. "We told you we're not down with a lot of the shit that goes on here. We prefer to stick with Abigail and Penelope and do our own thing. We fly in for a weekend, fall a little more for these two, then fly home. But while we're back in society, we really miss and worry about our girls."

Stewart looked down at the auburn-haired girl, Pen, on her knees before him. He cupped her head with longing. "You asked us why we don't buy flesh at home if we're rich enough to party at Vic's. The answer is, we're watched. We said as much. In fact, the past month has been a total shit show with our board, but…we can't keep doing this."

"This being visiting our jewels and then having to leave them here," Ben said. "Last time we visited, Abby had been whipped so badly by another Master, she spent most of my time in the recovery ward, and after what they told us about the Temple of Facets? We can't…we're not able to…w-we're done."

"Done?" I asked.

"We went to Victor and asked if we could buy Pen and Abby off him. We offered a decent price. Not as high as what you paid but generous all the same."

"Let me guess. He didn't take it?" I threaded my fingers through Ily's sapphire-black hair, making it seem as if I held her in place.

"No. He said it wasn't about the money. He'd love to accept. He's a businessman, yada yada. He refused to let Pen and Abby off his island because they'd spill his secrets."

"We assured him we would take responsibility," Stewart rushed. "We wouldn't let them tell anyone."

"Bet he didn't believe that." I snorted.

"Nope." Ben sighed. "We already have the right of their nights. They spend every hour with us when we're here, but…it's not enough."

"It's not enough because you're in love with them." I studied each man carefully.

Both of them flinched. "Can you blame us?"

"Blame? No. Believe? Also no."

"We have feelings, same as you."

"I never came here intending to fuck a prisoner."

"Yet you stayed, and that's exactly what you're doing."

Rage crawled up my throat.

Ben cut through my temper. "Look, all we're saying is…yes, we came here with unhonourable intentions. But we've seen too much. Witnessed too many atrocities. We came here for companionship and sex, but what we get is fear and abuse. Plus, we know what happens to jewels when they reach their use-by-date, and Pen and Abby—"

"We're not getting any younger," Penelope whispered over her Master's flaccid cock. "I've never seen a jewel over the age of twenty-nine. I…next year I turn thirty and Abby the year after."

Abigail kept rocking. "We've been helping with the Christmas presents. We…we told—"

"You *what?*" Ily hissed, swooping upright on her knees. "You told your Masters what we're planning?"

Both girls slouched. "Yes, but…they're trustworthy."

Ily shot both men a horrified look. "Have you…are you…will you tell Victor?"

My right hand slipped into my pocket. My fingers curled around my switchblade, warm and heavy at the bottom.

It'd be easy to kill them.

Not so easy to explain away their bodies.

"You better keep talking," I snarled. "Now."

Ben nodded. "We only ever discuss Christmas in the shower. It wasn't the girls' fault. We caught them putting something under the bed of the rooms we use. Later that night, I investigated. I have a background in chemistry myself and figured it out without making a scene." He flicked Stewart a look. "We asked our jewels for the truth, and we got it. We'll admit we wondered if we could buy Victor's favour by telling him. Perhaps he'd let us have Pen and Abby, after all. But we'd already offered money. What would information do that money couldn't? And so…we figured—"

"That you'd help free them so you can trap them in your own houses?" I snapped.

"No." Stewart stroked Pen's cheek. "Even if we wanted to do that, we'd be caught eventually with how much we're watched. The only way it will work is if our relationship is legitimate."

"Legitimate?"

"Marriage," Ben murmured.

"You…you agreed?" Ily asked, resuming her rocking but shooting the two jewels a look.

"We did." Penelope nodded. "I was a foster kid and was taken when I was ten. I belonged to another before Victor traded me, so I have no one. And Abs…"

Abigail winced. "My brother accidentally killed my parents in a drunk-driving incident. My world ended, and I hit the road after their funeral. I was trafficked from a dirty motel where I spent the night. There's no one waiting for me. We both have a clean slate. We could become completely different people."

"That's no reason to marry the men molesting you," Ily whispered coldly.

"You can't talk." Abigail sniffed. "You're in love with the man molesting you. Is it so hard to believe we are too?"

Ily wrinkled her nose. "But…"

"Out of all the Masters we've had, the moment Ben and Stewart started visiting, we could finally breathe. We could sleep without pain. We felt cherished and listened to and protected. We hate when they leave. We count the days until they're back. They've offered us freedom as well as wealth. We want to take it."

"No prenup," Stewart muttered. "We're loaded and lonely. If we can atone for participating in this place by giving everything we have to the two girls who love us regardless of how we met, then we'll happily be penniless because we're fucking miserable without them."

Ily looked up my body, her fiercely intelligent gaze catching mine.

What do you think? She licked her lips.

I'd never been so thankful for the strange, eerie connection between us.

Not sure. I ran my thumb over her cheekbone.

Looking at Ben, Ily whispered, "Are you willing to help?"

"Of course. That's why we're here. We know you won't trust us, but you need more Masters. And…" Ben shrugged. "We don't just come on our own."

"What do you mean?" I narrowed my eyes.

"We're friendly with three guards."

"What? How?"

Stewart winced. "I'm a smoker, you see. I loiter outside a lot, and when you loiter around guards, you inevitably start talking shit. 'What's it like working here? Do they enjoy their job?' That kinda thing." He sighed. "Turns out, they're as much a prisoner as all the rest."

"What are you saying?" I went deathly fucking still.

"They're housed in barracks down Victor's long driveway by his helipad. They have their own jewels that are kept separate. They also have care packages flown in. They have luxuries and are treated well but they can't go online. They can't visit family. The day they signed their contracts, Victor flew them here and refuses to let them leave. He keeps them obedient by reminding them that it's better to be the one holding the gun than the one wearing the collar. Each one is mostly a millionaire with how much Vic pays them, but what good is money if you can't spend it?"

"Why haven't they revolted before now?"

"They haven't dared. Money is far better than rape. But…a lot of them are sick of it. They came as young men who were only thinking about pussy and money, but they're older now and wanting more."

"You're saying they'd be open to a coup?"

"The three I'm friendly with just want off this fucking island. So yes. If they could be assured we'd win, they'll start hiding weapons around the place. There's an armoury attached to the barracks. They have access to ammunition and a stack of other shit that would ensure success. Hopefully."

My heart pounded.

I hated that the longer we talked, the more I wanted to believe them.

The more I *needed* to believe.

I hadn't wanted to voice my fears, but the closer we crept toward December, the worse my panic grew. For all our plans, it would most likely be suicide.

The jewels were powerless. The cleaning staff mostly useless. The gardeners only less so with their spades and rakes. Even the knives that the kitchen staff gave us only worked if a Master didn't electrify a jewel before they got close enough to stab.

We need guns.

We needed lots and lots of guns.

And these two bastards are offering them to us...

Pinching the bridge of my nose, I did my best to find that calm centre. I grounded myself. Sucked in a cleansing breath. Willed myself to spot any lies or traps.

Victor could've put them up to this.

He might be waiting to entrap me.

But…

What if their offer was real?

What if we had an actual fighting chance at doing this?

Ily broke through my thoughts, whispering to the girls, "Do you swear on the lives of every jewel in here that this is real? That you trust your Masters like I trust mine?"

Abby and Pen looked at each other and nodded. "We swear. You can trust them."

"In that case…" Looking at me, she shrugged. "Your call."

I studied the two couples.

I looked deep into their eyes and judged the flickerings of love I saw there.

And I made a decision.

One that I hoped wouldn't kill us.

"Fine."

Both men exhaled heavily. "Thank God."

"On one condition."

"Anything." Ben nodded. "We're not about to mess this up."

"We don't talk about this ever again. *You* don't talk about this ever again. Tell the guards to leave weapons in as many places as possible and have them inform you of the locations, but that's it. *Do not do a damn thing to make Victor suspect*. You're aware as much as I am how smart and cunning he is."

"Done." Stewart balled his hands in Penelope's hair. "Once the guns are in place, I'll tell Pen, and she'll tell the rest."

"Good."

"Pleasure doing business with you, gentlemen." Ben grinned as if a weight had lifted off his shoulders. "And now for the finale." His grin turned to a grimace, his hips jerked, his shoulders rolled. He faked the throes of an orgasm before tripping away from Abby and tucking himself away.

Without a word, he gave us all a look, snapped his fingers, and vanished into the dark with his jewel.

"Ho ho ho." Stewart smiled, faking his own release before tapping Penelope on the head and shoving his unspent cock back home. "Let's hope Santa doesn't have us on his naughty list this Christmas."

The night snatched him and his jewel as they disappeared into the maze.

I stood staring after them, hoping like fuck I'd made the right choice.

The sound of my zipper coming down jerked my gaze to Ily still on her knees. "What are you—?"

"You're still hard." Her eyes flashed. "And if I have my way, you won't be faking anything."

Chapter Thirty-Three

Ivy

HALOWEEN

I TUGGED AT THE GAUZY, DIAPHANOUS material. So sheer it hid nothing, so many layers it made my physical body look as if I'd become a creature made of light.

Turning in front of the mirror in our bedroom, I plucked the floaty whiteness, watching as the fabric whispered back to the other layers, looking like closed flower petals. The halter top wrapped tight around my throat, the train behind me as translucent and cobweblike as the rest.

Set against the black of my hair and rich tan of my skin, I had to admit…pure white rather suited me. The small crown I wore glittered with a million cubic zirconia. I might not have gotten my wish to wear the Crown Jewels, but tonight, I'd been transformed into a princess.

Victor had spent the past few weeks planning this masked ball for Halloween.

Our costumes had arrived this morning.

The energy in the fortress buzzed with anticipation and intrigue.

Last Monday, most of the Masters flew back to their families and despite it being a weekend now—the busiest time here at Joyero—only ten Masters had flown back in. The rest were either celebrating in their own way or not invited to Victor's event.

Ben and Stewart had nodded at us over breakfast.

Abby and Penelope had become invaluable as they whispered the locations of five guns that'd been hidden in the foyer, library, games room, ballroom, and kitchens. Peter and the rest of the jewels knew where extra bullets were stashed along with a few lighters May had given us from the kitchens. We also had two butane torches used to melt sugar on the regular crème brûlées Victor ordered.

We had guns.

Ignition.

And bombs.

We still hadn't made the larger, more dangerous presents that would take out certain structural integrities of the fortress, but we'd done enough that waiting for Christmas started to grate.

Every day was painful.

Every night was terrifying.

Victor didn't act like he guessed anything was afoot but…we could never know for sure.

At least he'd been distracted with organising this ball.

He'd joined Henri and me for lunch, giggling like a freaking loon as if he genuinely couldn't wait for this evening.

I'd never expected the dominating psychopath to place weight on something as silly as a dance. He actually believed the jewels were excited to be dressed and paraded, then abused and fucked as the evening went on.

Scooping the delicate mask from the bed, I secured the ribbon behind my head and blinked through a million facets of light. Every inch of the mask blinded with shimmering crystals, turning everything into rainbows.

"Are you ready?" Henri asked, striding from the bathroom where he'd dressed.

With his eyes on the floor as he tied his own mask behind his head, I had a quick moment to study him without his stare on mine.

And good grief…

Could someone fall in love multiple times?

I'd never seen a more handsome man.

Never had my breath stolen by another just for existing.

Dressed head to toe in black, he wore a heavy velvet cape that flared from his shoulders and whispered against the floor. Glossy black shoes, mandarin collared black shirt, and a mask covered in glittering black tourmaline.

The light-sucking gemstones drew every illumination in the room to his eyes, ensnaring me, killing me—

"Je-*sus*." He froze as his hands dropped and his gaze landed on me.

His mouth hung open.

He shuddered on the spot.

And then he prowled toward me, his grey eyes erupting with silver flames. The familiar starfire between us built and billowed, igniting every piece of our bodies, hearts, and souls.

"*Tu es et tu seras toujours la plus belle femme que j'ai jamais vue.*" (You are and always will be the most beautiful woman I have ever seen.) He cupped my cheek, running his thumb over my unpainted bottom lip.

He forgot our pantomime. Ripped up our script.

And kissed me.

The moment his mouth met mine, I slung my arms around his cape-draped shoulders and clung to him.

Just for a single moment.

A stolen second.

Then I let him go and broke the kiss.

I dropped to my knees for the cameras.

He sighed heavily as if my submission annoyed him, all while understanding why I surrendered.

His energy switched from rosy and warm, full of love and connection, to mean spirited and cold. Raising his voice so the cameras would record, he chuckled. "I have a good mind to make you blow me. A necklace of cum would really set off that dress."

I didn't look up.

I didn't answer back.

I played the role of a good submissive jewel.

Henri's hands landed on his belt.

I *instantly* hummed with need.

If he took me over the chair before we went to this stupid ball, I would not complain.

After so many weeks of giving in to animalistic urges—of encouraging my system to be dirty and bad and crave such despicable things, I couldn't get through a day without some form of pain and release.

I needed it.

I grew itchy for it.

I craved him and his unique brand of torment.

God...

My insides clenched.

My breasts became painfully heavy.

A gush of wetness—

Yep, now he'd done it.

No way could I go down there without him fucking me.

A shadowy part of my mind judged me. The old me pitied the creature I'd become.

I feared I'd become an addict to fear and pain and suffered regular nightmares of going home, moving back into my family's house, hugging my brother and kissing my parents, all while crave, crave, *craving* the absolute fucking madness that only Henri could cure.

My fingers sneaked across the carpet and latched around his ankle.

He sucked in a breath.

I looked up.

My body put on a performance for the cameras, but my eyes…they spoke the truth.

I need you. Badly.

He shuddered. *Now?*

I nodded.

Bending over me, he grabbed my elbows and hoisted me to my bare feet. "You know what? A cum necklace would be a waste. How about I fill you up, so you drip for me all night long?" Cupping me roughly between the legs, he drove the wispy fabric directly into my soaking core. "Would you like that? My cum oozing down your thighs? Knowing you've been fucked by me. That you belong to me?"

I convulsed.

My knees stopped working.

God, yes please.

"Fuck you," I snapped.

"As you wish." He smirked.

I love you, his eyes whispered.

Tossing me onto the bed, he flipped me onto my stomach and flipped the hem of my dress over my back. Kicking my feet apart, he unbuckled, unzipped, and fisted himself.

My heart pounded in my ears, my fingertips, my clit.

Every cell in my body wanted to submit and arch for him.

I *needed* him to fill me.

I wasn't whole without him inside me.

But I had a show to put on.

A show we'd perfected, and Victor had bought hook, line, and sinker.

Pushing up off the bed, I made to feint to the side.

He snatched me and threw me back down. "Where the fuck do you think you're going?"

Pressing a fist against my lower back, he kept me pinned.

"Get off me!" I struggled.

"Still so strong." He dragged my hips off the edge of the bed. "Still so unbroken."

"Get your fucking hands *off* me."

"Either beg or scream. Your choice."

I screamed.

He laughed.

Grabbing my ass cheeks, he spread me wide, and impaled himself deep, *deep* inside.

My pussy fisted around him, not making his takeover easy.

The pinch despite my arousal.

The thickness of his size.

It all pushed me into mania, and I lost it.

I fought the urge to surrender to him.

I forced myself to thrash and cry.

And my Master and twin flame understood both sides of me, both the act and the truth, the lust and the love. His fingernails dug into my hips as he grabbed me and pumped fast and fierce into my body.

His thumbs stroked me in those wonderful Morse code circles.

His cock punished me over and over again.

The bed creaked with his every vicious pound.

My ears rang.

My womb tightened.

A release percolated and popped in my blood.

"Fuck…" I couldn't breathe. "*You*." I gasped as he rode me like a manic beast.

He didn't reply. His pace absolutely unhinged, his hipbones bruising me, his cock punishing my G-spot over and over and over…

Every inch of me prepared to leap.

Yes.

God yes.

I stopped fighting him.

I gave him everything.

I screamed for real as his hot hand slapped cruelly against my ass.

"Five strikes for making me so goddamn hard for you. You've got your juices all over me. How am I supposed to last the night knowing you're this fucking wet?"

He hit me again.

Pain.

Glorious, frenzied pain.

I moaned.

He groaned.

Our pace reached delirium.

"Fuck, little nightmare." He spanked me again all while his cock grew and throbbed, claiming me, maiming me. "Feel that? Feel how much I need to come?"

I nodded.

I gasped.

I yelped as he struck for the fourth time, sending me hurtling toward heaven.

"You and that damn tattoo. You've cursed me for life."

I hovered on the cliff's edge.

The fall looked so deep and black, full of starbursts and supernovas.

I just needed one tiny push.

A single little—

Thwack.

I combusted on his fifth strike.

I grew wings and flew.

My entire body came.

Waking and rippling, milking and fisting.

I made noises.

I begged for things. Nonsense, unknown things.

I wasn't human as I shattered and fractured and—

"Ily. *Goddammit.*" Henri dragged me onto him. Crawling inside me as deep as he could go. "Ily. Fuck. *Fuck!*"

His release spurted and coated, branding me in hot, ropey liquid.

His grunts as he kept feeding me his orgasm threatened to push me into another.

I could barely see, hardly think.

He destroyed me.

When he finally shuddered and held himself locked inside me, I shivered at the sensation of him marking me forever as his.

I wore his cum.

I had his scent all over me.

With a breathless groan, he withdrew, tripped backward, and fought hands that no longer worked to stuff his spent erection into his black slacks and buckle up.

Twisting upright, I sat primly on the edge of the bed.

A wet patch soaked into my dress, matching the silvery trails of my arousal glinting on the black fabric over his fly.

He caught me looking. "Told you your juices were all over me."

I smiled, embracing the flood of possession. *You're mine. My body says so.*

He nodded and placed a fist over his heart. *Forever.*

"Come along, little nightmare." Snatching my wrist, he dragged me off the bed and carted me toward the door. "Time to party."

A flood of moisture oozed hotly down my thigh.

I cringed.

He wrenched open the door and laughed at my screwed-up face. "Bit of a mess down there? Maybe if you're a good girl tonight, I'll lick you clean."

I stumbled.

He caught me.

He whispered into my ear, "You still with me, *mon cœur?*" (My heart.)

I caught his gorgeous grey eyes.

I fell into even deeper feelings. "Always."

He shivered.

I smiled.

Together, we descended into a night where ghosts and demons came out to play.

And hoped we'd still be alive come morning.

"Something doesn't feel right, *jaanu.*"

I spun and caught Peter behind me.

He shifted on the spot, pressing his lips to my ear. "Victor has a smug look in his eyes. It's giving me the fucking creeps."

I shot a glance at Victor laughing with Roland across the room.

Slim and tall, with his own dark cape, Victor looked like a distinguished art gallery curator or slightly eccentric benefactor. The mask cutting his face in half hid a lot of his sins, but Peter was right.

His navy eyes seemed particularly pleased, kind of pompous actually.

"Come." With a quick look at Henri who stood talking to Ben and Stewart not far away, Peter snatched my cuffed wrist and dragged me into the alcove draped with white netting that'd been hung on all the walls of the Great Hall.

For two hours, we'd mingled, all while I did my best to forget about the stickiness between my legs. Henri kept giving me knowing glances as Masters ate, drank, and grew merry.

Victor had spared no expense.

The Great Hall travelled almost the entire length of the east wing. Its polished parquet floors, sweeping high brimstone and devil painted ceilings, and hundreds of stained-glass windows made it seem as if we truly were in hell. Each stained-glass window depicted some sort of erotic carnage. From women skewered on a spears, to girls burning at the stake. Each one died a slow, painful death all while being fingered, fucked, or whipped.

The scenes were so barbaric, so brutal, I hadn't been able to eat a thing.

Interspersed amongst the sickening windows, Victor had ordered his decorating team to drape white and black swathes of material on every wall. The black absorbed the candlelight flickering from the many candelabras while the white glittered like stardust.

I still couldn't figure out his theme, but every Master wore the same black cloak as Henri. The same black tourmaline mask. The same aura of grim reaper gliding around the room sipping blood-red wine and laughing as they tormented their jewels.

The jewels…

If Victor had intended to make them seem like angels, he'd succeeded.

Every one of us wore the same white gossamer fabric. The girls in wispy petal dresses with trains long enough for Masters to stomp on, and the boys in trousers and shirts so fine and sheer, the shadows of their bodies were visible, teasing bastards to touch.

I looked up at Peter's face.

His matching mask of crystals glittered with rainbows, casting pinks and greens over his lips.

I hated that we hadn't had much time to talk.

I missed him even though he was standing right there.

I wanted to tell him I loved him but...I had a feeling that would hurt him too much. Not because I had such deep feelings for him but because those feelings were purely platonic.

He was my friend and soulmate. Just like my brother.

If I hadn't found the missing part of my soul, then perhaps we would've ended up as a couple.

But...in this life, this incarnation, I was Henri's.

Do badan, ek jaan: two bodies, one soul.

My gaze drifted from Peter's handsome face to the swollen welts on his chest, glowing red beneath his angelic white shirt. "Oh, Paavak...I'm so sorry."

He flinched and rubbed the lashes as if he could erase them. "I'm fine."

"Who hurt you?"

"Branson's back. But don't fret—"

"Bastard."

I wished tonight was Christmas not Halloween.

I wanted to leap forward two months and stop him from ever being abused again.

"I can give you the rest of the arnica tablets I took after Emerald Bruises. They really helped heal all my paintball marks."

He smiled distractedly and shook his head. "Don't worry about it. I didn't drag you here to talk about my injuries—"

"Do you want to talk about what happened the night of Topaz Tor—"

"Nope." He rubbed his mouth. "Definitely not."

I winced, remembering how we'd stood side by side on that dance floor.

How we'd climaxed at the same time to different Masters.

How he'd been dragged off by a Master named Wilson and Henri had carted me the other way.

Despite my wariness of telling him I loved him tonight, I'd told him during that game.

I'd given him what he asked for and...we hadn't mentioned it since.

Rubbing the goosebumps on my arms, I shrugged. "We need to talk about it. It's been awkward between us for weeks."

He dropped his hand with a heavy huff. "Ily...please don't."

Flinching, he watched a black-caped Master drift past our transparent wall of stardust. "I know what I asked you to do, and I know why you went along with me. I know it didn't mean anything and..." He gave me the saddest smile all while his eyes glossed with grief. "We're all good, *jaanu*. Seriously. I'm fine."

The cavernous echo in his voice.

The aching despair.

Henri shot a look in our direction. He swayed toward me, his entire body bristling with protectiveness.

But I subtly shook my head.

We were safe.

We weren't far.

And Peter needed me.

I owed my wonderful friend some company. Especially when his entire energy felt...empty.

Worse than empty...desolate.

Peter's white outfit suddenly no longer looked like an earthbound angel but a shroud—grave clothes even while he still breathed.

Grabbing his hand, I squeezed. "Paavak, what is it? You're scaring me."

Running his thumb over my knuckles, he exhaled. He didn't reply for the longest time but finally, he sniffed and gave a tattered laugh. "I told myself I wasn't gonna do this. I've choked on the words since the day I fucking met you but..." Fisting my hand so hard it hurt, he groaned, "You know I'm in love with you, right?"

Everything dropped away.

The classical haunting music of Victor's soiree.

The sensation of Henri watching us like a hawk.

"I don't just love you, Ily," he murmured. "I'm *in love* with you and fuck, I wish I wasn't."

Ego ordered me to deny it. To act surprised. To give him a semblance of dignity.

But...I couldn't.

I'd never lied to him, and he'd never lied to me.

Even on that first day when he asked me to reveal myself, so he had a mental picture to cling to while he was being hurt, I'd sensed he felt something I didn't.

I wished things could've been different and I had the power to make him happy.

But...I belonged to another, and it wouldn't be fair.

To any of us.

Struggling for words, I opened and closed my mouth a few times, praying I said the right thing, but Peter beat me to it.

"You don't have to say anything back." He shot Henri a look. "I know how you feel about him. You only have to be in the same room as you two to feel it. To see it." He chuckled painfully. "He'd literally kill himself for you and you...well, you'd bring him back to life because you can't live without him. If I didn't know any better, I'd say you shared the same fucking heart and...I won't deny that hurts. It hurts worse than all the whips, the rapes, the beatings. It hurts because I'll never get to know what that feels like, and I'll die before I'm ever loved in return."

Stepping into him, I wrapped him in the biggest hug. "I love you, Paavak. I think I have for lifetimes. I'm yours as well as his. I'm just not the missing piece of your soul. But you will find her. I know you will. Of course you won't die. She's waiting for you outside this place. By next year, you'll be free and healed and you'll meet each other on the train or in the supermarket and she'll take one look at you and just know."

He gathered me to him, his heart thundering between us. "I love you, Ilyana Sharma."

I dug my fingers into his back. "I know but you'll love someone far deeper than me. When you find her, you'll understand."

Sniffing back grief, he murmured, "Do you know he said he'd step aside if you ever chose me?" He pressed a kiss to my temple. "Fucking bastard showed me in one sentence he wasn't faking how he felt. He didn't threaten me. Didn't even tell me to back off." He stepped away and rearranged some of the layers of my dress with tender fingers. "The fact that he put your own happiness above his own told me everything. He loves you, *jaanu*. So much. And...fuck, if I can see it, then everyone can." He flicked a look at Victor who toasted Roland as a waiter topped up their wine goblets. "*He* can see it. He knows."

Henri brushed aside the fabric, his eyes narrowing at how close we stood to each other. "Everything okay?" His hand twitched toward me, but he snatched it back.

Giving me space.

Giving me to Peter for a few seconds.

If I didn't love him already, I would've for that alone.

"We're fine. Just...two minutes."

It cost him.

I saw it in his eyes, but he nodded and turned his back, guarding us from cameras and Victor.

"You think Victor knows more than what he's showing?" I whispered, a cold draft howling down my spine.

"I think he's used to keeping his cards close to his chest and likes the hunt." Peter slouched. "In the five years I've served him, he's always the happiest when he's got a winning hand. H-He's hiding something." He crossed his arms, hugging himself. "I just don't know what."

"If he knew about our presents and plans, surely he would've—"

"Nah, I don't think it's that." He shook his head. "Faiza checks the locations each time she cleans. Nothing has been touched or moved."

"Then what?"

"I don't know. But something doesn't feel right. It feels like a storm gathering on the horizon. Don't you sense it too?" He ran his hand over his arm, rubbing at goosebumps. "It's building. The energy in here is off the fucking charts."

"Give me a sec." Grounding myself, I visualised silver roots growing out of my feet and feathering deep into the ground. Closing my eyes, I shivered as golden light cascaded through my chakras and—

"Oh my God, how could I be so blind?" Peter gasped.

My eyes ripped open just in time to see him stagger back, his gaze locked on my face.

"What…what happened?" I reached for him.

Henri suddenly appeared. "See what? What didn't you see, Pete?" Grabbing Peter by the elbow, he fought the urge to shake him. "Spit it the hell out."

Peter let out a guttural groan that tore at my insides. "The masks. The crown she's wearing…they're…he's dressed us in fucking diamonds."

Henri gave me a horrified look.

I touched the crown atop my head and swayed as I studied Peter.

His mask.

His outfit.

Not an angel.

A diamond—

"He knows." Henri grabbed me. "He knows about the chit."

I trembled. "But—"

"Gentlemen!" Victor's voice cut through the classical strings and stopped my heart. Through the hazy shimmering fabric, all three of us froze as Victor stood on a small stage and raised his goblet. "Happy Halloween!"

"Happy Hallows' Eve!" Roland smirked.

"Tell us you have a good game tonight!" Ian grinned.

Victor preened and waited for the murmurings to die down. Flicking his velvet cape to cover his feet, he smiled like a dark magician about to bring all those he'd damned back to life. "As it so happens, I do have a particular game in mind."

A roar of approval.

A splattering of applause.

"But first, allow me say a few words." Victor smiled as silence fell again. "To start, I wish to announce some housekeeping, along with a new business opportunity. You were selected to attend tonight as you're the most accomplished and have high pedigrees out of all my guests."

Henri grabbed my left hand.

Peter my right.

We stood as a frozen trio as Victor shot us a look through the material and tipped his glass in our direction.

"First, and possibly the best piece of news this evening is...*I'm going to have a son!*"

Every Master broke into over-the-top cheers. "Congrats!"

"Now your Jewelry Box can continue for generations!"

"Do our memberships transfer to our boys, Vic?"

Victor nodded along. "Yes, yes. Okay, that's enough. Hush. *Quiet.*"

Silence fell.

He smiled graciously. "Thank you for your joy on my behalf. It was confirmed this morning by Dr Belford. I'm so glad the equipment arrived early, and we now have a fully equipped maternity ward." He smirked. "It might seem a bit over the top to create an entire medical ward for just one birth, but...that's where you all come in, my friends."

Striding around the stage, his cape flaring behind him, he pointed at each man. "Most of you have offspring already. You've proven you can sire. Up till now, my jewels have been forbidden to get pregnant. Partly for my benefit and for yours, but...if any of you wish to share your proven seed, then tell me who you would like, and I'll arrange it."

"Wait, what?" A few Masters turned up their noses.

"We don't want fucking kids running around here, Vic." Roland sneered.

"Speak for yourself. I'm down with raping for a purpose." Wilson stepped forward. "Count me in!"

Victor looked at each man. "I'm aware you'll enjoy the baby-making part but will want nothing to do with the results. Once you've achieved impregnation, the jewel in question will be sequestered until she is able to return to her duties."

"So you'll be introducing more stock if you're planning on turning most of them into brood mares?" Travis asked.

"I will. In fact, my team is already gathering more gems as we speak."

"Hell yeah." Branson snickered. "Love getting my dick wet on new supplies."

Peter shuddered beside me.

I squeezed his fingers.

"What are you going to do with the babies once you get them, Vic?" Ben dared to ask.

Victor smiled like a snake. "Sell them of course."

"*Sell?*" Stewart choked on a mouthful of whiskey.

Henri bristled, most likely wanting to slap the only Masters on our side and order them to stay silent.

If they revealed how much they abhorred Victor.

If they exposed the lengths they'd go to in order to free Abby and Pen...*we're all screwed.*

Luckily, Victor kept revelling in his monstrosity. "Yes, sell. And now for the fun part. Because I have an heir on the way and I'm not getting any younger, I have asked a very good friend—a man who I consider my protégé in so many ways—to be his guardian. If I don't live long enough to finish his education, another will take my place. Henri." Victor pointed at us in the shadows. "Come join me if you please. Come on now, don't be shy."

Henri swallowed a snarl.

He fisted my hand so hard my fingers went numb.

Then...without a word, he let me go, swatted away the fabric curtain, and stalked toward Victor. With a gravity-defying leap, he shot onto the stage and stood beside the sickest, vilest man I'd ever known. "You summoned."

"You came." Vic patted Henri's cheek. "Such a good lad."

Henri smiled.

It looked so genuine. So real.

But my heart saw past the lies and the truth beneath.

I saw how close Henri was to purging this entire night up.

How close he was to the end.

Peter threw all caution to the wind and wrapped his arm around my waist. Pulling me into him, he whispered, "You need to run, *jaanu*. I don't know where, and I don't know how, but…you really need to fucking run."

Ben and Stewart turned to look at me.

Their eyes.

Their fear.

Peter was right.

The energy in this place was all twisted and wrong. Building, gathering, hissing and slithering…growing sharper and colder and—

"Henri." Victor raised his glass. "You have continued to impress me these past few months. We have so much fun together, and…I truly mean it when I say I see myself in you. I see you growing into who you truly are. I see the man you will be when you're finally free. So…just like I've taken it upon myself to push you along your journey, consider this my final push."

Heavy anticipation filled the Great Hall.

Peter snagged my wrist and pulled me toward the exit.

I tripped and stumbled, all while I looked back and caught Victor's noxious eyes. He waved. He chuckled. Four guards cut in front of us and stopped us in our tracks.

Henri stood frozen on the stage.

"You asked me for a lifetime membership?" Victor smiled at Henri. "Tonight, I will grant it. Your probational period is over, *mon ami*. I am ready to welcome you completely. And, in a show of good faith and to prove how grateful I am for your friendship, I won't take all your money. We'll split it. Fifty-fifty. Not only will you inherit my home, but you will also have the funds to look after my boy if need be."

Peter stood panting beside me.

Prickles of terror stabbed down my legs.

The urge to flee grew stronger, *stronger*.

My heart stopped as Victor snapped his fingers at a waiter

then pointed at Henri.

A glass of alcohol was placed into Henri's slack hand.

It woke him up.

Fury blazed in his gaze before he covered it up with a look of respect and gratitude. "*Merci*, Vic. I'm…honoured."

"No, no, my friend, it's me who is honoured. I'm aware you haven't given me your answer but I'm making it for you. Congrats on being my son's godfather. He couldn't have a better one. Now, drink." Clinking his glass to Henri's, he didn't take his eyes off him as Henri shot it back and cleared his throat.

"*Fabuleux!*" Tossing his empty glass at Rachel, Victor spread his arms. "And now, gentlemen. If you'll leave your jewels behind and all follow me. The final part of tonight is ready." He strode off the stage, his cape wafting like the night as he swooped toward me and Peter.

He reached us before the crowd.

He sucked us into his evil the second he arrived.

Dropping the gentile persona and revealing his true murderous colours, he fisted my wrist and pressed his mouth to my ear. "Did you honestly think I didn't know, *Ilyana*? Did you truly think you could get something as *ridiculous* as escape past me?" He pulled back, clucking his tongue. "And you, Peter." His eyes snaked to Paavak. "You've disappointed me. You've *gutted* me. This is the loyalty you show me after everything I have done for you?" He shrugged and yanked me into him. "So be it. So fucking be it, you two ungrateful *little shits*. Just remember you're the ones who forced my hand. *You* did this. You are responsible for tonight." His lips pulled back, his voice low and trembling. "You two fucking *sicken me*. Running around like mice in the dark. Visiting my kitchens. Turning my jewels against me. You must be suicidal to believe you could hide your little games from me. The cleaners? The chemicals? *Ha!*" He laughed and looked over his shoulder as Henri came toward us.

Keeping his voice too low for Henri to hear, he hissed, "I'm done letting you cause rot in my home. You and your little whispers and rebellions. It was pointless. *Useless*. You've lost and I'll punish all those you dragged into this fatal little scheme. You want freedom so badly? Well then, you shall fucking *have it*."

The guards broke their wall in front of us as Victor stalked forward, dragging me beside him.

Peter let me go.

He fell back.

But Victor said politely, "Guards, please ensure Peter joins us. He's a guest of honour tonight."

"Yes, Sir."

Seamlessly, two black-suited men slipped into place, stepping into line behind me and Victor, blocking Peter between us and preventing Henri from getting too close. Victor grinned over his shoulder. "Are you ready, *mon ami*?"

Henri vibrated with energy.

His lifeforce didn't fit inside his suit anymore, his lines blurring with rage.

But he still managed to follow our script.

Managed to act and simper and lie. "Of course, Vic. Looking forward to it. Whatever it is."

I choked on a sob.

I opened my mouth to scream for him to run.

But two more guards slipped behind Henri before a procession of guests fell behind them.

We were trapped.

Corralled.

Livestock heading to the slaughter.

He didn't know.

Didn't hear what Victor had said.

Didn't hear Victor's low chuckle as he dragged me through his castle. Or his whisper as cold as snow. "Time to die, little diamond. Let's go set you free."

Chapter Thirty-Four

Henri

FUCK.
Fuck.
Fuck!
My mind overloaded as the clip of polished dress shoes marched over stone pavers and the rustle of velvet capes whispered in the dark. Every Master came. Multiple guards interspersed with black-masked men.
All male apart from one.
Ily.
The only splash of white came from her and Peter at the front.
No other jewels.
It was as if Victor didn't give a rat's ass about them. Single-minded and entirely focused on whatever horror he had planned.
Stalking at a fast pace, Victor guided us down a corridor, through an archway, across a courtyard, and into a tower with a flag fluttering high in the star-studded sky.
Every metre, I tried to figure out how to stop this.
Every heartbeat, I begged for supernatural powers to surge through me and smite Victor where he stood.
This would be so much easier if I could kill with just a thought.
A bolt of sorcery.
A well-placed curse to the brain.
I had no idea which guards were on our side.
Ben and Stewart trailed a few men behind.
My back prickled as they stared at me.
I wanted to fall back and talk to them.
Plan a siege as we walked because tonight was the fucking night.
There would be no Christmas.
No coup.

No bombs, no bullets, no freedom.

Victor knew.

How much he knew, I didn't know.

But he knew *something*.

And none of this was fucking good.

Stone swallowed us whole as Victor vanished into the tower and we all followed. Echoes throbbed with ice. Eternal coldness bit into my bones with fangs.

A guard stepped forward and pulled out a ring full of brass keys from his pocket.

They jingled painfully loud.

The scratch of metal on metal as it slipped into the ornate lock. The creaking hinges as the door opened.

I couldn't fucking breathe.

The door screeched, dragging over the stone pavers as the guard wrenched it wide and stepped aside for Victor to climb down the stairs.

We followed.

So many stairs.

A winding corkscrew of never-ending stairs.

Electrical torches flickered like fire on the walls, granting just enough light not to trip but not enough to get my bearings.

Where the hell is he taking us?

Musk and dankness billowed like a swamp.

The air turned dense and earthy, growing colder and colder until my toes turned numb, and claustrophobia clawed at my throat.

The glow of Ily in her stunning white gown was the only thing keeping me sane.

She was my beacon.

My north.

My only.

She glowed, not because of her dress, but because of her spirit. The light in her that tempered my black. Her goodness to my darkness. Her redemption to my remorse.

Peter didn't say a word as Victor reached the end of the stairs. His shoes clicked and hissed on rock. The sound bounced around us, the tunnel we'd reached as narrow as a fucking coffin.

I swallowed hard.

My skin itched.

It felt as if he'd buried us alive.

Lights snapped on as Victor triggered sensors.

One after another, disrupting the never-ending black with pinpricks of illumination.

I passed by a shadowy tomb to my left.

I crashed against the wall to my right.

A cell.

Bars.

Shackles on the wall and a drain in the middle.

The dungeons.

We're in his motherfucking dungeons.

Victor snickered from his place at the top of the line. His voice was cool and collected like any good tour guide offering facts to his tourists. "I hope you like the aesthetics, Henri. I spent many hours poring over the blueprints from Linlithgow Palace and its ruins. I ensured my builders gave me a replica. Right down to the sandstone, granite, and oak."

I couldn't have talked, even if he held a gun to my head.

A few Masters behind me chuckled. "Always love the vibe down here, Vic. Especially love a nighttime play. You can almost feel the ghosts of the tortured highlanders who suffered in the real one."

"Thank you for saying so, Larry. I'm glad someone appreciates my attention to detail." Victor looked over his shoulder and smiled. His eyes caught mine. "Are you quite well, my friend? You're looking a little pale."

I choked, coughed, and cleared my throat. "I-I'm fine. Just…taking it all in."

"Plenty more to see. Plenty more. This way."

Picking up the pace, he yanked Ily along with him.

Her bare feet would be so cold.

Her body icy from the bowels of this earth.

The tunnel meandered like a labyrinth. Widening in places and forking off in others. Dungeons large and small appeared in the gloom. Some with typical looking torture equipment, others with brand-new BDSM crosses, leather tables, and racks full of salacious toys.

I completely lost my sense of where the fuck we were as we stopped at another barricaded heavy wooden door. A guard opened it with another set of clinking keys.

"I thought access this way wasn't possible anymore?" Ian enquired behind me, his dark skin soaking up the night.

"It wasn't." Vic nodded, patiently waiting for the guard to wrangle the damp-swollen door open. "But I've had a team evacuate the cave-in and they managed to clear it last week. Just in time for this."

"Perfect! Much easier going this way," Larry said.

"I agree." Victor smirked.

My racing mind latched onto the fact that Larry was here.

The weedy little wretch I'd almost slaughtered.

I thought Vic wasn't a fan.

The day after I'd killed Daxton, he'd mentioned he'd sent the snivelling man home.

I jerked, remembering what Peter had said.

Larry had a guard on his retainer.

A guard who would happily give up his gun when and if Larry wanted to shoot me.

Christ, can this get any worse?

Boxed in beneath the earth, surrounded by enemies, utterly powerless, completely useless, all while the love of my life was manhandled by the worst bastard to ever exist.

I *hated* myself.

Fucking despised myself for putting her in this situation.

We should've gotten out sooner.

What the hell were we thinking, waiting for Christmas?

We should have fought the moment Victor flew away for a month.

Fuck!

"This way, gentlemen." Victor descended yet another staircase.

My knees trembled as I followed.

Down and down, the musky earth turned sharp with rock.

Pebbles and dust crunched beneath my shoes as we finished descending and stepped into yet another corridor. My black cape tugged my shoulders as it caught on the jagged sides.

If the last tunnel had been a coffin, this one was a casket.

Not just any casket.

One made from stone and ions of pressure from above.

The same overbearing heaviness of the caves a few months ago returned, crushing my head, my spine, driving me into the dirt beneath my feet.

No.

Please tell me we're not—

"Almost there, friends." Victor shoved Ily in front of him and pushed her along. The tunnel was only wide enough for a single person.

I lost sight of her apart from a flash of her transparent ivory dress.

I wanted to be sick.

My guts churned; sourness splashed over my tongue.

I swallowed the urge.

I balled my hands.

I forced myself to think.

Peter was here, along with Ben and Stewart. If luck favoured us, perhaps one of the guards Stewart knew was also in this procession.

We could fight.

Here and now.

I could kill Victor. Finally.

Let myself go. Completely.

We could be free tonight.

Free or dead…either choice was better than this.

This scratching anticipation.

This nerve-wracking apprehension.

I couldn't fucking stand it.

My blood bounced.

My muscles bunched.

I vibrated with war, all while unable to see what side my enemy would strike first.

No one talked as we cut through the earth like worms through soil.

Lanterns decorated our journey.

No glow worms.

No stalagmites or stalactites.

Just chiselled rock that'd been forced to part, leading us closer and closer to the heavy crash of surf smashing itself against stone.

No.

Fuck no.

Peter tripped and went to his knees.

Victor turned and sneered at him on the ground. "Get up, *Paavak*. Now."

Peter sucked in a gasp.

"What? You didn't think I knew your real name? I hear everything, little Peter. I know *all*. Why give me a false one, hmm?

Yet another thing you've kept from me."

I wanted to barge past the two guards in my way.

To haul my friend to his feet.

To beg him to be with me when the time came.

But the guards didn't move, and Peter stumbled upright with a bow. "Sorry, Sir V."

Victor chuckled and patted him on the cheek. "You know…you have my permission to say what you truly feel, my pet. Enough of these charades. I'm sick of them."

For a moment, Peter did nothing.

But then, he dropped all his obedience and cocked his chin. "Fuck it." Baring his teeth, he snarled, "Do whatever you want to me. I won't do a thing to stop you. But…leave her out of it. Whatever you think we've done? It was all me. She had nothing to do with anything."

My heart fucking sank.

And I knew.

All of it.

Everything we'd planned.

All our hope.

Over.

Victor smiled. "That's not how this works, Peter dear. You're on clean-up. As always. Only once you've done your duty shall I deal with you."

I almost threw up on my shoes.

Despair howled down the tunnel and pounced.

Every ounce of depression.

Every horror and misery, every desolation and melancholy found me, snatched me, and turned off every flicker of light left inside me.

I would die down here.

We would *all* die down here.

This wasn't a procession to whatever game Victor had planned.

It was our funeral march.

And I needed to get on my knees and repent.

To confess and atone so when the time came for my life to end, I might stand a minuscule chance at following Ily into the next life.

Because Peter and her…they'd travel together.

They'd find each other again.

Both of them pure enough to deserve a worthwhile existence.
But me?
Fuck *me?*
After the things I'd done.
The things I wanted to do.
Twin flame or not…I wouldn't be allowed to go with her.

Sighing happily, Victor twisted to face the front, pushed Ily between her shoulders, and we were all moving again.

Closer and closer.

Nearer and nearer…

Until finally—

"We're here," Victor announced, his voice echoing off stone.

With my heart already turning over in its grave and my skin slick with icy sweat, we all spilled out into a familiar cave.

One with an altar.

A cupboard full of skulls.

And seats for devils to watch.

Chapter Thirty-Five

I DIDN'T SCREAM AS VICTOR snapped his fingers and two guards grabbed me around my arms and legs and plucked me from the ground.

I didn't scream as they spread me on the stony, icy altar with its grooves for blood and cauldron to catch my essence.

I didn't scream as heavy, thick straps were tossed over my ankles and buckled down tight.

I didn't scream as my golden cuffs were tethered onto hooks and my collar snapped into place with a mechanism in the stone, choking me, keeping my head down, my chest exposed, and every part of me ready to be sacrificed.

I didn't scream.

In this dimension.

But in all the rest?

I screamed and *screamed* until my soul was hoarse, and every lifetime rippled back.

Tears trickled down my face as my heart cracked and bled.

I'd never see Krish again. Never kiss my mum or hug my dad. I'd never cook with my auntie again or ride my bike to visit my cousin at the local gemstone. I'd never get to kiss Henri again or dance with Peter again or breathe fresh air or see the night sky again.

I had minutes.

Mere minutes.

And I wouldn't waste them by screaming.

I couldn't raise my head, but I could turn.

I looked for him.

Needed him.

I shuddered with relief as our eyes touched.

Henri.

God, Henri.

His grey gaze looked like ash. The fire in his soul burned out until nothing but coal and char remained. His skin pulled tight around worn eyes, his mask unable to hide his fear. His mouth so thin and his cheeks so stark, he looked skeletal in the harsh light.

I might live in terror, but he wore it.

Both of us painted forever by horror.

Now I knew why the velvet black capes all the Masters wore looked so familiar.

I'd seen them before.

In the chest where Caishen and I had found the torches and the chipped knife.

The Masters all fanned out around the cave, taking their places on the carved amphitheatre, their black tourmaline masks making them seem like spectres from hell.

Peter stepped stiffly to my side.

He grabbed my hand on the altar and squeezed.

Victor didn't stop him.

He merely smiled as if all our secrets were exposed, and he took such pleasure in winning.

Henri dropped his stare where Peter held me.

He trembled as if he was moments away from snapping.

I was proud of him.

So fucking proud that he hadn't lost his temper. Hadn't revealed himself.

Victor knew Peter and I were up to something, but he hadn't said anything about Henri.

I sent up a prayer that he didn't suspect him.

Didn't know that Henri was as complicit as us.

He would survive.

He has to.

There'd been too much death.

Far, far too much death.

It was over for me.

I knew that as surely as I felt the binds holding me on this altar.

But it wasn't over for Henri.

He could go on.

Could do what we had failed.

Please don't give up. I begged with my twin flame-connected heart. *Please get them out...somehow.*

Henri staggered and came toward me.

No one said a word as he took my other hand, looking at Peter across the table as both men crowded over me and gave me the same heart-wrenching look.

*I'm going to get **you** out of here.* Henri's ashy gaze vowed.

You can't. I shrugged. *Don't give yourself away.*

His lashes snapped closed as if he couldn't breathe.

He clutched my fingers with agonising pain.

And then, Victor started the countdown on my life.

"Friends, welcome."

The Masters stopped rustling.

Their breathing quietened.

Even the surf outside seemed to soften.

"It's an absolute pleasure to bring you all here this evening. I'm sure you've been wondering what my theme for tonight has been, and…I'm ready to tell you."

Coming toward Henri, he cupped his elbow and tugged him away from me. "Mercer, if you will. Come stand with me, please."

Henri stiffened.

For a second, I saw a different reality where he whirled on Victor and ripped out his throat. I pictured him as a hurricane of violence like the night of the treasure hunt. He transformed into something unbeatable and slaughtered every Master and guard in here.

But then reality replaced that fantasy.

Eight guards.

Ten Masters.

Completely outnumbered.

Even with Ben and Stewart as our silent accomplices.

We didn't stand a chance.

Please… I breathed hard. *He doesn't know you're involved.*

Henri looked away and allowed Victor to drag him to the head of the cave where the shelves and its sapphires, and the cupboard with its skulls flanked them.

Victor sighed happily. "As you all know, this man has become rather special to me. Not only has he agreed to be godfather to my only child but he's also trusted me to free him so he can find his ultimate happiness." Giving Henri a doting look, his eyes through his mask radiated absolute peace. "He has continued to grow and step into the man he was always meant to be, and I pride myself on having something to do with that. He hasn't been happy with my meddling. He's fought my pushes and sometimes made me doubt, but with every scream of his jewel and every drop of blood he has drawn, I know he truly is a monster, so…tonight is entirely for him."

"Me?" Henri choked.

"The theme, *mon ami*, is light and dark. Death and life. Monsters and diamonds. I warned you that love is holding you back. I told you what you needed to do to reach that final frontier of freedom."

"Victor, I—"

"Don't interrupt." Victor clucked his tongue. "You're in love with her. Any fool can see it, and I am not a fool. She has been a toxic presence in my home ever since that first night. She has wrapped you in her spell. Beguiled you until you are lost. You can't see what I do. You aren't aware how much she is using you. She's nothing but manipulation and greed. She's turned Peter against me. She's scurried around and convinced my well-behaved jewels to plan an uprising that they can't possibly win. She schemes and plots, and I'm so sorry to tell you this, but…she doesn't love you back, Henri. It's all a ruse—"

"That's not true." I jerked on the table. "I haven't done a thing. None of the jewels—"

"You *will* remain quiet, Ilyana," Victor hissed. "Otherwise, I will cut out your ungrateful tongue."

Hot splashes landed on my arm.

I looked at Peter.

He cried silently, clinging to my hand as if he'd collapse at any moment.

God, my heart broke for him.

How many times had he seen this?

How many times had he held the hand of one of his friends as they lay waiting to die on this godforsaken altar? How many times had he cleaned up their blood, their viscera, and placed their bleached skull in that awful cupboard?

I wished I could communicate with him like I did with Henri.

I wished I could tell him I wasn't afraid.

Not truly.

I was afraid of the pain.

Afraid I wouldn't be able to stop myself from fighting, thanks to the animalistic instinct to survive.

But I wasn't afraid of actual death.

I knew there was more than this.

I knew this wasn't the end.

I just hated that it would be a while before I saw him again.

Before I found him and Henri again.

Brushing aside his velvet cape, Victor reached into his waistband and pulled out a long red bag. Holding it horizontal in two hands, he looked gravely at the Masters.

"Tonight, you will witness a ritual we have perfected over the years. A ritual that turns a prospective friend into a Joyero member. A kiss that not only frees a jewel but frees a Master too."

Placing his hand into the red velvet bag, he slowly, dramatically—with the flair of a born showman—pulled out a diamond-handled knife. The exquisitely sharp blade glinted in the light. The handle glimmered with crystalline fractals.

Dropping the empty bag on the floor, he stepped slowly toward Henri and grabbed his slack hand. "Here."

Henri didn't react.

He looked as broken as I felt.

Victor curled Henri's fingers around the blade and stepped back as Henri stared blankly at the knife.

"This place is called Temple of Facets as you will deliver one hundred cuts to turn her from human into gem. Each cut will drench her blood with adrenochrome, which will be collected and sold. Her kidneys have already been purchased. Along with her lungs and eyes. But it was her heart that fetched the biggest price. A price I will give to you, my friend, so you will always remember the value of this lesson. A lesson that you are worth far more than she could ever hope to afford. You are above her in every way. She is yours to do whatever you wish. That is how this world works. That is what you are. And love has no place in it."

Moving to stand behind Peter, he placed his disgusting hands on Peter's shoulders.

Peter choked on a sob, bowing his head.

"Tonight, gentlemen, Peter will perform his final duty as our cleaner. He has disappointed me and lost my trust. The other jewels will be punished for their role in their futile little war, but I have no doubt the unrest stems from these two. And so…if any man present would like to give him a Diamond Kiss later this evening, you are more than welcome to bid once he has cleaned up what will be left of Ilyana."

Reaching over Peter's shoulder, Victor kissed him softly on the cheek. "I'm being kind to you, Paavak. I could keep you alive after this. I could make you live a long, long life haunted by the memories of the girl you love. The girl you watched be turned into a jewel. The girl whose intestines slithered through your hands as you tossed them into the sea."

He sighed and let Peter go. "What do you say, my pet? Come now, don't be shy."

With tears dripping down his cheeks, Peter raised his chin and tore off his crystal mask. Throwing it onto the floor, he hissed, "Fuck you to *motherfucking hell*."

Victor nodded. "I expected you were holding that in for a while." He chuckled and patted his cheek. "Doesn't that feel better?"

"I fucking *hate* you. I hope you fucking *rot*."

"Not before you, I'm afraid."

My own tears spilled.

I looked back at Henri.

He hadn't moved.

Gaunt and blinking at the knife in his shaking hands.

Victor returned to him.

He slung his arm around Henri's waist. "Come now, my friend. You won this. I saw you find the chit and also saw you tear it up. That was the moment I knew you had to do this. Not because I wish to cause you pain but because this is the only way you can be free of her."

Grabbing Henri around the nape, he said kindly, "I know this is hard. Believe me, I loved once too. And you know what cured me of that nasty affliction? Death. The moment I drove a dagger into her heart, I felt such relief, *mon ami*. No more humanity holding me back. No more doubt. No more fear. I stepped into my power. And now…it's time for you to step into yours."

Taking Henri's wrist, he dragged him toward me.

He pushed and directed until Henri stood over the altar, his shoulder brushing Peter's.

I couldn't look away from him.

I couldn't read him, hear him, feel him.

He'd checked out. Burned out. Gone.

Please be okay.

Please don't let this break you.

No response.

Not a single blink.

"It's time, *mon ami*." Victor guided Henri's hand and the knife to my belly. "Allow me to tell you how this will go. With that knife, once you've faceted and transformed her, you will cut right here." He drew a line with his finger over the softest part of my belly.

I gasped.

Twitched.

Bit my bottom lip until I tasted blood.

"You will slice through her stomach and reach up through her ribcage. While she is still alive, you will grab her beating heart and tear it from her. As she dies in your hand, you will kiss those beautiful lips and let her go. And then..." Pulling a huge diamond from his pocket, Victor held it up. "You will insert this into her empty cavity. A heart for a heart. Meat traded for a gemstone. She'll become priceless, and you? You will finally be free."

With a wicked smile, he backed up and bowed. "She's ready for you, my dear friend. Make the first cut. Let's begin."

Henri and Ily's tale concludes in Diamond Kisses...
Hope is gone, pain is coming…it's not a question of if someone will die but who…

www.pepperwinters.com

Want to know what happened in Topaz Torment? I deleted a scene from Sapphire Scars as I felt it wasn't needed. BUT if you'd like to read it, keep scrolling! I've included the chapter at the end!

Also, if you haven't met Q and Tess yet (Henri's half brother), their New York Times Bestselling Dark Romance is available and complete now! Start with Tears of Tess
READ NOW

DIAMOND KISSES

"I hoped we'd have luck on our side. Goodness over evil, right over wrong. I'd prayed for a miracle, but in the end…the darkness won."

I knew what it felt like to reach rock bottom.
To do things I could never repent.
To want things I could never absolve.
I've wanted to die for so long.
I deserve to die for what I've done.
But not until I finish this.
Not until I repent.
And so, I make a decision.
A cascade of decisions that will bring about the end of my world.
The darkness wants to be fed.
So I'll feed it.
With blood.

Deleted Scene: Topaz Torment

VICTOR SMIRKED AT HIS GUESTS and tormented jewels. "To refresh your memory of this particular game, my friends, the rules are simple. No pain. No abuse. The first part of this activity is for them."

"Never liked that rule," a Master muttered.

Victor chuckled. "Yes, well. You will play by my rules, or you won't play at all."

"I've never played," a Master quipped in the dark. "What *are* the rules?"

Victor clasped his hands and smiled. "Topaz Torment is basically a game of economics."

"Economics?"

"The study of how people—jewels in this case—behave and how quickly they can make decisions when faced with certain…influences."

"Influences being…?" another faceless Master asked.

He winked. "The aim of the game is to torment the jewels as much as you can. But not in the usual method we so love to indulge in."

"How do you mean?"

"I mean…it's rare that sex focuses on their pleasure. But tonight, that is what this game is about. You must edge them to an orgasm, make them weak-kneed and wet. Every Master will have a turn. He can only use his fingers or tongue. The Master who earns the jewel's favour and makes them come wins the game. He's then entitled to have his own pleasure by whatever method he prefers."

A splattering of murmurs.

A few chuckles.

"I know what I'm gonna indulge in." A Master snickered.

"Jewels…if you'd be so kind." Victor squinted through the dark club, the strobe lights still spearing with colour. "Assemble on the dance floor please."

Slowly, collared jewels left their Master's side and stepped warily onto the dance floor. Masters fell back, forming a circle around the mix of bare skin and lingerie all trembling in the centre.

My heart seized.

I wanted to run.

But this was just another night.

And we had no choice but to play.

Unclipping my leash with shaking fingers, I went to join the others.

Henri snatched my wrist.

Jerking me against him, he hissed, "Faint or do something. Anything so I have an excuse to get you out of—"

"Henri," Victor barked. "Let Ilyana join her fellow jewels."

Henri's gaze locked on mine. *Please, Ily...*

I fake swooned.

My knees buckled. I pressed the back of my hand to my forehead and—

A guard caught me. "She's light-headed, Sir. Should I take her to Dr Belford?"

Henri didn't breathe.

The club grew terrifyingly quiet.

And then Victor chuckled, his voice amplified with a microphone. "Know what I think? I think she's trying to get out of it. No matter. It's jewel's choice, after all. Did everyone hear that? Including the new ones?" Victor beamed. "If you prefer a Master or have certain kinks you know a Master can fulfil, then I suggest you give your chosen one your orgasm. If you can hold off coming from another's attempt, then do so as long as you want. Or...enjoy a night of pleasure. Your choice. That's part of the fun. Now, Richard, please stand Ilyana beside Peter." Holding up a finger, Victor added, "I almost forgot. My Rachel will not be involved into tonight's activities. Proceed."

Henri swayed toward me as the guard scooped my legs out from under me and carried me onto the dance floor.

I didn't struggle.

There'd be no point.

My eyes locked with Peter's as the guard crossed the small space and dumped me onto my feet next to him.

"Hi." He gave me a quick smile.

"Hi." I couldn't stop my trembling.

His fingers twitched by his side as if he was about to take my hand. He stopped himself, whispering under his breath, "Out of all the games, this one is the only one you don't have to worry about." He flicked Henri a look.

He stood frozen and stony eyed, watching our every move.

"He won't like it, though."

"W-What do they do?" I whispered.

"Everything." Peter shrugged. "They'll try to make the jewel they want to play with come as fast as they can." He sighed. "It's damn hard holding on to that climax, *jaanu*, especially when you've been fucked for months and denied the slimmest sensation of pleasure."

"So if someone comes, this is all over?"

"Yep."

"I'm first!" A Master stepped onto the dance floor.

"Fuck off you are." The Masters pushed and shoved like children. Immediately, a line formed.

Masters elbowed and kicked each other, fighting for a favourable position.

I kept my eyes on Henri as he stalked forward and merely glowered at some of the men in front of him.

I didn't know if his reputation of killing or his title of in-house exterminator gave him clout, but a few Masters stepped out of his way, letting him jump the queue.

Once the shuffling and positioning had finished, I counted how many men I'd have to endure before Henri touched me.

One, two, three, four, five…

God.

Five men.

Five touches, five licks, five…whatever they wanted.

My heart flurried right out of my chest.

All the wetness Henri had conjured just by existing slowly dried and disappeared.

Peter brushed the back of his hand against mine. "Hey, it's okay. I've got you, alright?"

I choked and fought tears. "Sorry, I—"

"I know the thought of another touching you is probably twisting you up, but…I'm before you in the line-up. I'm rock fucking hard already. I won't take much." He sniffed. "Especially standing next to you."

I shot him a wide-eyed look.

He didn't drop his gaze. "God, Ily…if you let me stare at you while they do whatever they're gonna do…I promise I'll come first, and the rest of you will be free."

"But then the Master will hurt you. He'll win—"

"With how desperate I am to come? I don't really care at this point." He sighed. "Just…be here with me, okay?"

"What if the Masters don't pick you? What if they go straight to me or—"

"The rules state they have to touch each jewel."

Wait, what?

My eyes flew to Henri.

It was a Rachel situation all over again.

Not only did he have to watch me be touched but he'd also have to do the touching…

I shook my head, catching Peter's dark, soulful stare. "So Henri will—"

"Have to touch me?" He half smiled. "Yep."

"But—"

"I have four chances before it's his turn. I know Travis is good with his hand. If he rubs me, I'll probably be able to—" He rolled his shoulders, dropping his voice to a barely-there whisper just as a Master I thought was called Branson stepped toward the first jewel. "If you want to avoid this whole game, *jaanu*...all it will take is for you to say three little words in my ear and..." He sniffed and couldn't look at me.

My forehead furrowed as he flicked me a glance full of embarrassed shame.

"Shit." He sighed. "I didn't mean to say that. I sound as manipulative as they are." He scrubbed his face with his hands. "Ignore me. You don't have to. I'll...yeah. Forget I said anything."

Shoving his shoulders back, Peter didn't look at me again.

But I looked at him.

I couldn't take my eyes off him even as Branson slowly made his way down the line of six jewels before us. Six pretty girls who all stood trembling with their fists balled and collars gleaming.

Branson kissed the first three.

Groped the fourth.

Fingered the fifth and sixth.

Peter's bare chest rose and fell as the Master stopped before him and grabbed him around the nape. "Remember all the fun we had together a few weekends ago?" He ran his tongue over Peter's cheekbone. "I have half a mind to make you come so I can continue my little experiments on you, but...I have my eye on Chloe tonight, so..." Dropping his hand, he cupped Peter's erection through his white boxer briefs. Rubbing him twice, Peter shut his eyes as if willing himself to find pleasure and climax.

Branson chuckled and tore his hand away. "Greedy little sod."

And then it was my turn.

Fuck...my turn.

My ears rang with white noise.

My heart smoked; blood turned to ash.

He kissed me.

Grabbing my jaw, he angled my head up and planted his grotesque mouth on mine.

And...that was it.

No tongue.

No torture.

He kissed me platonically, and when it was over, he whispered, "Tell your psychotic Master I didn't hurt you. I don't want to end up as another one of his corpses."

And then he was gone...groping the next jewel.

Fingering the next.

Peter gave me a questioning look.

I swayed on my feet.

Another Master appeared.

Ian.

Giving Peter a nasty grin, he dove his hand into Peter's briefs and fisted him.

Peter groaned as Ian jerked him roughly.

No one could come from that.

It was abuse, not teasing—

Ian cursed under his breath as he tore his hand away. Studying the slickness on his palm, he raised his hand to strike. "Why, you little horny cunt. Is that precum?"

"Ah, ah, Ian." Victor purred over the microphone. "No hitting. Pleasure only, remember?"

"Fuck's sake." Dragging his glistening palm on Peter's bare chest, Ian smeared whatever fluid marked him onto Peter's skin, then turned to me.

I waited for him to hurt me.

To touch me in ways I wouldn't be able to forget, but...he gave me a half-hearted nipple twist.

And then, he left.

He fondled the girl next to me. One of the new girls, Laura.

She moaned under her breath as he actually attempted to conjure bliss in her, dropping his head to her breast and sucking her nipple into his mouth.

Peter's sharp gasp ripped my eyes back to him.

A dark-skinned Master who I only knew as Master G kissed Peter roughly.

Biting Peter's bottom lip, he made him bleed all while his eyes lit up with cruelty.

But he didn't reach between Peter's legs.

Didn't attempt to make him come.

Satisfied with making him bleed instead.

Peter staggered back as the Master finally let his bottom lip go.

I froze as Master G stepped into me.

With a savage smirk, he drove his hand between my legs.

I soared onto my tiptoes—

A snarl echoed over the music.

Animalistic.

Unhinged.

Looking over his shoulder, he stared at Henri, who was restrained by two Masters, preventing him from turning the dance floor into a blood bath.

Victor didn't seem to care that Henri's true feelings were showing. He merely smirked from his place on the podium, his reptilian eyes far too calculating, knowing, and sly.

I didn't dare move.

I'd been so lucky up till now.

I felt guilty for not being tormented like the other gems.

It wasn't fair I had Henri protecting me. My very own guardian angel, all while we were surrounded by so many fallen ones.

But Master G suddenly let me go, held up his hands, and made his way to Laura.

My bones rattled as Travis—the whole reason we were playing this game—oiled his way up to Peter.

"Hello, little Pete. I see you're packing tonight." He clucked his tongue. "Fancy playing with me, is that it?"

Peter sucked on his bleeding lip and shrugged. "Make me come, and we'll see."

Travis chuckled. "What happened to your politeness? Master T this, Master T that. You're usually so good at grovelling."

"I'm a little on edge, *Master T*. But if you want me to beg? Well then." He grinned. "Get on your knees and make me."

My heart stopped.

Travis froze.

For a horrible second, I envisioned him killing Peter for such insolence, but then he laughed and shook his head. "I think I like you feisty."

"Good. Choose me, then. I'm a sure thing if you want me."

"Still trying to protect the others, huh? Figure you'll take the game tonight so the others don't have to?"

Peter bared his teeth. All signs of the obedient jewel I knew vanished. He looked as if he didn't give a shit anymore. "Or I'm just so fucking sick of not getting mine that I'm willing to endure a bit of sodomy to get it."

Grabbing Peter between the legs, Travis stepped into him. "Tell me, Pete. How many strokes would it take?"

Peter looked at me, his eyes glowing brown and fathomlessly broken. "Three…maybe four."

I wanted to wrap him in the biggest hug.

I wanted to take him far, far away.

I loved him, yet I couldn't help him.

My eyes flared.

That's what he wanted me to say.

Three little words.

Words that meant entirely different things to the ones I said to Henri.

Words that meant entirely different things to Peter.

My chest grew tight.

I'd known Peter had feelings for me.

He wasn't exactly shy at hinting them.

But…I hadn't thought it was love.

I thought it was affection. Maybe lust.

The fact we spoke the same language and came from the same culture.

We'd bonded so fast because of that.

Peter groaned under his breath as Travis pumped him once, twice…

And then Travis stopped and moved on to me.

"Hello, pretty gem. Tell me. How much would it take to get you off?"

Swallowing hard, I tipped up my chin. "I wouldn't even bother. I won't come for anyone but my Master."

"Tempting to try but…" He shot a look at Henri who stood in front of a jewel. "I've heard rumours of what happens when someone touches you, so…" Kissing me chastely like Branson did, he pulled away after a few seconds and moved on to Laura.

She cried out as he dropped his hand between her legs, touching her like a lover all while his arm looped around her shoulders and held her close.

Perhaps she'd come first and—

Peter gasped as yet another Master grabbed his cock.

This one I didn't know.

He didn't speak.

With cold eyes, he jerked Peter twice, then let him go.

His gaze shot down the line to a jewel farther away, his goal obviously not either of us. Grabbing both my breasts, he squeezed me roughly, then pushed Travis off Laura and groped her too.

"Thank you for looking after Ily while I couldn't."

That voice.

That energy.

My gaze shot to Henri.

He stood before Peter.

I hadn't seen what he'd done to the other jewels, but I had no doubt it would've been as perfunctory as what I'd endured. Perhaps a gentle kiss, a very short grope—just enough to avoid Victor from demanding more.

Peter narrowed his eyes. "I have no power. I wasn't able to stop them."

"But your presence would've kept her mind intact." Henri tipped his chin. "So thank you."

"I don't think you'd be thanking me if you knew what I asked her to say."

Henri went stiff.

He flicked me a look. "What did you—"

"You better touch me and move on to her," Peter huffed. "Seeing as I failed to come first, you two are gonna be the ones to take the win." He swallowed hard. "Can't say I'm looking forward to standing right here while you make her shatter. But…I'll endure it."

Henri glowered at him, questions all over his face.

But…with a quick glance at Victor carefully watching from the top of the dance floor, he leaned in and kissed Peter extremely swiftly on the cheek.

My entire world righted again as Henri stepped into me, gathered me into his fierce, furious embrace, and pressed his lips to my ear. "How do you want me? Fingers? Tongue? It has to be quick. I'm losing my fucking mind."

"Fingers." I breathed.

Whatever pull he had over me tugged deep, deep in my belly.

The wetness returned.

The flurry, the steam, the crackle.

Cradling me in one arm, he dropped his hand between my legs.

Pushing aside my purple G-string, he inserted two fingers, boldly, unapologetically.

My body clamped around on his touch.

I bit my bottom lip.

Not looking away from me, he pumped his wrist, slowly to start with, his thumb pressing against my clit.

Even in this awful situation, he conjured such despairing desire.

My heart pounded with his.

The nightclub and Victor's awful game faded.

All I focused on was Henri's eyes.

His smoky tortured eyes.

Our souls entwined like always.

Our minds synced.

My body opened.

My breathing came faster, shallower as he increased his pace. Mimicking the action of sex, he made me rock in his tight hold.

Come for me, Ily. His gaze dropped to my mouth. *Come.*

I flung myself into the pleasure.

This wasn't just about us.

If I came first, the other jewels would be safe and—

"Long enough!" Victor barked, "Move it along, everyone."

"Fucking hell," Henri snarled.

I was close, but…not close enough.

I tried to fall.

I considered faking it.

Peter grunted beside me as another Master jerked him off.

His eyes met mine.

I fell into my friend as well as my lover.

And Henri noticed.

His touch turned violent.

A growl echoed in his chest.

And his teeth clamped into my throat, sinking hard, deep—

Peter grabbed my hand.

Henri thrust into me, Peter squeezed me, and…I shattered.

I cried out as the first ripple crashed like lightning.

Henri's teeth punctured harder, delivering that maddening pain and slick release of blood.

I couldn't stop it.

The intensity.

The primordial reaction of succumbing.

I came.

Hard.

Star-burstingly hard.

Peter shuddered as the Master went to let him go and shove Henri aside. He cursed in frustration. His face twisted up from being denied the only thing he needed in that moment.

I kept coming.

He didn't.

I transcended every mortal bone and decided to give Peter what he needed.

To find a smidgen of bliss in this awful place.

To be free, just for a moment.

"I love you," I breathed.

I barely spoke the words.

Peter's reaction was instantaneous.

He jack-knifed in half as the Master took his hand off his cock.

It didn't matter.

Ribbons of white pulsed from him, arching through the bright, colourful lights of the nightclub and splashing onto the polished dance floor.

We came together.

Two friends.

Two soulmates.

All while my twin flame sent me spiralling into a barbaric release.

Victor clapped his hands as I slowly dropped from the stars and slammed back into my body.

"It seems we have two winners, gentlemen." Striding toward us, he patted Henri on the shoulder as he removed his fingers, slick with my climax. "Your winners are, Henri Mercer and a fairly recent acquaintance, Wilson Optin. Congratulations, gentlemen. Go claim your spoils."

Striding off, the music switched on again, far too loud and pounding in my skull.

The jewels were grabbed by different Masters, and the night unspooled with fresh debauchery.

Without a word, Henri snagged my cuffed wrist and tugged me through the crowd.

I looked back at Peter.

He gave me a single wave as Wilson dragged him the other way.

Sickness rushed up my throat.

I'd tried to give him something good.

Instead, I'd delivered him into something awful.

Again.

He'd be hurt because of me.

And no pleasure was worth that.

I hung my head in grief as Henri squirrelled me away.

**Hope you liked it!
I didn't include this scene in Sapphire Scars as I felt the book was already long enough BUT it was a rather sweet scene between Ily, Peter, and Henri so didn't want to delete it forever.
Henri and Ily will be back in Diamond Kisses!!**

Printed in Great Britain
by Amazon